Praise for A HOUSE OF CRANES

"Adept storytelling and rich characterizations make this work a significant contribution to the literary fiction genre. Its introspective exploration of human emotions and relationships will likely engage readers who appreciate nuanced, character-driven narratives."

—Literary Titan

"An intricately woven plot that is emotional, sensual, and, at times, achingly poignant—a true literary gem."

—Stephanie Elizabeth Long for Reader Views

"A slow-burning white-hot tale of obsession and desire."

—Jennifer Jackson for Indies Today

"A House of Cranes is a beautifully written exploration of longing, passion, and the enduring quest for understanding the intricate dance of the heart."

—K.C. Finn for Readers' Favorite

Also by James Walter Lee

Kilómetro Cero

Tooth and Talon

A HOUSE OF CRANES

Z

Zennea Press

www.zenneapress.com

First Zennea Press paperback edition April 2024

Library of Congress Control Number: 2024901795

ISBN 979-8-9885153-2-6 (paperback)
ISBN 979-8-9885153-3-3 (ebook)

Cover illustration by Stefan Dimitrov
Author photo by James Walter Lee
Cover design by James Walter Lee
Interior design by James Walter Lee

For Ronald S. March

ONE

1

She would always be a phantom. When Lucius Cook arrived at the Wynn Funeral Home, memories of Eleanor once again dominated his thoughts. Uncertainty and regret attempted to dig their claws into him as they did the last time he saw her at the Crane's grand house. That evening, she stood in the doorway as he drove away. Her silhouette backlit. Shadows denying him a last glimpse of her. He remembered one night they shared when she sat behind a one-way mirror to watch him. He knew she was there beyond his reflection. Now, in the funeral home bathroom, he glared into the mirror.

"Are you there?" he whispered.

He slipped his hand in the hip pocket of his blazer and gripped an old, narrow child's belt. It rested deep in his pocket like a coiled serpent. He found it days ago while cleaning out the attic of his modest single-story rancher and was astounded he had kept it all these years. He slipped his fingers through the center of the rolled leather. As he made a fist, the leather stretched tight over his knuckles. His first inclination was to lash out and smash his reflection. To shatter the mirror into tiny shards so he could disappear within their many fractions.

He sighed and held his free hand under the running faucet, then ran his wet hand down his clean-shaven face and finger-combed his dark brown bangs. Droplets fell from his chin onto his lapel and tie, a tie which once belonged to a famous New York fashion photographer.

The door swung open. He slipped the rolled belt back inside his pocket. Kenneth Crane squeezed Lucius's shoulder before he went to stand before one of the wall urinals. At six-three, Kenneth stood half a head taller than

Lucius. He came to live with the Cranes when he was a boy, and he often, even to this day, felt like that same boy around Kenneth.

As he dried his hands, he glanced in the mirror at Kenneth's broad-shouldered back. Kenneth was a well groomed, highly sought-after corporate lawyer, named partner seven years ago at the law firm of Morris and Langtree in Hartford, now Morris, Langtree, and Crane. Time had dulled the rich brown color of Kenneth's hair, and ribbons of gray followed its perfect contours.

He washed his hands in the neighboring sink. His gold wedding band absent from his finger.

"You okay?" he asked.

Lucius only glared at himself in the mirror. Kenneth spoke over his shoulder as he dried his hands.

"We can't change the past. Today, we pay our respects and then get on with our lives. It's best to let go. C'mon, let's get this over with. You can be angry at her later—today is not the day."

Kenneth held open the bathroom door, and they went down the hallway. Lucius sucked in a breath as they approached the open doorway to the viewing room. When Kenneth squeezed his shoulder to guide them forward, Lucius drifted to the moment as a boy of eleven when he first met a younger Kenneth who, back then, like now, guided him into a viewing room to grieve a different loss.

It was 1963. Eleven-year-old Lucius wore a white dress shirt and black trousers that the Edgewood Foster Home provided him for the occasion. The shirt fit, but the legs of the trousers fell short, leaving his white socks visible.

Kenneth, known to him as Mr. Crane back then, towered over him and tugged his hand. He glanced upward ever so often to see the man's grim, tight-lipped smile and gentle nod. It was the only comfort he had in all the confusion.

"It's okay, son. I'm here with you. Let's go in and say our goodbyes," Kenneth said.

"Okay." It was all Lucius could say. His voice was small, hollow, and dry.

His gaze scanned beyond the people who sat in the rows of chairs or stood around the room, to the two ornate carved mahogany boxes with gold plaques fixed to the fronts. The boxes sat atop a rectangular, rich-stained cherry wood table with curved legs positioned at the far end of the room. A weight fell over him like a heavy blanket, as those in the room stopped to watch him. Some familiar faces. Friends of his mom and dad. A few of the women dabbed tissues to their cheeks to catch their tears. A large, husky man with a brush-cut and broad face nodded at Kenneth and Lucius. He was the police officer who drove Lucius to the station, where later Mrs. Davis from the Edgewood Foster Home retrieved him. They made their way to the table where the urns sat. He peered at the names on the gold plaques.

Darius Riley Cook (1932-1963)
Paulina Carol Cook (1935-1963)

"Let's close our eyes for a moment and say a little prayer for your mother and father, then you can tell them anything you like. I'm right here with you. Don't be afraid," Kenneth said.

He scowled at Kenneth. "How can my mom and dad be in there? They would never fit in there."

Kenneth crouched down on one knee, his eyes glassy. He held Lucius's slender arms in his big hands.

"I'm sorry Lucius, they were in a terrible, terrible accident."

Lucius scowled, and his bottom lip curled. The police already told him his parents had died when they picked him up from school. They forced him to stay at the foster home until Kenneth came for him, but now he wanted to see his parents.

"Do you mean all that's left of them is their heads? Are only their heads in there?"

His eyes widened, and his mouth opened, prepared to scream.

"No-no-no, that's not it at all. Listen to me."

Kenneth glanced around the room as if he were looking for an answer or an escape.

"Look, Lucius. These urns—that's what they are called—are only symbols of your parents. I'm sorry, but they could not save their bodies so that you could see them one last time."

Kenneth's words trailed off. His lips tightened, and he looked as though he wanted to curse.

"So you see Lucius, for their funeral, this is the best they could do for you."

His face softened and his pain, confusion and anger seemed to have flowed into Kenneth. He gazed at the urns and reread the names, but they were only words. How could there be love and memories inside those boxes?

He closed his eyes instead and pictured his parents. "Dad, you always told me to be a good boy. I will try my best. Goodbye."

He peeked at Kenneth, who nodded. He turned to the wooden urn with his mom's name.

"Goodbye, Mom. I'm sorry for all the bad things I've done. I love you and miss you."

When he turned to Kenneth, tears wet the man's cheeks.

Kenneth scooped him into his arms.

"As a friend of your mother's, I want to take care of you, Lucius. I spoke to your aunt Phoebe. She's agreed for you to come live with me, my wife Eleanor, and my daughter Beatrice. You need to be around a loving family and not back at the foster home. Okay?"

Aunt Phoebe? His eyebrows knit together, but he nodded. Kenneth took his hand and before they left the viewing room, he glanced back at the urns. No tears came, not the two days he spent at the foster home and not now. He wondered if they ever would. A numbness took over his body. He felt like the cricket he saw on the grounds of the Edgewood Foster Home cocooned in a spider's web. No, he would never go back there. Any place other than the foster home would suit him. All he had to do was hold on tight to Kenneth's hand.

The ride to the Crane's house was quiet and solemn, like the funeral service and burial for Lucius's parents. As Kenneth drove at a leisurely pace the saddened faces of those who attended the funeral floated through

Lucius's thoughts. He listened in a daze when the preacher said a prayer. Some of his mom and dad's friends got up to say a few words. Most of them attempted to make Lucius smile. Some succeeded. Most of the women hugged him at the cemetery and the men patted his shoulder or rubbed his head. He hated when they messed up his hair. He wanted his hair combed perfectly, like Kenneth's.

A sleepy sigh escaped past his lips. He recognized the drive through town, but they had entered a neighborhood unlike anything he had seen before. The houses were grand and yards stretched wide and deep. Lucius sat up straighter. His gaze flittered from one house to the next. He thought the car was grand enough with its broad chrome grill and double stacked headlamps. It was a beautiful machine, both inside and out. The rich leather interior even smelled expensive, and was far superior and better maintained than the ripped and torn vinyl covered seats in the junk cars his dad owned. He understood now. The car matched the houses, and the houses matched the car.

The Mercedes floated as Kenneth turned the wheel and eased the big sedan down the driveway to a grand Victorian-style house with yellow siding, white trim and slate-colored shingles. There were three floors. Lucius's mouth hung open, his eyes wide. Thoughts of kings, queens, princesses, and knights distracted him from his sadness. Kenneth parked the Mercedes in front of the doors to a two-car garage. The prospect of adventure and terror took hold when Lucius no longer heard the soft purr of the engine nor felt its vibration. The cabin fell silent.

Lucius opened his door after Kenneth got out. The long paved driveway was unbroken, unlike the short driveway at his parents' house with its cracks and weeds. Flowerbeds filled with gladiolus and daffodils ran the length of the side of the house, and hydrangea shrubs with their globe-shaped snowy white flower-heads broke up the row at pleasing intervals. Below one window, a large rose bush with full, vibrant heads crested the bottom white trimmed frame. Lucius squinted at the bright summer sun. When he glanced at the window above the rosebush, he thought he saw shadows move inside, but it was difficult to tell with the reflection of the sky. An occasional bee buzzed among the flowers and disappeared inside the velvet pedals.

Lucius stiffened when Kenneth squeezed his shoulder.

"Don't be afraid, Lucius. This is my home. I'm excited for you to meet Eleanor and Beatrice."

Kenneth held the door for Lucius and he stepped inside the foyer. His eyes widened at the height of the ceiling, which rose to the second floor.

"Hello, I'm home," Kenneth shouted, then whispered to Lucius, "Where the heck is everyone?"

"Hello Daddy."

A girl's sweet, musical voice came from above. She stood at the top of the stairs in a yellow dress with puffy sleeves. A headband separated her dark chestnut brown bangs from her shoulder length curls. She skipped down the steps. When she reached them, she gave Lucius a wide-eyed glance, then she smiled at her father.

"Hello Beatrice dear, this young man is Lucius Cook. He is the boy I spoke about. He's going to live with us. Lucius, this is my daughter Beatrice."

Lucius's eyebrow rose. He tried to imagine what they might have said about him. Beatrice smiled at him as she held out her hand. His hands were still dusty from the dirt he dropped over his parents' urns at the cemetery. He looked at her hand for a moment, and patted his own on his pant leg before he took hers. This would be perhaps the second time in his life that he shook a girl's hand, maybe even *his first*, as he had trouble recalling the other time.

"Nice to meet you Lucius," Beatrice said.

The corners of his lips curled slightly. He liked the sound of her voice and the way she said his name.

"Uh, nice to meet you," Lucius said.

He finally noticed her hazel eyes and stared at the soft curl of her lips when she smiled. Kenneth swooped her up into his arms and they kissed one another's cheeks. Finally, he put her down and rested his hand on her shoulder.

"Where is your mother, Dear?"

"She's in the kitchen. Ms. Käthe and Ms. Mila were here earlier to tidy up and prepare dinner, but they've gone."

Lucius glanced at Kenneth.

"Mrs. Käthe and Ms. Mila are our maids and Ms. Käthe is our cook as well. Shall we go see what's for dinner?"

Kenneth put his big, warm hands on the children's shoulders and led them to the kitchen. Lucius was hopeful, but struggled to smile. These people were definitely rich. Their warmth covered the hole in his heart. But for how long?

A woman's bold voice came from the kitchen, her tone one of dissatisfaction. Kenneth glanced at Beatrice, then Lucius, then at Lucius's hands.

"Beatrice, take Lucius to the hallway bathroom and you both wash up for supper. Afterwards, join us in the dining room. I suppose your mother is having difficulties cutting the roast or whatever we're having."

After Kenneth left them, Beatrice rolled her eyes. Lucius smiled and followed her.

As the children returned to the dining room, Kenneth placed a platter with the roast on the table. Eleanor brought in a bowl with a mix of carrots, peas, and small white potatoes. The woman gazed at Lucius as if he were some oddity she attempted to comprehend.

"Eleanor, this is Lucius. The boy I mentioned to you. Lucius, this is my wife Eleanor, Mrs. Crane, that is."

"Hello Lucius," Eleanor said.

She held her hands in front of her and bent slightly toward Lucius. He stared at her, his lips slightly parted. There was something unsettling about the way she looked at him with those eyes. Her irises were a pale sky-blue. The narrow opening of her mouth, a sliver between her lips, drew his attention. Could she be an angel or a devil? His mind worked like a mouse sniffing the bit of cheese on a trap. She must be an angel, he concluded, but in the back of his mind doubt swirled like distant storm clouds. Her shoulder length hair was golden brown with soft curls, like rolling waves on an ocean.

"He's shy," Kenneth said. His voice broke the spell.

"Uh, hello. Nice to meet you, Mrs. Crane."

His words tumbled out. Kenneth chuckled, and Eleanor smiled at Lucius. Her smile conveyed not acceptance and understanding of a child's clumsy social graces, but a hint of subtle disappointment.

"Sit everyone, please," Eleanor said.

Lucius sat in the chair where she gestured with a slight wave of her hand.

"After we eat, Beatrice can show you around the house. Don't go upstairs or down in the basement, though. Would you do that for me, Dear?"

Beatrice smiled at Kenneth.

"I would be pleased to."

She glanced at Lucius and nodded. Lucius only looked at all of them and wondered when he would wake from this dream. There was something fantastic about all of this, and he thought of Alice, from *Alice's Adventures in Wonderland*. If this was a fantasy, could he stay here, or would he have to escape?

After dinner, Kenneth loosened his tie and unbuttoned his collar, then followed Eleanor to the screened in patio, each with a second glass of wine in hand. Beatrice and Lucius followed so she could first point out the three-season patio room as not to later disturb her parents, who took seats on the cushioned wicker chairs. Lucius looked out the screen panels at the well-groomed back yard with its many towering trees. In the fading light, the property appeared to go on forever. Beatrice touched his arm and motioned for him to follow.

Kenneth took a cigarette from the open pack that sat on the wicker coffee table. He lit it while he watched Eleanor. She drank her glass of wine and gazed out into the moonlit backyard. The way she held the glass was always pure elegance, and the way she sat comfortably poised with her shoulders straight and her chin lifted, she carried herself like the sophisticated heiress she was. Even after five years of marriage, he wondered how he had ever won her over. Being a single parent to Beatrice should have totally put her off, but she seemed to relish the idea of an instant family since she could not bear children of her own. He had one concern, though. She lacked gentle motherly qualities, but her sophistication enamored him with the prospect that she could raise Beatrice to be a well mannered and refined woman.

"Beautiful night," he said.

Her lips curled into a tight-lipped smile when she looked at him.

"The boy got through his parents' funeral better than I could have imagined," he said.

She stroked the notch at the base of her neck.

"You're a saint for taking him in, but it is still unclear to me how you knew his parents."

"I knew his mother, Paulina. She worked at one of the law offices when I first started out. I heard that her husband, Darius, Lucius's father, was a mean drunk. I never saw him raise a hand to her, but he got loud and abrasive at one of the firm's Christmas parties."

"That's a shame."

He took a sip of wine and felt her gaze bore into him.

"Anyway, I met the boy the few times when she brought him to the office. A quiet but inquisitive boy. After I moved on, I hadn't seen Paulina for some time, then when some of my colleagues and I were having lunch at the Beacon Diner, she happened to be our waitress."

"Is that so?"

"Yes dear. Apparently, her husband didn't much care for lawyers, so he forced her to look for other employment."

"How unfortunate—for her."

"Indeed."

They sat quietly and gazed out into the dark. A beetle fluttered its wings against the aluminum screen. Kenneth took a drag on the cigarette. His wineglass balanced between his fingers. Eleanor raised her chin, but her gaze remained some place out in the darkness.

"Now the boy has dropped into our lap. It is a sad circumstance, but why is it our responsibility to care for him? We are not his family."

"He has no one, except—"

Kenneth expelled the smoke from his lungs. Eleanor gazed over at him.

"Except there is an estranged aunt living in Indiana. I spoke to her. She is not keen on taking the boy."

"An aunt? Why his mother's sister should be quick to care for him, one would think."

"The aunt is Lucius's father's sister."

"I see. Another angry drunk, like her brother?"

"I don't think that's the case. She sounded more like she lacked the financial means to support the boy. Besides, how would I know if she was a drunk?"

"I don't know Kenneth, how would you?"

He huffed at her implication, took a drag, then tilted his head and blew a stream of smoke toward the ceiling.

"Eleanor dear, you're being silly."

"And I think you're being irrational. Why not let the foster care system have him?"

"Don't be cruel."

"Kenneth, you were never much for charity. When did you all the sudden jump on a save-the-children bandwagon? I say, 'children' with the deepest fear that you might bring home more strays."

Kenneth took another drag on the cigarette and cocked his head.

"Just this one. He needs a good home, and I intend to help him."

Her eyebrows rose, and then her eyes narrowed.

"Folly, I say."

She drank. Her narrow, suspicious glare softened and her eyelids appeared heavy. Lights came on in the windows of Kenneth's study. He put out his cigarette and sat his glass of wine on the table.

"I'm going to see how Beatrice and Lucius are getting on."

Eleanor huffed.

"Let's hope—not too well."

He chuckled, then smirked at her. She gazed out at the shadowy moonlit landscape of their backyard. She held her empty wineglass. A tinge of crimson crawled the bottom.

"Let's not get melodramatic. They're children, after all."

He stood and left her to her quiet contemplation.

Lucius followed Beatrice down the hallway. He was relieved to find out that she was younger than him, albeit by only a year. Another person older than him to boss him around would have been too much for him to stand, especially another child. Beatrice ran her fingers along the wainscoting that spanned the walls between the rooms and only once had to step around a narrow hallway table with a vase that held a bouquet of flowers. Lucius mimicked her. When he passed the table with the flowers, he imagined he would be happy not to see another flower for the rest of his life. He almost ran into her when she halted in front of a darkened doorway. The sun had set and shadows filled the room. The ceiling light in the hallway was of no help. She slipped into the shadowy room. The hem of her yellow dress disappeared in the gloom. A muted click came and two Tiffany floor lamps lit the space. His eyes widened. She stood with a broad smile.

"This is my father's study. He's a lawyer. He works at the best law firm in Hartford—Morris and Langtree."

Lucius's eyebrows rose.

The walls were a moss green and the wainscoting, baseboards and crown molding were white, giving the room a masculine feel. Lucius inhaled and sighed. The Tiffany floor lamps were at each end of a button tufted leather sofa. A bronze statue of a mermaid sat on top of a coffee table that was in front of the sofa. Lucius gazed at the bare breasts on the statue until Beatrice nudged him. Heat rose and prickled his cheeks.

A Persian rug spanned much of the rich dark-stained hardwood floor. Shelves filled with books rose from floor to ceiling. Framed photographs, mostly black and white prints, adorned the walls. A richly stained, heavy wooden desk with stout legs commanded the space between the two windows that looked out onto the backyard.

Before they stepped further into the room, the wooden floor creaked in the hallway. Kenneth appeared in the doorway. Beatrice stiffened and looked up at him.

"Hello children," he said.

Lucius stood silent with parted lips. Beatrice fussed with the skirt of her dress.

"I wanted to show Lucius your study. I was getting ready to tell him we mustn't enter without your permission," Beatrice said.

Kenneth's lips tightened, his eyebrow rose, then his lips curled into a soft, tight-lipped smile.

"Well, Lucius knows now. Thank you for making that point, Beatrice."
Her lips curled into a subtle smile.

"Can I look at the pictures?" Lucius asked.

Kenneth lifted his chin and examined the boy.

"Oh? Do you have an interest in photography?"

Lucius shrugged. Kenneth chuckled.

"Come, have a look."

Lucius came forward. His loafers tapped on the wood floor until he stepped onto the Persian rug. It was as if he had become a ghost in that moment, until his feet were again back on the wood floor, and he again existed. He went to the first picture of Eleanor and Beatrice at the beach. It was black and white. Eleanor wore a sun hat with a broad brim and a one-piece bathing suit. Her arm was around Beatrice's shoulder. They stood side-by-side, instead of Beatrice in front, as most parents might pose lovingly with their child.

He gazed mostly at Eleanor. The angle of the sunlight cast subtle shadows that indicated where the bones of her pelvis protruded on both sides of her hips. His gaze followed the lines of her bathing suit to where they ended between her legs. Beatrice tugged at his arm.

"Come see this one."

He got a brief glimpse of the picture of shells and driftwood before she had them positioned in front of the third picture. It was another black and white. One of Beatrice alone in an elegant formal dress. When he glanced at her, she beamed.

"You look like a little princess," he said.

She giggled. Kenneth gestured at the pictures.

"All the pictures are mine, except the three you see over there. I also print my own photographs."

The other three pictures were also black and white, but they were of fashion models.

"A friend of mine, a famous New York City fashion photographer named Otto Schenker, took those pictures. Aren't they marvelous?"

A tone of admiration rose in Kenneth's voice. The richness of blacks and whites captured Lucius's attention. He stepped closer.

"Don't you want to see the rest?" Beatrice said.

"He will, give him a moment," Kenneth said.

Lucius stood before the professional photographer's prints. Beautiful, tall, elegant women in two of the pictures appeared to be photographed at some exotic location on narrow streets or alleyways, with architecture unlike anything he had seen before. In one picture, the model stood surrounded by white with a soft curving shadow behind her.

"Notice the wall and floor, Lucius. See how it flows together without a hard break? That is done with a paper backdrop extended long enough for the model to stand on. They call it a seamless."

"Oh."

"The other two pictures he shot in Monaco. That's in Europe, Lucius. The fellow gets around."

A soft trailing hum in Kenneth's voice, a twinge of jealousy.

Lucius gazed at the fashion photographer's prints.

"Daddy?"

"All right, Lucius, come see the rest."

Lucius looked at the rest of the black and white pictures that Kenneth had shot. There were two color portraits, one of Kenneth, and the other of Eleanor. The one of Kenneth was from his chest up. The one of Eleanor was a full-length picture of her.

"I was experimenting with color. The one of me is a self-portrait."

"How did you do it?" Lucius asked.

"I used the camera's timer with the camera mounted on a tripod. It's tricky. You have to set the timer and hurry back to your position and pose."

Lucius nodded. Beatrice rocked back and forth on her heels with a smile.

"Lucius, I think we have confirmed that you do indeed have an interest in photography."

He smiled at Kenneth. For the first time in the past few days, he felt sure of something.

"Is this your camera?"

He pointed at one shelf where there were no books. The camera sat on display next to a conch shell and an old brass compass. Kenneth went to the shelf and retrieved the camera. He smiled at Lucius as if the boy had won some sort of contest. He then knelt in front of Lucius. Beatrice sat on the buttoned leather sofa and tapped her shoes together. Kenneth glanced at her, his face wrinkled briefly, then he held the camera up to show Lucius.

The camera was silver with a black grip that wrapped around the body. Its dials were knurled to make them easier to turn, and it had a slender film advance lever.

"I shot all the pictures in this room with this camera. This is a Leica M3. It's a 35mm camera with a 50mm lens. Once you have it loaded with film, the main things you have to think about are your exposure settings, focus, and how smooth you press the shutter button."

Lucius stared at the camera. Kenneth removed the lens cap.

"Here you can feel the weight of it. One important thing to always remember is to never touch the lens."

Lucius nodded. Kenneth handed him the camera. He looked through the circular viewfinder, but everything was blurry.

"Uh. It's broken. Did I hurt it?"

Kenneth laughed.

"No, adjust the focusing ring on the lens."

Kenneth demonstrated, then Lucius tried. The room came into focus. Lucius smiled.

"I see. I see now."

He panned the camera around, first at Beatrice. She still sat on the sofa, her arms now crossed and she wore a scowl. He swiveled and panned the camera some more. He paused when Eleanor filled the frame. He quickly adjusted the focusing ring, and she came into sharp focus. She stood in the doorway.

"Having fun?"

She braced her body against the frame, which made her look vulnerable, like a starlet in one of the romance movies his mom loved to watch. Lucius also remembered how his mom stumbled and braced herself when she had too much to drink. He lowered the camera and Kenneth took it from him and returned it to the shelf next to the conch shell.

"Lucius was admiring my photographs. I think we might have a photographer here in the making."

Kenneth grinned. Eleanor snorted.

"Is that so?"

"I'm certain of it."

"Well, it's late. Time for bed."

Beatrice got to her feet and yawned. Her arms hung slack at her sides.

"Dear, why don't you go on up and I'll tuck Beatrice and Lucius in?"

Eleanor turned, and her heels made unsteady clicks down the hallway.

2

It was a girlie room, the Crane's guest bedroom, what little Lucius saw of it before Kenneth turned out the lights. Lucius held the flowery printed comforter and satin edged cream-colored sheets up to his neck. He wore boxers and a tank top to bed, provided by the Edgewood Foster Home, along with the dress clothes he wore to his parents' funeral. The clothes he wore the day the police picked him up—his clothes—sat folded in one of drawers of the otherwise empty dresser. He stared at the ceiling through the open top of the canopy bed with its top corners wrapped with frilly decorative poplin. Moonlight filtered through the trees outside and created soft shadows across the ceiling. The room was twice the size of his bedroom back home. The word *home* no longer existed.

He thought of his aunt Phoebe. Who was this woman? He struggled to remember her. Perhaps the only memory he had was an infant's memory, a lost memory. He snorted. Tears wet his cheeks and tickled his face. While at the foster home, he fought his tears to avoid any displays of weakness for the other boys to seize upon. Now, he let it all out. His mouth opened and his lips wrinkled, his chest rose and shuddered. He covered his mouth with the comforter, and hoped none of the Cranes would hear him moan, or worse, find him crying.

Voices from down the hall silenced him. He tilted his head to listen. Nothing. He sat up in bed. There. Were Mr. And Mrs. Crane arguing? There was laughter. Her laughter—musical and taunting. Her words were soft and shapeless, but her tone was playful, then silence. He waited. He laid back down and rested his head on the pillow. His gaze returned to the ceiling. Soft moans came, muffled, then came again, fast and abbreviated. A siren's song. Aroused, he held himself. When silence filled the hallway, he rolled on his side and peered out the open doorway until sleep found him.

When morning arrived, an early summer breeze swept through the open bedroom window and woke him. He looked around the room with half-closed eyes, unable to imagine someone opening the window while he slept. He snorted as he took in the room. Definitely a girl's room. The walls were a pale peach color. The moldings and trim were white, the same as the rest of the rooms in the house. Kenneth appeared in the doorway.

"Up-up-up."

He clapped his hands. Lucius propped himself up on his elbows and rubbed the sleep from his eyes.

"I hope you slept well, and hopefully you're up for some photography today. The court gave me the okay to take you to your parents' house to get your clothes. I wish I could give you another day, but come Monday, I'll have to contact your school and see what they require. With two weeks until summer break, perhaps they will excuse you and let you stay—here." He knew Kenneth wanted to say, "home."

The Cook's house was a two bedroom single-story rancher in an area closer to Hartford. An area the affluent members of the private golf club that Kenneth belonged to referred to as "the other side of the tracks," because of its elevated crime rate and low income housing. After Kenneth carried two empty suitcases up the cracked walkway, with its tufts of sprouted grass, he unlocked the front door. Lucius darted inside. Kenneth shouldered his way in with the suitcases. He winced when the screen door slapped his elbow.

"Let's go to your room and get your things."

He pushed past Lucius into the living room, where he bumped the coffee table with one suitcase and upset the few women's magazines that were neatly stacked there. The boy looked around as if he were in some strange mausoleum.

"Don't worry Lucius, we'll be back. Let's get your clothes and whatever you need for school, everything else can wait."

Lucius scampered down the narrow wood paneled hallway to the first open doorway and disappeared inside. When Kenneth brought the suitcases to the bedroom, he found the boy sitting on a twin-size bed. The bed's length spanned the tiny room. Lucius stared up at him with an anguished expression. He should have never brought the boy here. Maybe it was too soon. He put the suitcases down and sat on the bed next to Lucius.

"I'm sorry Lucius."

He put his arm around the boy.

"It's going to be okay, son. I'm here. I won't let anything happen to you. Okay?"

His voice trailed off. Lucius only stared at the floor with his hands cupped in his lap.

"Losing your parents. It's unfair, especially for someone your age. I know your sadness. My parents died before I finished college."

Lucius trembled and whimpered. Kenneth held him tight.

"That's it. Get it out. It has to come out. Don't be afraid or ashamed."

After Lucius had his moment, he became silent. His cheeks were puffy and reddened. He lifted the boy's chin to look at him.

"I'm okay."

Kenneth laid open both suitcases on the bed, while Lucius opened the closet doors. Between the narrow closet and dresser with four drawers, He imagined most, if not all, of Lucius's things should fit in the suitcases.

"Pack the things you wear most often, including shoes. You can put your school stuff in the smaller suitcase. I'm going to look around the house and make sure everything is secure."

He went to the kitchen first to see if any food sat out. It was warm out. He was grateful the windows were open, otherwise the place would have been stuffy. He put in the trash a near empty carton of milk. Also in the squat refrigerator, Lucius's mother, Paulina, must have taken down some ground beef from the freezer to thaw. Kenneth dumped it in the trash and tied up the bag to take out. He then went around and closed the windows, although he knew if someone wanted to get inside, the locked windows would only slow them down. When he turned around, Lucius stood outside his bedroom.

"Done?"

"No."

"Don't worry, I'm still here. I'm not going to leave without you."

The boy popped back inside the bedroom. Kenneth found the laundry room.

"I don't have any dirty laundry. My mom washed everything."

When Kenneth turned around, Lucius stood in the doorway.

"All right."

Kenneth started down the hallway to the boy's parents' bedroom.

"There's nothing down there."

"Are you done packing?"

Lucius shook his head.

"Well, hurry, so we can get some lunch. I'm starving, aren't you?"

"Yes."

Lucius went back inside his bedroom. Kenneth shook his head. When he gazed down the hallway to the other bedroom, a chill caused his shoulders to tighten. He glanced back, but the boy was still in his room. He needed to see the bedroom where Paulina slept with the man who mistreated her. Was there ever any love there?

Paulina and Darius's bedroom was three times the size of Lucius's room, but that only allowed for a queen-size bed and room for two modest size dressers. The closet had two accordion style doors. The living room, the hallway, the boy's room, and the parents' room, all had the same dull light blue inexpensive low pile carpet covering the floors. There were stains and visible wear on the carpet throughout the house, mostly in the living room, where he imagined they often ate in front of the television. The folded snack trays in the living room added to that impression.

Kenneth slid open the top drawer to the nearest dresser. The drawer rode rough on its tracks. If it belonged to Darius, he thought he would see similar things that most men kept in their top drawer, instead he found Paulina's undergarments. He took a pair of her panties and held them to his face. He tried to imagine her in them, but all he could think of was that she would never wear them again. He put them in his pocket and closed the drawer.

When he turned, Lucius stood out in the hallway. How long had he been there, watching?

"Did you get your things packed?"

"Yes. Are you looking for something?"

"Um, no, just curious about your parents. C'mon, let's get out of here."

Summer break started early for Lucius. Kenneth had spoken to the school principal, who sent his condolences and excused Lucius for the last two weeks of school. Kenneth and Lucius wandered the backyard with the Leica camera. The summer air was fragrant, warm, and thick. Towering white oaks and elms provided ample shade. Late afternoon rays filtered through the trees, and created cloud-like shadows across the lawn. An occasional bumblebee or fly buzzed past them. At the far end of the property stood an enormous sycamore. It must be the pride of the Crane's backyard, or so Lucius believed. His eyes widened at the girth of the base of the tree. Its thick branches curved and rose like arms. The tree beckoned to be climbed and taken up into its embrace.

As the two walked the property, Kenneth demonstrated how the Leica functioned and explained the Sunny 16 Rule to set the camera's exposure. He then let Lucius adjust the settings and take a picture of anything the boy found interesting: the trees, the log pile, a beetle or butterfly, or some flowers. Kenneth even posed for a few pictures. When Lucius raised the Leica to his eye, Kenneth held up his hand to stop him.

"You've seen how easy it is to press the button, but you have to slow things down. Be deliberate. Wait for the moment. Patience, Lucius. We are artists. We are not *taking* pictures, we are—*making* pictures."

He lowered the camera. He double checked the position of the dials, made one minor adjustment to get the correct exposure, returned the camera to his eye, focused the lens, then framed the composition carefully—and waited.

"Beatrice will be home anytime. Maybe she can pose for us."

When he stopped speaking, but before he could smile, Lucius pressed the shutter button. Outside, among the singing birds and buzzing insects, the camera's shutter was inaudible. He lowered the camera. A surge of exhilaration filled him.

"I think I like to photograph people the most."

Kenneth grinned, and his nostrils flared.

"Me too."

Beatrice waved from the living room window.

"Just in time," Kenneth said.

He waved back at her and motioned for her to come outside. Lucius spotted Eleanor in one of the master bedroom windows. She stood off to the side, aligned with the drawn back heavy drapes and sheer curtains, her expression flat and detached. The windows were open. She probably heard them talking in the yard when they were near the house. Kenneth seemed not to notice her.

"There you are, my lovely."

He swept Beatrice up into his arms. She still wore her Leighton Day School uniform. It was a sleeveless Black Watch tartan dress with a green and blue cross-pattern, over a white blouse with rounded collars, white ankle socks and glossy black shoes with T-bar straps. Lucius almost took a picture of their embrace, but a twinge of jealousy crept in. He rarely received a hug from his dad, but one every day and always from his mom. The few pats on his head or back, or a squeeze of his shoulder from Kenneth, was something. He never felt that connection with his dad, or any man. While Beatrice told Kenneth about her day at school, Lucius glanced at the open windows on the upper floor to see if Eleanor was still there, but the windows stood dark and empty. The sheer white curtains swayed against the heavier drapes.

"Hello Lucius," Beatrice said.

She and Kenneth stood there.

"Uh—hi."

She giggled.

"Did you take some good pictures?"

He looked at Kenneth.

"Dear, this is serious business. Lucius and I are enjoying nature and *making* pictures. Isn't that right, Lucius?"

"Yes. Yes, that's right."

Lucius held up the camera, but quickly lowered it, for Beatrice probably knew more about photography than he did.

"Dear? How would you like to pose for Lucius?"

Kenneth raised his eyebrows.

"Sure daddy, but for only one picture. I have to change my clothes before supper."

"All right, Lucius. You heard her. This is actually good. You've got one shot at this."

Lucius nodded.

"Can we go over there?"

He pointed to one of the elm trees to the side of the house near the fence that separated the Crane's property from their neighbors. There was a small patch of delicate fuchsia, white, and yellow flowers at the base of the fence.

"Excellent," Kenneth said.

He motioned for Lucius to lead on. Lucius had Beatrice sit on the lawn with her legs folded under her to one side. He stood back and shook his head. He then had her move to the right, near the edge of the tree's shadow, where more sunlight filtered through. After he looked through the camera's viewfinder, he hunched down to be at the same level as her.

"There, that's good," he said.

She looked up and smiled. Lucius imagined Kenneth was doing something behind him to draw her attention. He kept the camera's current exposure settings, and adjusted the focus ring until the two images of Beatrice came together as one. She smiled, laughed, and fidgeted. He waited. She took one glance up toward Kenneth, but when her eyes lowered—click.

Lucius held the camera to his face for a moment and prayed he got the shot. After a brief pause, he lowered the camera and his lips curled into a soft smile.

"I got it. Thank you."

Kenneth's big hands cupped his shoulders.

"Splendid. I believe you did," he said.

The three walked back to the patio. Eleanor sat on the stone steps with a cigarette between her fingers.

"Hello, dear. Have you come outside to enjoy the air with us?" Kenneth asked.

Lucius stared at Eleanor. She sat with her knees together and ankles crossed. The hem of her light blue dress sat above her knees and revealed her sheer stocking clad legs, with her feet in taupe heels. The light breeze lifted her golden brown waves. As she looked up at Kenneth, Lucius hurried and raised the camera to his eye. He ignored the exposure settings, and put her in focus, then waited. A fraction of a second, her gaze with her penetrating pale sky-blue eyes lowered to look into the camera's lens. Mesmerized, he almost missed the shot. He pressed the camera's shutter release button, but nothing happened. He quickly lowered the camera and tried to advance the film.

"Uh?"

A subtle smirk appeared on her face. Kenneth squeezed his shoulder.

"Sorry, Lucius. Looks like you've reached the end of the roll of film. I guess she's the one that got away," he said.

Kenneth looked over at Eleanor and smiled.

"Maybe Mrs. Crane will sit for you another time."

"We'll see," she said.

She stood with a cocked eyebrow, brushed her hands over her skirt, and went inside the house.

"Cheer up. You'll be ready next time. After supper, I have a treat for you. We can develop the film and see what we got. How would you like that?"

Lucius's eyes brightened and he grinned. Kenneth held the shoulders of both Lucius and Beatrice.

"C'mon, let's go inside," he said.

As dinnertime drew near, Lucius glanced in the open doorway to the kitchen, careful not to be spotted, so he could watch Eleanor direct Ms. Käthe, who did the actual cooking. The aroma of the baked chicken, thyme and other spices thickened the air.

Eleanor, Mrs. Crane, ruled the house like a queen. It was difficult to fathom how she and Mr. Crane ended up together. Lucius longed to see her eyes, to lose himself in the pale blue so he could float among the clouds there, but the intensity of her gaze also frightened him.

He jumped when Ms. Mila passed behind him in the hallway. She must have lifted her heels to sneak up on him like that. Then again, her thin frame made her appear light as a bird. He pressed his back into the wall outside the kitchen. Her lips curled into a warm and patient smile, like the smile of his English teacher, Ms. Evert. Ms. Mila had her fine blonde hair pinned back under a white ruffled headpiece, and she wore a knee-length gray dress with a white apron. Both women dressed alike, but Ms. Mila was never as polished as Ms. Käthe.

Ms. Mila's simple low black heels made soft but crisp strikes on the hardwood floors. Lucius watched her calves flex while she walked away and disappeared around the corner into the dining room to set the table. Both Ms. Mila and Ms. Käthe would depart after they placed the food on the table, cleaned the kitchen, and washed the dishes. They would always say, "Gute Nacht," to Mrs. Crane, before they left, and she would say, "Gute Nacht," to them. Beatrice later explained that they said good night.

When he peeked inside the kitchen again, Ms. Käthe and Ms. Mila were cleaning up. Mrs. Crane had disappeared. Lucius felt the weight and warmth of Kenneth's hand on his shoulder.

"Suppertime Lucius."

He peeked into the kitchen with a curious expression as if he struggled to figure out what held Lucius's attention. He guided them to the dining room. Dinner was on the table. Beatrice and Eleanor sat waiting. Eleanor looked at them with narrow eyes.

"You two are late."

"Sorry dear," Kenneth said.

They sat with their heads lowered. Beatrice smirked at them. Lucius expected her tongue to poke out at any minute. He wanted to look at Mrs. Crane, but was afraid of her critical gaze.

After dinner, he and Kenneth descended into the shadowy murk of the basement. Kenneth cradled the Leica in his big hands. At the bottom of the stairs, he flipped the light switch so they could see. He took out his keys and unlocked a matte black painted door and flipped the light switch inside. Two banks of florescent lamps that hung from the ceiling lit the space. Inside it looked like some kind of laboratory with long tables that lined both sides of the room, a metal sink with a large basin, and a separate table on which sat an imposing odd looking contraption like an oversized microscope. Next to it was a black square timer. There were three large shallow trays lined in a row near the sink. Shelved below were white opaque and dark brown jugs of various liquids. Above the tables were wall mounted shelves with books and flat orange and black boxes with the Kodak logo on them. Everywhere Lucius looked, it appeared cluttered yet tidy. *Organized chaos*, he recalled his dad would say about his tools and their garage.

When Kenneth shut the door behind them, the windowless room shrank. One of the florescent bulbs flickered as if to wink at Lucius. A single red bare bulb hung from the ceiling like a meaty heart at the center of the room, with a dangling pull-string attached to the socket to bring it to life.

"Well? What do you think?"

His eyes widened as he took in the room, unable to decide what to focus on. Kenneth went to the far table, sat the camera down, and pulled two stools from underneath the table.

"Come sit."

Lucius sat, and Kenneth explained how to rewind and remove the film from the camera.

"Easy?"

Lucius nodded.

With the camera still open, Kenneth got a fresh roll of film from the shelf and talked Lucius through the process of loading the camera.

"Got it. That was easy."

Lucius grinned.

"Now the tricky part: to develop the film, we have to do it in complete darkness."

"How can we see what we're doing?"

"We won't. I'll get a junk roll of film for you to practice with. Eventually, you'll have to do this in complete darkness, or you'll lose everything."

Kenneth gathered the development tank, a black container with a lid that contained a spool inside, some scissors, three glass containers near the sink, and three bottles of various chemicals. He explained the entire process, instructed Lucius to stay put on his stool, then he turned off the lights and all Lucius could do was listen to him move around in the dark. Every few moments, he explained what he was doing, and Lucius tried to visualize the process. The lights came on and Kenneth stood by the door.

"The film is now spooled safely inside the processing tank. Now for the chemicals."

He watched as Kenneth filled the three glass flasks: developer, stop bath, and fixer. The chemicals had a strong odor, like vinegar or cleaning supplies. Then, one by one, Kenneth applied the chemicals, using the square timer to let them know when to dump one out and apply the next. Eventually they had a long strip of developed film hanging from a clip attached to the wall mounted shelves. Kenneth glanced at his wristwatch.

"It's late. Maybe tomorrow we can develop a contact sheet from the negatives. All the pictures will be on one sheet of paper, then we can decide which ones are good enough to make into larger prints."

"Oh? Okay."

"Don't be sad. I know how you feel. I am eager to see how your pictures turned out just as much as you are. You head up. I'm going to tidy up down here."

"Can I help?"

"No, you have to brush your teeth, wash your face, and get into your pajamas."

He was about to protest, as he knew they both had to prepare for bed, but when Kenneth's eyes narrowed, he slipped from stool and left Kenneth in the darkroom. As he lumbered up the basement steps, he wondered how long Kenneth would be down there.

The moon had taken the night off, as his mom used to say, for the Crane's guest bedroom felt like a tomb. A feeble band of light came from the master bedroom down the hall. It lit the edge of the guest bedroom doorway. As in the previous nights, Lucius stared at the ceiling. This night, he thought of other things besides how much he missed his mom tucking him in. His mind played over the day's picture taking with Mr. Crane. Lucius saw each picture, clear as when he peered through the camera's viewfinder and pressed the shutter button, even the one of Mrs. Crane, which Mr. Crane said he missed because he reached the end of the roll. The picture of Mrs. Crane would exist in his mind if nowhere else.

As sleep approached and his eyelids became heavy, a tall, shadowy figure passed the guest bedroom doorway. Mr. Crane? A subtle creak of hinges and the light from the end of the hallway brightened, then dimmed. Hushed voices accompanied the dim light from the master bedroom, voices of Mr. and Mrs. Crane. Mrs. Crane dominated the conversation. Her voice rose and the tempo of her words quickened. Mr. Crane's voice responded. First, it matched hers in tone and pitch, then became low and heavy. A dead silence followed.

Lucius lowered the comforter, propped himself up on his elbows, waited, and listened. The light from down the hall went out. The guest bedroom, with its feminine trappings, the polished wood floors, the walls in the hallways with the wainscoting that lead from room to room, all swallowed by shadow. When the light returned, it seemed brighter than before. A few hushed words came from the master bedroom, then girlish laughter as if Mrs. Crane was being tickled. Soft moans followed. Lucius sat up on the edge of the bed. When he heard the moans come again, he stood and stepped to the open doorway to the guest bedroom.

Down the hallway, the master bedroom door sat open a sliver, allowing a narrow band of light to escape. Beatrice's door stood closed and appeared impenetrable. Lucius stepped heel-to-toe as light as he could toward the master bedroom. The wood floor was cool on the bottoms of his bare feet. He ran his fingers along the smooth wainscoting. With each step he took, he tested his forward weight for any tattletale creaks in the wood.

A grunt, then an audible slap, came from the narrow open doorway. Lucius froze feet from the door to the master bedroom. He waited, muscles tensed, for the door to swing open. Soft, sensual moans returned, followed by hushed, unclear words.

Lucius had the idea that he should move to the opposite side of the hallway before he glimpsed into the room. He saw this on spy shows and knew it was the right thing to do. He dashed a step and a half across the hall and collided with the narrow hallway table that stood in the dark. A vase full of flowers fell into his arms, smothering his face with soft velvet pedals. He grasped the edge of the tilting table and straightened it. He expected to hear silence from the adults beyond the door, as they might listen for interlopers. The soft, sensual moans continued. He exhaled. The flowers, white gardenia pedals, tickled his nose. Their scent, a creamy coconut and spice, captured him in that moment. It was the rise in activity beyond the door that again drew his attention. He stepped enough inside the narrow open doorway and attempted to steal a glimpse. At first, all he could see was Mrs. Crane's dress, which hung from a free-standing gentleman's wooden valet, and her stockings that were folded over a chair next to an elegant gentle lady's mirrored vanity. When his eyes reached the bed, his lips parted.

A nightstand lamp with an opaque cloth shade lit the corner of the bed. Mrs. Crane was on her back with her chin raised and her mouth open as if she were preparing to whisper into God's ear. Her bare milky white breasts slid gently on her chest like two enormous dew drops. Raised areolae with small pointed nipples like raspberries atop of pillows of toasted meringue. The bottom half of her hidden beneath the bedspread and sheets. An extended heavy moan rose from within her and out through the open aperture of her mouth. The curve of her lips reminded him of some flowers around the house, their pedals open and inviting. Her bent knees under the covers created two peaks with a wide valley between her spread legs.

The covers rose near her feet and amassed between her parted knees. She released a sudden outburst of laughter when Mr. Crane's head appeared from under the covers at her abdomen. He kissed her stomach around her navel, then his head descended back under the covers. The bedspread crawled between her legs, and her moans returned.

"Come to me," she gasped.

He rose from beneath the covers, his naked shoulders and back exposed between the peaks of her knees like a wave about to descend over her. His torso was held upward by muscular arms and supported by locked elbows. Their bodies shifted to make an unseen connection, which caused their mouths to open in awed surprise. He bent and kissed her neck as he moved. His body crashed into hers, slowly at first, like a steam locomotive as it built momentum. She raked her fingernails across his back. His shoulder blades drew together. He seized her wrists and pinned her hands to the mattress, then slammed his body into hers with greater vigor. Beads of sweat shimmered down his back. When he reached full speed, her cries quickened and drove him into a sprint. She threw back the covers, then hooked her leg around his thigh, and drove her heel into his pasty white buttock. With a grunt, he arched his back, then paused. His weight pinned her. He drew back his hips with his cock still half inside her. She had a look of anticipation with parted lips and heavy eyelids. Seconds hung in the air.

In a mere glimpse, like the shutter of a camera opening and closing, Lucius saw for the first time. Mr. Crane's cock half inside Mrs. Crane. Between her legs, a patch of golden brown hair hid uncertain folds. Somewhere in the thicket was a passage.

Mr. Crane kissed her between her breasts, then rested his head on her far shoulder. Her nails left angry red marks on his back.

Lucius gasped, then covered his mouth. He realized he must have stopped breathing. Mrs. Crane's gaze rolled slow and lazy toward the door. His body stiffened and his mouth hung open. He gripped the doorframe for fear he would tumble into the bedroom. She blinked softly. He was sure she saw him. He backed away slowly into the gloom of the dark hallway until he could no longer see her.

When Lucius returned to the guest bedroom, Beatrice stood framed in her bedroom doorway. Her sleepy eyes were on him. She closed her door before he could say anything. His eyes now accustomed to the dark. He slipped back into bed.

3

The grand house stood empty and silent like the giant conch on the shelf in Mr. Crane's study. Earlier, Lucius woke to the chitter of dishes and silverware as the Crane's conducted their morning weekday breakfast ritual. No dreams came to him as he slept last night. The guest bedroom's dresser and closet, now filled with his clothing and things, felt as foreign as when he first arrived. He walked down the hall to the dining room in his stocking feet. He poked his head into the kitchen. The sheer curtains that fluttered at the open window were the only life he found there. The soft chime of silver and china came from the dining room. Mrs. Crane sat at the end of the table in her usual spot in a navy and cream patterned dress with a scooped neck and abbreviated sleeves that only covered her upper arms. She had pinned her hair up into a pleasing modest shape, unlike the spill of curls that he witnessed last night that remind him of octopus arms stretch across her pillow. As he moved into the room, her penetrating pale blue eyes watched him.

"Good morning," he said.

His voice was low and careful.

"Good morning."

She had prepared for them a simple breakfast of eggs and toast.

"Come sit, and have breakfast with me," she said.

Her voice was softer than usual, like a stringed musical instrument tuned down to a lower key. Her lips curled into a gentle, tight-lipped smile. Lucius swallowed, then took his seat at the side of the table. The way she watched him, like a snake perched in a tree with its body cocked and ready to strike. When he peered at her, she busied herself. She unfolded and placed her cloth napkin across her lap and buttered her toast without a glance at him. He mimicked her while they ate. When she sipped her coffee, he sipped his orange juice.

"Mr. Crane went to the office today, and Beatrice is at school, as you know, so today that leaves us to enjoy each other's company," she said.

His narrow shoulders knotted. He watched her until her gaze met his, then his attention retreated to his plate of food.

"I have things I need your help with today."

He heard his mom's stern voice inside his head, chiding him to look at whoever was speaking to him. His gaze met hers.

"Okay."

Trapped in her gaze, her pale sky-blue eyes offered nothing, but her polite smile reassured him. He drank his orange juice, and made several quick glances at her, only to find her gaze still on him, even when she raised her coffee cup to her lips.

After breakfast, she ascended the staircase, and he followed. He watched her take each step in her modest sling back heels, how her ankles bent and created creases in her stockings. She turned around when they reached the top of the stairs and he almost bumped into her.

"There are a few boxes I need from the attic. If I'm right. A young and adventurous boy, such as yourself, should have no trouble maneuvering in the tight space."

She went to the nearest hallway closet with a door narrower than the rest. She retrieved a long metal rod with a hook at the end the circumference of a quarter.

"We need to pull down the stairs."

She raised the rod and with ease hooked a metal eyelet recessed in the ceiling. The rectangular outline of a door he had never seen before appeared like magic. When she pulled on the metal rod, unseen hinges and springs protested as if they awoke from some ancient slumber. As the attic door angled down, steps became visible. She handed the metal rod to him while she unfolded the segments of hinged wooden steps until they reached the floor. She looked at him with an energy of excitement, as though they had found some mystical entrance. His eyes widened as he peered up the wooden steps and into the gloom of the attic space.

"Take your time and be careful climbing up."

"I don't know. It looks pretty dark up there."

His chest tightened. He took a step back and his feet took root.

"In the attic, there are two lights with pull strings to switch them on. The first one should be close."

She sounded uncertain where the lights were, and he wondered when she had last climbed up into the space, if ever. She may have, at most, climbed to the top of the steps and only peered in. If the space was that constricted as she described, Mr. Crane, a mountain of a man over six-feet, must have great difficulty maneuvering up there. Her pale blue gaze, and her expression of his certain victory, lit a small fire within him, large enough to move him to stand before the folded stairs. He held both sides of the steps and climbed. They felt more like rungs on a ladder than steps.

"There are five dress boxes I would like brought down. They are rectangular and of a certain depth."

He glanced down at her. She drew outlines in the air of the approximate dimensions of the boxes, then she then held the unravelled staircase with its metal hinges locked in place. He wanted to please her, so he nodded and continued to climb. The wooden steps were rough, so he felt for splinters and hoped not to get pricked.

"If I recall correctly, they are near the far left corner."

He wondered who put them there in the first place. He glanced down at her. She held her hand to the side of her face with an expression as though she were watching some circus high-wire act.

"Okay."

It was all he could think of to say as he reached the top.

"Mind your head while you're up there."

At the top of the steps, the mouth of the attic emanated a breath of warm, thick, dusty air. He hunched over and reached in to feel for anything he might hit his head on, and immediately grabbed hold of the main beam that ran straight into the depths of the attic. The pull string for the first light made him lurch back when it fell across his face. It felt like a spider's web. He pulled the string. The bare bulb bleached spots in his vision, and for a moment, darkened his surroundings.

The attic space ran the length of the roof with a track of boards to stand on. He recalled his dad once told him how his old buddy, Randy Jeffries, fell through the floor of an attic space, only to have his leg stick out of the living room ceiling. "Dumb ass," his dad added after telling the story. His dad explained there was no support in an attic other than the beams and joists. Lucius stuck to the track of boards, but still tested his weight with each step. The low ceiling forced him to crab walk on bent knees and duck his head low enough to avoid contact with the above joists. The further in he went, the dustier it seemed, and the hotter.

Tucked in the pitched spaces on both sides were cardboard boxes of various sizes and in erratic piles. There were two without tops filled with Christmas decorations. He imagined it would be his duty to come and fetch them when the holidays arrived, if he still lived with the Cranes.

"Did you find the boxes?"

Her muted voice called up. He turned and shouted back toward the opening.

"Not yet."

His wet bangs stuck to his forehead, and beads of sweat stung his eyes. As he ventured deeper into the attic, his own shadow cast in front of him made it almost as difficult to see as when he first entered. He ducked to allow light from behind to cast over his shoulder until he spotted the pull string to the other light. There were more boxes deeper in the attic, a few trunks with reinforced brass corners, and old suitcases. He found what he thought were the boxes she wanted, but there were only three. He opened the topmost one to find a dress inside. These must be the boxes. He turned about, cautious not to hit his head or step off the support boards. He found two more similar size boxes wedged beneath a pile of smaller ones. When he removed the topmost boxes, there sat a flat yellow and black box with the Kodak logo on it, like the photo paper boxes in Mr. Crane's darkroom. He peered down the length of the attic space, his footprints on the dusty raw wooden planks, to the opening where Mrs. Crane waited. Her silence and patient anticipation crawled on him like tiny spiders.

He knelt and opened the Kodak box, curious and certain to find photographs inside. Inside were prints sheathed in a protective frosted vellum. He glanced up and waited for her to call to him. Seconds past. He slipped the photographs from the vellum and his eyes widened.

The black and white prints were pictures of her. A younger naked Mrs. Crane. A Mrs. Crane in only stockings, a garter belt, and a large rim hat. She was leaning back on an unrecognizable sofa with her legs open. Her full bare breasts with pointed nipples exposed. He fixed on the dark, triangular patch of pubic hair between her thighs. Her expression, not sated like what he saw after her having sex with Mr. Crane, but one of desire and a dare to come hither, an offering to the camera or to anyone who gazed at the photograph. He went to the next print. In the next picture, she wore a bra and panties, her back to the viewer, an elegant spine, hands behind her set to undo the clasp to free her breasts, those two enormous dew drops. His throat became dry, in part from the dust, which he tasted every time he licked his lips to wet them. His prick stiffened in his underpants.

"Lucius?"

He jerked upright and bumped the back of his head on one of the overhead joists. A crown of pain radiated around his skull. A muted tock tock tock staccato of her heels as they struck the wooden steps and short shrieks from the stressed springs and hinges rose from the open doorway to the attic. He hurried to put the photographs back in the box. He skipped putting them back in the vellum sleeve and instead placed the vellum over the pictures and secured the top of the box.

"Lucius?"

He knelt behind the steamer trunk as if to shield himself from enemy fire. Her head and shoulders appeared backlit in the open attic doorway at the far end.

"What are you doing back there? I see the dress boxes. Come out from behind there and come back this way."

"Uh? There were only three. I think I found the other two."

He snatched the two boxes, but upset the Kodak box and the prints spilled out behind the steamer trunk among the joists and insulation. His eyes widened at the seductive images of Mrs. Crane bearing all. Her legs open for some lover to have her.

"Uh-uh. I think these are the other two boxes."

He held them up to the light.

"Bring them to me so I can have a look."

He shuffled on bent knees back to the open attic doorway, back to her—a breathing, in-the-flesh, in color, warm-blooded, adult female body—Mrs. Crane.

He twisted his hips to hide the awkward front of his pants where his erection poked forth. She took the top box from within his arms and smiled.

"Yes, that's what I'm looking for."

She sat the box at his feet and gazed inside the other one.

"Excellent. Can you fetch the other three? Thank you."

She descended the steps with the two boxes. He scurried back to the scattered nude pictures. He ducked behind the steamer trunk and gathered the photographs as quickly as he could and placed them in the box. He imagined her examining the contents of the two dress boxes, but then the tock tock tock of her heels came. Soon she would appear in the attic doorway. He lifted the top of the Kodak box and took one print and slipped it in the back of his pants and tucked his shirt in over it. He returned the two boxes that sat over the box of photographs and shuffled to get the last three dress boxes. Tock. Tock.

"No time to dally. It's far too hot up here for us to linger. You especially. You're in the belly of the beast."

He struggled to wrap his arms around the three boxes.

"Bring them to me one at a time so you don't drop or crush them."

He did as she asked. With each trip, she held out her open arms as if she were waiting for him to run to her so she could embrace him. The spell broke each time she took a dress box from him. When she had all five boxes, he turned out the two bare bulb lights and climbed down the fold-away attic staircase. She folded the segmented sections of stairs and pushed the door upward. The springs and hinges did the rest. They shrieked and the door made a final clunk when it shut flush with the ceiling.

She brushed the dust from his hair and shoulders.

"You're going to need a bath after today. What took you so long? I wouldn't want to be up there any longer than necessary."

He shrugged. Sweat tickled his neck at his collar and pinned his shirt to his back. His underpants clung to him. His erection, to his relief, departed before he climbed down from the attic. He excused himself to use the bathroom and waited for her to head downstairs with some of the dress boxes. He went to the guest bedroom and untucked his shirt. The photograph tucked in his pants stuck to his lower back. He carefully peeled it free, then he slipped the rumpled photograph between the mattress and box spring, then smoothed out the wrinkles in the bedspread. Afterwards he brought down the two dress boxes she left at the top of the stairs. When he got downstairs, she was nowhere to be found.

He found the side door open. Beyond the outer screen door, he saw her in the driveway. The trunk was open on her little silver coupe convertible, a Mercedes-Benz 300 SL Roadster. The underlined chrome *300 SL* badge on the automobile's trunk lid emblazoned in his memory. As she headed back to the house, he got the two dress boxes he left on the entranceway table and met her at the door.

"Perfect. We're going to run these dresses to the church to donate them."

"Okay."

He followed her to the car and put the boxes in the trunk next to the other three. She closed the trunk lid and eyed him for a moment with her penetrating pale sky-blue eyes, then took him by the shoulders and rotated him around. She huffed, then patted and brushed the attic dust from his hair and clothes, which were more visible out in the sunlight. His shirt stuck to his lower back, where the hidden photograph once clung. He stiffened when she patted the dust from the seat of his pants. His shoulders curled, and he held his hands in front of him to hide his arousal. She held his upper arm to steady him. His underpants, damp with sweat from his adventure in the attic, clung to his body. The skin of his penis pulled and stuck to his sweaty abdomen. He fought the urge to tug at the front of his pants. The tip of his penis ached for a destination his youth had yet to possess the map to.

"I guess that will have to do. I'll put the top down and maybe the wind will do the trick."

She smiled. It was the first time he saw her smile. It was a real smile, one of sincere joy.

It was a simple there and back to St. Paul's Evangelical Lutheran Church. Mrs. Crane seemed pleased that Father Lawrence Hagen was out, so she could avoid any lengthy conversations. She instead left the dress boxes with Mrs. Helen Chadwick, an elderly widow, organist, and a local volunteer who was busy dusting and polishing the woodwork. Lucius remained quiet during their time with Mrs. Chadwick. There were questions about him, but Mrs. Crane only gave brief answers and stressed that he and she had a busy day ahead of them. She wanted to get to her gardening, or so she told him on the drive to St. Paul's. No dallying, like she told him, when she admonished him for his time in the attic. During the ride to the church and back, he stole glances at her. She held the wheel to the Mercedes with gloved hands and shifted the little silver convertible coupe with the confidence and determination of a race car driver. Even in heels, she managed the clutch, brake, and accelerator with ease. On the ride back, she drove faster. With the top down, the rush of late morning air loosened her pinned up hair. The curls that came free lifted in the wind and she became a goddess.

They sat in the driveway in the little silver coupe with the top down. She combed her fingers through his wind-swept hair. It was a moment where he was free to stare at her moist red painted lips without suspicion.

"There. Not perfect, but you look like you've spent the day at the beach."

He touched his hair and curled his lips into a soft smile. He got out of the car while she put the top back up. Ms. Käthe and Ms. Mila walked up the driveway, their purses hooked over their forearms. Both wore their usual knee-length gray dresses with white aprons, and their hair pinned back under white ruffled headpieces. The slender Ms. Mila glanced first at him and smiled before she turned her attention to Mrs. Crane. Ms. Mila had a more elegant gait than the boorish, older stout Ms. Käthe.

"Hello, Mrs. Crane."

Both women spoke. Their greetings staggered.

"Hello."

Mrs. Crane slipped off her driving gloves and tidied up the loose curls that fell from her hair.

"Mrs. Crane, can we help to carry anything in?" Ms. Käthe asked.

"Oh no, thank you Ms. Käthe. We were only out for a little drive."

"Very good," Ms. Käthe said.

Ms. Mila only smiled and nodded. The two maids held the side door open for Lucius and Mrs. Crane to enter the house.

"Lucius, I want you to head out to the backyard while I change my clothes and you can help me with the gardening."

"All right," he said.

He heard her talking to the two women before he went out the door that lead to the stone patio and the backyard. They had spoken his name. That much was all he recognized.

He waited on the stone steps. Mrs. Crane came out in denim pants and a white button-down cotton shirt. She also traded her heels for canvas oxfords and let her hair down. A yellow headband kept her hair out of her eyes. She wore what his mom often wore when not waitressing or working at some office. The memory made his chest hurt and caused his stomach to knot. Mrs. Crane touched his shoulder. A hug would have been better, but anything had to be better than nothing. In her defense, she knew nothing about the pain he felt, or perhaps she was trying to help him take his mind off of things.

"Come along. We need the gardening tools from the shed."

She handed him a pair of brown cotton work gloves. He followed her to a small wooden structure next to the woodpile. Its roof tapered downward and its size was too small to store even a small sports car. The weathered wood siding, dark with moisture in areas where the shade of the trees blocked the sun, reminded him of campground outhouses. The metal door latch worked better than he expected, but the hinges creaked.

The entire afternoon, he followed her around the property. He was happy to trade, shlepping a garden rake and pale for her, as opposed to going to school. Random, gratifying moments came when the sun illuminated her light golden brown hair, and the breeze animated her soft curls. Those moments intensified when she glanced over at him with her pale sky-blue eyes. Each missed opportunity without the camera struck madness inside him. He wanted to cry out for her to stay put so he could photograph her. Mr. Crane had loaded the Leica with a fresh roll of film, but where was it? Had he left it in the darkroom? Without the camera, he tried to internalize the images of her so he might peer at them later in his mind. There was another alternative. The black and white photograph of her under his mattress.

She snipped the dead or dying leaves from the flowers and bushes around the house. When she focused on her pruning, he snuck glances at her and imagined her body. It astounded him how her clothing hid her true shape, her naked private shape only known to him in black and white. Under her white cotton button-down shirt, her breasts took the shape of her bra in the form of two missile heads. Even her heels and toes, which he has never seen without shoes, he had seen sheathed in sheer stockings in the attic photographs. He longed to see them bare.

After they ate a brief lunch of sandwiches and lemonade set out on the wrought iron outdoor patio table by Ms. Mila, they continued pruning until it was time to fetch Beatrice from Leighton Day, a private all girls' school. Before he came to live with the Cranes, he had never heard of such places. All he knew was public school, and Wilton Saunders Junior High in particular. He sat on the stone steps with Mrs. Crane after they put the garden tools back in the shed.

"Lucius, why don't you play outside while I get Beatrice. Ms. Käthe and Ms. Mila will look after you."

"Can I go to the darkroom?"

Visions of his developed film strip that hung in the darkroom called to him.

"No, you must wait for Mr. Crane to get home."

Her pale sky-blue eyes bore into him. He shrunk inside.

"Okay. Can I take pictures?"

"I don't know where Mr. Crane's camera is, and I think it's best that you wait for him to help you."

Her lack of trust in his ability jabbed at his pride.

"Okay."

It was all he could say. He avoided looking at her and his gaze roamed the backyard and made brief stops at the trees and flowers as a bumblebee might.

"When we get back, I'm sure Beatrice would love to keep you company."

He smiled with his gaze off in the distance.

"That would be nice."

He saw her legs and shoes from the corner of his vision as she walked away. Then he heard the shriek of the door springs when the door opened and closed. Unseen birds chirped from the trees. A cloud of gnats floated near the shade of a hydrangea shrub, and single flying insects flew determined on random flight paths.

He saw Ms. Käthe in the window on the upper floor. She peered down at him. Her expression stone faced like a prison guard in a tower. He snorted, but then a tightness crawled up his spine. What if they were cleaning the rooms and making the beds? The photograph. He stood and hurried into the house.

Lucius stood in the guest bedroom doorway. His eyes were wide and mouth open. Either Ms. Käthe or Ms. Mila had made the bed, dusted the room, and placed items back to their rightful spots. This was more alarming than finding either of them in the bedroom. He rushed to the side of the bed, and half slid on his knees, pulled up the bedspread and sheets, and thrust his hand between the mattress and box spring. Nothing. He gasped.

Footsteps clomped in the hallway, brought on images of the boxy black low-heeled loafers both women wore. He plunged his hand in again, stretched until his fingertips touched the edge of paper, photo paper. After he pulled his hand free, he tugged at the sheets and bedspread to straighten them.

"What are you doing in here?"

The stern, heavy voice of Ms. Käthe boomed from the doorway. He peered at her with wide eyes. She filled the doorway with her stout frame. Her arms crossed, which barely circled her large bosom.

"Uh?"

"Out boy. You'll have plenty of time tonight to mess things up when you go to bed."

Her thick German accent pronounced 'out' as 'hout'.

She waved him from the room. He stood, but remained fixed in place until she backed out into the hallway to give him space to exit. She followed him to the top of the stairs, where he felt her eyes on him as he scurried down to the ground floor. He worried she would return to the bedroom, curious to know why he was in there, kneeling at the side of the bed. It would be a stretch that she would believe he had been praying, even if she caught him actually praying aloud.

After dinner, Ms. Käthe and Ms. Mila departed. Lucius stood in the hallway. Ms. Käthe gave him a look as though she might know his secret. His stomach knotted. A late arriving Mr. Crane stood outside the door as the women exited. He held his briefcase with his sleeves rolled, necktie loosened, and collar unbuttoned. The three exchanged both greetings and goodnights. Mr. Crane smiled as he passed him and squeezed his shoulder.

"Hello, Lucius."

The look on his face was joyful, yet secretive, with the way he cocked his eyebrow. Uncertain how to respond, Lucius raised his eyebrows.

"Hello."

His greeting sounded more like a question. He followed Mr. Crane down the hallway to the study, where Mr. Crane deposited his suit jacket and briefcase. Beatrice greeted her father, and he swept her up into his arms. Lucius's heart ached at the sight of them. He stepped away unnoticed as Mr. Crane asked Beatrice how her day was.

He wanted to run upstairs to the bedroom and check if the photograph remained hidden under the mattress, but found Mrs. Crane at the bottom of the stairs.

"Hello, Lucius. Where are you off to?"

"Nowhere."

It felt like nowhere was his destination, and maybe where he belonged.

"Let's go to the dining room. Mr. Crane has yet to have dinner and has some news for you."

Mr. Crane and Beatrice sat at the table. Mrs. Crane went to the kitchen to get his plate of food that Ms. Käthe had prepared for him and kept warm in the oven. Lucius took his seat and listened to Beatrice go on about how she bested her schoolmate, Cassandra Martin, in their French class. He snorted and tried to fathom why anyone would want to learn French. He knew of no one who spoke French, except for now Beatrice.

Mr. Crane ate and spoke while everyone sat and listened. Mrs. Crane curled her hand under her chin.

"Lucius, I spoke to your Aunt Phoebe again. It was a brief conversation, but we agreed we would talk again tomorrow, and you would get a chance to speak to her. We all want what is best for you. I hope I can speak for everyone at this table. We've enjoyed having you live with us."

Beatrice bobbed her head in a bold, exaggerated nod. Mrs. Crane only glanced at him with her pale sky-blue eyes. A subtle sadness in them.

"What does it all mean?" he asked.

He sat with his hands under the table, his fingers interwoven in a tight grip. Mr. Crane finished chewing and rested his fork on his plate.

"It means your Aunt Phoebe may want you to come live with her. She is your father's sister and next living relative. That is typically how the law works. I would like you to stay with us, unless after speaking to her you would like to live with her. We would all like you to be happy."

His eyebrows knit together, and he looked down at the table.

"I know it's a lot to think about. Don't be sad. I have some fun things planned for us tonight."

He glanced up at Mr. Crane.

"That's right. I developed a contact sheet with all of your pictures and some of mine as well. We each shot half of the last roll of film. You can choose a few of your pictures and we can make some larger prints. How does that sound?"

His eyes brightened, and he grinned.

∾

Lucius knelt on the stool. His body stretched over the table, with the loupe to his eye to inspect the postage sized images on the contact sheet. Kenneth sat next to him, arms crossed, and smiled inside.

"See any good ones?"

"Uh huh," Lucius said.

The boy never lifted his head. Kenneth chuckled.

"Are you going to let me see them?"

His tone was playful. Lucius finally looked up and slid the contact sheet and the loupe toward him. He repositioned the table lamp over the contact sheet and brought his eye down to the loupe to have a look. He already looked over the contact sheet the other night, after he had sent Lucius to bed.

"Oh? Ah? I see. Mm. Oh. Hm."

"What? What is it? Are they terrible?"

He took his time to keep Lucius on the edge of his seat. He raised his head slowly and stared into the boy's questing eyes. As a hint of doubt seeped into the boy's gaze, Kenneth smiled.

"These are superb, Lucius. I shot the first half of the roll, but the second half of the roll, the ones you shot, are as good, if not better."

"Really?"

"Yes, really."

He slid the contact sheet and loupe back to Lucius. He reached into a cup of pens and pencils and handed him a thin black marker.

"Pick three. Circle the ones you like the most and we'll make some prints."

It took Lucius seconds to select three.

"Let me see."

He slid the contact sheet back to him. Even without the loupe, he saw that Lucius picked a picture of him, the single shot of Beatrice, and one of a dragonfly balanced on a tall blade of grass.

"Good, good, these will make for some lovely prints."

He then took the loupe and looked over the other images. After he marked little x's on three of the shots he had taken, he showed the boy the plastic sleeve holding all the negatives, cut in groups of six.

"These sleeves protect the negatives and keep the dust off. When you take more pictures, you'll want to store them like this."

The boy's keen attention made him smile. Lucius spoke little, but when he nodded, he knew the boy understood, especially how he handled himself behind the camera. Kenneth talked him through the process. He prepared the chemicals and poured them into the three flat trays: developer, stop bath, and fixer. He expected Lucius to wince at the smell as he did the first time, but the boy was stone faced. His eyes, though, watched every move. The boy never seemed to blink his eyes. Kenneth removed one of the negative strips and placed it into the enlarger. He smiled at Lucius before turning off the lights and turning on the red bare bulb safe light. He lowered the enlarger to make an eight by ten print, then brought the image into focus. From the shelf, he retrieved the box of photo paper and carefully inserted one sheet into the holder, centering it under the projected image. He set the timer and exposed the paper, then slipped it into the tray of developer chemicals, and again set the timer. They watched as the black and white image appeared.

"Whoa," Lucius said.

Kenneth slipped the print into the tray with the stop bath and waited ten seconds. He squeezed the boy's shoulder, then finally slipped the print into the fixer and set the timer for thirty seconds. Afterwards, he rinsed the print in the sink. It was over-exposed and too dark.

"Let's try that one again."

He adjusted the time under the enlarger and ended up with a more pleasing exposure and a more balanced light to dark tonal range in the overall image. He used the same settings for the remaining images and figured any adjustments Lucius made in-camera were minor. All six prints, including the three pictures he shot, all developed with less effort than he anticipated. He turned on the lights and turned off the red safelight. Both leaned over to inspect the prints.

"Hm," Kenneth said.

Lucius looked at him with his head tilted as if he were waiting for Kenneth to render his verdict. All six eight-by-ten black and white prints sat out on the table. The ones Kenneth shot were the top row, and Lucius's the bottom. The boy has an eye for photography. He glanced at Lucius from the corner of his eye to watch the boy's reaction. He was quiet. His head turned slowly and his eyes even slower as he took in the photographs. Kenneth crossed his arms and rested them on the tabletop. A sliver of jealousy pricked him. The boy can see, not as a child, but with maturity beyond his years.

"Wait here."

He left Lucius in the darkroom and hurried to his study to retrieve the Leica. When he returned, Lucius was where he had left him, leaning over the photographs. The boy never glanced up when he entered the darkroom with the camera. He sat the camera on the table behind them, then stood alongside Lucius with his arms crossed.

"Not bad I'd say. What do you think?" Kenneth asked.

"I really like them. When can we take, I mean, *make* more pictures?"

Kenneth laughed.

"You're making them. That's for sure. The pros use the word, *shoot*, as in when can we schedule another *shoot*?"

"Okay. When can we shoot again?"

He shook his head and laughed.

"You're something, Lucius. Quiet. I guess still waters indeed run deep."

Lucius wrinkled his face.

"Never mind, it's a good thing."

A timid and unsure smile formed on the boy's face.

"I have to say, Lucius, your one portrait of me is the best portrait *anyone* has ever taken of me."

"Really?"

He smiled at the boy.

"Yes, and your picture of Beatrice is excellent."

He wanted to add, "beginner's luck," but remained silent, as he knew better. Such a joking accusation would be silly, and the joke would be on him.

"Tell me what you think about the light on the faces in both portraits."

"I wanted it to be bright, but soft and even."

"Good."

They both looked at the picture of the dragonfly.

"You shot the dragonfly in direct sunlight. Why?"

"I liked how its wings glittered in the light."

"Okay. Interesting."

The boy knew the most important thing about photography. The quality of light. They looked at Kenneth's photographs. Two of Beatrice, one of her standing in the hallway near the open doorway to Kenneth's study, and one of her at the beach in a bathing suit standing in front of a large piece of driftwood. The other photograph was of Eleanor. She sat in one of the patio wicker chairs with bands of light from the setting sun over her shoulder. A near empty glass of wine sat in front of her on the coffee table. Kenneth remembered that evening. Beatrice stayed the night at her friend's house. He and Eleanor, after dinner, had sex on the kitchen table. Her nipples were still hard, and she was bra-less under her blouse in the photograph. There was a playful tilt to her head, a private quality of hers that he adored. Lucius appeared to consider the two pictures of Beatrice, but stared at the picture of Eleanor. He waited for the boy to say something, anything. His pride was on the line. What was taking so long? What did the boy see? Was he staring at Eleanor's nipples?

"Well?" Kenneth asked.

Lucius turned and met his gaze.

"These are incredible."

He smiled and patted the boy's head.

"Gee kid, give a guy a scare. What do you like about them?"

Lucius pointed at the picture of Beatrice in the hallway.

"The light from the study is soft, the hallway behind Beatrice is dark. It's spooky."

"Please don't tell Beatrice the picture of her is spooky. That's a good way to get her to never pose for you again."

He laughed. The boy's face reddened.

"This one is nice, too."

Lucius made no further comments about the picture of Beatrice at the beach. Kenneth thought he nailed the exposure. There were rich blacks and creamy whites. Could it be his age, or the fact she is wearing a bathing suit? The boy leaned to the side, as if to allow Kenneth a better look at the third photograph, his own photograph of Eleanor, as if it was some museum piece and Lucius was about to lecture on it.

"I really like the light."

Lucius pointed to the bands of light that came through the patio window and over Eleanor's shoulder. The edge of it touched her hair and brightened that side of her silhouette.

"I like the light, too."

He turned to face Lucius.

"I was thinking about something all day today."

Lucius tilted his head and raised his eyebrows. Kenneth went to the table behind them and retrieved the Leica. The boy's eyes brightened.

"Lucius. I want to give you this camera, but we have to have an understanding. This is an expensive and fantastic device. I know you understand the fantastic quality of it, but you must also know all the care needed to keep and maintain such a device. Will you promise me you will take care of this camera? I will show you all the maintenance, although minor, that needs to be done to keep it clean and functioning properly."

It was an odd question to ask, since he already knew the answer, but he needed to hear the boy say it. He needed to hear Lucius's promise.

"Oh, yes! Yes, I promise."

He smiled and nodded.

"Good."

He held the camera for a moment to feel its weight and to remember all the images he captured with it. His familiar tactile intimacy with the Leica's dials was like that of an old lover. He looked over the camera with deep consideration and sighed.

"Lucius, take good care of her. She's a beauty. You and her will capture some amazing pictures. I am most certain of it."

His voice trailed off as he handed Lucius the camera. Lucius held the Leica with both hands and Kenneth squeezed his shoulder and patted his back.

"Thank you. Thank you."

The boy sat the camera on the table and hugged Kenneth.

"You're going to be an amazing photographer."

Lucius beamed as he looked at the camera. He turned it slowly around on the tabletop to examine all of its sides.

"Remember, we put a fresh roll in it. Tomorrow, you can have some fun. Be thoughtful before you press the shutter button. If it's not worth it, save yourself a shot."

The boy nodded. Kenneth looked at his wristwatch.

"Oh, gee. It's getting late. You best head up and get ready for bed."

The boy's eyes looked heavy, as if he were already dreaming. No protest came from the boy. Only a soft question.

"Can I take the camera with me?"

"Sure, it's yours now."

He handed Lucius the camera and watched the boy step quietly from the room. He left the six prints out on the table to finish drying and cleaned up. When the door opened, he glanced up, expecting to see Lucius, but Eleanor stood in the doorway with a glass of Chardonnay, with one arm cradling the other.

"I came down to check on you boys, but then I met Lucius on the stairs, heading up to bed. Did you give him your camera?"

Kenneth leaned his hip against the table next to the prints.

"Yes. You should see the boy's pictures. He's meant to be a photographer and I intend to help him."

She tilted her head.

"Is that so?"

"Come see."

He sat on the stool. Her heels clicked on the tile floor when she came over to the table. He loved the sound of women's heels, especially when they approached. She stood over and inspected all six prints. He was certain she knew who took which pictures simply by the logistics.

"He has your eye."

"Do you think so?"

"He does."

She hummed softly as her gaze slowly scanned each print. She ignored the photograph of the dragonfly and focused on the portraits.

"We spent the day together, Lucius and I. He watched me with curious eyes the entire time. We took a short drive over to St. Paul's so I could drop off some dresses to donate, and when we returned, he helped me tidy up the flowers in the backyard."

"So he was helpful? That's good."

"Yes, and he is quiet and reserved for now, but you know how rowdy boys can get?"

"He'll be fine. You'll be fine."

"What about Beatrice?"

"She'll be fine too."

She took a drink of her Chardonnay, then handed the glass to him, and he took a drink and handed the glass back to her. He then went and locked the door, turned off the lights and turned on the red safety light, which bathed them and everything in the room in shades of red. She sat on the stool and unbuttoned the top of her dress. The scooped neckline allowed him direct access to the flesh of her neck and collarbones, now unbuttoned, allowed access to other things. He planted soft kisses on her neck before their lips met. Her skin had the scent of bergamot, pear, and gardenia. Her breasts poured into the molds of her bra cups and yielded to their shape like the heads of missiles. Kenneth slipped his hand inside her unbuttoned dress, first to touch her breast, then to venture under her bra to find her hardened nipple.

Her lips parted, and her breath warmed his cheek. A soft hum rose from within her as he rolled her nipple between his fingertips. She unzipped his trousers and unbuckled his belt, and everything except his boxers fell to his ankles. The belt buckle made a clunk on the tile floor. The front of his boxers stood out, a declaration of his arousal. She knelt and pulled down his boxers so they joined his trousers at his ankles, then her hot mouth encircled him, first the head, then half of his length. He groaned. Her tongue expertly ran over the contours of the tip of his cock and caused his buttocks to flex. She grasped one of his buttocks in one hand and held his cock in the other. He grunted.

"Wait, wait, not yet."

She stood, turned around, and bent over the darkroom table. She lifted the skirt of her dress and slid down her panties enough to suggest he slide them down further and have her. He did as she beckoned. Her soft moans echoed in the small darkroom, and their bodies moved and molded in shades of red.

4

In the study, Mr. Crane sat behind his desk with the phone to his ear. Lucius sat opposite him in a guest chair and listened to the chirpy voice that came through the receiver. His Aunt Phoebe's voice, so he was told. A woman he never met, at least not at an age he would remember. Her words, he struggled to make out, but her tone was energetic.

"Yeah, uh-huh. Yes, he's been doing well here, all things considered."

Mr. Crane looked at him and smiled. It was not a smile of joy, but one of assurance.

"No-no. His school was kind enough to excuse him for the two weeks before their summer break."

Mr. Crane leaned back in his padded swivel executive chair. Lucius held his hands with his fingers knit together in his lap. He looked at the tall bookshelves, mostly filled with neatly shelved leather bound law books. There was another shelf, with various size books, the one where he first saw Mr. Crane's Leica on display. Only the spiny large conch and antique brass compass remained, pushed closer to fill the gap where the camera once sat.

The conversation with his Aunt Phoebe droned on. He tuned them out. He put his head back on the chair and his arms up on the armrests. It reminded him of visits to the doctor's office with his mom, where the conversation between her and the doctor never seemed to end. Who would be his mom now? Aunt Phoebe? Mrs. Crane?

He squeezed the leather armrests.

"Lucius?"

He sat up, stunned, as if hit by a bucket of cold water.

"No, he's fine, just daydreaming. I'll put him on."

Mr. Crane held his large palm over the mouthpiece and leaned forward with his elbows on the desk.

"Lucius. Your Aunt Phoebe would like to talk to you."

Mr. Crane held out the phone. Lucius stood at the side of the desk, but was slow to grasp the phone. He moved with trepidation when he brought it to his ear.

"Hello?"

His voice sounded small and distant, like hearing it from the other side of some tunnel.

"Hello Lucius. I'm your Aunt Phoebe, your daddy, Darius's older sister. We've never met, but your daddy sent me a picture of you when you were a baby."

Her voice was warm, rich, and husky—sexy even—like those women in some of the classic movies his mom liked to watch. She spoke slowly, each word offered with care. Her delivery reminded him of Ms. Hart, his English teacher. She spoke slow and clear as if he was some much younger child. Unlike with Ms. Hart, his aunt's voice was welcoming and lacked any tone of resentment.

Mr. Crane watched intently. Occasionally, he raised a curious eyebrow. Lucius turned his gaze away and traced the writing mat on top of the desk. He had no words for his Aunt Phoebe. She probably sensed that and went on.

"Mr. Crane and I have been discussing what is best for you regarding whom you should live with. I live in Bradford, Indiana. It's a quiet, small town. Do you know where Indiana is?"

"In school, I've seen it on a map of the United States—Indiana. I don't know where Bradford is."

She chuckled through the phone. Her laughter was rich and musical. He felt closer to her because of it.

"I suppose you wouldn't. Silly of me to ask you that. Indiana is far from Connecticut. I live in a one-bedroom apartment above a laundromat. Not very glamorous, huh? From what Mr. Crane has described, you're living in a mansion."

Her voice differed from his mom's, but had a similar soothing quality.

"Oh, it is, and the backyard, it's like a small park with trees, flowers, birds, and bugs."

Speaking to her reminded him of conversations he had with his mom. Conversations he would no longer have. Emotional fatigue settled over him and he fell silent.

"Hm. That sounds terrific. I'm glad you like it there."

Something in her voice spoke of home. Mr. Crane was staring at him when he glanced up from the desk, and he lowered his eyes again.

"Aunt Phoebe?"

Her title felt as foreign as her place in his life.

"Do you think I should come live with you?"

"Oh, Lucius."

Her heavy breath in and exhalation followed by the rumble of her clearing her throat came through the receiver.

"Since your parents' funeral, I've been asking myself that very question."

She paused.

"I'm not sure if it's the best thing for you. You're very lucky the Cranes have taken you in."

"I know."

"Also, don't you want to go to school with your friends? It's always tough making new friends."

"Beatrice is my new friend, and that was easy."

"Who is Beatrice? Hey, are you telling me you have a girlfriend? That's more the reason to stay."

"She's not my girlfriend. She's Mr. and Mrs. Crane's daughter."

"Oh. Well, I'm sure she's nice. Is she pretty?"

He wrinkled his face.

"Um? I guess."

"Wouldn't you miss her?"

"No."

She laughed.

"That's not nice. I'm sure she would miss you."

"I don't think so."

"Look, there are other things to consider. I work crazy hours and might not be home to look after you. Also, I'm not much of a cook. I'm sure Mrs. Crane is a much better cook."

"Mrs. Crane doesn't cook. Ms. Käthe does."

"Who is Ms. Käthe?"

"She's one of the maids who cooks and cleans."

"Is that so? One of? How many do they have?"

"Two. Ms. Käthe and Ms. Mila."

It was quiet on the other end of the line.

"Lucius, you should be so lucky. Be grateful you have such an amazing place to live."

"I guess."

Mr. Crane touched his arm and motioned for the phone.

"Hi. Yeah, I guess he's a little mopey, but he deserves to be."

Mr. Crane's voice dropped to a whisper.

"I don't think he's grieved much."

He glanced at the Tiffany table lamp on Mr. Crane's desk. The domed lampshade had a fruit motif composed of abstract pieces of tinted glass fitted together to create images of golden pears and green apples.

"It will be good for you to see him, regardless if he remembers you. He'll know his family when he sees you. I'm sure of it. I'm sorry you have to go through your brother's things, but it has to be done. Oh no, it's my pleasure. All right. Looking forward to meeting you, too."

The tone of Mr. Crane's voice rose and, when he laughed, it caught Lucius off guard. It was an overly familiar, even flirtatious, laugh. What could she have said to induce such a reaction? Mr. Crane put his feet up on his desk. Lucius's eyebrows knit together.

"Yes, we can certainly get a drink somewhere. With all that's happened, I'm sure we can all use a stiff one."

Mr. Crane chuckled.

"All right, yes—yes, of course. You too. Goodbye."

Mr. Crane put the receiver back on its cradle. He stood and squeezed Lucius's shoulder.

"Are you okay?"

He nodded.

"Your Aunt Phoebe will be in Connecticut in a few days to take care of your father's and mother's affairs. We'll all go to your parents' house to figure out what to do with their belongings and the house. You can see if there's anything you would like to keep. It's a sad time. If you think it will be too much for you, you can stay here."

"I'll be fine."

He was unsure of his own words, but he wanted to put on a brave face. Mr. Crane only nodded and stared into his eyes. Soon Aunt Phoebe will come to Connecticut. The thought echoed in his head. He tried to imagine a face that would go with her voice, that husky, witty and playful television damsel voice. After he left the study, he worried for Mrs. Crane, and an overwhelming urge to protect her came over him.

5

"Look at the camera, or off to either side of me," Lucius said.

He lowered the Leica and held it with both hands at chest-level. His eyebrows knit together when Beatrice's eyes wandered toward the house. She stood in the shade of one of the majestic elm trees, her loose hair and summer dress lifted and animated by the breeze. Her hair fell across her face and she brushed it away. An awkward smile came and went as she settled into the pose.

"Ok, I'm ready," she said.

When he looked through the camera's viewfinder, her gaze was once more upward and toward the house. He huffed and turned to see what she was looking at. Ms. Käthe stood at one of the bedroom windows. She gazed out at them, then disappeared into the shadowy gloom. He turned to Beatrice.

"What? What's wrong?"

"I don't like her in my room."

"Who? You mean Ms. Käthe? Why?"

Beatrice glared at him. A fire in her eyes. She cocked an eyebrow and smirked.

"Daddy likes you, and I've concluded you're not a spy, so I'll tell you."

Up to this point, she gave no signs that she had been unsure of him. She saw him peeking in her parents' bedroom, or at least he thought she had. He lowered the camera, so it dangled above his belt buckle, then he put his hands on his waist.

"Thanks, I guess."

Her eyes darted back-and-forth between Lucius and her bedroom window. "Spies. The both of them."

"Huh? That's crazy."

She narrowed her eyes. His shoulders slumped, and he put his hands in his pockets.

"I'm not sure about Ms. Käthe, but Ms. Mila is really kind to me. Ms. Mila can't be a spy."

"Don't be fooled. Ms. Mila can act sweet, but she tells Ms. Käthe and Mrs. Crane everything. As for Ms. Käthe, I know she snooped in my bedroom. Things in my drawers were disturbed after she cleaned my room."

"Mrs. Crane? You mean your mother?"

Her arms straighten, and her hand balled into fists.

"Mother? Heh. Stepmother."

His face went slack.

"Eleanor is my stepmother. Some eye you have, as my father seems to believe. I don't look anything like her. Thank God. My real mother was beautiful. And she was kind and gentle."

Her shoulders slumped, and she cradled her arms in front of her. Even though her gaze lowered, her glassy, wet eyes were visible. Lucius raises the Leica before the moment had vanished and he captured her. She seemed not to notice.

"Sorry."

Her lips formed a subtle, soft smile.

"I'm the one who should be sorry. You have no one."

Ever since he arrived at the Crane's house, he tried to immerse himself in their lives, so he could forget his own. Beatrice glanced once more toward the house.

"I miss Anna, our previous house maid. She was from Paris, a *real* French maid. Eleanor fired her, but my dad said, 'we let her go.' And Eleanor hired Ms. Käthe and Ms. Mila, those German witches. Don't trust them. I don't."

"Okay, got it."

She held her hand out to him.

"C'mon on, I have something to show you."

When he took her hand, she tugged him until they ran out to the edge of the property where the enormous sycamore stood solemnly rooted. Its branches stretched out wide and welcoming. They ran to its wide trunk like when she rushed to be swept up into her father's arms. They leaned against the great trunk and laughed as they fought to catch their breath. The bark of the tree was like the hide of an elephant. The wide trunk of the sycamore was such that if they held hands, they would circle less than half its diameter.

While she laughed, he brought the camera to his eye, focused, and pressed the shutter button before she made too much sense of what he was up to. He smiled, certain he got the shot. She smiled and dashed around the backside of the sycamore. He circled around the great trunk in the other direction, only to find himself alone. A giggle floated down from above. She knelt on a broad lower branch and glanced down at him.

"C'mon. Climb Lucius."

She smiled, then pulled herself up to the next branch. The skirt of her dress flared, and he saw her white panties. A thrill surged in him. He slipped his arm through the camera's strap and positioned the camera to his back to protect it, and then he climbed. As she climbed, she glanced back with a coy smile. He looked at her wide-eyed. He wrestled himself up the next branch only to watch her climb two more. The tree's skin higher up became mottled with patches of lighter green and tan against darker grays. As the sycamore's limbs decreased in diameter, he finally caught up to her. Two limbs cradled her, and she held on to the one that supported her back. He crept to her, hunched over like when he was in the Crane's attic. When he sat next to her, he struggled to catch his breath.

Their feet dangled in the open air. She kicked her bare legs. Her feet with her ankle socks and rubber-sole cotton oxfords floated out in space. Less bold, he fluttered his legs gently, as if he were treading water. His Buster Browns made slapping sounds when he tapped his feet together. He frowned at the scuff marks on his dark gray pants and hoped his shirt had no rips or lost buttons. It was a new outfit the Cranes got him. He slapped at the scuffs on his pant legs, but the open air beneath his feet mesmerized him and he stopped to take hold of the branch he sat on. The height provided a grand view of the deep back yard that lead to the house. From the distance and elevation, the enormous house appeared less monumental.

"Beautiful, isn't it?"

She closed her eyes and her chest rose as she took in a deep breath. The moment would have made for a nice picture of her, but he was slow to bring the camera from around his back. The angle could have been better, so no great loss, he figured. He panned the camera around. The tree's branches and leaves made for dreamlike vignettes of the world beyond the great sycamore. It reminded him of when he held his curled hands up to his eye when he pretended to be a pirate with a brass collapsable spyglass, scanning the seas for ships to plunder.

When he lowered the camera and turned, she had slid in close next to him. Their lips touched briefly. He drew back, wide-eyed. Her lips curled into a thin smile. His chest rose and fell, methodically, as if he considered every breath.

"Do you like me, Lucius?"

He swallowed.

"Um. Yes."

"Then why don't you kiss me?"

He wet his lips and leaned toward her. When he was close enough to feel her breath, he closed his eyes. His eyelids trembled like cheap roll-down shades. Their lips touched again. This time long enough for thoughtful consideration. Her lips were the softest thing he had ever felt. He wished the moment would last forever, but she broke their kiss. When he opened his eyes, she giggled.

"Remember when I told you I was going to show you something?"

"Uh-huh."

She dug in the left pocket of her dress. From within her palm, out slithered a short black beaded necklace with silver joints holding tiny jewels and a single large opal at the middle of the length of it all. The end captured between her thumb and forefinger.

His eyes widened.

"Where did you get that? It's not real, is it?"

"Yes, it's real. Its Eleanor's. I'm borrowing it. My father bought it for her. Do you like it?"

"Eh—yeah, it's nice—too nice. Does she know you have it?"

"Of course, silly."

"Oh?"

He chuckled, but his smile faltered. She swung her leg over the thick branch and straddled it.

"Put it on me."

She brushed her hair aside and held both ends of the opal choker, so all he needed to do was secure the clasp behind her neck. When he got it fixed, she turned around and sat facing him. She touched the necklace with her fingertips. The choker sat loose near the notch of her thin neck and collarbones. He had seen necklaces like this, not jeweled ones, but ones made of ribbon with a locket at the center.

"How does it look?"

She smiled, and her eyes brightened. He struggled not to tell her how ill fitted the choker was on her. He smiled instead.

"Like you're a princess."

"Why don't you take my picture?"

He considered her request, but the light was all wrong. His lips pulled to one side and his eyebrows knit together.

"What's wrong?"

"The light's not right. We need to find better light."

They both glanced around.

"Where? There's no place we can move around up here."

It seemed like her way of saying, "just take the picture."

"Let's climb down."

She looked as though she was contemplating the idea.

"C'mon, you look so nice. We have to do it right."

He grinned, which made her smile.

"Okay?"

"Okay."

They both descended the great sycamore. He moved carefully, despite her impatience. Twice, he worried she might step on his hand or push him out of the way. She passed him as they got closer to the ground. He took a different route and would have had to jump ten feet to the ground. Before he decided what to do, he saw where she went and climbed back up and around to follow her. She gave him a smug smile when he reached the ground.

"Well, where would you like me to stand?"

She crossed her arms and stared at him. It was too much for him to look her in the eyes. Instead, he glanced around the tree, then stepped here and there and scanned and searched. When he went around the sycamore, he shouted.

"Here."

She came around the tree, her impatient expression had softened. He pointed to the base of the tree.

"I want to get the tree in the shot. This side seems to have the best light. Here. Sit here."

Beatrice sat and straightened her dress around her legs. He gestured for her to lean back against the tree. She did, but at first she had an uncomfortable look on her face. Before he could direct her, she bent her legs, interlaced her fingers, and looped her hands around her knees.

"Perfect."

He held his hand up in a gesture for her to hold the pose, then he squatted down to her eye level, and turned the ring on the lens to bring her into focus. He sighed. The angle could be better. He got on his elbows and stomach like one of the plastic toy soldiers he used to play with when he was younger. There. He turned the aperture ring on the lens to get what Mr. Crane called 'deep depth of field,' or a picture that captured more overall details. After doing so, he turned the shutter speed dial to a slower speed to compensate. She sat framed with the trunk and lowest branches of the magnificent sycamore behind her. He brought her into focus and waited.

Her dark brown locks lifted, and her dress rippled in the breeze. With the black-beaded opal choker around her neck, she looked sophisticated and more mature.

"Don't move. Look around, but don't turn your head."

He continued to look through the viewfinder. He licked his lips. His heart thudded against the ground. The grass provided little cushion. It was as though Mother Earth had put her ear to his chest to listen to his heartbeat.

"There."

Click. The shutters, as they opened and closed, made a soft metallic whisper. Judging by her expression and how she fidgeted, she was unaware he had taken the picture.

"Stay still. I want to take a few."

She settled into her pose.

"Don't be too stiff."

She wrinkled her face and glared at him. He laughed, and she smiled. Click. He thumbed the lever to advance the film. Gusts of warm summer air swept across the yard, patches of grass bowed as if stroked by a giant invisible hand. The wind picked up, and she fumbled to control her hair. Click. The hem of her skirt fluttered, lifted, and glimpses of her bare thighs and white panties came in half seconds. Click.

"Did you take the picture yet?"

He cycled the lever to advance the film. He got on his knees and crawled closer to her. As he came closer, the coy smile she wore earlier while up in the tree returned. When he stretched out on the ground once more, his heart thumped harder into the ground and his stiff bound erection pinched between his body and the earth. She closed down her eyelids to give them a dreamy bedroom appearance. His lips parted, and he sucked in a breath. She playfully and slowly drew up her skirt. Where had she learned to do that?

"Better act fast."

He made a quick focus adjustment and pressed the shutter release button. Click. She laughed. When he lowered the camera, her devilish persona had vanished, and he wondered if he saw it in the first place. Had he got the shot? Was there even a shot to be gotten? His erection remained. That was real enough. When he stood, he held the camera in front of him to hide his excitement. He sat under the shade of the sycamore next to her. While he cycled the film advance lever, she hummed, then sang in a sweet hushed tone. The lyrics and words were foreign, unlike anything he had ever heard.

"What's that?"

"It's a French song, Parlez-moi d'amour."

His face sagged.

"Huh?"

She giggled, then smirked and raised an eyebrow.

"It means tell me about love."

"Oh."

"I only know some of it. Anna would sing when she cleaned the house. My father liked it when she sang. We both loved her until my father met Eleanor and they married."

"What happened to your mother? Your real mother?"

She plucked several blades of grass and held them in her lap. She gazed downward as she pulled the blades of grass between her fingers as if she tried to stretch or straighten them.

"She died in a car accident. A man who had been drinking crashed his car into hers while she waited at the stoplight. The policeman told my father he was sure she didn't suffer."

She raised her chin, her eyes glassy and wet, and her lips formed a tight line. He moved closer and put his arm around her.

"We couldn't even see her at her funeral to say goodbye."

Her voice a whisper. He put his hand over hers and one of her tears fell and wet the back of his hand.

"I couldn't see my mom or dad either."

She looked up at him.

"I didn't know that. That just makes it worse. I'm sorry Lucius."

"I don't know what I'm supposed to do, or where I'm supposed to live. My Aunt Phoebe is coming here in a few days to take care of my parents' things. Am I supposed to live with her? She sounded nice on the phone, but I don't even know who she is."

"No Lucius. You have to stay here with us."

Her hazel-eyed gaze penetrated him and his gaze turned to wander the patches of green in front of him. He took his hand from hers and patted the dust from his pant leg and then picked at the sole of his shoe. From across the great span of the yard, Mrs. Crane had come outside and stood on the patio. Beatrice tossed the blades of grass and unclasped the opal choker from her neck and shoved it into her pocket.

"It's Eleanor. She must have gotten back early from shopping."

His eyes widened at her fright. Mrs. Crane spotted them, for she waved her hand high above her head.

"C'mon, and don't forget what I told you about Ms. Käthe and Ms. Mila."

Beatrice tugged his arm, and they stood and walked back to the house. Mrs. Crane waited for them with her hands on her hips. Beatrice glanced at him with her eyebrows raised. She patted her skirt where the opal choker hid in her pocket.

"Don't say anything about the necklace."

Her voice hushed and tense. He snorted.

"Why would I?"

His voice matched hers.

"Thanks."

Mrs. Crane waited for them on the outdoor patio as they walked toward the house.

"It's time for you two to clean up for dinner."

Her eyes narrowed when she looked him up and down.

"What on Earth did you do to your new clothes?"

In the bright sunlight, grass stains tracked down the front of his button down short-sleeve shirt. Dust powdered his pant legs. He slapped at and fumbled with his clothes, but it was hopeless. She scowled.

"Stop that. They'll need to be washed, and that is all there is to it. Beatrice, go inside and clean up for dinner."

Beatrice hurried past him without a word or a glance back.

"You're marching straight to the laundry room."

She held the door open and followed close behind him. His shoulders slumped. As they went through the kitchen and down the hall, her heels struck the wood and tile floors with an oppressive staccato. She directed him down the open wooden staircase into the basement where, past the locked door to the darkroom, was a narrow utility room with a single window near the ceiling that perhaps a child might fit through. Dusty bands of light from the window cast across the room to where a washer and dryer sat abreast against a concrete block wall. Mounted on the ceiling were two bare bulb lights with pull cords.

"Undress, but first, give me the camera."

He gazed up at her. His lips parted. As he lifted the camera strap over his head, she snatched it away.

"Wait. I promised Mr. Crane I would take care of it."

Mrs. Crane put her hand on her hip. Her face dipped into the band of light that came from the single small window. Her pale blue eyes had turned to ice.

"Judging by how well you took care of your new clothes, how could anyone trust you to take care of such an expensive camera?"

He started to raise his hands, but lowered them.

"I promised."

His eyes watered.

"Take off your dirty clothes and put them here on the floor. Ms. Mila or Ms. Käthe will wash them. I will discuss with Mr. Crane if it was a good idea for him to give you this camera."

He wanted to argue that the decision was Mr. Crane's and his alone, but he remained silent. Instead, he unbuttoned his short-sleeve shirt and tugged it free from his waist. Without his shirt, he felt smaller. Although he still wore his pants, he felt fully naked in front of her. He unlaced his shoes and slipped them off. The scuffs on his shoes made his heart sink. She waited. Her glare was enough to force him into motion. He unbuckled and undid his pants. With a couple of wiggles of his knees, they fell to the floor, and he stepped out of them. He stood there in his boxers and socks with his arms crossed to cover his small nipples.

Mrs. Crane moved his soiled clothes in front of the washing machine and slapped and brushed her hands together as if she feared she might get dust on her. She sighed.

"All right, back upstairs."

He eyed the camera, but she took him by the arm, turned him around, and gave him a gentle push to get him started. His stocking feet pattered on the basement's wooden stair treads, while her heels knocked softly with each step.

Ms. Mila appeared in the hallway. Lucius tightened his arms around his chest and sandwiched his hands under his armpits. His face prickled with heat when she looked him up and down. A smirk appeared on her face. He worried Ms. Mila would laugh, but Mrs. Crane cleared her throat.

"His grass stained shirt and pants are by the washer. Could you please put those in right away?"

"Yes, Mrs. Crane."

Ms. Mila glanced down at him, an unspoken glimmer of sympathy shown in her eyes before she headed off. Mrs. Crane put her hand on his shoulder and directed him down the hall to the second floor stairs. A clatter of cooking activity from the kitchen came and went as they passed the open doorway. The metal clasps on the camera's strap made tiny metallic chimes he knew well from handling the camera. They stopped at the foot of the stairs.

"Up you go. Clean up and put on some fresh clothes. Don't be long. Dinner will be ready soon."

She held up his camera near her shoulder, where she would typically hold a glass of wine. The steeliness of her pale sky-blue eyes had softened, but not entirely.

"When can I have the camera back?"

The words caught in his throat and sounded dry and hollow.

"That will be up to Mr. Crane after we've spoken. Perhaps he'll decide that you need a break from photography, or he might come to the realization that it was a mistake to place so much responsibility on you."

How could she say that? The camera was in the same condition as when Mr. Crane gave it to him. He stood breathless and silent. Her gaze was hard and electric. He turned and climbed the steps. When he got to the top of the stairs, he wanted to shout down at her and tell her she wasn't even Beatrice's mother. Eleanor, huh! That's what Beatrice called her. When he glanced down the stairs, she was gone.

6

Kenneth emerged from the bathroom. The slit where he held a towel around his waist revealed his pale, round buttock. Eleanor sat at her vanity in a lace bra, panties, and sheer stockings. She watched his reflection in the large ornate carved wooden framed mirror attached to the back of the elegant French-style vanity, which had curved legs and multiple small drawers that stored her jewelry, makeup, and hairbrushes.

He stood naked as he dried his dark brown hair, then lowered the towel to his side. Although he was tall, he was the shortest rower on his team in college. At thirty-five he had kept his lean muscular rower's body. She caught his gaze in the mirror. He raised a single eyebrow. His cock lengthened and hung heavy at a slight angle. The corners of her lips curled upward.

She ran her brush through her golden brown hair and watched him drop the towel over the arm of one of the sitting chairs and glide up behind her without a sound. He took the brush from her and brushed her hair. She put her hands behind her and ran her fingers up and down his thighs as he continued to brush. If he were fully erect, his cock would have touched her spine. The thought delighted her. She opened one of the small felt-lined shallow drawers on the vanity where she kept her black-beaded opal choker. It was one of the few extravagant and most touching gifts he had ever given her. She recalled that evening in Paris, the fierce lovemaking they shared. Peering now in the drawer at the choker, her eyes widened and her breath froze.

"Sorry, dear. Did I pull your hair?"

She put her hand over his, squeezed his fingers, and gently patted the back of his hand.

"No, love."

She lifted the choker from the drawer. Her eyebrows knit together. Her prize lay hastily tossed in the drawer, and not neatly placed, as she had always kept it. Not even respectively folded to best display the opal in the middle of the necklace, like when that snoop Anna, that French whore of a maid, must have taken it out. Eleanor's breath caught when she imagined *that* woman trying on her jewelry, especially the choker. How many women, and now possibly a girl, had worn her prize, Kenneth's gift to her, not to them? Her own thoughts stabbed at her until she sneered. Her face softened when she caught his gaze in the mirror. She held up the choker between her thumbs and forefingers.

"Put it on me."

Her voice purred. He put down the brush and took the choker.

She raised her chin.

"Now, I'm going to fuck you."

7

It had been over an hour since they picked up his Aunt Phoebe at Hartford's Bradley International Airport. She was nothing like Lucius imagined. Her voice during their phone conversation brought on images of Elizabeth Taylor or Audrey Hepburn, but not Brigitte Bardot. His late dad whistled every time Brigitte Bardot appeared on the television. He expected Mr. Crane to whistle when his Aunt Phoebe slinked up the sidewalk to greet them in her polka-dot pencil dress with ruffled sleeves. His eyes certainly popped. Before they departed, Lucius took a picture of his aunt with the airport in the background. She seemed pleased and impressed with Mr. Crane's sedan. The two adults chatted on the drive back.

Lucius sat in the back seat. Aunt Phoebe's hand occasionally slipped across the opening between the two front seats to touch Mr. Crane's arm as if to add emphasis to what she had said. Laughter followed between the two. He had never seen Mr. Crane so happy. Even though Mrs. Crane took his camera, he felt a sadness for her. Mr. Crane had given it back to him the afternoon they set out for the airport. More laughter came from the front seats. Although the car moved at a leisurely speed, he held tight to the armrest with his eyes narrowed.

"How ya doing back there—Lucius?" she asked.

She said his name as though she had to remind herself. She twisted her body and her face appeared between the two front seats to look at him. Her big blonde curls hung past her shoulders. Every time she moved, they bobbed lively like springs. She had fancy painted nails. Mrs. Crane's nails were always painted, but in less striking colors. Aunt Phoebe's were a robin's egg blue and long like those of a coffee shop waitress. Perhaps it was part of their dress uniform, since she worked as a waitress at some diner in Indiana. His mom, Paulina, sometimes painted her nails bright red, but his dad, Darius, would make strange comments in a bitter tone about her walking the streets at night and then made her repaint them before she could leave the house, even once before a parent-teacher conference at his school.

A subtle smile appeared on his face.

"I'm fine."

She squeezed his slender knee. Her silver bangle bracelets jangled around her wrist and forearm. Her sapphire blue eyes were bright and cheerful, unlike Mrs. Crane's, which hid something curious, something secretive. Aunt Phoebe returned her attention to the surroundings and to Mr. Crane. The Mercedes glided down a spiderweb of streets, eventually turning on the street to his parents' house. After a gentle bounce, when they turned into the driveway, they eased to a stop in front of the garage.

"Looks like the lawn will need tending to soon," Mr. Crane said.

Aunt Phoebe only hummed with delight. His parents' empty house seemed so small and impotent now. Mr. Crane pulled up near the garage door and turned off the engine. They got out and stood alongside the Mercedes, on the concrete slab driveway with its long, erratic cracks. Lucius looked over the Leica that hung from his neck. He turned the shutter speed dial, not because it needed adjusting, but more so because it put him at ease.

"Oh, hon, why don't you leave that in the car," she said.

"Why can't I bring it with me?"

"Because it doesn't seem right."

"Why?"

Mr. Crane came around the front of the car.

"I think it's okay. Lucius is going to be a famous photographer."

He smiled at Lucius, then at Aunt Phoebe. Her face wrinkled for a moment, then a hesitant smile appeared.

"I suppose it's all right."

Mr. Crane took the house keys from his pocket.

"Shall we go inside?"

The house was stuffier than when he visited it last with Mr. Crane. A sour odor came from the kitchen. Mr. Crane and Aunt Phoebe opened a few of the windows, one in the kitchen and two in the living room. A delicate cross breeze pushed through. The air seemed hesitant to enter and quick to exit. His aunt inspected the kitchen cabinets. She held up two bottles of liquor.

"Care for a drink, Kenneth?"

Mr. Crane smiled and glanced at Lucius.

"Maybe another time."

She sat a bottle of gin and a bottle of whiskey onto the white speckled charcoal laminate countertop.

"I think I'm going to need a drink after going through my brother's things. I never met Paulina. Darius was upset that I missed their wedding, but we were never close."

Her voice trailed off into a whisper. Lucius considered venturing to his old bedroom while the two adults talked, but when she took out a tissue to dab at her eyes, Mr. Crane went to her. Lucius snorted. Her tears confused him. Shouldn't he be the one crying?

"Maybe you should sit down."

"No, I'll be fine."

She swayed on her heels as though she might faint. Mr. Crane caught her.

"Oh."

"Steady, it's all right."

Mr. Crane took hold of her with his arm around her waist and helped her to the couch. She rested her head on his shoulder. Her big, bouncy blonde curls sprung against his face. After he sat her down and turned away, her lips curled into an impish smile. She seemed not to care that Lucius saw her. Perhaps it was her intent.

"Oh thank you Kenneth, you're too kind."

"Lucius, can you get your Aunt Phoebe a glass of water?"

When he brought her a glass of water, she took a single sip and sat it on the coffee table. Then she sat up as if her moment of overwhelming grief had suddenly passed. Mr. Crane glanced at his wristwatch.

"I guess I should leave you to it. Are you sure you want to stay here? Mrs. Crane and I have room if you would like to stay with us."

"Oh no, I don't want to impose. Besides, I have a lot to do here."

She glanced around the room, then chuckled.

"I don't know where to start."

"You mentioned putting the place on the market sooner than later. Think of it like moving. Pack up one room at a time until you're done. I wish I could stick around and help you. Are you sure you wouldn't like to come to the house for dinner? I could drive you back afterwards."

"That's very sweet, but I'll be fine."

Lucius wondered if Mr. Crane enjoyed being referred to as *being sweet*. Mr. Crane sat one of the two house keys on the laminate counter and took one of his business cards from a silver card holder and scribbled on the back.

"In case you decide to go out, here's the house key. The phone is still in service if you need to call a taxi. Also, here's my card with the house number on the back. Please call if you need anything."

He slipped his silver card holder and gold pen into the breast pocket of his jacket.

"Thank you. I should be fine. There's plenty of food still in the house. I have everything I need here."

"All right. I'll bring in your suitcase. Come along Lucius, we'll be just in time for dinner."

Lucius stood at the other end of the living room, with the hallway to the bedrooms behind him. The Leica hung at his waist from the leather strap around his neck.

"I want to stay and help Aunt Phoebe."

"Dear. Why don't you go with Mr. Crane? I'm not much of a cook. You'll get a much better meal at the Cranes. I imagine you'll sleep better there, too."

"But *this* is my house."

She put her hands in her lap and tilted her head. Her eyebrows rose and her lips formed the makings of a sincere smile. Mr. Crane stood near the kitchen counter with his hands in his pockets.

"Oh, sweetie. I know. It is your house. You've lost your mommy and daddy, and I lost my brother. These are terrible terrible things to deal with, but we must. We unfortunately can't bring them back. All we can do is grieve, then do the best we can to move on."

Her earlier tears, if they existed, had dried up as soon as they came. Her worrisome eyes turned to Mr. Crane.

"She's right Lucius. Although, I think it would be good for him to stay and help. He was fine here before, and he'll be fine now."

Mr. Crane winked at Lucius and gave him a confident smile. The same smile he gave him when he showed him how to use the camera.

Her expression hardened. She ran a fingertip down her jawline.

"I supposed you're right."

"Great, I'll grab your suitcase."

Mr. Crane tapped the kitchen countertop, then headed out to the car.

"Well, Lucius, this gives us a chance to get to know one another."

When she raised her eyebrows, they seemed to pull up the corners of her lips. A moment later Mr. Crane returned with her taupe-colored suitcase and flower-patterned cosmetic train case. He sat them near the dark walnut stained colonial style dinner table.

"Thank you, Kenneth."

"It's no trouble. Phoebe, call me if you need anything, and Lucius, help your aunt."

Mr. Crane winked at Lucius and smiled at her before he departed. Lucius went to the door to watch Mr. Crane back the Mercedes, with its broad chrome grill and double stacked headlamps, out into the street. Mr. Crane drove off without a glance back. Lucius lowered his hand. He wanted to wave goodbye, but Mr. Crane would have never seen him. She called to him from the living room.

"Are you sure you want to hang out with your Aunt Phoebe?"

He came back to the living room.

"Yes. What are we going to do?"

"Are you hungry?"

He nodded.

❦

The sky darkened earlier and dulled every color. A light rain came down. A black Pontiac sedan sat parked at the mouth of the Crane's driveway. Mr. Henry Kraus, Ms. Käthe's brother, sat behind the wheel. He gave Kenneth a subtle wave as Kenneth drove past. Ms. Käthe and Ms. Mila were near the end of the driveway with their heads lowered when he pulled in. Both women stepped out of the way of the Mercedes, nodded and waved politely. Raindrops wet their uniforms. He waved back, then glanced at his wristwatch.

After he parked, he grabbed his suit jacket and briefcase from the passenger seat and got out of the car. The black sedan pulled away with the two maids. Ms. Mila glanced out from the backseat window. Their eyes met and their gaze held until the car got further up the street and vanished. The rain once again picked up and woke him from his reverie. He hurried to get inside the house.

"Sorry I'm late."

Eleanor and Beatrice sat at the dinner table and had already started eating when he came into the room. Beatrice's face brightened when she saw him. Eleanor smiled, but with a chilled look in her eyes. He lowered his head and took his seat at the dinner table.

"Hello Daddy. Where's Lucius?" Beatrice asked.

"Hello Dear. I was beginning to think you weren't going to make it," Eleanor said.

Kenneth situated himself. A plate of roast and potatoes sat prepared for him. He offered them both a weary smile.

"Lucius's Aunt Phoebe's flight arrived forty-five minutes late. She wanted to go straight to the house to see what she was in for. Lucius wanted to stay and help her sort through his parents' belongings. It seemed like the practical thing to do, so I agreed and left them both at the house."

He cut into the roast on his plate and took a bite. Eleanor raised her wineglass and took a sip.

"What's she like?" Beatrice asked.

Her voice was excited, as though her father had driven the Queen of England from the airport. He chewed and raised his hand for her to give him a moment.

"Yes, Dear. What is she like?" Eleanor asked.

Her tone was flat.

"Oh, she was nice."

"Nice like Lucius?" Beatrice asked.

He chuckled.

"I suppose so."

"Is she pretty?" Beatrice asked.

"Dear, eat your dinner," he said.

"I think Beatrice asked a valid question. So Kenneth, is Aunt Phoebe pretty?"

He popped another bite of roast into his mouth to delay his response. Eleanor's eyes narrowed, while Beatrice waited wide-eyed with a knife and fork in her hands as if it was unclear to her how to use them. He pointed at her plate while he chewed to get her attention on her dinner. She cut the small serving of roast on her plate into smaller pieces and poked at a potato, but nothing stuck to her fork.

"Okay. Yes, she is an attractive woman."

Beatrice smiled as she looked down at the table. It was a smile that young girls made when they fantasized about princesses. She started eating with a distant gaze, off in her thoughts. Eleanor raised her eyebrows and put down her wineglass. She ate, but picked at her food like someone on a diet, or someone accused of being fat, which she had never been. He glanced at both of them while they jousted with the food on their plates. He cleared his throat.

"She won't be staying long. Her employer only allowed her a few days off."

The brightness in Beatrice's eyes faded.

"Oh, how sad? Even with the death of her brother? That's not very generous." Eleanor said.

He wrinkled his lips.

"Indeed. But that's what she told me."

"I see."

A winter chill settled in her pale blue eyes.

"Maybe this is an inconvenience for her. You said that her and her brother were not close."

He wiped the corners of his mouth and sighed.

"Hard to say. She seemed compassionate and spoke nice things about her brother on the drive to the house."

Eleanor picked up her wineglass and took a sip. Beatrice straightened up in her seat.

"Was Lucius happy to see her?" Beatrice asked.

Beatrice's voice was now more measured. Eleanor sat back in her chair. She cradled her arm that held her wineglass. Kenneth looked at Beatrice with a sombre smile.

"I think so. He was quiet after we picked her up at the airport, maybe a little shy, I guess, but he *did* want to stay at the house with her. He probably wants to get to know her better."

He smiled at Beatrice, then glanced at Eleanor.

"He's protecting the castle," Eleanor whispered.

She gazed off into the room and she appeared not to focus on anything in particular.

After dinner concluded, Beatrice went upstairs to prepare for bed, and Kenneth and Eleanor retired to the screened in patio with fresh glasses of wine and cigarettes. The rain came steady but light and cleansed the air. A fresh scented breeze came gentle through the screened panels. As the light faded, the amber glow of the cigarette they shared brightened with each drag. Most nights, they sat in silent contemplation, allowing their thoughts to roam until one of them spoke. Tonight, Kenneth needed that silence. His gaze roamed the darkness. Low cumulus shrouded the moon and made it impossible to see much of the property. Without the moonlight, they were like two prisoners huddled together in some dark hole, one waiting for the other to speak, so they would know if they were alive, or even there.

An amber dot floated bright in the air and the subtle sound of singed paper and tobacco came from the darkened corner where she sat. He instinctually felt her hand reach out to him to hand him the cigarette. Her breath as she exhaled came smooth. He envisioned the smoke push past her lips.

"So, tell me more about *Aunt* Phoebe. What kind of woman *is* she exactly?"

Kenneth took a long drag on the cigarette. The smoke singed his nostrils when he exhaled. He could feel the weight of her anticipation.

"There's not much to tell. She grew up near Hartford, like her brother Darius. Then met a guy, a trucker, who she fell in love with and moved to Indiana to be with. He left her shortly after, but she stayed there and tried to make the most of it."

He handed the cigarette back to her. She took hold of it in the near dark.

"This man she followed to Indiana—was there not a marriage proposal?"

"I guess not."

She snorted.

"She sounds like a fool. And she is making the most of it—waitressing? I thought you said she was pretty."

He cleared his throat and took a drink of wine.

"She mentioned secretarial work, too."

"Splendid. You said she was pretty. How pretty? I know you have a good sense of beauty, Kenneth. Let's not beat around the bush."

An exhausted breath slipped past his lips.

"She is stunning, but with her current job, that won't last."

She huffed as if he had confirmed her suspicions.

"All this time she hasn't found a man?"

She took a drag.

"She impresses me as being the *independent* type."

"Hah. She sounds more like the survivor type. I'll give her that much. Not a bright girl, I dare say."

He drank his wine and peered out into the dark gray landscape of their backyard. He hoped she gazed outward into the gloom as he did, and not at him, but knew there was little hope in that.

"You want to photograph her, don't you?"

He knew his silence was telling, but he was unable to speak.

"I've allowed you freedom in the past to explore your *artistic* endeavors, but no more."

The wicker chair creaked when he shifted in his seat.

"Don't you ever bring her here, into our home. Do you understand me, Kenneth? Treat her as a legal client if you must, but nothing more. It's bad enough that we've taken in the boy."

"Yes," he whispered.

His voice was hollow and dry. He licked his lips and picked up his wineglass, but it was empty.

"Would you like another glass of wine? I could use one, or perhaps something stronger?"

Her heavy escaping breath came from the shadows.

"Why not?"

8

"I'll make us some sandwiches and then you can show me around. How does that grab you?" Aunt Phoebe asked.

"Okay," Lucius said.

They shared a mutual smile. He sat the camera on the dinner table and rushed to the kitchen to get out everything they needed to make the sandwiches. For a moment, she stood by the counter and watched while he took the lead. Then she found the cupboard where the glasses were shelved. With her back to him, she poured two glasses of orange juice. When she brought the drinks around, he noticed the broken seal on the bottle of gin. She gave him a tightlipped smile when they sat down at the dinner table.

"I can't imagine what you're going through, Lucius."

There was his name again. When she said it, it made her seem more like a stranger than his aunt.

"Are you really a waitress? You should be on television."

She bursted out laughing, and almost spit out her orange juice. Her eyelids closed when she laughed, to reveal the mysteries of how she painted her eyelids. She had covered her mouth until she regained her composure.

"Oh wow, that's funny, but very sweet. I'm sorry to disappoint you, but I've been a waitress for almost five years. Bradford, Indiana sure ain't no Hollywood, California, so don't expect to see me on television. I can't complain much, I'm lucky to have a job. A gal like me, single that is, needs to be able to take care of herself. I'm not fortunate, like Mrs. Crane, to have a lawyer for a husband."

"Mr. Crane is the lucky one."

Her eyebrows drew together.

"What do you mean?"

"Mrs. Crane is rich. At least that's what Beatrice tells me."

"Beatrice? Um, that's Kenneth and Eleanor's daughter?"

"No."

"Oh? Huh?"

"Beatrice is Mr. Crane's daughter. Mrs. Crane is Beatrice's stepmother."

She wrinkled her lips and raised her eyebrows.

"I see. Mrs. Crane is rich, huh?"

She nodded slowly and took a small bite of her sandwich. Her glass of orange juice was half empty. She went to the kitchen and topped it off with gin, but this time not seeming to care if he saw her. She stood at the counter that separated the kitchen from the dinner table and cradled her drinking arm. A light rain pattered outside the open windows.

"That's what Beatrice tells me."

"Interesting."

"What is?"

"Oh, nothing, adult stuff. Speaking of lawyers, I used to be a secretary at a law office."

He sat up with half of his sandwich in his hand. His eyebrows raised. She had her glass to her lips and waved her hand until she finished swallowing. He waited. She held her hand in front of her mouth as if to stifle a belch, but nothing came.

"Nothing like where Mr. Crane works. At least I can't imagine he would work in a dumpy wood paneled office with only one window. Besides, there was only one lawyer, Donnie Dix, where I worked. Mr. Crane said he had *colleagues*."

She rolled her eyes. He laughed. It was unclear whether she was making fun of Mr. Crane or her former employer. Regardless of who she meant, she looked goofy. She even crossed her eyes to make him laugh even more. She topped her glass off and came back to the table. Her blonde curls and bosom bobbed when she sat down hard. Her glass of gin and orange juice, now more gin *than* juice, sloshed but remained upright without losing a drop. She giggled, and he smiled.

After they ate, she followed him so he could show her around the house. She lumbered behind him with her drink in hand. The brief tour ended in his parents' bedroom. She livened up when he turned on the lights. She seemed particularly interested in going through his mom's jewelry.

"That's it? I guess that's what I should have expected from Darius, always a cheapskate. Well, some of this has to be worth something."

He knew to stay out of his parents' bedroom, but he knew little of what was in there to begin with. When she dug through his mom's things, it made him tense. Her drink created wet rings on his mom's dresser. A big no-no, at least for him. He went to take the glass and hold it for her. She grabbed his hand.

"Oh, no, mister, that's not for you. If you're still thirsty, why don't you get another glass of orange juice?"

Her eyes were wide in a bug-eyed glare, and her words were mushy. She sounded sleepy. She waved her hand in the air and pointed out the door as if he needed directions to the kitchen. He crossed his arms and sat on the bed.

"Never mind."

"There, that's perfect. Sit on the bed."

The more she spoke, the more he thought she needed to sleep.

"Do you have to go through everything?"

Her hands rested inside one of the open drawers.

"Yes, we have to go through everything. That includes all of your parents' private things."

He squeezed his crossed arms together.

"Have you done this before? What makes you qualified?"

"My, aren't you a smart one? Unfortunately, I have done this before. It's not an enjoyable task."

She laid out more of his mom's jewelry that she found tucked and hidden below the folded clothes.

"Oh hey, these are nice."

He had never seen the silver opal teardrop-shaped earrings before. Were they real? She held up one earring to her ear and glanced at her reflection in the mirror. The teardrop opal dangled at her earlobe. He huffed, and his eyes narrowed. He got up and started for the door.

"Where are you going?"

"Bathroom."

She fluttered her hand to wave him away. He went down the hallway to the laundry room. After he glanced out the door to make sure she was still in his parents' bedroom, he took the step stool and went through the cabinets that hung over the washer and dryer. Nothing. Hm. There was a fold-a-way ironing board. He pulled it down from inside its recessed cavity. Wedged back in the space—there it was—his mom's diary. He shoved it in his pants, then straightened and tucked his shirt over it. He lifted the ironing board back into place. It squeaked and his shoulders tensed. He peeked out the door again. No sign of his aunt. He crossed the hallway to his bedroom and slipped the diary under his mattress. His room seemed miniature compared to the Crane's guest bedroom.

When he came out, his Aunt Phoebe stood in the hallway with her empty glass. She held her hand against the wall and teetered her way to the kitchen. He followed. The rain had picked up and came down steady now and wet the sills of the open windows.

"Be a dear and go around and close the windows."

When he returned, she poured herself another drink, mostly gin with a splash of orange juice. She poured him a glass of milk.

"Did your mom give you a glass of milk before bedtime?"

"Sometimes."

"Here, drink up."

She slid the glass of milk on the countertop towards him. Her bangle bracelets made a dull clink when they touched the laminate surface. They stood across the counter from one another until he finished his glass of milk, and she her mixed drink. After she poured herself another, she stepped cautiously, still in her heels, to the couch. She sneered at the old beat up dark green recliner, and probably knew it belonged to his dad. He sat in it with his arms wide so he could grip both armrests, while his elbows hung in the air.

"You're the man now."

She raised her glass, then took a drink. When he put the footrest up, the chair tilted back like a giant green vinyl mouth, ready to swallow him whole. She slumped on the couch and grinned at him. Her eyes were glassy.

"Why dontcha turn on the television, hon?"

He wiggled to the end of the seat to get enough leverage to push the leg rest down, then he went over to the television and switched it on. The table top set sat on a simple blonde stained wooden table, unlike the one at the Cranes, which was encased in a dark stained fine wood cabinet. It surprised him that the Cranes watched little television, and a bigger surprise that his interest had waned. He glanced at the Leica he left on the dinner table. It called to him to come and pick it up. He recalled Mr. Crane's lighting formulas, and what he said about speeds slower than two-fifty or one hundred, which might result in a blurry shot.

"See if Ben Casey is on and sit down so I can see."

His mom used to watch Ben Casey when his dad would allow it. It was some show about a brain doctor. Boring. Maybe his dad thought so, too. He turned the television knob until he found the show, then bounded back to the old green recliner. She sat slumped on the couch cushions and only struggled to sit up to take a drink of her gin and orange juice. When she sat back, she put her elbow up to brace her head, while her heavy-lidded eyes glared at the pulsing light from the television.

By the time Ben Casey ended, she was half slumped over asleep on the couch. Lucius got up and turned off the television. The house fell silent, except for the slow, heavy breath that passed her lips. He watched her breast rise and fall, and her lips open as she breathed. It felt like they were the last two survivors on some raft adrift at night with only the moonlight to see. He slipped off her heels and sat them next to the couch. She shifted her shoulders and muttered something that sounded like a man's name, followed by a subdued giggle.

He knelt by her feet, and carefully put his hands under her calf and her ankle. Her leg was fleshy but firm, warm and heavier than he imagined. The texture of her stocking stretched over her flesh felt different from the loose, limp ones he touched in the laundry basket. He lifted her leg up on the couch cushions. The hem of her dress slid up her leg and exposed the clasp of her garter. His muscles coiled, ready to jump away if she woke.

She slept, heavy and motionless, except for her breathing. He poked at her leg, but she remained asleep. He pinched at and flipped her skirt away, then sat on his knees with wide eyes. His gaze became focused, direct, and anxious. Her white panties spanned her hips and a gentle hill rose in the middle where the mound of her pubis lie hidden. Brown pubic hairs curled and peeked out from the edges. Her white garters stretched taut down her thighs and ended in clips secured to the broad darker beige welts at the tops of her sheer nude-colored stockings. He slipped off his shoes and put them next to her heels, then he stepped quietly in his stocking feet to the dinner table to get the Leica.

He thumbed the film advance lever to make sure he was on the next exposure, then opened the aperture as wide as the lens would go to let in as much light as the two lamps in the room offered. He crept back and knelt in the same spot. What speed did he need? Two-fiftieth of a second? A hundredth of a second? A fiftieth of a second? Twenty-fifths of a second? Lower? Anything under two-fifty, Mr. Crane said was tempting fate. Lucius sat the camera on the coffee table next to her drink. He went to the dinner table and brought back a chair. It was much heavier carrying it than sliding it. After he got the chair positioned, he placed the camera on the seat, tilted his head sideways against the surface of the seat in order to look through the viewfinder, adjusted the lens focus ring, and waited. She moved her arm, and he nearly knocked over the camera and the chair as he prepared to stand and run off. He waited a moment until he could breathe again. She remained still. He quietly and slowly moved the chair back into place, looked through the camera's viewfinder while it sat on the seat, reestablished his focus, and pressed the shutter release—click. The shutter blades made their delicate metallic whisper. He thumbed the film advance leaver, rotated the shutter speed dial down one, checked his focus and click. He repeated the cycle— click and click—until he reached the twenty-fifths of a second setting on the speed dial. With each shot, the camera's shutters moved half as slow as the last. He held his breath for each shot. He adjusted the speed dial back up to two-fiftieth of a second, where he always kept it, then stood and surveyed his subject. Since he was done with the chair, and it would only be a liability if she woke, he carried it back to the dinner table. When he returned, he pinched the hem of her skirt and lowered it to return her modesty.

He got on his knees and placed the camera on the coffee table to shoot her sleeping portrait. He set the speed to two-fiftieth of a second, then he got her into focus. Click. Without moving the camera, he cycled to the next frame. He set the speed to a hundredth of a second. Click. He cycled to the next frame. He set the speed to a fiftieth of a second. Click. He cycled to the next frame. He set the speed to twenty-fifths of a second. Click. She muttered something incoherent. He put the camera aside and slid close to her. A soft, heavy, sweet alcohol breath passed her lips. Her makeup had caked from all the traveling she had done and all the unnecessary laughter between her and Mr. Crane. What would Mrs. Crane think of his Aunt Phoebe? He touched her blonde springy curls, but when he bent to smell her hair. Her hair had the scent of stale smoke and a faint hint of perfume. Her hairspray perhaps.

He stood with the camera slung over his shoulder and went to the kitchen. The open bottle of gin sat empty. He stuck his finger in the opening and touched it to his tongue, then wrinkled his face and groaned. After he turned off the kitchen light, he sauntered to his bedroom. He emerged in an old pair of pajamas, went to his parents' bedroom and turned off the light, then poked around in the hallway closet until he found a blanket to cover his Aunt Phoebe. When he came out to the living room, she had rolled on her side. He covered her and turned out the lights.

The rain obscured the view from his bedroom window. He lie on his back and stared at the ceiling. Familiar and distant shadows from the street lamp painted the walls. It seemed unreal that he saw his Aunt Phoebe's panties. Did she look like Mrs. Crane with her panties off? Was she really his aunt? How could she be? She was too pretty. He had touched her, this strange beautiful woman. The texture of her hair, her warm stocking covered legs, made him stir and stiffen below the waist. His fingers slipped under the waistband of his pajamas and his underpants.

He covered his penis with his flattened palms and moved his hands up and down with increased pressure. With each stroke, his shoulders tightened. His legs opened and flexed straight with his heels driven into the mattress. A few shuddered breaths, and he spilled out hot onto his stomach. He used the bedsheet to wipe himself off. His skin chilled and tightened where he came. With the bedspread raised to his chin, he released a sigh. His mind raced with possibilities. The Leica sat on his dresser with the leather strap coiled around it. The camera's lens pointed towards him. His new friend. One he intended to share and create new secrets with.

Thoughts of Mrs. Crane came. The naked black and white picture of her hidden in the Crane's guest bedroom churned in his mind. Was the hair between her legs a different color or shade than the golden brown hair on her head? Even with her spread out, there was no way to tell from the black and white photograph. He listened to his own breathing, in and out, and thoughts of Mrs. Crane—Eleanor—followed him into sleep.

9

When Lucius woke, his Aunt Phoebe appeared in the doorway. She must have showered while he slept. She had her hair pinned up, and she wore capris and a button up short-sleeve shirt. Her face was fresh with a lighter application of makeup. She wore no jewelry and looked ready to tackle the house.

"Oh good, you're awake. Thank you for being a gentleman last night."

He sat up on his elbows and rubbed his eyes.

"Huh?"

"Thanks for taking off my shoes and covering me up. That was sweet of you."

"Ah? Sure."

She glanced around his room. Now that the sunlight came through the window it was easier to inspect, not that there was much *to* inspect.

"We have a big day ahead of us. Lots to do. Mr. Crane told me of some estate management businesses that can pick up the furniture, clothes, dishes and such, and pay me, or us, for those items. So get up and let's get started. I'll make us some breakfast first. I think I saw a carton of eggs in the refrigerator."

"Okay, sure."

She left his doorway as quick as he was to reply.

After breakfast, they went outside to inspect the garage, since they skipped it yesterday evening, due to last night's rain. The lawn and the driveway were still wet, but would be dry by noon if no more rain came. They stood before the garage. It was only a single-car garage, but it took both of them to open the heavy wooden door, which made Lucius wonder if that was the reason his dad usually kept it open all day. Its windowless cinder block walls sat hollow and vacant of his parents' old Buick. Aunt Phoebe brushed her hands together after she lifted the dusty door. She went inside and poked around. He found his dad's flashlight. It had a rugged steel casing with a knurled diamond pattern grip.

"Do you think you would like to work on cars someday like your daddy use to?"

He shook his head, no. He turned the flashlight on and off. The butt end of it, as well as the fine recesses of the grip, held some grease and dirt, which got on his hands. He caught himself before wiping them on his pants.

"Can I keep this?"

She barely looked up at him. He could have held a large knife, and doubted she would have noticed.

"Oh, sure hon. Are you sure you wouldn't like any of your dad's tools?"

He sat the flashlight on the small wooded bench his dad had cobbled together with two-by-fours and plywood, then he shifted through the wrenches, screwdrivers, and hammers that were carelessly tossed into an open metal tool caddy. He kicked at the greasy jack on the floor.

"I guess not."

She stood there with her arms crossed and raised her eyebrows.

"All right, I'll have them take the tools."

He found a half soiled shop rag and did his best to wipe down the flashlight.

Back inside, he put the flashlight in his bedroom and went to the kitchen to help her clean out the cupboards. They piled the dishes and cookware on the counters and left the empty cabinet doors open. By late afternoon, when Mr. Crane phoned to inform them he was taking them to dinner, they had the kitchen and the master bedroom cleaned out and had filled trash bags full of clothes, bedding, and an assortment of other things. The bags filled the living room. They sat at the dinner table to take a break. His mom's jewelry was missing from the items, and he wondered if the jewelry had found its way into his Aunt Phoebe's suitcase. He should be boiling, but he felt a cool detachment, followed by anxiousness. He was certain Mrs. Crane and Beatrice would be there for dinner, and he was curious to see if Mrs. Crane liked his Aunt Phoebe.

"You'll get to meet Mrs. Crane and Beatrice. You'll like them."

Her eyes narrowed, and she smirked.

"If you say so, I'm sure I will. Mr. Crane mentioned Beatrice. She sounds sweet."

He returned her snide smirk.

"I have to say, Lucius, you surprised me."

"How?"

"You're not the boy I would have imagined my brother having as a son. I imagined you would be tough and athletic. A boy who liked sports—not photography. Maybe even a boy who wanted to be a grease monkey like his old man."

She snorted and smiled sympathetically. He was unsure what to say, so he stared at her and remained silent. She peered out the window and her eyebrows rose.

"It's awfully nice that the Cranes took you in, but I wonder what's in it for them? Why should they trouble themselves, especially if they are as rich as you say?"

She got up from the dinner table and milled about in the kitchen. She tossed the empty bottle of gin into the trash. It made a dull thud when it hit the bottom of the plastic container. She then picked up the whiskey bottle and seemed engrossed in the label. He went down the hallway to the bathroom, and when he returned, he saw her sneak a taste from the bottle and return it to the counter. He snorted.

"I'm going to go get cleaned up before Mr. Crane gets here to take us to dinner. I suggest you do the same. With all the cleaning we've been doing, at least wash your hands and face."

He followed her down the hallway. The sway of her hips was more rhythmic and pronounced than Mrs. Crane's, but also less elegant and less graceful. She clomped on her heels while Mrs. Crane floated. She slipped into his parents' bedroom, glanced back at him, then closed the door. He turned into the bathroom and washed his hands and face as she asked, then went to his bedroom and shut the door. While he sat cross-legged on the floor next to his bed with a comic book in his lap, the clunk of the bathroom door came from down the hallway. He waited and after a while assumed she had climbed into the bathtub.

At least she had been patient enough and gave him some privacy, but eventually he would have to pack up the things in his room. He slipped his mom's diary from under his mattress and held it in his lap. It was silent in the hallway. His fingertips traced the gold, elegant lettering. "Diary." The faux leather cover was a cream color. The edges cracked and the spine creased. A lock with a hinge held the book closed and secured it from prying eyes. He pressed and slid the flat button latch and the lock sprung open. Tucked inside the back cover was a red ribbon with two tiny gold keys tethered to it. He untied the ribbon and slipped the keys into his pocket.

The cover made a dry crackle when he opened it. He expected his mom's ghost to fly out. He had seen her writing in it a few times before, but she always avoided his question as to what she wrote. Thoughts. That was the only answer she ever gave. His mom had written her name inside in pencil, Paulina C. Livingston. The scrolling graphite letters made him smile, but he wondered why she used her maiden name. He flipped through some pages and the number of entries surprised him. Singing came from the hallway. He sat up, his back straight against the side of the bed. His bedroom door swung open.

10

Beatrice came down the hallway when Kenneth came in the house. Her oxfords clicked on the tiled floor. She was still wearing her school uniform.

"Hello Darling," he said.

"Oh? Hello Daddy. You're home early."

He smiled and knelt down inside the entranceway, then sat his briefcase on the floor and slung his suit jacket over it. She stood with a broad smile, and held her arms up, ready for her father to scoop her up. They hugged, and he kissed her cheek.

"Yes. I wanted to see if you both wanted to have dinner with Lucius and his Aunt Phoebe."

"Oh, can we?"

She hugged him tighter around his neck.

"It's up to Mrs. Crane. Do you know where she's at?"

"Upstairs, I think."

He wrinkled his lips, worried that he had misspoke.

"Thank you, Dear. I'll head up and check on her. Please don't be sour if she says no."

She looked into his eyes. Her hopeful smile faded, but not completely.

"Okay."

"Thank you for your understanding. So, how was your day at school?"

"Good."

"Good to hear. Now run along, while I go speak to Mrs. Crane."

He left his jacket and briefcase near the entranceway and headed upstairs.

11

The bedroom door swung open, Lucius covered his mom's diary in his lap with two comic books that were on the floor next to him. Aunt Phoebe stood in the doorway wrapped in his parents' cheap, tattered bath towels. One wrapped around her head, and one around her body clenched to her breast. Her shapely bare legs, fresh from her bath, exposed. Her painted toenails matched the robin's egg blue on her fingernails. He stiffened against the hidden diary in his lap.

"It's your turn, Mister."

He looked at her with wide eyes, and when he was able to compose himself, he held up his open palms toward her.

"I washed my hands and face like you asked."

She raised her eyebrows.

"Not good enough. Your hair's greasy. You're going to need a shower or bath, or you might as well stay here."

He touched his head and wrinkled his lips. She pulled the door handle and glanced around the backside of the door to inspect what was there. Through the narrow slit where the towel overlapped, offered a glimpse of her upper thigh. She clenched the towel to her breast. The fine coils of chestnut brown hair that appeared at the sides of her panties while she slept on the couch slipped into his thoughts. Her voice shook him from his daydream.

"What are you up to in here, anyway? You should be cleaning and packing your things."

"I was reading my comics."

He held up the *Fantastic Four* comic he had in his lap, while his mom's diary lay hidden under *The Amazing Spider-Man*. She rolled her eyes.

"You'll have time to read your comics after we get this house in order. Now give me those."

She held out her hand and struggled to hold the towel wrapped around her. His breath caught and his heart pounded. He put his hand over *The Amazing Spider-Man* comic in his lap and his mom's diary underneath pressed against his erection.

"Uh?"

"Give it, Mister."

She took a step towards him. The cheap, thin ragged bath towel contoured to the curves of her torso. He put both hands over the comics to shield himself. She knelt down to take the comics, but a knock came at the front door.

"Oh great. I bet that's the man from the consignment store. Go answer the door while I get dressed. Let him know he can load up what we have in the living room, including the furniture."

She went down the hallway to his parents' bedroom. The knock came again.

"Lucius," she shouted.

He stretched and swung his arms under the bed until he found what he needed, an worn hardcover copy of *The Adventures of Tom Sawyer*. He tossed his mom's diary under the bed. It flew deep and clunked against the wall. He slipped the Mark Twain novel under his two comics, then hurried to the front door.

After the truck eased out of the driveway and disappeared down the street, Lucius returned to the empty living room. The dining table, its chairs, the couch, the television and the small table it sat on, even his dad's ugly dark green recliner were all taken away along with the dishes and cookware. Only the furniture's footprints remained on the shag carpet that spanned the living room. Back in his parents' old bedroom, Aunt Phoebe had the two men take everything but the bed. The older of the two men told her they only take headboards and bed frames, but not the mattresses or box springs. They had cleared out the garage as well.

He was relieved they left his bedroom alone. The slender younger man with sinewy arms told the older man the truck was full, which meant good fortune for Lucius, at least for today. Aunt Phoebe made it clear they would have to take his things tomorrow. It felt as though his life, his past, everything, was being erased on consignment.

After the men had left, she insisted he take a shower, and threatened to leave him at the house by himself if he refused. He relented and did as she asked. After he dressed, he sat on the bed with the Leica, made some adjustments to the shutter speed dial, thumbed the film advance lever, then crept down the hallway with the camera strapped around his neck. He watched her as she applied her makeup in the bathroom. He raised the Leica, focused the lens, then pressed the shutter release button. Click. The camera's delicate shutters made a soft metallic whisper. He stiffened and prepared to dash down the hallway, but she seemed unaware.

"You can come in, it's okay," she said.

Her eyes never left her reflection, yet she somehow knew he was there. He stood in the bathroom doorway, the camera in his hands.

"Can I take your picture?"

Her gaze remained on her reflection in the mirror.

"Sure, after I finish getting ready."

He laughed when she puckered her lips to apply her lipstick.

"Want to try some?"

His eyes widened, and his lips wrinkled.

"Uh? No."

She laughed.

"Come here."

He stepped slowly into the bathroom. She grabbed him by the arm and kissed his cheek and left a red lipstick print. He squirmed away and brought his hand to his face.

"No, don't rub it off. It looks good. Now you're a real ladies' man. Come see."

They stood side-by-side in the bathroom and both peered at their reflections. He tilted his head this way and that until his lips curled into a smile and his eyebrows rose. He stared at her reflection, his gaze met hers. She indulged him for a moment, a smirk appeared across her lips, then she swung her hips and she hip bumped him away from the sink and the mirror.

"Whoa," he cried.

They both chuckled.

"Go on, get out of here, Casanova, while I finish up. Why don't you sit outside and wait for the Cranes while I finish getting ready?"

He rushed down the hallway, excited to see Mrs. Crane, Beatrice, and Mr. Crane waiting in the Mercedes, but the driveway was empty.

"They're not here yet," he shouted.

He went out and sat on the poured concrete porch with the camera hanging from his neck. His fingers followed a ragged crack in the concrete. The summer sun had completely dried up the puddles, and the dew soaked grass, which appeared taller than the day before. Mr. Crane's Mercedes came down the street silent like a ghost with only the driver. It slowed, made the turn into the driveway, then glided to the house. He wrinkled his lips at the empty seats. When Mr. Crane stopped in front of the garage, Lucius finally heard the purr of the car's engine. He stood and dusted off the back seat of his pants. Mr. Crane got out and stepped around the front of the car. He had on a casual polo shirt, cotton trousers, and loafers.

"Hello Lucius."

"Hello."

"How's the photography business?"

"Good."

"You've got your shutter speed set for a longer exposure. Did you get some indoor shots?"

"Ah? Yeah, I tried."

Mr. Crane tilted the camera to inspect the frame number.

"I would say so. You're almost at the end of the roll of film. Anyway, I can't wait to see them."

He swallowed. Mr. Crane squeezed his shoulder and patted him on the back.

"Is your Aunt Phoebe inside?"

"Yes, she's getting ready. Where's Mrs. Crane and Beatrice? Didn't they want to come?"

"Oh, Ms. Käthe had dinner started and Mrs. Crane didn't want it to go to waste, so they both stayed at the house."

From the short time he knew Mrs. Crane, she never ate leftovers, but it was too early for Ms. Käthe to have started dinner.

"Oh? Okay."

He followed Mr. Crane inside the house. The screen door slapped shut behind them. Mr. Crane glanced into the kitchen with its cupboard doors all ajar. For such a large man, his loafers made no sound on the tiled floor, or even as he stepped into the empty living room.

"My God, your Aunt Phoebe wasted no time. If you stay any longer, you'll have to sit on the floor."

Mr. Crane chuckled, then raised his eyebrows and glanced at Lucius.

"I trust you helped her out?"

He glanced up at Mr. Crane.

"Yes."

"Good boy."

The master bedroom door opened, and light spilled into the darkened hallway. When Aunt Phoebe came out wearing a yellow with white polka dot form fitting dress, coco-colored stockings and cream-colored pumps, Mr. Crane's eyes brightened and his smiled broadened. She had brushed her hair and pinned parts of it up while spiral curls trailed down the sides of her face. There was less bounce in them from the day before. When she played with the curls near her shoulders, her earrings glittered and dangled. Lucius's eyebrows knit together. They were his mom's silver opal teardrop-shaped earrings. The ones she had tucked away in a lower drawer under her clothes. Ones he had never seen until his Aunt Phoebe found them. Mr. Crane's smile waned.

"Phoebe, good to see you. You look—very nice," he said.

She smiled and lifted her shoulder and lowered her chin, like a schoolgirl having difficulty accepting a compliment.

"Thank you Kenneth. Where's the missus and your daughter?"

His face wrinkled.

"Um. Like I told Lucius, dinner was almost ready and Mrs. Crane didn't want it to go to waste."

"I see."

Her eyebrows rose and fell. She glanced at Lucius. Mr. Crane put his arms out as if he were a realtor presenting the space.

"Well, you've certainly made quick work of getting the house cleaned out. Lucius said he helped."

"Yes, but he hasn't touched his bedroom. I hope to at least get his dresser emptied so the men could take it. They'll have to get it tomorrow."

She caressed the ends of her hair near her shoulder. His eyes looked tense.

"I see. But your flight back to Indiana is before noon, and we'll need an hour to get you to the airport."

"The men from the consignment store are set to come back in the morning. We should be fine."

He looked over at Lucius.

"Lucius, you have to get your room packed up tonight."

His voice was stern. She tugged at her earlobe. The earring attached danced, and the opal caught the light that came into the living room window. Mr. Crane was quick to notice before he returned his attention back to Lucius.

"I'm sorry Lucius. I think you should stay here and get your room ready. Your Aunt Phoebe put in a great deal of work. I would like you to pack all of your clothes. We'll bring them back to the house and whatever doesn't fit, we'll donate to the church."

Mr. Crane paused as if to gauge his reaction. Lucius stood there without a word and held the Leica in both hands. He was unclear how he felt and wondered how that must look on his face. It was a moment he thought someone should take *his* picture. Mr. Crane was not his dad, Aunt Phoebe was not his mom, he was not back at school frightened that a police officer had come for him, yet this felt like the day his parents died. He blinked.

"I'm sorry, but it's for the best. We'll bring you back something to eat."

Mr. Crane's voice was low. He glanced at Aunt Phoebe.

"Is there cereal still in the house?"

She nodded.

"Good."

"He'll be fine," she whispered.

She smiled a soft, conciliatory smile.

"Oh, come on Lucius, you said you wanted to take my picture. Let's go outside."

He wrinkled his lips in a smile of uncertainty. She grabbed his arm and guided him to the front door. Mr. Crane followed them out into the sun.

"Okay, Lucius, where would you like me to stand, and how would you like me to pose?"

She put her hands on her hips, bent slightly forward, and pursed her lips. Mr. Crane laughed.

"Oh, don't tease the boy. He's a professional. Right Lucius?"

He glanced at Mr. Crane. A subtle smile formed on his face.

"That's right," he said.

He glanced around the property with his fingertip pressed to his lip. The porch where he sat earlier was now cast in a swath of shade created by the pitch of the roof. His eyebrows rose.

"There."

His voice hushed but certain. He went around them and stood at the base of the concrete steps. He stepped back to allow his Aunt Phoebe to occupy the space. Mr. Crane stood with his arms crossed and appeared intrigued.

"Fold your arms like this."

He demonstrated, and she mirrored his pose. He then adjusted the aperture ring, then the shutter speed dial, then brought the camera's viewfinder to his eye. After he got her in focus, he stood there for a moment.

"Don't smile so big."

She wrinkled her lips.

"Don't do that either."

Mr. Crane laughed. Lucius stepped in a semicircle to check which angle he liked the best. Finally, he stood on the lawn a step off of the walkway from the porch to the driveway. He glanced at Mr. Crane. He had moved to lean against his car. Another idea formed, but he turned back to his Aunt Phoebe and brought the camera to his eye and focused. They stood frozen as they waited for him to press the shutter release. As soon as her smile faltered—click. He got the shot he wanted.

"All right, just one more," Mr. Crane said.

Mr. Crane tilted his head as though he were eager to get in on the action. Lucius wanted to keep control of the camera.

"Okay, over here. Can you lean against the car?"

He held out his arm and pointed to where he wanted her to stand. She raised her eyebrows and smiled when she glanced at Mr. Crane. He moved away from the car, so she could lean against the front quarter. The sunlight was much brighter in the driveway.

"Put your elbow back on the hood and, with your other hand, shield your eyes."

She did as he directed.

"Move your right foot out."

She did. Mr. Crane rubbed the side of his face. It was a pose Lucius had seen on a calendar with bare breasted women that hung in his dad's garage. The ease at which she took and held the pose seemed to be telling. Had Mr. Crane noticed? He hurried and got her in focus before anyone could protest, held for a brief moment, then click. The wisp of the Leica's shutters was like a whisper in his ear. It was the secret he shared with his mechanical companion.

"Bravo," Mr. Crane said.

He clapped as she stood. She squinted from the sun in her eyes, but smiled with a broad grin on her face, then fussed with her dress as the pose had caused the hem to ride up her thigh. Mr. Crane went to Lucius and squeezed his shoulder.

"You, young man, you are dangerous."

He looked up at him with wide eyes, and his lips parted. Mr. Crane chuckled, then lowered his head to whisper to him.

"I'm sure you got a great shot. I can't wait to see the negatives and make some prints."

Mr. Crane gave his shoulder another squeeze. After Aunt Phoebe got in the passenger side, Mr. Crane turned to him.

"Oh, I almost forgot, get that room cleaned up."

His shoulders slumped.

"Okay."

"Lucius, what kind of pie do you like?"

He scratched his head.

"Cherry—or apple."

"I'll get you a piece."

He grinned. Mr. Crane gave him a friendly salute before he got in the car. Lucius saluted back and watched the Mercedes back out of the driveway. After the car disappeared down the street, he peered down at the Leica strapped around his neck. How was he ever going to get his film developed without Mr. Crane seeing the pictures? The worst that could happen was Mr. Crane would take the camera from him. It made his stomach turn to think about it.

12

Kenneth Crane and Phoebe Cook sat in a booth at the Rally Diner in Rock Hill. It was a place he sometimes took clients, those of lesser financial means. He brought the legal documents for her to review which pertained to the selling of her deceased brother Darius's house and his and Paulina's belongings to be dispensed with. The proceeds later to be distributed, which he felt the lion's share should go to Lucius. The papers sat in his leather portfolio case on the table to the side of their glasses of ice tea. She only glanced once at the leather case. It was a small insurance policy if anyone he knew saw him. Sure, he sat with a beautiful woman, but with his case on the table, it suggested a modest business dinner.

She sat with her elbow on the table and played with the dangling opal earring. He smiled.

"Those are *some* earrings. The chap that you moved to Indiana with, did he get you those?"

The corner of her lips curled up and one of her eyebrows rose.

"Pfft. No, not Danny. He was exciting in other ways. He would never buy me jewelry. Maybe flowers, but never jewelry."

"Oh?"

She flipped her hair over her shoulder. The teardrop opal earring dangled and jiggled. She pinched her earlobe and a devilish smile appeared across her lips.

"I got these from another suitor."

He tilted his head, and his brow furrowed. Under the table, he pressed his hand against his thigh. His palm was like a clothing iron, hot and steamy.

"Do you mean Donnie Dix, the lawyer you worked for?"

She covered her mouth as she burst into laughter. An elderly woman at a nearby table looked up from her plate.

"Oh, heavens no. Sure Donnie had money, but he was a cheapskate. He could have done much more with his practice, but he could never get past his small town mentality. He *was* small in a lot of ways."

Her voice softened. He shifted in his seat.

"Were you seeing him?"

She raised her hand in front of her and examined her nails.

"We had a few moments, but he was terrible in bed."

She chuckled, waved her hand dismissively, then sipped at her ice tea. He raised an eyebrow. His lips drew into a tight line and then he snorted.

"So a mystery suitor gave you the earrings?"

"You could say that. What does it matter?"

She peered into his eyes. He looked away and sighed.

"It doesn't. I'm sorry. It's none of my business."

She glanced around the dining room. The Rally Diner had all booths. When the waitress came to take their orders, he felt embarrassed for bringing her to a diner, since she worked at one. There was a small German restaurant, nothing fussy. He should have taken her there.

After the waitress left, he took the legal papers from his leather case and went over them with her. She signed the papers to allow Morris and Langtree, the firm that employed him, to make the necessary arrangements to sell her brother's house. They would confirm with her all offers prior to the sale. She seemed satisfied and grateful. The food came as she signed the last of the documents. As Kenneth slipped the papers into his leather case, a familiar voice came over his shoulder.

"Miss, I hope you know you've got one of Hartford's most expensive lawyers, and he's worth every penny."

The man's voice was rich and boomed, and his chuckle that followed matched. Kenneth grinned and turned.

"Oh, hey Lloyd. Nice to see you. How's things?"

"You know me Kenny, I'm always doing well, but—"

Lloyd Jenkins glanced at Phoebe, who grinned with bright eyes at the near bald, barrel-chested man. Lloyd touched the edge of the table with his sausage sized fingers. He wore a three-piece navy pin-stripped suit with his tie loosened at the collar.

"You, my friend, are *always* doing great."

He winked at Kenneth. Kenneth smiled and glanced at Phoebe.

"Ms. Cook, this is Lloyd Jenkins, one of my colleagues and friends at Morris and Langtree. Lloyd, this lovely client of mine is Ms. Phoebe Cook."

Lloyd shook her hand with both hands. Her hand disappeared in his large mitts. Kenneth had never seen the man grin as much as he did. He feared Lloyd's face might crack in two. Lloyd continued to hold her hand while he extended his hand to Kenneth, and they shook. Finally, Lloyd released them.

"So what brings you here?" Kenneth asked.

"The wife's out with her girlfriends playing cards, so I popped in to get something to eat before heading home. They've got a great turkey and mashed potatoes plate. Kenny knows how much I love Thanksgiving, and their cherry pie is real good."

He winked at her, almost to suggest if she played her cards right, Kenneth might buy her dessert. He smiled at Lloyd.

"Well Kenny, great to see you, and Ms. Cook, nice to meet you. I won't keep you."

Kenneth shook Lloyd's hand, while Phoebe simply nodded and smiled. After Lloyd departed, they ate, and she giggled. She leaned in as if to impart some sensitive information to him.

"Kenny? Do the ladies call you Kenny as well?"

He smiled and snorted. His face warmed. A coy smile crossed her lips.

"Not when the lights are on. Well, maybe then as well."

They both chuckled. When the waitress returned, he put in a takeout order for Lucius, which included a slice of cherry pie. He finished eating. The entire time he could feel her eyes on him.

"You're so sweet," she whispered.

He barely heard her. His back stiffened when he felt her stocking clad toes enter the opening of his pant leg. Her toes climbed his shin and playfully pulled his sock down to his ankle. She giggled softly. His gaze rose to meet hers. She leaned back into the booth's cushions and traced the notch at her neck with her fingertips. It was something Eleanor did to signal she was ready to be fucked. It was Phoebe now who had given the signal. Her eyelids lowered, heavy and seductive. She smiled and parted her lips enough so he could see her tongue trace her top teeth.

His breath caught and he put down his fork and lowered his hand to his thigh to hide what he felt must be an enormous bulge at the front of his trousers. He ached to have his cock sunk deep inside this woman and her delicious legs wrapped around his ribs. When she slid her foot between his thighs, he jolted upright. Her toes pressed and dug at the front of his trousers. He gripped the edge of the table. She teased his cock with her toes, and his body told her everything she needed to know.

She withdrew her advances, and leaned into the edge of the table, no doubt to slip her foot back into her shoe. He gazed at her. His breath was heavy. She snorted and chuckled softly at his expression. He lowered his head and glanced out into the dining room. Thankfully, no one caught on to this spectacle. He swallowed down a dry knot in his throat. The waitress came with the takeout order and the check. How was he supposed to walk to and stand before the cashier with a hard-on? Phoebe offered no solutions or any sympathy. She instead touched up her lipstick and sat with nonchalant ease across from him. Her now cavalier demeanor confused him. Did she want him to take her to some nearby hotel so they could fuck until their bodies melted into pools of orgasmic transcendence?

"I'm ready, are you?"

She snapped her compact case shut and slipped it into her purse. He adjusted himself to pin his erection under his waistband. It would protrude less, he hoped. He intended to use the takeout bag for cover, but she snatched it up.

"Oh, I can carry it."

She smirked at him. She must know he needed the bag to cover himself. She grabbed his leather portfolio case as well. There was no getting out of the diner without the risk of humiliation. She slipped from the booth and headed for the entrance. Her hips swayed for his entertainment, and it was only to his detriment that he eyed her round ass. He stood as if he had thrown his back out and tried not to make eye contact with any of the other patrons, but it happened anyway. He imagined their judgement, but they only gave him a cursory glance.

While in the parking lot, after he opened the passenger door for her, he imagined he looked as though they had already been to a motel. When he went around the back of the car, he nearly fell over as he skipped on one leg to pull up his sock. He shook his head and mumbled incoherently, then opened the driver's side door and got in behind the wheel.

13

Lucius ate several fistfuls of cereal, then he left the open box on the counter and wandered into his parents' bedroom. His Aunt Phoebe's suitcase sat on the bed. He flipped open the latches, and tucked down alongside her clothes, he found his mom's jewelry. His mom would never wear it again, so why did it matter? At first he wanted to offer it to Mrs. Crane, but he knew deep down that she would never wear it, accept it as a gift maybe, but never wear it. He explored his Aunt Phoebe's clothes. He laid out a pair of her coco-colored stockings on the bed, then two pairs of her panties, one a deep red, one a dark beige, both with satin crotches and lace edging. It was difficult to imagine them being as nice as what Mrs. Crane might wear. Mrs. Crane was a much more elegant woman. In that moment, he longed to see Mrs. Crane. To watch her walk about the house, to see her body move through space. The corner of his lips turned down. He rolled up his Aunt Phoebe's stockings, folded her panties, put everything back in her suitcase, shut it, and snapped the latches closed without another thought or feeling.

The sunlight that came into the living room windows had faded and no longer was bright enough to reach the kitchen. The wall switch to the kitchen light made a loud snap when he flipped it on. He dug his hand into the open cereal box and stuffed a handful into his mouth. The opened bottle of whiskey sat pushed back on the counter, its label faced the wall. Would she get sloshed again tonight? Sloshed, that was a word he heard at school. Some of the other boys would use it when they referred to their parents or other adults who they had seen drunk. His dad drank much more than his mom. She only drank when they had friends over to play cards, and when she wanted to fit in. He had a glass of milk, then put his empty glass in the sink. He had tasted liquor before, its foul burning and biting taste. It was amazing anyone would find it appealing. He lumbered to his bedroom carrying an empty trash bag he got from the cabinet under the sink.

He sat cross-legged on the floor. The closet door hung open. The remaining clothes from the closet sat tossed on the floor and on the bed. A limp, yet to be filled, garbage bag with its mouth open in a yawn sat next to him. He took the clothes from the floor and stuffed them into the large black plastic bag, then reached behind him and did the same with what lie on the bed. He then scissored his legs and stood in one motion, as was the providence of young boys. After he dragged the garbage bag, less than half full of his clothes, to his dresser, he began unloading each drawer into the bag until the dresser stood empty.

The *Carnival of Souls* poster on the wall caught his eye. He gazed at the blonde woman in distress. Her blouse nearly coming off of her, and threatened to expose her breasts at any moment. His parents argued about whether he should have it, but like always, his dad won out and he had it taped to his walls ever since. His dad got the poster last year from some kid he knew who worked at the movie theatre. Lucius always wanted a horror movie poster, but that was the best his dad could do. He carefully removed it from the wall. Four sticky tape marks remained. It was a question if Mr. Crane would allow him to put it up in their guest bedroom. As for Mrs. Crane, that would be a definite no. He rolled the poster and sat it on the floor next to the bag of clothes.

He smiled when he looked at the Leica that sat on top of his dresser. It called to him to pick it up, but something else also called to him. He turned around and peered at his bed. It was without a bedspread. A green and black plaid blanket with a tattered satin edging covered the sheets and pillow.

He took his dad's flashlight and lie at the side of the bed to see what he collected and hid under there over the years. He dragged out a few more comics, two *Hardy Boys Mystery* novels, an old comb, pencils, a notebook, until he saw the edge of his mom's diary. It sat furthest in against the wall. He squirmed on his back, his arm stretched out, fingers pointed, but the diary remained out of reach. He dropped his arm to the carpet to rest it. The muscles in his shoulder burned, and the metal bed frame weighed on his chest and scratched his face. The springs underneath clawed at his clothes. His breathing slowed. It was like before each picture he captured. He slid his body further under the bed. His lips wrinkled, and he tried to ignore the discomfort. His middle finger touched the faux leather spine of the diary enough to rotate it until he had a hold of it. He squirmed slowly back out and sat against the bed. After a deep exhalation, he tugged at his shirt to straighten it. A dull ache came from his scalp. He raked his fingers through his hair to part it in its usual direction.

The dust from under the bed brought on a sneeze. After he rubbed his nose against his shirt sleeve, he thumbed the button on the diary's hinged lock and the latch sprung free. He lifted the faux leather cover and turned the pages. The first few pages mentioned the time before he was born. How happy his mom was to be pregnant and her dreams of having a family had finally come true, the many arguments she had with Darius over family and money, his friends and their wives and girlfriends, most of them scoundrels, cunning survivors like hyenas. She had questioned whether any of these wives or girlfriends, "loose cunts," as she referred to them, had slept with Darius. There was pain and trepidation in her words. He reached some blank pages and was sure he had come to the end of the entries until he thumbed past them to find others. It seemed she wanted to bury her deeper secrets in the depths of the diary.

The first few written pages, followed by many blank ones, mentioned a man. No first name. No last name. His mom described him as tall, handsome, and, most of all—kind. She wrote of a moment where she screwed up some paperwork, no office or company name mentioned, and this man calmed her boss down and persuaded him not to fire her. Afterwards, she worked hard not to draw the ire of her boss. Any stress at work seemed to be alleviated by the kindness of this unnamed man. He scanned ahead some pages only to read that his mom no longer loved his dad.

The familiar squeal of the screen door's springs and the wooden clap when the door slapped shut, shot from the front of the house, through the living room, and down the hall to the bedrooms. A click of heels echoed on the linoleum floor in the kitchen.

"Lucius?"

Aunt Phoebe called to him. He flipped the diary closed, thumbed the hinged lock, and snapped it in place. He dug into his pocket and took out the diary's tiny golden key and secured the lock. The button held firm and would not budge. Good.

He had a hold of the garbage bag when she appeared in the doorway. He had stuffed the diary among his clothes, and was about to add the rest of his comics and books when he looked up at her. She had one hand on the doorframe and the other on her hip.

"Wow. You've been busy."

"Yeah. The dresser and the closet are empty. These are my clothes and books I want to bring to the Cranes."

He lifted the mouth of the garbage bag.

"Great. Well, you can take a break now. Your dinner is out in the kitchen. Come out and eat."

"Okay."

He stuffed the rolled *Carnival of Souls* poster into the bag and loosely twisted the top shut, as if he was worried something might fall out.

"Is Mr. Crane here?"

"No, he seemed to be in a hurry to get home. I think I gave him a fright."

"Huh?"

She chuckled.

"Never mind. Come out and eat."

He got up from the floor and she stepped aside so he could exit his bedroom. He walked slowly to be sure that she followed close behind him. They crossed the dark, empty living room. A large paper sack sat on the kitchen counter. She opened the bag and set out the wrapped up cheeseburger and fries. She also put out a styrofoam cup of soda and handed him a straw to unwrap.

"When you're done eating, Mr. Crane also got you this."

She took from the sack a final styrofoam container and sat it on the counter before she crumpled up the paper bag.

"It's a slice of cherry pie."

She winked at him. He grinned and his eyes widened. He unwrapped the cheeseburger, and she leaned back against the counter as she watched him eat. She tilted her head as if she were contemplating something. Since the men from the consignment store took the chairs, they both stood with the counter between them and glanced at one another. She let out a heavy sigh, and went on and on about how lucky he was to live with the Cranes, and how nice of a man she thought Mr. Crane was. He took hungry bites of the cheeseburger and nibbled at the french fries, while he only half listened to what she said. When he finished, half his soda remained along with a handful of french fries.

"Done, already?"

He covered his mouth and burped.

"Sorry."

She chuckled.

"That good, huh? Gonna save your pie for later?"

He nodded. She nibbled at his remaining french fries and sipped at his soda.

"Since we no longer have a television and you picked up most of your room, I guess you can read one of your books or go to bed early if you're tired. I'm going to take a nice, long, luxurious bath."

She grinned, and her eyes beamed when she mentioned the bath. He returned to his bedroom and took off his clothes to get ready for bed. Beyond his closed bedroom door, he heard his parents' bedroom door close. He wrinkled his lips when he glanced down at his skinny body. With no pajamas to wear, he figured he would sleep in his boxers. He had stuffed the old pair of pajamas he wore the other night into the bag with his other clothes and everything else he owned. If he dug in the bag with his mom's diary, he might draw his Aunt Phoebe's curiosity. A chance to read it would have to wait until he got to the Cranes.

The sound of doors opening and closing out in the hallway gave him an idea. He opened the door as quietly as he could and slipped into the hallway. The sound of running water from the bathtub faucet came muffled from behind the closed bathroom door. He crept into the adjacent laundry room, and left the lights off, otherwise she might suspect he was there. In the past, when he took baths and his mom was doing laundry, he would see the light in the laundry room through the shared vent near the floor. He sat on the floor and tilted his head to peer into the bathroom from the vent. The running water sounded thunderous as it echoed in the adjacent bathroom.

She sang and hummed from somewhere in the room, probably at the sink. Then her bare legs appeared. She dipped her toes in the bathwater and hummed with delight. The towel fell to the floor and hid her feet and ankles until she stepped into the tub. She released a long, low moan of satisfaction.

When he turned on his side so his head was closer to the laundry room's cement floor, he could see her arm rested on the side of the tub, and occasionally she would lift and bend her leg out of the water. The laundry room floor had a chemical smell, and there were bits of hair and dust that tickled his nose. He felt a sneeze coming. He pinched his nose shut and covered his mouth. A muffled wheeze passed his lips and his body jerked. She stopped singing and sat still in the bathwater. He froze in a fetal position on the laundry room floor. He took shallow breaths and his eyes remained fixed on her through the other side of the vent, at least from what he could see of her. Her arm disappeared. He waited for her to sit up in alarm, then he would have to dash back to his bedroom, but he was sure he could beat her there.

The wait seemed forever. Or had time stopped? He swallowed. Soft moans filtered through the vent from the bathroom.

"Mmm. Kenny-Kenny-Kenny."

Her voice came through the vent in a metallic echo, as if heard through a tin can. His eyebrows drew together. Did she say, "Kitty-kitty-kitty?"

"Oh, Kenny. You were ready to go, weren't you?"

Kenny? Kenneth? Mr. Crane?

She laughed. Her soapy leg extended up and out of the water. White bubbles and suds ran down her milky calf and thigh. She pointed her toes and tiny suds clung to them. Her leg eased back into the foamy bathwater. The whiskey bottle appeared horizontal in her hand. She drank straight from it. The glass bottle clunked crisp and amplified in the small enclosed space when she sat it down on the porcelain tiles.

"Oh, Kenny. That look in your eye. I know *that* look. You want me, Kenny, don't cha?"

She laughed and took another drink from the bottle.

"I wonder—"

She let out a soft hiccup.

"You must know I want you, too. Sure, it could have only been a tease. I do that sometimes to entertain myself. But—but in your case, I don't think it takes a mastermind. Whew! Was your cock ever so hard? I bet you never had a foot job before. I could have popped your cork right there."

She laughed.

"Anyway, I forgive you. I'm sure you didn't intend to take me to a diner. God, I'm going to hate to go back to work."

She sighed and drank. This time, she took a long slug. He blinked his eyes slow and softly as if he was afraid she might hear him. The light from the bathroom painted a waffle shadow pattern on his chest and arms. His arm hurt, pressed against the cool floor. A loud rush of water came when she turned on the faucet, presumably to raise the water level in the tub or to adjust the temperature. Her robin's egg blue painted toes curled as she placed both of her feet apart on the edge of the tub. Sounds of swirling water echoed off the bathroom walls when she repositioned herself. Her soapy knees stood out of the water. Her legs glistened wet and the way the bathroom lights hit her skin, they looked electric. He imagined photographing her. His index finger bent as if to press the shutter release button.

She released a sudden deep moan. Her breath drew in and out erratically. Then another moan and another, each built in volume and quickened in tempo. The balls of her feet pressed firm against the bathroom tiles. She let out one long, low moan before she slipped her feet back into the water. Then she crooned.

"Oh Kenny? What am I going to do with you, now that I have you? Because Dear—you *know* I have you."

His eyebrows drew together, and he wrinkled his lips. Not Mr. Crane. Never Mr. Crane. What about Mrs. Crane? His mom's written words came to mind, "loose cunts." Did Aunt Phoebe have a loose cunt?

He rose carefully and crept back to his bedroom, closed the door, and climbed into bed. When he was nearly asleep, his bedroom door opened. He counted the seconds where she must have peered at him before she closed the door.

14

"Oh, Kenneth. What has come over you? To what do I owe gratitude for this most delightful amorous attention?"

Eleanor hummed and moaned. Kenneth lie next to her, his chest rose and fell as he fought to catch his breath. His skin glossy wet with sweat, her breasts, one exposed where he tore her negligee. He took and kissed her hand that lie on his chest. She traced her fingers down his body, past his navel, to find him still fully erect. His cock was thick and as firm as she had ever known. He groaned as she tugged on him. When she slipped her fingertips between her folds, they came back slick with his semen.

"I want you again."

She was about to straddle him when he adjusted her knees, and she knew he wanted her from behind. She bent forward and offered her ass to him. Before she could grasp the sheets, he took her by her hips and thrusted his entire length inside her. His semen ran down her inner thigh like warm honey. She released a long modulated, "Ooh." He dug his fingers into her buttocks. She, to her delight, was certain he had marked her. Did he forget how soon they might visit the beach? Bruises on her buttocks would be telling. She laughed inside at herself, but then pushed her thoughts aside. Tonight he offered pure bliss, and she knew not to squander it.

After he had come a third time with her insisting on being on top, his body lie entirely wasted, wrecked on her shores, and asleep. She covered him. Her torn negligee lie on the floor next to the bed. She threw the covers over herself. The smooth silk sheets slipped cool over her naked body.

15

The faint roar of jet engines filled the open air. Lucius swiveled his head to catch sight of the departing flights. The Leica dangled from its strap around his neck. Planes that taxied down the runway appeared like tiny metal toys. As they rose into the sky, they shrank until he could no longer see them.

"Stand here, Aunt Phoebe."

He pointed to a spot near a railing where there was a clear view of the planes connected to the terminal, with others landing and lifting off in the background. He had adjusted the camera to a daylight exposure on the ride to the airport. With the film advanced to the next frame, he was ready. All that remained was to focus the lens and press the shutter release.

Aunt Phoebe stood in front of the railing. He directed her to shift her body slightly, then he held the camera vertically to get her entire body in the shot.

"No, wait."

He held up his hand.

"Bend your leg like you did when you turned. No, no. Go back to how you were. Okay, turn again. There!"

Mr. Crane laughed, but when Lucius glanced at him, his eyebrows shot up and his smile flattened. He returned Lucius's serious gaze, then nodded. Mr. Crane stood to the side with his arms crossed. One arm cradled the other. His closed hand touched his lips, like a spectator who waited and hoped for something extraordinary to happen.

She grinned when he peered at her through the camera's viewfinder.

"Less of a smile."

Her eyes widened, and she glared at him. He was undeterred by her impatience. He was making pictures, as Mr. Crane said. There was something basic and amateurish about her direct gaze.

"Maybe look at Mr. Crane."

She gazed off to where Mr. Crane stood. Her expression, first serious and inquisitive, transformed. Her eyebrow rose and one corner of her lips curled up. He waited. A plane rolled slowly on the tarmac in the distance. Her lips parted as if she were about to be kissed. He wanted to know what expression Mr. Crane had made to illicit such a response. He fought his curiosity and kept his gaze through the viewfinder. She lifted her chin slightly. Another plane raced down the runway, tilted its nose upward, its back arched before it left the Earth. Click. He lowered the camera and thumbed the frame advance lever. He expected it to be the last shot, but the roll advanced to the next frame. Mr. Crane clapped softly a few times.

"Now that's going to be a great shot."

She put her hand on her hip.

"All right Lucius, I have a plane to catch."

"No wait. Just one more shot. I'll make it quick. I promise."

"Okay, make it quick. Why don't you take a picture of Mr. Crane and me?"

Her voice climbed. He wrinkled his lips.

"Kenneth, if you don't think the missus will mind."

She waved for Mr. Crane to join her. He paused before responding.

"Ah? No, of course not. That would be great. What do you think, Lucius?"

He seemed to grapple for a way out. Lucius tilted his head and glanced at the both of them.

"That sounds interesting. Sure. Mr. Crane, if you can stand next to her, that would be great. Maybe you both can lean against the railing."

Maybe the railing will break. The thought lingered as he raised the camera to his eye. It was a candid family-photo type shot. The composition was flat and uninspired, but the subtle tension between Mr. Crane and Aunt Phoebe drove him to press the shutter release button. The image held in his mind's eye. Their eyes were tense as their faces contorted into discreet masks.

He lowered the camera. The roll was complete.

The Mercedes took the broad, curved exit ramp from the airport with ease. Lucius stared out the window at the departing planes. Which one might his Aunt Phoebe be on, if she had even boarded yet? She told Mr. Crane she hoped to see him again, which made little sense since she was in a hurry to take care of her brother's estate and get back to *life* in Indiana, whatever life there was for her there. Lucius assumed she liked him. Would he ever see her again? Did it matter to her? She seemed the type who had little desire to visit family, especially if there was nothing to gain. She had his mom's jewelry and soon the house would be up for sale. Her one visit was perhaps her final and only visit.

Mr. Crane reached over and squeezed his shoulder.

"I can't wait to see your pictures. I'm sure you have some amazing shots."

He pushed and agitated Lucius's shoulder until he smiled. His smile faded when he thought of all the pictures *he made*. Some were his private pictures, at least ones he wanted no one else to see. The Leica sat in his lap with the strap still around his neck. The weight of its metallic body felt heavier. How would he explain to Mr. Crane some of the pictures he shot?

By the time they arrived at the house, he convinced Mr. Crane they should wait to develop the film. When he carried in the garbage bag filled with the last of his clothes from his parents' house, Ms. Käthe and Ms. Mila were busy in the kitchen, and, to his relief, had already cleaned the bedrooms. Beatrice was happy to see him, as he was to see her. She was eager to see what treasures he brought from his parents' house.

"It's nothing really, mostly clothes. I have some comic books."

He beamed with his declaration while she wrinkled her lips.

"What else you got?"

"I can show you after dinner. How's that?"

She raised her eyebrows. She still followed him to the top of the stairs and when he glanced back, her gaze was still on him when he lugged the garbage bag into the guest bedroom. Once free of her prying eyes, he dug into the bag until he found his mom's diary and stashed it. When he stepped into the hallway, she was halfway to the bedroom. She stood with her arms crossed and her eyes narrowed.

"What took you so long? Ms. Käthe called up the stairs to say that dinner was ready. My father and—Eleanor are waiting for us."

"Oh? Sorry."

"Did you hide something? I bet you did."

She had a smug smile.

"No. Why?"

She huffed and turned on her heels and he followed her down the hallway, then downstairs to the dining room, where Mr. and Mrs. Crane sat at the table. Mrs. Crane glared at them with her pale sky-blue eyes. He desperately wanted to know what was behind her stoic mask.

"Sit children," she said.

Two words, but her tone had teeth. They took their seats. She gave them both a sympathetic smile. The four ate, and afterwards Mr. and Mrs. Crane retired to the patio with wine and cigarettes, as usual. Beatrice and Lucius went upstairs to the guest bedroom, and as he promised, he showed her what he brought from his parents' house.

They sat on the floor with the open garbage bag between them. He took out the rolled up movie poster.

"Do you think your parents will let me put this on the wall?"

She leaned forward with her legs folded under her. He unrolled the poster.

"*Carnival of Souls*? What's that?"

"My dad got it for me. It's a horror movie. Have you seen it?"

"No! My father would never let me see a movie like that. Have you?"

"Uh—well, no."

She tilted her head and wrinkled her lips. He rolled the poster and set it aside. Its glamour gone. The books he pulled from the bag held more interest to her, but not much more, being they were of boys' interests. As for his comic books, she only looked at the covers, then sat them on the bed.

"Hey, that one is *The Fantastic Four*."

She crossed her arms.

"I can be Reed Richards. He's Mr. Fantastic, and you can be Sue Storm."

"What makes you so fantastic, and who is Sue Storm?"

"Mr. Fantastic can stretch his body into different shapes and lengths."

She raised her eyebrows.

"Sue Storm. She can turn invisible."

"I can already do that."

She stood and peered down at him. He still held the open garbage bag. Only his old clothes remained. The show was over. He wrinkled his lips. He expected her to tell him to put everything back in the bag and sit it outside with the rest of the trash.

"I'm going to my room."

She marched from the room. Her light footfalls were a polite adieu. He wrinkled his lips. She could have at least closed the bedroom door on her way out. He gazed up at the Leica on the dresser, pregnant with his sins.

16

At the dinner table, Mrs. Crane spoke little, only to mention that Mr. Crane was working late and they would dine without him. She also mentioned he may stay overnight at the apartment in Hartford he had for such occasions. Although Mrs. Crane spoke in an even tone, there was a tightness in her voice.

After dinner, Mrs. Crane went to the study. She stood with her buttocks pressed against the top edge of the desk, and her long elegant legs braced outward. She had the phone cord wrapped under her arm and twirled around her fingers. From the dark hallway, Lucius stood motionless. He took half glimpses of her from the hallway, and his ears pricked to catch her words.

"Dear, you were a beast the other night. I have to have you tonight. Let me arrange for an overnight sitter and I'll drive up," she said.

She paused and coiled the phone cord around her finger. What was Mr. Crane's reply?

"Why yes, it's raining."

The wet windowpanes distorted the light from the street lamps.

"Don't be silly, Kenneth. I am quite adept at driving in the rain. Yes, Dear, even at night."

She could do anything as far as Lucius was concerned. She could sky dive out of an airplane.

"My hair will be fine. Remember the times when we made love in the rain? It's been a long time since we've done that. If it's still raining when I get there, we can—"

The wood floor in the hallway made a dull pop when he shifted his weight. His eyes widened. He straightened up so he could no longer see her. He expected to hear her approaching footsteps on the wood floor. Instead, she cleared her throat.

"Oh? It's not—raining there."

She released a tense chuckle.

"You're tired, I understand. Won't you let me take care of you?"

He peeked around the door frame, only enough to see her legs and feet. She sighed. She dropped her hand and brushed her fingers across her skirt. He leaned further so he could see all of her.

"Is this about Lucius's Aunt Phoebe? Your flames have died down after she left. The day you had dinner with her, that night, was I the consolation prize?"

She unravelled the phone cord from around her finger and stood up from her perch on Mr. Crane's desk.

"I'm not being silly. Let's not play games, Kenneth. We both know you have a wandering eye. You said yourself, you thought she was stunning. Stunning, single, probably desperate to have you between her legs."

Where ever Mrs. Crane's gaze was in Mr. Crane's study—the bookshelves, the leather sofa—Lucius imagined would catch fire at any moment.

"Enjoy your night alone, if you are indeed alone."

She hung up the phone after she spoke, which no doubt denied Mr. Crane any goodbyes if he had any. She huffed, then marched toward the door. Lucius hurried down the hallway as quietly as he could and ducked into the kitchen. Her heels struck the wood floors in the hallway close behind. When she stepped into the kitchen, he had fled into the adjacent dining room. His heart pounded like a rabbit's and he tried to silence the gulps of breaths that pushed past his open lips. He trembled as he glanced into the kitchen. She opened a fresh bottle of wine, filled her glass from dinner that sat on the counter, retrieved a pack of cigarettes from an upper cabinet above the countertop, and retired to hers and Mr. Crane's after dinner locale. He followed. From the doorway to the screened in patio, he watched her.

A steady rain came. Its voice and presence were more pronounced through the screens, and brought with it cool damp air. Even from the doorway, he felt it on his face and arms. It then came sweetened with the smoky scent of Mrs. Crane's cigarette. She sat alone in one of the cushioned wicker chairs, with her elbows on the armrests. In one hand, she held out a cigarette smoked close to the filter, and in the other, she cradled a wineglass. She lifted her chin and blew a stream of smoke upward toward the ceiling, then took a drink. He watched her repeat the cycle several times before she leaned forward and set down her glass to refill it. The wine bottle she brought with her was less than half full. It sat on the wicker coffee table next to the open pack of cigarettes and a porcelain ashtray filled with crushed rose-lipstick stained cigarette butts. She blew out a final stream of smoke, bent forward, and put out her cigarette in the ashtray. She sat her wineglass next to the pack of cigarettes before she relaxed back into the chair cushions.

Her head rolled from side to side as if she tried to unravel a knot from her neck, then she rested her head on the back of the chair. The rain continued without slowing. It made a dull pattering rumble as thousands of droplets landed on the screened in patio roof and masked her breathing.

At first it was difficult to tell if she had fallen asleep until soft moans came from inside the ever darkening patio space. All of its colors and shapes cast in a gloomy gray. Her nylon covered knees rose, and she braced her stocking feet on the edge of the coffee table.

Mrs. Crane released a heavy breath followed by a series of drawn out, ooo's and mmm's. There was a subtle shift of her knees and the placement of her feet on the table. Her moans rose above then sank below the growl of the cascading rain. She faced the backyard away from the doorframe where Lucius watched. The intricacies of her performance were a mystery, but her vocalizations were familiar to what he heard when he witnessed her and Mr. Crane in bed. He tightened his grasp on the doorframe's moulding as her moans and cries quickened and raced to a long groaning release. She held her knees together. Her stocking feet lifted and hung in the air for a moment before settling to rest on the coffee table. Her final soft hum faded out into the dull groan of the rain.

He swallowed and his eyebrows drew together as he watched her. A short, sudden burst of crazed laughter bellowed from her. She exhaled long and slow.

"I know you're there."

Her voice was smoky, raspy, and low. He took a step back, but the floor creaked. She sat up, filled her wineglass with what remained in the bottle, and lit a fresh cigarette before she relaxed back in the chair.

"It's past your bedtime. Run along."

He crept up the stairs. Before he slipped into the guest bedroom, he saw Beatrice barefoot at the top of the stairs in her nightdress. Where had she come from? He watched her step towards him without a sound like a ghost. She seemed to float down the hallway.

"What are you doing?" he asked.

His voice was a tense whisper. She huffed.

"*Me?* You need to do better if you're going to spy on Eleanor, or anyone else, for that matter."

He said nothing. He watched her continue down the hallway and slip into her room. As her door closed, the knob turned, and the latch seated without a sound.

17

A week passed where Mr. Crane was either too distracted or disinterested to process Lucius's roll of film. Maybe it was the several spats with Mrs. Crane over his Aunt Phoebe and the handling of his parents' estate. Maybe Mr. Crane was as nervous as he was to see the pictures. There was a strong likelihood that Mrs. Crane would want to see them as well, or, if denied, would find them herself. As a consolation, Mr. Crane gave him two fresh rolls of AGFA ISO 100 black and white film. He talked him through the process of how to rewind the roll he shot and how to load one of the new rolls. He did so with ease, which delighted Mr. Crane.

Tonight, he gazed at the Leica on the dresser, loaded with a fresh roll. An abundance of possibilities. The roll he shot of Beatrice and his Aunt Phoebe, which sat next to the camera, overshadowed his excitement. What could he possibly shoot now to get himself into even deeper trouble? He wanted to photograph Mrs. Crane more than anything. The nude black and white photograph of her, which he had tucked behind the dresser, called to him. He sighed, and instead, stretched his arm down the side of the bed until he felt the butt of his dad's old flashlight.

He squirmed on the bed until his shoulder pressed against the headboard. He slipped his hand between the headboard and the mattress to the box spring. There he had hid his mom's diary. Since Ms. Käthe and Ms. Mila always lifted the sides of the mattress when they made the beds, he thought it would be safer there. He hid two of his comic books under the mattress, positioned so they lined up with the quilted pattern to see what would happen. The comics, shifted from their original position, confirmed his suspicion.

He opened his mom's diary as he lie on his side and brought the flashlight up from under the covers to illuminate the entries. The flashlight's cool metal barrel left a chill on his skin where it had touched his side. He flipped the pages in an attempt to find where he had stopped reading. An occasional creak came from the sleeping house. His gaze went to the darkened doorway, and his ears pricked up. He pointed the flashlight near the door to make sure it was closed, then he returned his attention to the diary.

His mom had left out names, important names, specifically the name of a man she had feelings for. This man she wrote about worked at the office where she worked before she became a waitress. She called him more than handsome. She wrote the word—*dashing*. She said his hair was perfect and his nails always trimmed. An elegant man, one who took pride in his appearance, which came with his profession. What profession? His mom never mentioned what *his profession* was specifically. His looks, this man she wrote about, had an equally matched gentle demeanor.

He sighed, turned the page, then aimed the light. She wrote that she had dinner with this man. It was on one of her claimed to be *working late at the office* evenings, to which his dad accused her of things. Things that she wrote in her later entries that she knew to be true of his dad. She used the word *fucking*. Darius is fucking that woman again. She said she saw them, but no mention of the woman's name or where she saw Darius and the woman—fucking. It was difficult to read the f-word written in her hand, but there it was, written several times. The corner of his lips tightened. He turned the page and rubbed his heavy eyelids.

"What are you doing? You should be sleeping."

A hushed but sharp whisper came from the shadows of the room. He bolted upright and flipped the diary closed. The silhouette of Mrs. Crane stood in the doorway. He never heard her open the door. Damn Ms. Käthe or Ms. Mila for oiling the door hinges. He raised his light, then lowered it when she shielded her eyes. She stood there in a silk nightgown with an ostrich feather collar and cuffs, and silk house slippers.

"Its late. What are you doing?"

She crossed her arms.

"Um. I was reading."

She took a step into the room. His eyes widened. He put his hand over the diary.

"What is it you're reading that is so interesting to keep you up at this hour?"

"Ah. Nothing."

She would never buy his answer.

"Um. *The Adventures of Tom Sawyer.*"

He pressed the diary into the mattress as if he feared it would somehow float to her.

"Put your book away and go to bed."

She waited. He swallowed, held his breath, and his heart hammered. He turned off the flashlight and placed it and the diary on the nightstand. The room was dark enough not to tell what he had been reading. She waited until he slipped under the covers and put his head on the pillow before she left the room and closed the door. She made no sound in the hallway, so he waited several minutes before he got out of bed, found *The Adventures of Tom Sawyer* among his small stack of books, replaced the diary with the novel on the nightstand, and returned the diary to its hiding place between the headboard and the box spring.

18

Ms. Mila and Ms. Käthe were in the kitchen preparing dinner. Mrs. Crane moved between the dining room and the kitchen to manage both women. Beatrice sat out on the screened in patio reading a book, while Mr. Crane had yet to arrive home from work. Lucius took the opportunity and snuck to the guest bedroom. He was sure Mrs. Crane knew he was hiding something, and worse, where. It would be only a matter of time if she became curious enough to search the bed he slept in. He would have put the diary behind the dresser with the nude photograph of Mrs. Crane, but the gap was too narrow.

After he stretched his arm down between the headboard and box spring and pulled up his mom's diary, he examined it for a moment as he sat on the bed. Bright warm bands of early evening sunlight came in through the windows and fell across the bedspread. They warmed the skin on his arms. Seeing the diary in the daylight dispelled some of its mystique.

"What do you have there?"

Beatrice stood in the bedroom doorway. He put his hand over the diary and lowered his head.

"Nothing."

Her eyes narrowed.

"It's not nothing—it's a diary."

"Go away."

"Lucius. Who does it belong to?"

Her sweet soft voice carried on the wind as it did the day they climbed the great sycamore in the backyard. He sighed and shut his eyes for a moment.

"It's my mom's diary."

She looked as though he told her he saw his mom's ghost. He expected her to beg him for a peek. Instead, she stood in quiet contemplation before she spoke. Her bottom lip curled under.

"Have you read it? If you haven't, and it's locked, you must burn it."

"Why would I burn it?"

"Because it's private."

She put her hands on her hips and lean forward as if the gesture would give her words more power.

"Did you read it?"

"I've read some of it."

He chose his words carefully to test her response. She stood upright, crossed her arms, and appeared conflicted.

"Those are her private thoughts. You shouldn't have read it."

"She's gone Beatrice. This is all I have left."

She snorted, wrinkled her lips, then turned and left him alone with the diary. She would keep his secret, he was sure of it. From what she told him about Ms. Mila, Ms. Käthe, and even Eleanor, she had no great love or connection for any of the women in the house. He held the diary in both hands and caressed the hinged lock with his thumb. In that moment, it occurred to him all the negative things his mom said about his dad. Did his dad know? Did his dad ever read any of the diary passages? He swung his feet over the edge of the bed and stood. He examined the geography of the room and considered where he might hide the diary.

The mood at dinnertime was sombre. Mr. Crane cleared his throat.

"Lucius, I want to let you know that your parents' house has sold. The proceeds, I mean the money, will go to your Aunt Phoebe, who will save and invest it for your future."

He glanced at Mrs. Crane, who gazed not at anyone, but off in her thoughts, perhaps hundreds of miles away. She only raised her eyebrows and then took a drink from her wineglass. It felt as though the tide that came in and swept his parents from him had returned to claim the rest of his past. Mr. Crane's voice got his attention.

"For some more uplifting news. I've spoken to Mrs. Crane, and Beatrice as well," he winked at Beatrice, "and we would love for you to stay with us. To make things more welcoming and permanent, Mrs. Crane, who has an excellent eye for interior decorating, will redo our guest bedroom to become your official bedroom. How does that sound, Lucius?"

His voice rose when he posed the question. Beatrice smiled at Lucius. The corners of Mrs. Crane's lips curled, and she smiled politely, but without sincerity. Her pale sky-blue eyes might as well have been the eyes of a reptile.

Over the next few days, Mrs. Crane transformed the guest bedroom to one suited for a boy of eleven and eventually a teenager when he reached his high school years. Before Mrs. Crane brought in the movers and painters, Lucius returned the nude picture of her to the attic, where he also stashed his mom's diary.

They painted the walls a warm brown and the wainscoting a satin white. He even got a new bed, nightstand, and dresser with a mirror. She seemed relieved to be rid of the old guest room furniture. Perhaps it belonged somewhere in the past and being tucked away in the guest bedroom was a concession.

The weekday while Mr. Crane was in Hartford and after the men who moved the new chestnut stained furniture into Lucius's bedroom had finally left, Mrs. Crane then left as well to pick up Beatrice. Mrs. Crane would be gone briefly, but long enough for Lucius to jump on the bed. The new mattress propelled him higher than the old one. He smiled and laughed as he jumped up and down and made a mess of the bedsheets that Mrs. Crane made. If he forgot to straighten them, Ms. Mila or Ms. Käthe would have to fix them when they came later in the day. He was sure if it was Ms. Käthe, she would mention it to Mrs. Crane.

After he settled down and sat crossed-legged on the new bed, he eyed the Leica he placed atop the new chestnut stained dresser. The lens faced him, but the camera sat in front of the dresser mirror so he could see the back of the camera in the reflection. He smiled at the notion he could see two sides of something from one angle. It would be something if he could do that without a mirror.

He stood and went to the new dresser and pulled out a drawer. There was slight vertical play as the drawer moved on its track. He pulled the drawer out as far as he could and tilted it. It became apparent to him that the drawer was removable. Inside the unstained cavity, he could hide his mom's diary. He glanced outside the window at the sky. How long ago did Mrs. Crane leave the house?

He carefully tilted the drawer to get it back on its track and slid it closed. He glanced at his reflection, then hurried to the top of the stairs. In the closet, he retrieved the pull-down rod used to grasp the metal loop to the folded attic stairs. With the stairs lowered, he sat the pull-rod against the wall. He listened for the return of Mrs. Crane and Beatrice, but he heard no car in the driveway.

"Okay," he whispered.

He hurried up the creaky extended attic staircase and into the dusty gloom. It took him longer to find the first pull cord. He was sure he passed it, so he went back and searched until he found it. Sweat from his forehead stung his eyes and his scalp felt as though he had been out in the rain. His shirt clung to his back and his underwear to his buttocks. Thankfully, he wore shorts, but they did little to cool him. The hot, thick air was simply too much.

The one bare bulb provided enough light for him to hurry to the deepest recess of the attic. His socks mopped the dust covered boards that lie across the floor joists. He stepped around the stack of boxes where he first found the dresses Mrs. Crane donated to St. Paul's Evangelical Lutheran Church. The box hidden beneath the other boxes that contained the nude photographs of her called to him. He glanced at the pile, then moved on to the far back of the attic. It was dark behind the raw wooden beams and supports. He knelt down and felt around the insulation where he thought he tucked the diary. Where is it? Not in this spot.

He crouched and crawled as far as he could to the open joists with insulation packed between them. It has to be here. He rubbed his nose with the back of his hand and a sneeze threatened, but never materialized. He pressed his open palm into the batts of insulation, then winced. The only thing he found was a few protruding nails that bit into his fingers and drew blood in two places on his right hand.

"Shit."

It was one of his dad's favorite words. His mom even said it once or twice around him, but she had been more cautious and sensitive to his young ears. Aways glancing at him to see if he heard her. He crawled backwards out from the low space where the roof sloped. After he sat back on his heels and examined the two bloody spots on his hand, he was about to wipe his hand on his shorts, but thought better of it. As he sat there, he swiveled his head around and took in the dimly lit attic. He knew he hid the diary further back for fear any of the Cranes might venture up here to dig through their forgotten belongings, but where? There were no other boxes this far back for him to use as a landmark, and he even forgot which side of the space he had stashed the diary. He wiped the sweat from his face on his shirt. All he could taste was dust. He wanted to spit. Instead, he swallowed his dry, gritty saliva.

He crept back to the stack of boxes and licked his dusty lips. A droplet tickled the end of his nose before it fell onto the raw wood planks. He slowly lifted and set aside the boxes that were stacked atop the Kodak box that contained the naked photographs of Mrs. Crane. After he ran his hand over the top of the Kodak box and brushed away the dust, he then carefully lifted the cover with both hands and set it aside. The black and white photograph he hid in the guest bedroom sat on top of the others. His sweat, when he first concealed the photograph under his clothing, had warped it. Its corners were curled, and the image threatened to separate from its paper backing. He looked beyond the photograph's condition. He parted his lips when he gazed at the image of her exposed in all her glory. His penis stiffened in his sweat soaked boxers. He lifted the photograph and set it next to the one underneath. In the other photograph, Mrs. Crane was kneeling on a bed with her back to the camera. She wore only stockings with lines that ran up the backs of her legs. Her bare back and buttocks exposed, and her head turned over her shoulder, so her profile faced the camera. It was a subtle acknowledgment of the camera and its operator, Mr. Crane. He imagined being the one to have captured the image of her. He imagined her knowing he was there—wanting him there, as she playfully posed. The light from the room's table lamps sculpted the contours of her body.

He squeezed and tugged at the crotch of his shorts until he gasped and released. He then knelt breathless and sat back on his heels. The sound of a car door shot into the vents in the attic eaves. His eyes widened, and he pushed both photographs back into the box and returned the cover. Something in the narrow space to his right caught his eye. Wedged between the insulation and the face of the joist, it was the spine of the diary. He grabbed the diary and tucked it in the back of his waistband, and tugged his shirt over it. There was no time to put all the boxes back in place, so he took two and sat them on top of the box of photographs.

He hurried down the length of the support boards, only to have to turn around and rush back to turn off the far light. With the dark attic behind him, he started down the attic steps. The storm door opened, followed by the front door. He nearly tumbled down the steps. He folded the stairs, and rather than allow the springs to retract the door and step back into place, he used the pull-rod to ease the door up. The springs still shrieked. He clenched his teeth and his shoulders tightened.

Beatrice hummed some song when she came through the front door. He glanced over the railing and watched her slip into the downstairs powder room. After he rushed to his bedroom, he removed the bottom drawer from the new dresser and placed the diary in the back, then replaced the drawer. He returned to the top of the stairs and watched Mrs. Crane enter the house. She had her hands full. In one hand, she hugged a paper sack full of groceries, and in the other she had Mr. Crane's white dress shirts from the dry cleaners. After she disappeared down the hallway, he crept down the stairs. He slipped out the front door and snuck around the house to the backyard.

From behind one of the elm trees, he saw Mrs. Crane in the kitchen. His gaze rose to the second floor, where he spotted Beatrice at her bedroom window. She peered in the backyard, as if she were looking for something. Her gaze met his before he could duck behind the trunk of the elm. He blinked, and she disappeared. He ducked behind the tree and slumped down until he sat at the base of the elm. A moment later, the squeal of springs came from across the lawn, followed by the familiar wooden clap of the screen door slapping shut. He sat cross-legged and picked at the blades of grass in front of him until Beatrice appeared at his side.

"Whatcha doing out here?"

He peered up at her with a squinted eye to pinch out the sunlight. She wore a pink summer dress with white canvas sneakers and had her dark chestnut hair braided into a long ponytail. Her grin could eclipse the sun.

"Nothing really. Climbing trees."

"I can see that. You look disgusting."

She chuckled at him. He wrinkled his face.

"Thanks."

Her smile broadened.

"You're welcome."

"Have fun at your friend Stephanie's?"

He said her name in a snide tone.

"Yes."

She knelt down next to him. Her eyes wandered to the top of his head.

"Gross. You need a bath."

He ran his fingers though his sweaty, dust-caked hair. He tried to smile, but was sure he looked ridiculous. Maybe like some kid who got struck by lightning.

"Okay-okay. What do you want?"

"I wanted to see what you were doing in the backyard, and to tell you about *Stephanie*."

"Um. Okay?"

"She wanted to know more about you and how long you were going to live with us. I told her you were living with us permanently. She asked if you were cute, and I told her she would have to figure that out for herself, so next time my father takes us out for ice cream, I'll see if I can invite her to come along."

He groaned.

"I know she's going to like you."

"Great."

"Beatrice!" Mrs. Crane shouted from the back patio.

Beatrice and Lucius peered from behind the elm tree.

"Come inside!"

She waved for Beatrice to come back to the house. Beatrice looked at him. A look of want in her eyes.

"Come on, you too."

He staggered as he got to his feet. Both kids headed back to the house. She skipped in the grass while he sauntered behind. Mrs. Crane gave him a hardened gaze.

"What on Earth have you been up to?"

"I was climbing."

She stopped him before he entered the house.

"What's all this?"

She patted the dust from his shorts and the sleeve of his shirt. He shrugged, and she wrinkled her lips. He was sure she knew he had been in the attic, or would soon come to that conclusion. She held him by his arm, before he could follow Beatrice into the house.

"Take off those clothes in the laundry room first thing, then I want you to take a shower before Ms. Käthe and Ms. Mila arrive, understood?"

"Yes."

"Good, now go inside."

She released her hold on him.

19

"Are you sure you lost the roll?"

Lucius sat on a stool in the basement darkroom, shrugged his shoulders and grimaced. His eyes darted around as if he were searching his mind for the roll of film. Kenneth raised his eyebrows.

"I don't understand. There had to be some great photographs on that roll. I could feel it."

He wrinkled his lips, then patted Lucius on the shoulder.

"Sorry, I don't mean to make you feel any worse. We all lose things we love. Maybe it was fate."

He rubbed his forehead.

"Damn shame, though," he muttered.

"Anyway, I have a roll I haven't yet processed. I'm going to let you do the honors and see if you remember how to process the roll, and perhaps we can make some prints, or at least a contact sheet. Are you up for it?"

The boy perked up and sat straighter on the stool.

"Yes! Can I?"

He smiled at the boy and handed him the roll of film.

"I'll sit here quietly and I'll only jump in if you need help. Don't be afraid to ask."

Lucius slipped off the stool. He gathered the chemicals and everything else he needed, all the while Kenneth nodded at him at each correct action he took. Occasionally he would say, "good." When it was time to turn off the lights, he offered to stand near the switch by the door, but Lucius insisted he do everything, which impressed Kenneth. When Lucius finished, the processed roll of film hung in one long strip on the clip attached to the cabinets.

As the wet strip of film hung to dry, Kenneth went to the shelf and took down one of the ring binders, with the current year labeled down the spine. It was more than half filled with negatives.

"These are some of my latest pictures, the negatives at least. Have a look and let's make a few prints."

Lucius stretched over the tabletop and retrieved the magnifying loupe to examine the strips of film stored in the clear plastic sheets. He smiled at Lucius as the boy leafed through the sheets, taking his time to examine each of the exposures. When Lucius stopped to examine a specific exposure more thoroughly, Kenneth leaned in to see which one caught the boy's eye.

After Lucius selected two of the negatives, Kenneth examined them, smiled, then sat upright and raised his eyebrows. Both were pictures of Eleanor, one when he took the family to the Finger Lakes in New York with rolling hills in the background, and the other here at the house in his study. She sat casually on the buttoned leather sofa with her shoes off and her legs tucked under her.

"Interesting choices. Mrs. Crane will think you have a thing for her."

He laughed. Lucius's face reddened. He took the two strips of film from the protective sheet and brought them over to the enlarger. He walked Lucius through the process of preparing the photo chemicals in the trays and setting up the timer and enlarger for the first print. Lucius watched him closely, so close each time he wondered if Lucius had blinked at all.

"All right. Turn on the red light and turn off the room lights."

Lucius did as instructed and was back by Kenneth's side as he projected the first negative on the empty holder in order to get the size he wanted and the image into focus. He then turned off the enlarger, took a sheet of unexposed photo paper from its box and protective black plastic inner bag. Lucius leaned over the table as Kenneth slipped the photo paper in the holder.

"I'll let you try the next one, okay?"

"Okay."

After Kenneth processed his print and observed Lucius process the second one, Kenneth laid out both prints so they could look at them before he hung them up to finish drying. Lucius leaned over the table, his eyes wide as he took in both photographs.

"You see things with mature eyes."

Lucius glanced at him.

"Huh?"

"You see things with much older eyes, maybe even as an adult might."

The boy said nothing, then returned his gaze to the two photographs. Kenneth was more interested in watching Lucius inspect the photographs than to inspect his own work.

"Any thoughts on my two pictures?"

Lucius's eyes remained fixed on the images. He touched the edge of one print.

"They're really good."

Kenneth smiled.

"Great, I'm pleased you think so."

He rested his chin on his hand with his elbow on the table.

"You did really well, Lucius. Processing the film and creating a print."

Lucius met his gaze.

"You think so?"

"I do. I do so much that I'm going to allow you to use the darkroom when I'm not home."

The boy's eyes brightened.

"Really?"

"Hold on."

His mouth fell open.

"Under the condition that if you can't lift something, especially the containers of chemicals, or if you forgot how to do something, you'll wait for me to help you. This is my special room. I want you to respect the equipment in here and be careful not to expose the photo paper. Can you agree to all of that?"

Lucius looked as though he had patiently waited for him to finish.

"Oh, yes, and I'll clean up in here if you want me to."

He smiled and squeezed the boy's shoulder.

"That would be great. First and foremost, we need to keep things neat and orderly in here."

"Okay."

Kenneth chuckled.

"Great."

Kenneth took both photographs and hung them from clips so they could finish drying. Lucius watched him with keen eyes. With the tips of his fingers, Kenneth felt the key to the darkroom in his pocket, but decided it needed to be the right moment to give the boy a key.

"It's time we head upstairs before they send a search party for us. I'm going to leave the door unlocked, so you can use the darkroom when you like. Just *remember* what I said."

Lucius nodded. Kenneth turned out the lights, and they both headed upstairs.

20

Weeks go by, and Lucius is unable to get Beatrice, or Mrs. Crane to pose for him. A few times he plodded around the backyard with the Leica strapped around his neck, but he found nothing to inspire him. He had no desire to waste film on subjects like nature or anything that was too weak to move him. People. He wanted only to photograph people, especially women, and one woman in particular.

He spent more time in the darkroom than behind the camera. Mr. Crane selected some of his recent negatives for him to make prints. All the prints turned out to Mr. Crane's liking. The only comment he made was he could have dodged and burned some areas on two of the photographs to enhance them. A technique Mr. Crane promised to show him when he had time, if he ever did *have time*. Mr. Crane's preoccupation with work required more nights in Hartford than Mrs. Crane and Beatrice would have liked. The nights when Mr. Crane stayed in Hartford, Mrs. Crane would phone the one-bedroom apartment to say goodnight to him, or maybe it was to see if he was there.

The rain seemed always present the nights when Mrs. Crane sat alone on the screened in patio with her wine and cigarettes. Mr. Crane was again in Hartford for the night. Lucius heard Mrs. Crane on the phone with him earlier. It was tense. She told him he was neglecting his wife and daughter and questioned if he needed to be in court as early as he stated. She argued he could do all of his work uninterrupted in the study and enjoy dinner with his family and sleep in his own bed, unless he preferred the bed at the Hartford apartment. The last was a jab, a soft stammer of her words, that he could tell she regretted before the call ended.

He stood inside the open doorway to the enclosed patio. Mrs. Crane sat in her usual wicker chair, a cigarette in one hand, a glass of wine in the other. Both near depleted. She took a long drag, then bent forward and stabbed her cigarette into the ashtray. She blew out a narrow stream of smoke while she filled her glass of wine. When Mr. Crane was home, the couple brought out a single glass of wine each to the patio, but alone, Mrs. Crane brought with her the bottle, which sat half full atop the wicker coffee table. She sat it down with a clunk after her pour, then eased back in her chair. Her head rolled back on the cushions.

"Join me if you like or go away, but stop lurking about."

Her voice reverberated within the enclosed space. He blinked and gasped. He stepped slow and cautious out into the screened in patio.

"Sit."

She pointed to the empty wicker chair where Mr. Crane usually sat. The rain was louder out on the patio. It roared atop the shingles of the patio roof and pattered on the stone walkway outside. A gust blew moist air through the screens. He sat in the wicker chair. She gazed at him through heavy sulking eyelids and only broke her gaze from him when she raised the wineglass to drink. He waited for her to speak and eventually eased back into the cushions. He gazed outside at the rain. June Norris, Stephanie's mother, picked up Beatrice after dinner to spend the night with them.

"We're two misfits, you and I, and you're not much of a drinking companion."

Her words lumbered out. She raised her glass and drank. Her gaze remained fixed on the rain outside. She sighed.

"Not much of a conversationalist, either. Then again, neither am I."

"I'm sorry," he whispered.

She huffed.

"So am I."

They both watched the downpour in silence. When her glass was nearly empty, he got up and filled it for her.

"Thank you dear, I knew you were good for something."

Her words were gentle and subdued. He sat the near empty bottle of wine on the coffee table and moved to stand behind her chair, then he massaged her shoulders. He expected her to bolt upright and shout at him. Instead, a soft hum passed her lips.

"Thank you, that's nice."

She patted his hands as he rubbed her shoulders. He wanted to touch her skin, but at least he could feel the warmth of her flesh and the sturdiness of her bones under her blouse. She slipped off her pumps. They made a dull sucking sound when her heels broke free. She dropped them casually on the patio floor. His lips curled into a toothless smile as he rubbed and she hummed. She rubbed her knee and calf before she crossed her legs. In the dim light, he was unsure if her stockings were black or coco. She usually wore coco.

He took in the flowery scent of her hairspray. He was unsure if she had fallen asleep until she raised her glass of wine to take a drink. When she swallowed and lowered her glass, he continued. Her hair tickled the backs of his hands. After the tension eased from her shoulders, he returned to the wicker chair and sat. He was jealous of Mr. Crane and the evenings he shared with Mrs. Crane out on the patio.

"Thank you, Lucius, that was very nice."

Her eyelids were heavy. The light had faded and her pale sky-blue eyes appeared gray. The corners of her lips curled into a soft smile. He returned her smile. Her eyes rolled in their sockets to peer out at the night rain. The roar of the heavy downpour had tapered to a drizzle. She massaged the arch and heel of her stocking foot.

He sat at the edge of his seat, then finally got up and knelt by her. She continued to stare out at the rain. Her chest rose and fell like a gentle wave. She glanced briefly down at him, like someone aware that their neighbor's dog had joined them, but not wanting to pet it. He took her foot in his hands and kneaded her arch and balls of her foot with his thumbs. There was no resistance or protest on her part. He gently squeezed the balls of her foot. Her stocking glided over her flesh beneath. He cupped her heel and ran his thumb over the bottoms of her toes, both veiled by the reinforced patches of her stockings. The second time he looked up at her, she peered down at him with a chill in her gaze. Her face, the placid mask she usually wore, cracked as the skin on her forehead tightened. She then spoke in a low but firm tone.

"I think it's past your bedtime."

He let go of her but remained hunched at her feet.

"Sorry," he whispered.

Her face softened. Her change in expression was subtle, but he could discern the tiny shifts. It was all he needed to know. He stood gracefully with decorum.

"Good night, Mrs. Crane."

"Good night, Lucius."

When he got to his room, he slipped off his clothes and got under the covers without brushing his teeth or washing his face. There was no photograph of her naked hidden in his bedroom for him to gaze at, so he tried to recall the evening on the patio. He cupped his hands over his face and blocked out the moonlight that came into the window. He breathed in deep and steady until he found her subtle scent cupped within his palms and fingers. Her spicy floral perfume came to him first, deep beneath that a hint of her nylon stockings. His penis stiffened. Under the bedsheets, he slipped his boxers down to his ankles and kicked them off. His naked body floated within the envelope of the covers. The texture of the cotton sheets felt electric against his skin. He closed his eyes and cupped his hand over his nose and inhaled the subtle remnants of her scent. The satin comforter tickled his chin while his hand moved beneath the covers. Breaths became shorter and faster until he came. The damp sheets stuck to his abdomen and chilled his body. Perhaps it was an hour later or less, when he raised his head in a half-sleep and heard Mrs. Crane pass by his closed door. Her heels struck the hardwood floor in the hallway, unsteady, but in a softer, considerate tone. A dull thunk came from down the hall. Mr. or Mrs. Crane almost never closed their bedroom door. He sighed and lowered his head to the pillow.

21

Lucius stayed at the house while Mrs. Crane left to pick up Beatrice at the Norrises. Prior to her departure, she warned him he would miss out on lunch if he stayed at the house. After she drove off, he went to the darkroom to process the roll of film he shot when his Aunt Phoebe flew in from Indiana. He calculated, if Mrs. Crane was gone long enough, he might have time to make some prints or at least a contact sheet.

The smell of chemicals circulated around the darkroom. He moved with confident fluidity. First, he processed the roll of film. As the strip hung to dry, he prepared the trays of chemicals for making prints, then returned to cut the long dry strip into smaller ones. Each of the cut negative strips contained six frames. When he glanced at the negatives using the loupe, he was uncertain which frames he liked, so he processed a contact sheet to include all thirty-six frames. He inspected the contact sheet as it dried, then decided on six frames: one of Beatrice, four of his Aunt Phoebe, and one of his Aunt Phoebe with Mr. Crane. He would have to be careful to hide the prints of his Aunt Phoebe passed out on the couch at his parents' house. After a quick glance at the clock on the wall, he got to work.

After a single mishap with the enlarger on his first print, the rest went faster than he expected and without incident. He snorted as he looked over the six black and white prints that lay drying on the table. He smiled at his work, but what would Mr. Crane think? Would Beatrice be mad that a sliver of her white panties showed? He was certain it would infuriate his Aunt Phoebe, the pictures he took of her, passed out drunk on the couch with her skirt raised beyond playful flirtation. He was sure Mr. Crane would like the two pictures of his Aunt Phoebe, the one of her leaning against his Mercedes, and the other when she was doing her makeup in his parents' bathroom. The one of Mr. Crane and her at the airport captured a tension. He knew or felt something that day, but was unable to put his finger on it. There it was now, in the photograph. Although the two were not touching, it showed in their eyes and on their faces. A certainty. Mr. Crane was in love with his Aunt Phoebe.

After he hung the six prints to finish drying, he tidied up the darkroom. Footsteps came from upstairs. His lips parted and his eyes widened. Mrs. Crane and Beatrice must have gotten home. He left the chemicals in the trays, and the box of photo paper on the table, then hurried to the door.

He glanced at the hanging prints before he switched off the lights to the darkroom. He twisted the lock on the knob. Voices came from upstairs. Soon they would look for him. He hurried to close the darkroom door and jammed his foot in the gap just in time for the door to slam against his foot. He winced. If he locked it, he would have to get the key from Mr. Crane, then Mr. Crane would see his photographs. Ms. Mila and Ms. Käthe would never enter the darkroom. Mrs. Crane only came down when Mr. Crane was down here, but only sometimes. Beatrice never came to the darkroom. He unlocked the door, then closed it without a sound and crept up the basement steps.

22

Kenneth stood naked, balanced atop a full-size mattress with his new Leica M4 camera. He struggled to focus the lens. Phoebe lie naked, giggling beneath him, and shifted about over the chaotic array of sheets. She teased him by covering and exposing her breasts and mound of pubic hair, all while he held the camera to his eye. They both laughed.

"Hold still, would you please? The light is perfect."

She shimmied her hips, and the bed shook, as it shook all night during their lovemaking. She held the sheet around her body and toyed with him.

Sunlight poured in the only bedroom window to the Hartford apartment and painted a rectangular swath of light across the bed and part of the far wall. Her tussled long blonde curls caught the light, and her sapphire blue eyes sparkled. He smiled, brought the camera lens into focus, and pressed the shutter button. The M4's shutters made an almost inaudible metallic click, like a whisper of sharp shears. He thumbed the film advance lever without lowering the camera to prepare for the next shot.

"You're perfect."

She bit her lip and drew back the sheets, exposing her body to him. He held the Leica steady and pressed the shutter release button—click. He again thumbed the lever and advanced the film.

"Did I say you were perfect? Perfect and beautiful."

She twisted her body, curled the tips of her hair around her fingers, then spread her legs. Her mound of pubic hair was a medium brown, not a dark brown, but a noticeable contrast to the blonde hair on her head. Her patch of hair separated like a hidden entrance among her shrubbery, to reveal delicate moist folds of flesh. Click.

He lowered the camera. His erect cock, heavy, engorged, angled upward and stood out firm like a high diving board, inviting him to plunge into her. She stroked his cock with her toes and feet and gave him a devilish smile. He hummed, then knelt on the bed between her legs, and carefully sat his camera on the nightstand. He fumbled in the drawer for a condom. She tugged at his arm and reassured him *again* that she was on the pill. The sun had moved and the rectangle of light shifted to cast their shadows on the wall in a rhythmic, silhouetted display of debauchery.

Afterwards, they had sex in the shower, like a couple on their honeymoon lazily starting their day. He first soaped up her breasts and buttocks, and she soaped up his cock until he ached to once again be inside her. She turned her back to him and he took her from behind. She moaned, and he grunted as they grasped at one another's soapy flesh. The bubbles clung creamy white to their skin as if covered by his semen.

Kenneth buckled his trousers. He adjusted his crotch, feeling another erection forming. His lips curled into a coy smile.

"I could call the office and inform my secretary I'll be out today."

Phoebe pulled the cups of her bra over her large breasts and closed the front clasp between them, creating a delicious display of cleavage. Her eyebrows rose and fell as she appeared to be contemplating his suggestion. After she glanced at the clock on the nightstand, her eyes widened.

"I have the interview you so generously arranged for me in less than half an hour!"

"Oh? Damn. That's right."

He threw his shirt on and quickly buttoned it. Half way, he realized the buttons were in the wrong holes, and had to undo them and start again. She chuckled. He shook his head and laughed as well.

"I can give you a lift."

"It's not on your way."

"Yes, but that's not a problem."

She went to him, her blouse half buttoned and her bra visible and inviting. After she adjusted the knot of his tie and ran her fingers under his shirt collar, she touched his face, then playfully patted his cheek.

"I'll get a cab. It's fine. We don't want to make a show of things, do we?"

He grabbed her by the waist and pulled her close to him; her breasts mashed against his chest. He wanted her to feel his erection. She gasped, and he smiled. His eyes narrowed.

"And what if we do?"

Her lips curled into a coy smile, and she raised an eyebrow.

"You flatter me, Kenny, but we don't have time."

He sighed.

"I won't be able to see you for a few days, and I won't be able to stop by your hotel room tonight."

He knew she knew why. Her eyes went to the clock on the nightstand.

"Well, you better fuck me fast, and I'm going to need that lift after all."

Their lips mashed together. He reached inside her blouse and squeezed her lace covered breast. They stumbled to the edge of the bed while she unbuckled his trousers and they fell to the floor. She raised her skirt and pulled her panties aside in time for him to enter her. Their mouths hung open and sucked in heavy breaths as they fucked.

23

Lucius dashed up the stairs to his bedroom to avoid Beatrice and Mrs. Crane. He suspected they were in the kitchen. He jumped in his bed with Tom Sawyer open and pretended to read. Footsteps came from down the hallway, light footsteps, Beatrice's footsteps, and there she was. She stood in his doorway with her arms crossed.

"There you are. Reading? I expected to find you outside taking pictures."

He peered at her over the top of the book.

"Can I help you?"

He thought she looked cute in her pastel violet dress and white frilly ankle socks that showed her bare, knobby knees. Her hair was in pigtails. He hid his smile behind the book. She huffed.

"No, I don't need anything from you."

Heavy angry footsteps, no doubt belonging to Mrs. Crane, came down the hall. Beatrice's mouth hung open as Mrs. Crane yanked her arm. Lucius dropped Tom Sawyer on the bed and sat up.

"Come with me, you little liar."

"What?"

She looked up at Mrs. Crane, horrified. Mrs. Crane poked her head into Lucius's room and glared at him. Her pale sky-blue eyes were pure ice. She held a photograph.

"Don't you go anywhere, mister."

She closed his door with a thud. Her words cemented him in place. The awkward sound of their footsteps in the hallway. He imagined her dragging

Beatrice. He sprung off the bed and went to the door, then carefully opened it a crack. Beatrice was on her toes, held upward in Mrs. Crane's grasp. They both disappeared into Beatrice's bedroom.

Voices, shouts, and cries came from her open door. He crept down the hall to peer through the narrow open doorway. Mrs. Crane stood holding the picture up for Beatrice to see.

"You lied to me. I suspected you took my opal necklace, and here's proof."

She rattled the print in front of Beatrice. He thought she might even hit Beatrice in the face with it. Beatrice stood, but looked unsteady. Her eyes were glassy, her mouth hung open, and her arms hung limp at her sides. He swallowed and bit his lip.

"Do you have anything to say for yourself?"

She shook her head, no.

Mrs. Crane slapped the photograph down on the dresser, grabbed Beatrice by the arm and pulled her to the side chair. She sat and tugged Beatrice across her lap.

"This is the only thing you seem to understand."

She held Beatrice down with her forearm on her back and smacked her bottom with an open hand.

"No," Beatrice cried.

She smacked her again, and Beatrice squirmed, then she tugged her skirt up over her back to expose her white panties with pink trim and the backs of her legs. She struggled even more. There was an audible smack when her hand hit Beatrice's buttocks. Beatrice cried out. Although she faced away from where he stood outside the door, the sharp tone of her cries softened and became slurred by unseen tears. Mrs. Crane hit the backs of her legs, then her buttocks again. She seemed determined that whenever the girl sat down, she would remember her crime. Mrs. Crane hit her again and again. Her pinned up hair came loose and a couple of her curls fell to the sides of her face. Lucius tensed at each strike. Mrs. Crane turned her gaze toward the door. Her lips drew into a wicked smile. He gasped. She got up and pulled Beatrice onto the bed, then stood and brushed her hair out of her eyes.

"Don't forget. Never touch my things."

"I hate you-ooh-oo."

Beatrice cried uncontrollably and buried her face into the comforter. He hurried back to his bedroom, but his body locked and he froze just outside the door.

"Get in there," Mrs. Crane shouted.

He sat on the bed and braced himself. Mrs. Crane appeared in the doorway with the photograph. The calm in which she closed his door scared him the most. She held the photograph up for him to see. It was the picture he shot of Beatrice posing next to the sycamore in the backyard. She wore the opal choker. His heart sank to his stomach. Did he have it coming? Was he always meant to have it coming?

She sat the creased bent photograph on the dresser as careful as if she were handling something of great value. She fixed her hair in the dresser mirror, then cleared her throat.

"I saw the rest of your handiwork."

She huffed and stifled a chuckle.

"Your Aunt Phoebe passed out on the couch, exposed. Not a woman of substance, by any measure. I think the word '*whore*' is appropriate. It's not a stretch to think a whore can be someone's auntie. Did you enjoy taking pictures of your Auntie Whore?"

He gazed at her reflection. He hoped his ass would grow roots like a tree and keep him from being whipped. Beatrice would never trust him again.

"Your picture of Kenneth and your whore Aunt Phoebe is quite telling, don't you think? Sure, you're just a boy, but I know you see things in people. It shows in your photographs. Maybe Kenneth is right, you are talented. I wonder, though, what he might think of your pictures hanging in the darkroom. When I'm done with you, you are to go down there and take them down—and destroy them. Do you understand me?"

He swallowed and only stared at her reflection. She whipped around.

"Do you understand me?"

She grabbed his arm, and he tried to go to his knees on the floor. He figured he weighed more than Beatrice, but she surprised him and went to the floor with him, then she rolled him over on his stomach. She held him down with his body pressed into the hardwood floor. She smacked his bottom harder than she did Beatrice, but his trousers protected him. An overwhelming desire came over him for her to pull down his pants and strike his bare flesh.

"Oh. Oh."

He grunted when she hit him, then he laughed. She rolled him over.

"You think this is funny?"

She unbuckled his pants, stripped his belt free, and yanked down his trousers. She nearly took down his boxers as well. He tried to cover himself but found himself facedown again. The unyielding hardwood floor felt even harder with the weight of his body pressed against it and with only the thin fabric of his boxers between his flesh and the wood. She smacked his buttocks. The blow carried and hammered the bones of his pelvis to the floor. His penis ached, crushed to the wood. He tried to anticipate her strike. He gasped and blinked his wet eyes when she finally hit him, but this time with the belt. The leather snapped and stung his buttocks, even through his boxers.

After a few times with the belt, his penis hardened. It felt as though he had a stick wedged between his body and the floor. Each time she struck him, he felt electricity jolt through his penis and into his testicles. She continued until he finally cried out. She hit him several more times. Each strike she paused, which confused him. When she stopped or paused longer than usual, he sucked in a breath with his cheek and shoulders mashed to the floor. His eyes rolled and his gaze fell on his closed bedroom door. Through the narrow gap at the bottom, he saw Beatrice's stocking feet. She stood there briefly, then disappeared.

"I hope you learned your lesson. After you've had your cry, clean up Mr. Crane's darkroom and destroy those pictures before he comes home."

She took her weight off of him and stood. He watched her heels as she stepped around him. There was a run in her stocking near her ankle. She quietly slipped out the door and closed it as casually as any other day. As painful as it was for him to lie there, he remain on the floor, as if he tried to capture and hold on to a memory. When he rolled onto his side, his breath caught and he released. His boxers clung to him where the warm rush of semen pooled. His belt lie casually on the floor like a snake bathing in the sun.

When he got to his feet, fixed his trousers and tucked in his shirt, he was astounded that she left the photograph of Beatrice on the dresser. It had creases and sat warped. He opened the top drawer and slid it inside to hide it for the moment. In the mirror, his eyes were glassy, and lips were dry and cracked. She wanted him to cry, but she did something else to him. All he knew, in that moment, was he wanted her to touch him again, no matter how brutal.

After straightening the darkroom, Lucius flipped the light switch and closed the door. He tucked his prints in the back of his pants even after he found several good places to hide them in the darkroom. The thought of having them closer to him made him more comfortable. He heard Ms. Käthe and Ms. Mila arrive earlier, and now, as he climbed the basement steps, he heard Ms. Käthe's voice. She asked Mrs. Crane if everything was fine. Mrs. Crane only mentioned that the children have been up to some mischief. He wrinkled his lips and waited for the two women to move away from the basement door. When it was silent, he slipped to the main floor, down the hallway, then upstairs, and only ran into Ms. Mila, who simply smiled at him as he passed her.

He closed his bedroom door, and was relieved to find that one of the two women had already made up his room. He took the photograph of Beatrice from his top dresser drawer, then tugged the others from the back of his pants. One clung to his skin, and he had to carefully peel it free. It was the picture of Mr. Crane and his Aunt Phoebe at the airport. He gazed at it for a moment. Was Mrs. Crane right? Was his Aunt Phoebe a whore?

He knelt down with the stack of photographs and opened the bottom dresser drawer. With his clothes and comic books inside, it made it difficult to tilt the drawer in order to pull it free, but after a few tries, he managed. He held the stack of photographs vertically and reached into the drawer cavity to stand them up. He hoped their vertical position would keep them from getting damaged when anyone opened and closed the drawers. The internal structure of the dresser allowed a perfect space to hide the photographs. Before he put back the drawer, he slid his fingers along the back inside track. His breath caught. He probed around inside, only feeling the edges of the photographs he put there. He bent down low to peer inside. There were the photographs, but to the left of them was only the raw wood back panel of the dresser. His mom's diary was gone.

24

They dined in near silence, except for Mr. Crane. It was almost as if he was talking to himself. Beatrice glared at Lucius only once and refused to look at him for the rest of the evening. Mr. Crane apologized numerous times for missing dinner and seemed to think he was the target of everyone's angst. He ate hardy, adding more chicken and peas to his plate, then he carried on about how much he missed dinner at home. Mrs. Crane expressed no feelings about anything to anyone.

Everyone seemed relieved when dinner ended. Mr. and Mrs. Crane retired to the screened in patio with their glasses of wine and cigarettes. Beatrice rushed upstairs to her bedroom, apparently to be alone. Lucius followed her upstairs, but gave her space. When he got to the top of the stairs, down the hall, she closed her bedroom door with a leave-me-the-hell-alone thunk. He went to his bedroom and changed into his pajamas, and left the door open the entire time. He waited for her to emerge, to brush her teeth before bed, but her door remained closed, so he took care of his own bedtime ablutions. Afterwards, he stood in front of her door, then knocked softly.

"Beatrice?"

Maybe she was asleep?

"Beatrice? Are you still awake?"

He put his ear to her door. There was no sound. Maybe she was sleeping. He wrinkled his lips, then sighed. The bedroom door opened a crack. It was dark inside. She squinted when the hallway light hit her eyes.

"What do *you* want?"

He felt bad about the photograph he shot of her wearing Mrs. Crane's choker necklace, but his lips tightened and he scowled when he thought about his mom's diary.

"I'm sorry about the photograph, but it was your idea to steal Eleanor's necklace."

It felt strange for him to say Mrs. Crane's Christian name.

"You didn't have to take my mom's diary. Now give it back."

She glared at him, but then her face softened.

"I didn't take your mom's diary. Did you leave it sitting out?"

He crossed his arms.

"No. You're the only one who knows I have it, so it has to be you."

She looked perplexed.

"I don't have it."

She closed the door in his face. He was sure her butt was still sore, and probably her pride as well, from Mrs. Crane's spanking. He would talk to her tomorrow. If what she said was true, then he was unsure what to do. As he lie in bed, he gazed at the shadows on the ceiling, and listened to Mr. and Mrs. Crane's lumbering, inebriated footsteps and muffled voices as they passed his closed door. He had seen Mrs. Crane going into his room a few times over the past week or two. Maybe she found the diary? Would she give it back once she realized what it was?

25

A week passed, then two. Mrs. Crane said nothing more about the pictures she instructed Lucius to destroy. Perhaps for the sake of art, his art, she let it go, or maybe she trusted he did as she requested. Either way, Lucius was relieved, but still baffled about his mom's missing diary. He gave up his suspicion that Beatrice took it. That left, Ms. Käthe, Ms. Mila, and Mrs. Crane. Ms. Käthe, he was sure disliked him well enough that she might have gone exploring his bedroom, like a guard searching a prisoner's cell for contraband. Ms. Mila liked him, he was sure of it. She always offered a polite smile. Occasionally, she would gently touch his shoulder or pat him on the head. Sometimes when he would play in the backyard among the trees, and with the gentle breeze caressing his face, he would see her in one of the bedroom windows, and it made him smile.

It surprised him that Mrs. Crane would venture into the basement when she and Beatrice got home. Maybe she wondered if he had been up to mischief? He struggled to imagine her capable of taking the diary. Did it matter anymore? He read most of it. She was dead and never coming back.

He surfaced from his thoughts when he reached the bottom of the stairs and went to the entryway to wait for the others. Yesterday, Ms. Mila had brought a bouquet of white gardenias for the entryway table. The Cranes always had fresh flowers in the house, Mrs. Crane insisted on them. It had been a year or longer since there were white gardenias in the house. He milled about the entryway in his tank top and swim trunks. The Leica dangled from its leather strap around his neck. They would all be leaving soon for one of their regular beach outings. He stood on his toes and leaned into the table to smell the white gardenias. His hips pressed against the edge of the table. The creamy white pedals tickled his nose. He closed his eyes and took in their fragrance until his head became light. Visions of the evening when he watched Mr. and Mrs. Crane in bed sent electricity throughout his body. His penis stiffened against the mesh lining of his nylon swim trunks.

"Do you like them?"

Mrs. Crane stood at the opening to the hallway. Her pale sky-blue eyes pierced him, but her face remained an emotionless mask. She wore a one-piece white swimsuit with a sweeping neckline and open-toe gold colored sandals that revealed her naked toes. In one hand, she held a navy and white striped tote bag stuffed with towels and a bottle of suntan lotion, and in the other, a tan wicker picnic basket. She sat both the tote and the picnic basket on the tile floor near the wall. He dropped back on his bare heels and held his hands in front of him to cover his arousal. The Leica dangled as if to direct her attention and to tell on him. He cleared his throat.

"Yes."

She took a deep breath, as if she could smell the flowers from where she stood. Her lips curled into a faint delicate smile, and she cradled her arms. Her breasts filled the cups on both sides of her swimsuit's plunging neckline, and her nipples stood out like landmarks on the highest points of her twin peaks. She was less buxom than his Aunt Phoebe, but she carried her sexuality like a movie starlet.

"So do I. They're called white gardenias."

"White gar-din-as."

"Gar-dean-yahs."

"Gardenias."

She nodded. The corners of her lips curled subtly upward. She then went down the hallway toward the study to see what was keeping Mr. Crane. The squared-off bottom of her one-piece swimsuit hid the bottoms of her buttocks, but the curves of her flesh filled out the swimsuit in the most pleasing way. She reminded him of the women in fashion magazines, elegant and classy. All of her clothing, even her swimsuit, fit her as if made for her.

The memory of his dad whistling at some girl in the street echoed in his mind. His lips puckered at the memory, and he was thankful that no sound pushed past his lips.

Hammonasset Beach had fewer people than usual. The weather report warned of an impending storm at noon or shortly after. The cloudless sky and radiant sun gave no indication of the foul weather to come. Mr. Crane, in his jovial demeanor, brushed off the news.

They got their pick of location on the beach. The four gathered under a large blue and white striped umbrella Mr. Crane erected. Mrs. Crane laid out a blanket for everyone to sit on. She massaged suntan lotion onto Mr. Crane's shoulders while Beatrice only wanted her father to touch her, so he applied the lotion to her while she sat between his legs. Lucius knelt in the hot sand beyond the comfort of the blanket and shade of the umbrella, and took a picture of them, one sitting behind the other, first Beatrice, then Mr. Crane, and finally Mrs. Crane. He chuckled after he got the shot. Mr. Crane and Beatrice looked at him, puzzled. Mrs. Crane's gaze was elsewhere. She only glanced toward the camera when he held it to his eye.

He came around the other side of the blanket with Beatrice in front, then Mr. Crane, followed by Mrs. Crane. After he advanced the film lever, he sat on the hot sand. He grimaced at first. With the Leica to his eye, he shut out the pain, and waited. The sun blazed on his shoulders and back. Beads of sweat trickled down his face and tickled his cheek and neck.

"Did you take it?" Beatrice asked.

He held his hand up to silence her. She wrinkled her lips at first, then smiled and looked directly at the camera. Mr. Crane smiled as well with his arms around her, but the only one Lucius focused on was Mrs. Crane. She was still on her knees behind Mr. Crane, with her hands on his shoulders. When the breeze caught her hair and she turned her head to near profile, he pressed the shutter release button. Click. He released a slow breath and hid his smile behind the Leica. He lowered the camera to let them know he got the shot. Mr. Crane grinned and nodded.

He joined them under the shade of the umbrella. Mrs. Crane was busy rubbing suntan lotion on her arms and neck.

"Need some help?"

She turned her head towards him, but the broad tortoiseshell frame sunglasses she wore with the dark lenses hid her eyes. Her sunglasses reminded him of a dragonfly's eyes. A subtle, sardonic smile formed on her lips.

"No, I'm sure Mr. Crane is up to the task."

Mr. Crane lifted Beatrice from between his legs, got to his feet, then took the bottle of lotion from her, and winked at Lucius.

"Sorry son, this job requires a professional."

The corner of Mrs. Crane's lips wrinkled. Lucius wanted to believe that behind her sunglasses she had rolled her eyes at Mr. Crane's comment, like his mom used to do when his dad made smart remarks. He chuckled regardless.

As Mr. Crane applied lotion to her back and shoulders, Lucius positioned himself to photograph them. He composed the shot so the pole from the umbrella divided the frame, Beatrice on one side peering out at the ocean in her own little world, and Mr. and Mrs. Crane on the other with Mr. Crane rubbing lotion onto Mrs. Crane's body. While the three were engaged in their personal activities, he pressed the shutter release button. Click. Mr. Crane glanced over at him.

"Lucius, I have something to show you."

His smile was broad and warm. Lucius lowered the camera and returned under the shade of the beach umbrella. When he sat on the blanket, Beatrice turned around with a curious look. The breeze blew her chestnut curls across her face, which she brushed aside. Mr. Crane removed his new camera from the tote bag, and Lucius's eyes widened. He crawled on his knees to have a closer look.

"Nice, eh?"

Mr. Crane handed the camera to him. It was beautiful with a sleek, all black body. It was a new Leica M4. He ran his fingertip over the recessed white lettering and immediately turned the crisp dials to feel how they operated. The frame indicator was on six. He thumbed the film advance leaver, but it remained locked on the sixth frame. Mr. Crane had shot five frames already. Of what?

"Go on, give it a try."

They all looked at him as if he held something magical, and wondered, and waited to see what he would do. He slipped the silver Leica M3 from around his neck and handed it to Mr. Crane, who coiled the strap around the camera's body. Lucius held the new Leica M4 at his chest and stared at their faces carefully. Beatrice wrinkled her lips and narrowed her eyelids when he looked at her. She made him smile. He glanced at Mrs. Crane and her hands. Her long elegant fingers. She wore two rings on her right hand, the hand she had struck him with. He felt the two rings when he looked at her. He only wanted to photograph her, but this was Mr. Crane's camera.

"Okay, Beatrice, sit here at the corner of the blanket."

He pointed. Beatrice only stared at him until Mr. Crane motioned for her to move. She plopped down at the corner of the blanket with her legs folded under her.

Lucius squatted like a crab at the other corner of the blanket and brought the M4 to his eye. The breeze and the sun favored him in that moment. The sunlight lit her chestnut hair with auburn highlights, while the wind lifted her curls. He waited until her expression softened. Click.

He lowered the camera to gaze at her for a moment and cycled the film to the next frame. Aside from her small and almost nonexistent breasts, narrow hips and spindly limbs, there was an odd, mature beauty about her. She tilted her head and glared at him.

"What?"

Her voice woke him.

"Are you done?"

"Uh? Yeah."

He turned to Mr. Crane, who held Mrs. Crane's shoulders. They both looked like spectators at some outdoor sporting event.

"That's it? Why don't you take a few more?"

He loved the new camera, but felt as though he was betraying an old friend.

"Okay, maybe a couple more. Mr. Crane, can you stand over here?"

He pointed to a spot on the sand, but positioned Mr. Crane so the sun would be over his shoulder. There were three young women, beautiful women, lying on towels facing skyward in the direct sunlight. Their less than modest bikinis accentuated the shapes of their breasts. Mr. Crane's height made it impossible to get the women in the shot, so Lucius had him kneel, then an idea came to him. He got the silver Leica M3 from the tote bag and had Mr. Crane wear it around his neck for the shot. The composition was perfect. The shot would include Mr. Crane kneeling with the camera around his neck, and the three beautiful women behind him, their collective six breasts like a beautiful mountain range of flesh shrouded by colorful patterns of nylon. He took the shot while Mr. Crane grinned, which was the cherry on top.

"Got it."

Mr. Crane got up, brushed the sand from his knees, and went over to him.

"Why don't you take one of Mrs. Crane," Mr. Crane whispered.

They both turned toward Mrs. Crane. She sat with her arms wrapped around her bent knees. Her head turned as though she were admiring the incoming waves.

"Ella?"

That got her attention. Mrs. Crane lifted her chin and gazed over at them. Lucius sighed inside when Mr. Crane called Mrs. Crane, Ella.

"Come pose for Lucius."

He beamed and motioned for her to join them. Lucius looked down at the dials on the black Leica M4. He turned the shutter speed dial, then turned it back, feeling the newness of the camera. Mr. Crane had yet to put the strap on it, so he gripped the camera with care. Mrs. Crane's toes first came into view, then her legs, hips, breasts, until he raised his head and there she stood, before him and Mr. Crane. She brushed her wind-swept hair from her face. The suntan lotion had given her skin a moist sheen. Mr. Crane touched her shoulder as if to console her.

"Dear, won't you pose for Lucius?"

"If you like."

"Thank you."

He shrugged his shoulders and smiled at Lucius as if he were a child who had been told he was getting ice cream.

"Lucius, she's all yours."

Mr. Crane squeezed his shoulder. His eyes widened. When he looked at Mrs. Crane, all he could see was his reflection in the dark lenses of her sunglasses. He went over to the blanket.

"Could you sit here?"

The edge of the blanket where he pointed was only half shaded by the beach umbrella. She sat where he instructed.

"Can you lie back on your elbows?"

"I don't think so, Lucius. That's a bit too cheesecake for me."

She turned her head slightly in the direction where Mr. Crane stood behind him. Then, to his surprise, she reclined back as he asked. What gesture had Mr. Crane made? Her legs extended out in the sunlight with her feet on the sand, while her upper body lie within the shade of the beach umbrella.

"Mrs. Crane, can you take off your sunglasses and hold them near your face?"

Mr. Crane chucked behind him.

"Ella! You've got a real professional here. Go with it."

He clapped. Was he trying to torture her? Lucius wanted to turn around to see if Mr. Crane was making faces. But when Mrs. Crane removed her sunglasses, everything was perfect.

"There!"

His own voice startled him. He held up his hand as if to freeze her position, then he stepped to the right until he found the angle he wanted. *There.* She held a pose similar to one he saw in one of the nude photographs of her in the attic. Mr. Crane was silent, but he felt his anticipation.

The bright sunlight allowed for a narrow aperture setting, which would capture a higher level of detail between near and far elements, like her feet, which were closer to him compared to her face. After he adjusted the aperture, he turned the speed dial to an appropriate setting. He brought the M4 to his eye and turned the focus ring on the camera lens until she fell into focus. Click.

He took the shot quickly, without waiting for the moment to happen. Doubt crept in. Had he got the shot? When he lowered the camera, he wished he had the older Leica M3 with *his* roll of film. He turned around and handed Mr. Crane the new camera.

"I think I got the shot."

The sun caused him to squint.

"I think you did, too. I'm looking forward to developing the roll."

Mr. Crane sounded only half excited. It reminded him of when his dad did something, knowing well that it would upset his mom. There was a knot in his chest for photographing Mrs. Crane in a pose she was reluctant to take. When he glanced at her, she was back under the shade of the umbrella, her eyes once again hidden behind her sunglasses. He recalled when Mr. Crane told him sometimes you'll only get one shot. That was his one shot. He somehow knew it was the last and only opportunity she would give him today, maybe ever again. Mr. Crane put his camera in the tote. Lucius stumbled on the sand and sat on a corner of the blanket. He hated that Mrs. Crane hid her eyes behind her sunglasses. The entire mood had somehow shifted. It felt like a funeral. Mr. Crane squeezed Beatrice's leg and nudged Lucius's shoulder.

"C'mon kids. Let's get in the water."

Beatrice smiled. It might have been her first *real* one today. She jumped up and led the three to the seashore, while Mrs. Crane stayed, comfortably or not, on the blanket under the shade of the beach umbrella.

26

In the spartan one-bedroom Hartford apartment, atop sweat-soaked sheets, Kenneth stretched out in bed with his arms tucked behind his head. His chest rose and fell and he sucked in each breath. Mila lie on her side next to him with her head rested on his arm. Her fingers glided over his chest. She glanced up at him with a soft, thin smile. The afternoon's late summer sun kissed their bodies. It illuminated strands of her sandy blonde hair like lightbulb filaments. Her belly was still wet, marked with his ejaculate. She pressed her dewy pubic mount to his thigh.

"I've missed you."

Her words purred in a warm coy whisper with that German accent he adored. He expressed on more than one occasion his desire for her to cry out in German when he fucked her. The thought stiffened her nipples, and she pressed her body to his. His amorous attentions made it easy for her to forgive him for missing their lunch date. He had phoned the restaurant where they were to meet with an apology that he had a client lunch he was unable to wrangle free from. The maître d informed her she could have whatever she desired with all expenses taken care of. Even then, she waited for him on a bench outside his apartment building.

Mila gazed at the topography of his face, his strong cut features, and tried to penetrate his thoughts. He seemed entranced or distracted by something. When he finally looked into her eyes, he seemed more distant than ever.

"I've missed you too."

His words robotic, calculated, with a subtle tone of surrender.

"Why haven't you called?"

He carefully slipped his arm from under her head, turned his body away from her, and retrieved a cigarette from the pack on the nightstand. He lit it, took a puff, then turned to her. She rested her head back on his arm and her hand on his chest. She waited for his answer. He took a long drag, then blew a stream of smoke toward the ceiling.

"I've been working crazy hours and taking evening meetings with clients."

He signed, and his tongue touched his top lip.

"Crazy billable hours. The firm should be happy."

She carefully pinched the cigarette from between his fingers, took a drag, then returned it to him. As she blew out the smoke, her breath sputtered and she coughed. His face contorted into a smug expression, then he took a long drag. She nudged him. He held the smoke for a moment before he released it in a hasty stream.

"You shouldn't smoke, my dear. I don't think it's *your* thing. You certainly don't need to on my account."

He took another drag, then reached over to the ashtray on the nightstand and crushed the cigarette. He blew out the smoke into the room, away from them.

"Good."

She choked out the word before she coughed again. His words, *my dear*, made her feel desired and somehow attached to him. If only his wife would fall off a cliff or burn to death, then she would release whatever hold she had on him. Mrs. Crane, *Eleanor*, that uptight, pretentious bitch. It was annoying when she insisted on being in the kitchen to direct the preparation of dinner, which Ms. Käthe and she were more than capable of executing without supervision. Ms. Käthe cooked every exceptional dinner the Crane family enjoyed. She deserved all the credit. It amazed her that Ms. Käthe never complained in private about Mrs. Crane. Mrs. Crane—that woman—had no motherly qualities about her. Kenneth must see that. Mila knew she could be a better mother figure for Beatrice and now Lucius if Kenneth still wanted her. That *was* the plan, or a possible plan. No promises, but there were encouraging words. But, now? She cleared her throat.

"You still could have called. I could have cooked for you here at the apartment. We could have made love before bed. I could have walked to the bus stop in the morning with no burden to you."

She whispered with a dry smoke-singed throat and was relieved her voice held. He sighed.

"I'm sorry. I have a lot on my mind."

She ran her fingertips up and down the length of his cock, which grew heavy, thick, and lengthened until the head strained, red, and tight.

"Let me easy your mind. If only for this moment."

He lifted his head and shoulders from the bed to kiss her lips. She slid her bent leg over his thighs until she straddled him. With her hands gently braced on his chest, she then moved her hips and stroked him with her sex. She was wet and ready for him. Even as she waited with anticipation outside on the bench for him to arrive, her panties clung wet to her flesh. She wet the tip of his cock at her opening before she eased back onto him. He had her shortly after they entered the apartment. Now it was her turn to have him. At first she rode him slow and steady to find her rhythm, then rough full movements to feel his entire length from head to balls plunge into her. He caressed her breasts, but as her movements shifted from gentle lovemaking to raw fucking, he took hold of her hips to steady her.

His eye widened, and his mouth hung open. Come inside me. Come inside me. Her thoughts and desires finally surfaced.

"Come inside me."

She cried and moaned while he groaned and grunted. His expression told her he was close.

"Come inside me."

His expression changed to one of hunger. Her demands seemed to set fire to him. He grasped her hips and raised his own so their bodies crashed together. She cried out as she came. His face twisted in an expression of alarm. He lifted her buttocks and slipped free from inside her. Ribbons of pearlescent semen shot up his belly. He held her hips tight to him so she was unable to reinsert his cock inside her. He reached to embrace her, but she climbed off of him and sat on the edge of the bed. Her face became warm and prickled as guilt crept in. It would do no good to force him into a relationship, which would no doubt turn into a disaster. Over time, he could come to regret her, even despise her. Tears wet her cheek and traveled down the side of her nose and tickled her top lip until she brushed them away. He moved to sit beside her, his warm hand on her back, which he removed after she tensed from his touch.

"What's wrong?"

"This. What *are* we doing?"

He cleared his throat.

"Mila, you must know I adore you, but things take time. My life is complicated. I am no longer a young man that can easily move from one relationship to another. We've talked about this before."

His words were dry and flat, and as dead as his explanation. How complicated did he think his life was? Being respectful and polite to his wife Eleanor, *Mrs. Crane*, all the while they kissed and carried on their illusion of a happy life while she witnessed and worked as a servant in their home, *that* was complicated.

She stood and pushed away his hand when he tried to take her arm. She felt the most out of place as she had ever been around him. When she bent to the floor to gather her clothes; under the bed she found a pair of black lace panties. Her lips wrinkled at the rip in them. She held them up for him to see.

"These are not mine."

When he said nothing, she tossed the black panties on the jumbled bed sheets, then huffed and dressed. She fixed her garter belt around her waist first as he sat there, then she snatched up her nylons. Her fingernail caught her nylon and created a run.

"Scheisse."

She pulled the nylon up her leg anyway and clasped it to her garter belt. She was more cautious when she put on the other one. The run ran up the inside of her thigh and screamed, whore. She could hear her mother's disdainful accusations in her mind. He slipped his boxers on and lit another cigarette, then went to the small galley kitchen to get a beer. He leaned against the counter and watched her dress. She knew that look. His eyes travelled the sight of her. He wanted to take pictures of her while she was half-naked. The multiple times he asked her in the past, she had always turned him down. It was one of the few things she was strong enough to deny him. She snorted and shook her head. His sometimes boyish gaze always softened her and made her want to giggle. Not today. Today, he was all man, refined and athletic, yet rugged, and she hated him.

"Have a good look. Maybe it's your last."

She supposed her accent caused his lips to curl into a satisfied smirk. His smile disappeared, and he took a long drag on the cigarette, but his gaze never left her.

"Patience, my dear. All good things come in time."

A steady stream of smoke passed his lips and followed his words. After she dressed, he opened his bottle of beer and took a sip.

"I won't wait for you forever. If you want to stay with your wife, then stay, but Kenneth, don't play games with me."

He took a short puff of the cigarette and put it out in the ashtray on the counter. He left his beer there as well, went to her, and stroked her upper arms.

"I'm not. Be patient Mila."

"It's time for me to go, and you should be back at the office if you are as busy as you *say* you are."

He snorted.

"I'm sure you're right."

He bent to kiss her, but she turn so his lips landed on her cheek.

"Goodbye Kenneth. I hope you're happy. I brought you what you wanted, but I don't know why—never mind, I don't want to know."

On her way out the door, she glanced at the cream faux leather diary with a gold metal lock. She had the urge to take it with her, to spite him. Stealing Lucius's diary was low. There was a lock on the diary. Did Kenneth have the key? She was astonished at the things, undeservedly, she did for him. The apartment door closed and clipped his muffled goodbye, or whatever his parting words were. After she marched down the hallway, she pushed the button to call the elevator. To her surprise, it was already there. If she had to wait, perhaps he would come out to chase after her, to make sense of things. To make her mind agree with her heart. It was ridiculous for her to consider, but she had.

The doors opened, and a beautiful woman with sapphire blue eyes and long blonde curls stood inside. The woman wore a fashionable sleeveless navy dress, beige nylons, and heels. She could be on television or in the movies. Mila waited for the woman to step off the elevator. They shared polite smiles. The woman even thanked her for holding the door. She lowered her head, like she often did around Mrs. Crane, before she stepped onto the elevator.

As the elevator doors moved, she pressed the button to open them, then she stepped out to glance around the corner and down the hallway. The woman stood before Kenneth's apartment door. When the woman knocked softly, Mila's body prickled with heat as she felt the temperature of her blood rise. She hurried back to the elevator car before the doors shut and pressed the button for the ground floor.

27

Friday evening, Beatrice was away for an overnight stay at her friend Stephanie Norris's house. Mrs. Crane remarked that perhaps the Norrises should adopt Beatrice. Presented as a joke, nevertheless a comment like many of her subtle jabs as a frustrated stepmother, exhausted Mr. Crane. Tonight, with Lucius at the table, Mr. Crane laughed it off. After dinner, Mr. And Mrs. Crane retired to the screened in patio with their wine and cigarettes. Instead of retiring to his bedroom, Lucius snuck down to the darkroom in order to process his latest roll of film. The roll contained the frames he shot of the family at the beach and whatever subjects he found around the house, lackluster as they were. Processing the roll was trivial. Finding the negatives or any prints Mr. Crane developed with his new camera was paramount. Those five frames Mr. Crane shot before letting him use the new Leica M4 burned bright in his mind like lost jewels and gold coins. He found it doubtful that Mr. Crane would take test shots of meaningless subjects merely to test out the new camera.

When he turned on the lights to the darkroom, there was no immediate indication that Mr. Crane had processed any film or prints. He walked around the space and glanced at everything to see if anything was out of place. Everything was as neat as always. The settings for the enlarger were in the same place as he last left them. He pulled the binder with Mr. Crane's latest negatives, only to find the same strips of film that they created several prints from weeks ago.

He sat on a stool, rewound the film in his camera, removed the roll, then ran through the development process. Within an hour, his latest roll of film hung in one long strip from the clip mounted to the cabinets. He stared at it for a moment, with no real desire to inspect any of the frames. He was certain his pictures of the Cranes at the beach were good, but other than that, he would be unfazed if the rest got lost or damaged. It hurt that Mr. Crane was reluctant to share his latest photographs. It was common to feel deserted by other kids in school, but now he felt deserted by Mr. Crane. Without a thought, he loaded a fresh roll of film into the Leica, straightened up the darkroom, what little it needed, then turned out the lights.

The sound of footsteps came from the upper floor. He closed the door to the darkroom and went to the stairs, but when he reached the bottom, the door at the top swung open and banged against the stairwell wall. Mr. and Mrs. Crane's laughter and loud voices, followed by their jovial hushed rebukes of one another's clumsiness, carried down the steps. Their shadows danced long down the basement stairwell walls. Lucius hurried and ducked under the wooden stairs. The Leica swung around his neck and he grabbed it before it struck anything. He moved back to the darkest corner under the stairs and crouched. Spiderwebs clung to his arm and in his hair and startled him, but not as much as when Mr. and Mrs. Crane came clopping down the steps.

"Shh. Shh," Mrs. Crane said.

She laughed. It was music to him. He never heard Mrs. Crane laugh in such a casual manner. It would have been easy to convince him she was another woman who descended the stairs with Mr. Crane.

"It's fine, no one can hear us," Mr. Crane said.

They laughed, and he hushed her anyway. Their words, their footsteps, came slow and heavy. They stumbled down the steps with caution, seemingly mindful of their inebriation. Mr. Crane's black wingtip oxfords, and Mrs. Crane's aqua blue satin pumps, appeared in the open spaces between the treads, feet away from where he hid. The two descended the stairs until they came into full view. He stiffened, alarmed by the delicate ghostly fingers that touched his hair. He quickly brushed a small spider from his forehead, not knowing where it landed.

The couple kissed and embraced at the bottom of the stairs. Mr. Crane pulled her up onto her toes and into his arms. Mrs. Crane bent her left leg and raised her heel off the floor as they kissed, like the women in films his mom enjoyed. He stared with an unblinking gaze. His breath shallow. A broken strand of a spider's web tickled his eyelash.

The two kissed, stumbled, kissed again as they made their way to the darkroom. He tried to make himself smaller as he hid in the shadows under the stairs. He was certain they could see him if they looked carefully in his direction.

Mrs. Crane unbuttoned Mr. Crane's shirt, and her hands ventured inside. His smile was dreamy and his eyes heavy as she caressed his chest. While she faced him, he unzipped her dress and pulled it down her shoulders and arms to expose her. She reached behind her and unclasped her bra, and slipped free of it. She let it fall at their feet, and his shirt followed. Her breasts appeared fuller in the dim basement lights. Her nipples pointed hard. Mr. Crane put his mouth over her nipple and she gasped and tilted her head back as he licked and sucked.

Lucius stiffened in his trousers at the sight of her breasts. He only looked away for a moment to ponder the hallway light above, then glanced down at the Leica. He adjusted the aperture to the widest setting to allow the most light into the camera, then lowered the shutter speed as well. With his elbows on his knees, he did his best to create a stable base, then strained forward to bring his eye to the viewfinder. He focused and waited. There was nothing he could do about the quality of light. He pressed the shutter release button. The shutter blades made their faint metallic whisper. He kept his eye to the camera's viewfinder and waited for either of them to look his way. When they kissed again, he thumbed the lever to advance the film, made a slight focus adjustment, and waited.

"I can't imagine what's come over you, Kenneth, but I have no complaints."

Mr. Crane buried his face between her breasts and grasped her buttocks. "You smell incredible," he said.

She smiled with heavy, wanting eyelids. They stood to the side of the door. He expected at any moment the two would slip inside the darkroom. They kissed with his hands on her waist and hers around his shoulders. He paused and gazed into her eyes.

"I want you."

His whisper was low, but carried to where Lucius hid hunched. She turned to face the wall and lowered her dress and panties to expose her buttocks. Mr. Crane unbuckled his trousers and let them fall to his ankles, then worked his boxers down his legs. His cock was long and thick and angled upward. She arched her back and bent at the waist, then he grasped her buttocks and positioned himself to enter her. Click. Lucius advanced the film. Then Mr. Crane slipped inside her. Her chin lifted, and she gasped. Click. He again advanced the film. He watched the Cranes from behind the camera. Mr. Crane plunged into her. His grunts and her moans filled the basement corridor. In a final deep thrust, his buttocks flexed into the shape of a keystone. Their bodies frozen. Click. After he advanced the film, he lowered the camera and waited. How long could they stay like that?

Mr. Crane kissed her back and shoulders as he massaged her breasts. He then slipped free from her. His glistening, semi-erect cock angled towards the floor. Lucius put his eye to the camera's viewfinder. She pulled up her panties, as he bent down to reach for his boxers and trousers. Click.

Lucius lowered the camera and held his breath. Mr. Crane paused as he bent over. Lucius closed his eyes as if that would make him invisible. When he opened his eyes, Mr. and Mrs. Crane were engaged in a deep, sensual kiss.

Mr. Crane opened the door to the darkroom and flipped on the light switch. A narrow band of light from the darkroom fell into the hallway. They disappeared inside. The door shut and the knob's plunger made a dull metallic clunk.

Lucius stood on unsteady legs. His thigh muscles were stiff and burned from crouching. As soon as he moved out from under the stairs, he hurried as quietly up them as he could, then through the house on the main floor, then up the stairs to his bedroom. He put the Leica on the dresser and got out of his clothes and into bed. As he lie motionless under the covers, he tried to slow his racing heart. A long sigh passed his lips. He tugged at the wet spot in his boxers as he peered at the shadows across the ceiling and fantasized about the things Mr. and Mrs. Crane must be doing in the darkroom. Were they lying across the work tables, or did they stand as they did in the hallway? As his heart slowed and thumped gently and his eyelids grew heavy, he cupped his testicles and drifted off to sleep.

28

When the summer ended and school started, it seemed all a dream. God had taken his parents and the simple life he had with them and the Cranes somehow found him, or rather Mr. Crane had, and now he exists in their world. His Aunt Phoebe was back in Indiana, probably never to be seen again. The only link to the past was his school and the few friends he had there. Both Tommy Perkins and Spencer Davies lived across town, so he never saw them during the summer. It made it difficult to be close to either of them, and they were best friends before they met him. His past life seemed to vanish before him like the man in the movie *The Invisible Man*.

One evening after school around the dinner table, Mr. Crane told him he had a surprise for him. The only hint Mr. Crane gave was it had to do with photography. Dinner went on forever. Beatrice seemed surprised that he turned down a piece of apple pie simply to quell his curiosity. Mr. Crane put his napkin on the table and glanced at Mrs. Crane.

"Excuse us dear. I best show Lucius his surprise before he bursts."

"Take your time. I'll be waiting out on the patio."

He smiled at her.

"Thank you. I won't be long. Come along Lucius."

They both headed to the study and left Mrs. Crane and Beatrice to enjoy their dessert. There was a pile of crumpled brown craft paper and twine to the side of the desk, and lined on the floor against the wall were a series of framed black and white prints. On the button sofa, leaned against the back cushions, were four more framed photographs. They went over to the sofa first. His eyes widened, and he smiled when he saw the photographs he shot at the beach over the summer. Mr. Crane printed only one of the two photographs Lucius shot of the three Cranes, one positioned in front of the other. The other three framed prints were: Mr. Crane with the young women sunbathing behind him, Beatrice by herself, and Mrs. Crane by herself reclining back under the shade of the beach umbrella. He gazed at them as if to search for some hidden message within each photograph. It surprised him that Mr. Crane would print and frame the picture of him with the young women sunbathing behind him. It was sure to draw Mrs. Crane's ire.

"Nice, right?"

Mr. Crane ran his fingers over the top of one frame, then stood there with a grin.

"Oh, yeah. These look amazing. I mean with the frames. Do you think they're good enough—my photographs?"

"I wouldn't have had them framed if I didn't."

Mr. Crane squeezed his shoulder.

"We can hang one or two in your room. The rest I would like to put up around the house. This one you shot of Mrs. Crane, though, I think would be best to hang here in the study."

His lips drew tight to one corner. Mr. Crane crossed his arms and raised his eyebrows.

"Since it is your photograph, feel free to come into the study to look at it, unless I'm in here working, which seems less and less these days."

He found that acceptable, but he wished the photograph could hang on a wall in his bedroom where he could admire Mrs. Crane in his own private space. Mr. Crane eyed him speculatively. Lucius smiled.

"Okay."

"Good. Which of the others would you like for your room?"

He glanced at the framed photographs.

"Just this one."

He pointed at the family picture with all three of the Cranes. Beatrice sitting between Mr. Crane's legs, his arms wrapped around her, and Mrs. Crane kneeling behind Mr. Crane, her hands on his shoulders.

"Great, I like that one too. I think it's the best of the two you shot of the three of us. We can hang it in your bedroom this weekend."

Mr. Crane smiled.

"Now that we got that settled, c'mon, take a look at *my* pictures, and tell me what you think."

The photographs Mr. Crane shot lined the floor on the opposite wall. There were five of them. They were all encased in the same style contemporary wooden frames. Could any of these be one or all of the five pictures Mr. Crane shot with his new Leica M4 camera? In his mind, Lucius could still see the M4's frame indicator on the sixth frame. He crouched close to the first one, while Mr. Crane stood and hung back with his arms crossed.

The photograph was Mrs. Crane at the beach. She was smiling, a rarity, but her sunglasses hid her eyes. She had her hands on her hips—playful, casual, without pretense. He smiled. She was definitely posing for Mr. Crane and Mr. Crane alone. He stifled a chuckle when he remembered his dad telling one of his dad's friend's wives who was drunk and laughing at one of his parents' cookouts, "Becky, about time you got that stick out of your ass." He imagined his dad would tell Mrs. Crane that she had a stick in her ass. He liked how Mrs. Crane carried herself, stick or no stick.

There were three more beach photographs, one of Beatrice, one of Mr. and Mrs. Crane (taken by Beatrice), and one of him. He had his head turned in the picture, but when he had glanced toward the camera was when Mr. Crane captured him. He knelt and lingered in front of his portrait.

"These are great."

"Thanks. I caught you looking there."

Mr. Crane chuckled.

"I look normal."

Mr. Crane patted him on the head.

"You are normal. As normal as a kid your age gets, but you're talented. That might seem strange to you, but it's a gift. Cherish it, because it makes you special."

The floor creaked out in the hallway. Beatrice stood in the doorway.

"Come in, Dear, and have a look at the photographs."

Beatrice glanced at the both of them and her gaze fell on him.

"I'll look another time."

She turned and disappeared. Her light footsteps faded. Mr. Crane's face looked flattened with guilt.

"I'm sure she's tired. I bet she'll love the pictures of her when she sees them. They'll be easier to see during the day."

He looked at the final framed print. It was a picture of Mrs. Crane sitting and smoking out on the screened in patio. He remembered her dress. Mr. Crane took the shot days or weeks after their visit to the beach. The light was soft, and the shadows were dark and rich in the photograph. Lucius tilted his head as he examined the image.

"This one is very nice. I like the mood."

Mr. Crane snorted.

"You're well beyond your years."

Mr. Crane made similar comments before, but he made little sense of them.

"Huh?"

"You've got a mature eye."

"Oh?"

Mr. Crane had a warm smile.

"All right. Time for bed."

Lucius got to his feet. His knees tingled and were blotchy red from being on the hardwood floor. He turned to Mr. Crane. He wanted to ask Mr. Crane about the five frames he shot before letting him try out his new camera. Maybe he should wait until Mr. Crane develops more prints.

"Thank you for showing me these. Good night."

Mr. Crane smiled a toothless smile.

"Good night Lucius."

TWO

29

A lanky, seventeen-year-old Lucius strolled the hallway toward the family room where music drew his attention. He passed two framed photographs that hung on the wall in the hallway. The first one was a portrait of Beatrice at the beach he shot four years ago, and the second photograph Mr. Crane shot of Mrs. Crane out on the patio. He slowed to glance at the picture of Mrs. Crane. Although he had examined it at length many times before, it was her gaze toward the camera that captivated him. How she looked at Mr. Crane. What would it take for her, *Eleanor*, to look at him in that way?

Stephanie Norris sat with Beatrice and Mrs. Crane in the family room. A record played on the turntable. It was "Sugar Sugar" by The Archies. Beatrice stood with her back to Mrs. Crane, who sat on the sofa and fussed with her homecoming dress. Stephanie Norris sat in one of the side chairs. Mrs. Crane wrinkled her lips.

"Where is he? I told him to come to the family room so you two could practice."

Beatrice's lips tightened.

"He's not taking me to the dance."

"I never said he was, but you might like to practice dancing with a boy whom you have no interest in before you dance with one you do."

Beatrice sighed and raised her eyebrows.

"Okay, good point."

Stephanie giggled, then went to the doorway to peek out into the hallway. She glanced back at Beatrice and Mrs. Crane with wide eyes.

"There he is, in the hallway. He's standing in front of one of the pictures."

Her voice was excited, but hushed. The corner of Mrs. Crane's lips tightened and her eyebrows rose. Stephanie took another peek, then hurried back to her seat.

"He's coming."

She straightened her dress and sat as comfortably poised as though she had been there for some time. Mrs. Crane tilted her head and gave her a subtle, tightlipped smile. Lucius appeared in the doorway, and she was sure her heart skipped a beat. Mrs. Crane gave him a hard but harmless glare.

"Lucius, we almost sent out a search party for you."

Stephanie would have gladly volunteered. He wrinkled his lips as he looked at Mrs. Crane.

"Sorry."

He glanced at Stephanie, and she grinned at him.

"Hello Lucius."

"Hi Stephanie."

Beatrice had told her he was shy, but she was sure he would like her if they could be alone and talk. The record ended, and the room fell silent. Beatrice wiggled her hips.

"Play it again."

Mrs. Crane sighed.

"If you must."

Lucius snorted and smiled at Mrs. Crane. Stephanie went to the turntable to start the single again.

"All right, you two."

Mrs. Crane stood and motioned for Lucius to join them. She instructed Lucius where to hold Beatrice if they were to slow dance. The music started. Mrs. Crane sighed.

"I'll find something slower and more appropriate after this."

Beatrice moved her shoulders and hips. She laughed, and Lucius moved with her, although he was stiff at first. After the song finished, Mrs. Crane put on another record, Ben E. King's "Stand by Me" played. She positioned Lucius and Beatrice and instructed them on how to move their feet.

"Take it slow. Listen, then move to the music."

Lucius raised his eyebrows and looked as though he might burst out laughing. Beatrice giggled. Stephanie stood.

"I'm going to use the powder room."

Mrs. Crane waved her away. Down the hallway, the music echoed softly off the walls. Stephanie paused at the picture she saw Lucius standing in front of. His gaze seemed lost somewhere in the black and white photograph of Mrs. Crane. She sat smoking out on the screened in patio. Mrs. Crane's gaze was seductive and her facial expression was one of a determined woman. Stephanie was aware Lucius loved photography. Beatrice mentioned it all the time, usually rolling her eyes as if he had some disgusting habit rather than a creative hobby. The picture though of Mrs. Crane, had he taken this picture? Why did Mrs. Crane give him such a look? What was going on? Her mouth went dry, and she hurried down the hallway to the bathroom.

When she returned to the family room, the song had ended and Mrs. Crane clapped, she assumed, at Lucius and Beatrice's performance. Mrs. Crane then switched the records on the turntable and put the needle down to start the music.

"Can I practice too?"

Beatrice and Lucius stood face-to-face with their hands in position to dance again. They all turned toward Stephanie. A warmth crept up into her face. Beatrice's face brightened, and she released Lucius.

"Sure."

Stephanie looked at him.

"Okay, sure."

Beatrice sat on the sofa, and Stephanie stepped to face him. Mrs. Crane changed the record, set the needle, then went and positioned them.

"Let Lucius lead you."

Stephanie smiled and melted inside. Her face became warm when he smiled at her, and warmer yet, when "Be My Baby" by The Ronettes played on the turntable. She was unable to tell who was stiffer, him or her. Beatrice was grinning when she and Lucius rotated their position. She wanted to stick her tongue out at Beatrice, but not in front of Lucius. She found it difficult enough not to giggle with his hand rested on her hip.

Halfway through the song, her nerves settled. She took a few opportunities to gaze into his eyes. He seemed emotionless, but his gaze was enough for her, at least for now. She wished he could hold her closer, but Mrs. Crane insisted on maintaining a space between them as they danced. She only witnessed Mrs. Crane's icy gaze once before, and wanted to avoid seeing it again. The song ended, and he released her. Beatrice clapped. Mrs. Crane stood near the turntable.

"Very nice. Beatrice, would you like to go again?"

"No, thank you. I'm sure Lucius has things to do. Thank you, Lucius."

Mrs. Crane put the records away and closed the lid to the turntable. Lucius gave her a look of anticipation, as if he hoped she would ask him to dance. Stephanie was sure he took the picture in the hallway of Mrs. Crane.

"Uh, sure. My pleasure," he said.

He turned and left. Both girls giggled wide-eyed. Stephanie lowered her head to whisper.

"I wish Lucius could take me to my homecoming dance."

"Leighton Day only allows the boys *who attend* Leighton Day to accompany the female students to various functions, including dances."

When Mrs. Crane stated the school's policy in a firm voice, both girls stiffened in their seats. Maybe there was something to the photograph in the hallway. Mrs. Crane still stood by the turntable. She flipped through the records and paused here and there to examine the album covers, reminiscing perhaps. Her face was as placid as ever. Whatever she was thinking, Stephanie was unable to tell if it was good or bad. Beatrice wrinkled her lips.

"Thank you for the dance lesson."

Beatrice stood, then Stephanie stood as well.

"Yes, thank you Mrs. Crane. That was fun."

"You're welcome. Won't you join us for dinner?"

"Uh?"

She glanced at Beatrice, who smiled and nodded.

"Thank you. That would be nice, Mrs. Crane. I have to phone my mother to let her know."

"I'll call her."

Mrs. Crane's lips drew into a tight smile.

"Okay. Thank you, Mrs. Crane."

She nodded, and Stephanie followed Beatrice from the family room.

"C'mon, let's go to my room."

She hurried to keep up with Beatrice. As they passed Lucius's bedroom, she peeked inside. Lucius stood in front of his dresser, examining his camera. He turned and saw her before she could slip past his door.

"Hi. Sorry. What are you up to?"

"I'm going to wander the backyard to see what I can find to photograph."

"Oh? Do you mind if we join you?"

With her arm hidden by the doorframe, she waved for Beatrice to come. His eyebrows rose, and he looked as though he had an idea.

"Sure."

She grinned.

"Great. Hey Beatrice, let's go outside and watch Lucius take pictures."

Beatrice stood in the hallway, out of his sight, her hands on her hips.

"You two go. I'll come out later."

"You sure?"

Beatrice disappeared into her bedroom.

"Okay, looks like it's just the two of us. Maybe you can show me how your camera works."

"Sure, that's easy."

He smiled, and they headed back downstairs and out to the backyard. She imagined Beatrice was at her window watching them. Maybe he would kiss her and make Beatrice's head spin. She walked alongside him and glanced at him as he led them to wherever they were going. His lanky limbs and body made her feel more comfortable about her own. They matched. He was a couple inches taller than her, and cute as when they first met, only a different kind of cute. Also, they were teenagers now, fast becoming adults.

She liked fast. Adults had all the fun, and they could do whatever they liked, and whenever they wanted.

They walked out to the towering sycamore tree at the far end of the yard. She had climbed it before with Beatrice, and hoped he had something else in mind. She had on one of her nicer dresses, and would hate to get it dirty, as she knew she would do just about anything he was up for, even climbing a tree.

"Do you see anything you want to take a picture of?"

She held her hands out in front of her with her fingers knit together as if to say, pick me. He did, or maybe that was what he had planned all along.

"Can you pose for me?"

"Sure. Where would you like me to stand?"

"Come behind the tree where the sunlight is less intense."

Maybe he did want to kiss her. Behind the tree meant out of sight. As much as she wanted him to kiss her, she moved with slow anticipation. When she stood with her back to the massive trunk of the sycamore, she waited for him to make his move.

"Can you turn this way and put your hands in front of you to brace yourself against the tree?"

Not what she expected, but she went along.

"Good-good. Hold that and turn your head towards me."

She did as he instructed. He stood there still like a statue with the camera to his eye. What was he waiting for? She smiled. Maybe that's what he was waiting for, for her to smile. He only stood there, frozen in space. A gentle gust of wind blew her hair in her face. When she brushed it aside and glanced at him, he lowered the camera. Had he taken the picture?

"Got it. Now, can you turn the other direction?"

"Okay."

After she got into position, he made her wait again before taking the picture. Curious, what was he waiting for? She turned with her back to the tree. She brushed her hair from her face as another breeze pushed past them. He held up his hand.

"There, that's nice. Hold your pose. I want to get a close-up portrait."

She liked the sound of that. When he came in close and brought the camera to his eye, she raised her hand to stop him. He lowered the camera.

"I saw you out in the hall staring at the picture of Mrs. Crane."

"Oh? Yeah, it's a beautiful photograph, isn't it?"

"That's a little boastful, don't you think?"

"Huh?"

He lowered the camera to his chest.

"You took her picture, right?"

"Uh? No, that wasn't me. It was a picture Mr. Crane shot."

Her face became warm and tight.

"I'm sorry. I thought you took her picture."

"Oh, I wish."

She raised her eyebrows. What did that mean? Maybe he has a thing for Mrs. Crane. Maybe a crush. She felt a pang of jealousy, but knew nothing would ever come of his fascination for Mrs. Crane. It would be absurd if he had a crush on her. Her being so—old. She stopped thinking and stepped closer, then kissed him on the lips. It was a soft peck, brief, but sent electricity from her lips to her toes. She gasped as if she had been holding her breath. His eyes widened. His lips parted as if he were about to speak. Beatrice appeared.

"There you are, hiding out behind the old sycamore."

Her tone was teasing and accusatory. Her face brightened at the sight of them.

"What have you two been doing?"

Each word came out punchy and excited.

"Just taking pictures."

They answered at the same time. He looked stunned, as if someone had slapped him in the face. She imagined she looked the same. Beatrice's smile broadened and her eyelids narrowed at the two of them.

"I bet."

"Can you two stand over there at the side of the tree?"

Beatrice tilted her head and wrinkled her lips at him, but he only gave her an insistent wave. She then gave Stephanie a curious glance. Stephanie ignored her and went near the tree as he directed. Anything to get past the awkward moment. Beatrice looked as though she might protest, then she went and stood next to her. They both stood at the side of the sycamore, where there was more direct sunlight. He busied himself adjusting the camera's settings. She, being almost a head taller than Beatrice, lowered her head to whisper into Beatrice's ear.

"I'll tell you later."

Beatrice smiled. She probably already knew what she would tell her.

"Okay, you better."

When both girls looked up, Lucius had the camera to his eye.

"Great, let's do another one. Beatrice, can you turn your back to Stephanie, and Stephanie, can you stand facing me?"

Beatrice glanced at Stephanie with a curious gaze. Stephanie was sure he took their picture while she was whispering to Beatrice. He cleared his throat, and both girls smiled at the camera. What's he waiting for? Beatrice said he was weird. Her parents rarely took pictures, but when they did, it was stand, smile, and say cheese. Her smile faded. He lowered the camera.

"I got the shot."

When he looked at her, his expression somehow told her he liked their kiss. Maybe he was as strange as Beatrice alluded, but he further stoked her curiosity. Also, she wanted to kiss him again.

Dinner at the Cranes that evening, Mr. and Mrs. Crane sat at opposite ends of the table, with Beatrice and Stephanie at the lengthy side, and Lucius and an empty chair across the table from them. It gave Stephanie an opportunity to glance at Lucius without her interest in him appearing too obvious.

Mrs. Crane wore a tense smile, but she raised her chin in a dignified manner and looked across the table at Mr. Crane.

"How was your day, Dear?"

Mr. Crane busied himself cutting the sirloin on his plate. He finally looked up and passed a smile around the table.

"Oh, the same old thing, only more of it. We got two new major clients, and I'm lead counsel for one of them."

"That's exciting news. How fortunate we are for you to join us for dinner. You've been so busy and compelled to stay at that dreadfully tiny apartment in Hartford. I can only image the toll your back must be taking sleeping in that bed. Anyway, we love it when you can make it home."

Mrs. Crane sounded as though she had more to say, but cut herself off, perhaps due to company being present. The tension in the air made Stephanie's shoulders tighten. Mrs. Crane smiled at Beatrice before she picked at her salad. She then nodded while he chewed and shared a brief smile with Beatrice.

"Yes, father, we love it when you're home."

Mr. Crane glanced around the table at the three teens.

"What has the youth of today been up to?"

30

It was a cool, rainy autumn evening. Beatrice was at her friend's house for an overnight stay, and Mr. Crane was away in Hartford over night, which left Lucius and Mrs. Crane to share each other's company. She instructed him to take the wineglass that was set out for Mr. Crane. She filled his glass. He sat in his usual spot at the side of the table, she at the end, and an empty chair between them. Ms. Käthe had prepared a lovely roast with carrots. Rosemary scented the air and hinted at the delightful dinner to come. A dinner for four, now a dinner for two. Although Mr. Crane and Beatrice's chairs sat empty, their place settings stood ready, expecting their arrival. It would surprise Lucius to see either of them. As equally surprised as seeing a ghost.

"There."

Mrs. Crane smiled briefly, then spread the cloth napkin across her lap. Lucius gazed at the glass of wine. His eyes widened. This was too easy. The other boys at school, his age of now sixteen, would be jealous if they knew Mrs. Crane offered him alcohol. They joked about stealing their old man's bottle of gin, only to be disgusted by the taste. None of them grew hair on their chests, as one of their dads had said. He never tried the gin himself, but now he smiled inside.

"It's a Cabernet Sauvignon," she said.

"Oh?"

He smiled, nodded, and acted impress, even though he had no idea what a Cabernet Sauvignon was, and he was certain she knew his ignorance. To him, it was a glass of wine. Beyond that, red or white was all he knew. The Cabernet

Sauvignon was a bold looking red wine. He was afraid to touch the glass, so instead he picked up his knife and fork after spreading the napkin across his lap.

"A toast first."

She held up her glass. He put down his silverware and carefully picked up the wineglass and held it as she held hers.

"To another sad evening with only the rain as our guest. Lucius, you and I have been forsaken yet again. We shall make the most of it. We will triumph."

He waited for her to glance at him with her pale sky-blue eyes and maybe offer a conciliatory smile, but instead she drank. So he drank. The wine had a bite to it, but went down smooth. He swallowed before any second thoughts could spoil the moment. She sat her glass on the table and picked up her silverware. Relieved, he did the same. He grew fond of the wine as he took sips between mouthfuls of the roast.

After dinner, she filled both glasses of wine. Her eyes were on him. He pushed in his chair and stood steady.

"It seems my dance partner couldn't make it. Would you like to join me out on the patio?"

There must have been a gleam in his eyes, for a wisp of a smile formed on her lips.

"Take your glass and bring the bottle as well. I think we're going to need it."

He followed her out into the screened in patio. She sat in her usual spot, and he took Mr. Crane's seat in the other wicker chair. At first, neither of them spoke. He was content to watch her smoke. When she need another, he was there to light it for her.

The downpour overtook the leaf-filled gutters and came down in sheets across the length of the eaves. It was unlike Mrs. Crane to forget to have the gutters cleaned. Ashes fell from the cigarette precariously held between her two fingers and drifted to the patio floor. She hid her emotions like no one he had ever known, but he could see the sour tension in her face, like aged, withered fruit soon to be discarded.

"Beautiful," she said.

Her tone was flat, but he felt her bitterness.

"We are yet another pair on Shakespeare's stage ready to act out one of his tragedies."

Her chest rose with long, steady breaths. He took in a deep breath as well. The moist, delicate breeze that passed through the patio screens filled his lungs. He sipped his glass of Cabernet Sauvignon. It was strong, too strong. At dinner it went well with the roast, but on its own the Cabernet Sauvignon was unbearable. He swallowed and fought the urge to wrinkle his face. She held out her empty glass for him to pour her another. She took a long drag on her cigarette while he poured. Her gaze remained outward at the steady rain.

"Two more years. What will you do then?"

When he sat the bottle of Cabernet Sauvignon on the coffee table, she drank and waited for his reply. He cleared his throat.

"I want to be a photographer."

She snorted.

"How will you do that? How will you make money?"

She eyed him over the top of her wineglass.

"You're growing to be an attractive young man. Perhaps you'll find some wealthy widow who will take care of you. Foster your art—your photography, and in turn—"

He took in her every word as he did with Mr. Crane's photography lessons. He swallowed and waited for her to finish her thought, but she drank instead and stared out into the shadowy rain beaten backyard. Her chest rose and fell, slow, gentle, steady, and the subtle pulse at her neck remind him of beating butterfly wings.

She took a drink, then slipped off her heels with her free hand. They made a soft thump when they landed on the patio floor. She massaged her calf down to her heel, then her arch, then her toes. His gaze followed her hand, and he watched her long slender fingers with well-manicured nails do their work. He could barely see her painted toes through her beige stockings. He was uncertain of the color. Perhaps red, like her fingernails.

"May I?"

He moved to sit at the edge of his seat. She gazed at him for a moment, then held her near-empty wineglass with both hands in her lap. He sat his half-full wineglass on the coffee table and knelt at her feet. Before he even touched her, she closed her eyes and relaxed her head back on the chair's cushion. His breath quickened and his body stirred. The hem of her sleeveless black and white patterned dress sat just above her knees. Her contoured legs, clad in sheer beige nylon stockings, were a spectacle. Although he remained at her feet, another part of him rose. From his kneeling position, his bound erection became painfully restrained within his boxers and trousers. He woke from his reverie when she nudged her shoe, and it made a soft clop when it toppled on its side. He took her foot in his hands and massaged her arch, heel, and toes, mindful to make his pace casual to avoid suspicion, or worse, anger. She drew in a sharp breath, followed by a slow exhale. After he spent a fair moment on her foot, he then worked his way up to her ankle, shin, and calf. Her breath was steady, and she released a hum, which sounded like a hum of pleasure. He felt as though he could boil over and come in his trousers. He squeezed her calf, then moved his hand further up her leg.

When he rested his hand on her knee, she looked down at him with heavy eyelids and a dreamy gaze. She looked resplendent and submissive. He licked his lips, then slid his hand under her skirt and his fingertips glided up her thigh. When he reached the middle of her thigh where her garter clasp held the top of her stocking, his eyes widened. He glanced at the wineglass she held in her lap, and expected, at any moment, she would throw it in his face. When his fingers ventured further to touch her bare skin, her hand shot out and captured his wrist wrapped in the fabric of her dress.

"Enjoying yourself?"

"Yes. Don't I make you feel good?"

She tilted her head and wrinkled her lips as if what he said was ridiculous.

"Mr. Crane is not here. It's just you and me."

Her eyebrows drew together, but she looked more puzzled than angry.

"Are you suggesting we have an affair while Mr. Crane is away?"

"Yes."

She pushed his hand away, and he withdrew it from under her skirt.

"I don't think that's a wise idea."

"Why not Ella?"

"You're not to call me Ella. Only Mr. Crane calls me by that name."

"But, Mr. Crane is not here."

Beatrice appeared in the doorway. Her hair matted in spots from the rain and her dress clung to her.

"There you are. I said hello when I got home, but no one answered."

He still knelt at Mrs. Crane's feet when he met Beatrice's gaze.

"And what are you doing down there?"

He stood casually and put his hands in his pockets, then balled them into fists to hide his arousal. Before he could speak, Mrs. Crane spoke.

"I'm a little tipsy, so I asked him to get my shoe from under the table."

Beatrice crossed her arms.

"And what about you? Are you tipsy too?"

He turned to glance at the glass of wine on the coffee table that he had been drinking from. Again Mrs. Crane spoke first.

"Since your father is conveniently away again, I offered Lucius a glass of wine and asked him to sit out here and keep me company."

"I see."

Beatrice's tone was sharp.

Mrs. Crane took a drink and addressed Beatrice again without turning around to look at her.

"What brings you home? Especially at this hour."

"The storm. The Norrises lost their electricity. Stephanie's family is going to Stephanie's grandmother's for the night. There isn't enough room for me, so they drove by and the lights were on, so Mrs. Norris figured it was best for me to come home."

"I'm sorry Dear. I know how much you like to spend time with Stephanie. Why don't you run along and get out of your wet clothes and dry your hair?"

Lucius gazed at Beatrice. How could Mrs. Crane know? She never turned around to look at Beatrice. Beatrice gave him a quick narrow-eyed glance, huffed, then marched off in her stocking feet. He watched her pass through the kitchen and disappear down the hallway, then he looked at Mrs. Crane.

"Do you hate her?"

She took a drink and stared out into the dark, rain-soaked backyard.

"I wouldn't say that. We have different personalities, but I believe she's jealous that I'm married to her father. A situation, I'm sure, she despises."

She shrugged her shoulders as if it was only a casual misunderstanding. When she finally looked at him, she first glanced at the front of his pants, then her eyes traced his body upward until she met his gaze. He withdrew his hands from his pockets and crossed them at the front of his pants.

"Be a dear and get me another cigarette and fill my glass. After that, you can take the bottle and your glass to the kitchen and head up to bed."

He parted his lips, but her gaze halted anything he had to say. He did as she asked and left her to contemplate the dark, rain-swept backyard.

31

In Mr. Crane's study, Lucius sat slouched in the middle of the button leather sofa with his head rested on the back cushion. If Mr. or Mrs. Crane saw him, they would immediately make him sit up properly. Fortunately, the house was empty. Mrs. Crane and Beatrice were out to lunch with Stephanie Norris and her mother, which would no doubt escalate to a shopping trip. Mr. Crane had to run to Hartford for some emergency.

After Mr. Crane's invitation to spend time in his study so he could enjoy the framed photographs, Lucius took every opportunity to do just that, and to explore.

Other times, when he was alone in the house, he searched all the shelves for his mom's diary, but as time passed, his desire faded. Much like the mental picture of his parents, he struggled to remember what they looked like, their faces like wax, softened by the heat of time.

From where he sat, his gaze always settled on the black and white photograph he shot of Mrs. Crane at the beach. Her name, Mr. Crane playfully called her, escaped his lips in a whisper, *Ella*. Although, that day, when she sat in the shade of the large beach umbrella, he recalled her pale sky-blue eyes. How she looked at him. She posed for him, and only him. His eyebrows drew together and his lips tightened. Had Mr. Crane hung his photograph of her in that spot on the wall for his own viewing pleasure? He huffed and pushed himself up so he sat properly on the sofa. The leather groaned.

He crossed his arms and glanced around the room. The house, a Goliath of wood and stone, its old bones creaked and popped. The cavernous study, filled with all of Mr. Crane's things, whispered to him, but not with words. In his mind, something told him to stand, and he did. He turned and peered at the bookshelves packed neatly with Mr. Crane's books, dusted clean by Ms. Mila. The walls with all the framed photographs, mostly pictures shot within the past few years, as Mr. Crane had taken down his old ones, the ones Lucius saw when he first came to the house. His gaze traveled the row of hung photographs that ended at Mr. Crane's heavy ornate wooden desk. It had six drawers, three on each side of various depths, and a shallow one in the middle. He opened the shallow middle drawer. It contained personal stationery, envelopes, and a few writing instruments. He felt as though he was sitting in a giant's chair whenever he sat in Mr. Crane's high-back leather executive chair. Although he had grown, he would need to be closer to Mr. Crane's height and build to fill such a chair.

He examined the side drawers and ran his fingertips over the brass keyholes. With a tug, he tested the handles. Locked. Both upper drawers on either side held firm. He kicked the base of the desk. The toe of his oxford made a dull clunk against the sturdy wood. He tugged at the handle on the bottom right drawer. Locked. He huffed and smirked. He was being silly. His quest, a fruitless one. He ran his fingers over the ornately carved edge of the desk. The carved ridges felt pleasing under his touch. After he sighed, he tried the handle of the bottom left drawer. It budged. The inside lip of the drawer was naked and stark compared to the dark mahogany stain that covered the exterior. The latch, misaligned when it was last locked, had missed its mark and had gone unnoticed. He pulled open the deep drawer, expecting a black cat or something evil to jump out.

Down inside the drawer sat a manilla folder and a large banker's accordion envelope. He took out the manilla folder, sat it on top of the desk and opened it. A plastic sheet with a frosted backing held a single negative strip with five exposed frames. Beneath it appeared to be prints. He recognized the edge of the photo paper, and considered that these must be the first five pictures Mr. Crane shot with his new, at the time, Leica M4 camera. He hesitated before he turned over the sleeve that held the negative strip. When he did, there was the first black and white print. A nude photograph of his Aunt Phoebe lying in bed.

Where was this? When was this? The angle was from above, so he knew Mr. Crane was standing on the mattress when he photographed her. His Aunt Phoebe lie with her back arched, which lifted her breasts. Her hard nipples cast shadows, which told him where the light originated. Her legs were open and, her expression was playful and seductive. The tangled ruffled sheets, and her heavy eyelids left no doubt that Mr. Crane had fucked her. The other prints were no different, except for two, where she, while dressing or undressing, wore his mom's silver opal teardrop-shaped earrings.

He removed the plastic sleeve containing the single negative strip. He closed the folder and set it aside. The large banker's accordion envelope looked heavier than it was. A string wound crisscrossed between two small plastic circular discs. He unwound the string and opened the large flap. He felt the thick papers inside—photo paper. More prints? He grasped the entire contents and slid it from the accordion envelope.

His eyes widened, and his mouth sat agape. He stood suddenly. His legs buckled, and he caught himself on the edge of the desk. The first of the black and white eight-by-ten prints peered up at him. His mom, Paulina Carol Cook, gazed at him, or rather at the camera and the man who photographed her—Mr. Crane.

His mouth went dry, and he swallowed. In the photograph, reclined bare-breasted on a sofa, was his mom. She still wore her skirt, which was drawn up to reveal the tops of her stockings and a sliver of her white panties. She had her legs hooked over the top back of the sofa. A cheesecake pose, he imagined Mr. Crane cajoled her into taking. She was much younger, her hair different from what he had last remembered. A slight timid reluctance on her face, unlike his Aunt Phoebe, who was ready and willing.

The other prints were stunning as well, but less revealing. In some she stood with her blouse buttoned, but with her skirt pulled up high to reveal her stockings and panties. He paused over the last print. It was a closer portrait. His mom's blouse was unbuttoned to reveal her bra and top of her breast. Her stiff nipple was visible on her blouse. On her earlobes hung the silver opal teardrop-shaped earrings. The ones he had never seen until he and his Aunt Phoebe cleaned up his parents' house. It took his breath away. There was only one person who could have given her those earrings—Mr. Crane. His dad was too damn cheap. Then again, he realistically was unable to afford such an extravagant gift, even for his wife.

His eyebrows drew together, and his lips tightened. His hands balled into fists, and he slammed his hand down ón the desk, which only made a dull thud, but sent a jolt of lightning up his arm.

"Fuck."

He rubbed his knuckles and cradled his arm. He wanted to destroy the photographs more than crumpling them in his fist. They needed to burn. He stuffed the prints back into the large accordion envelope, and placed the folder with the photographs of his Aunt Phoebe on top, and on top of that the plastic sleeve with the single negative strip.

A car door closed outside. His shoulders and back stiffened. He grasped the stacked items on the desk and nearly tripped over the open bottom desk drawer.

"Shit."

His shin stung from hitting the heavy wood. The door opened down the hallway, and soft voices came. It was Beatrice and Mrs. Crane. There was even a bit of laughter, which suggested a successful shopping trip. He put the large banker's accordion envelope and the folder back into the drawer as he found them and closed it as quickly and quietly as he could. He kept the plastic sleeve, folded it in half, made sure not to crease the negative strip, and tucked it into his trousers under his shirt.

The clomp of heels on the hallway wood floors rose. He hobbled to the sofa and fell onto the cushions, then positioned himself to give the appearance that he had been sitting and admiring the framed prints, even as his head ached and eyes burned. He lifted his knee to cross his legs, but his shin throbbed, so he kept both feet on the floor. As the footsteps clomped to an abrupt stop, he fought a wince, and managed a half-cocked smile as he looked toward the doorway.

"There you are."

Beatrice stood in the doorway with her hands on her hips. A shopping bag hung from around her wrist. He sat stunned as the pain climbed his leg.

"Hello? Don't you think about anything other than photography? Bor-ring. I can make it *not* boring. You can photograph me in my new dress."

She beamed. She shrugged her shoulder at the side where she held the shopping bag. He raised his eyebrows. She looked light on her toes as though she could float away. He chuckled. The sound that escaped his lips surprised him and helped to quell the rage within him. He blew out an exhausted breath.

"Okay, show me whatcha got."

When he got to his feet, she smiled and disappeared from the doorway. Her heeled sandals clicked and faded as she hurried down the hallway. He limped after her. He would need to retrieve his camera, and would hide the plastic sleeve with the single negative film strip in his room. Later he would move it to some place more secure.

32

After school, Lucius took the bus to the Sunny Grove Cemetery. He struggled to wrap his head around the photographs he found in Mr. Crane's desk. He needed to get back to the study. Destroying the photographs would only partially satisfy him. It was the negatives that concerned him the most.

The cool air filled his lungs. It had yet to carry the dampness and smell of decay, which would come later after the leaves fell. Autumn had added some color to the leaves, their full vibrancy certain in the coming month. A flock of geese flew overhead in an arrow pointing south. A harsh winter was on its way, his dad would say. The early evening breeze penetrated his shirt to his skin and chilled him. He stood in front of his parents' headstone. It was a single headstone with both of their names on it. Their union in death seemed more of a happier marriage than when they were alive.

He knelt and brushed the fallen twigs from the headstone. He read both of their names, slow as if in a trance, like he had done in prior visits to the cemetery. It was like a ritual to confirm their deaths. He usually spent more time in front of his mom's name. His eyes would follow each carved letter, caressing them, but today he found her name, Paulina Carol Cook (1935-1963), difficult to look at, and his eyes instead fell on his dad's name, Darius Riley Cook (1932-1963). He felt a stab of guilt for not considering what caused his dad's often foul mood.

"Dad? Did you know? Did you know she was with Mr. Crane?"

His voice was low, dry, ghostly and translucent. He envisioned his mom with her arms crossed, like when her patience had run out and she glared at him. He felt like a traitor to her, but now he considered his allegiance, perhaps misguided.

"No, I suppose you didn't—but I'm sure you suspected. That's why you had mom quit working as a secretary. Isn't that right?"

He tapped the toe of his oxford at the base of the headstone as if that would elicit a response from his dad.

"That's right. It's the only explanation."

He wrinkled his lips. His gaze shifted to peer at his mom's name on the headstone. His eyebrows knit together.

"If you left dad for Mr. Crane, would you have left me too?"

There was no answer, like every other time he visited his parents' graves.

"If you're looking down from Heaven as everyone says you are, I wonder what you think about Aunt Phoebe. Did you even know her, or know *of* her?"

When he glanced at his dad's name, he imagined him shrug as he did when he sat on a lawn chair with a beer in his hand, and stated matter-of-factly that there was nothing to be done. There came the urge to spit on his parents' headstone, but something told him he would go to hell for it. He thought of his parents and the Cranes. Was there *any* family that was honest and wholesome, or did every family have secrets? He stood and wondered why he even came to the cemetery. There were no answers here and there never would be.

33

From the upstairs window, Eleanor watched Lucius stroll up the driveway on his way home from school. She glanced at her watch. Usually she would arrive after retrieving Beatrice from Leighton Day, but today June Norris would pick up the girls. June assured her it was no trouble. The Norrises adored Beatrice. Stephanie had asked to have Beatrice stay overnight, and there was no objection, so that left her, Lucius, and Kenneth, if Kenneth could find his way home. She huffed and was conflicted as to what to believe. He was ambitious, especially when he first started at the firm, but that tapered off after a few years. Was his office that busy? She doubted his overnight stays in Hartford was merely to get a break from his family. Her gaze followed Lucius until he disappeared into the house, then she went down the hallway to the bathroom and expected to hear him climb the stairs at any moment.

She waited. It was silent in the upstairs hallway. He should have come by now. She headed downstairs. All the while, she stepped lightly as she listened for him. Subtle sounds came from down the hallway. Maybe he was in the study. The boy obsessed himself with the photographs that hung on the walls in there. Desire, obsession, she knew well of these things, especially when it came to Kenneth. She liked to control him. She enjoyed dangling the carrot. He liked when she dangled the carrot. It made him want her more. His obsession made her wet. Even after they first got married, he would call her from the office to tell her he would have her that night, and not to fight him. He would buy her lingerie—scandalous lingerie. She would model it for him, and sometimes he would masturbate while he watched her move about the bedroom in sheer lace panties and nylons. Sometimes she would bend over the bed to tease him. Now his obsession only came in fits and starts.

A few dull knocks came from down the hallway. She slipped off her heels and crept silently to the study, then peeked around the doorframe. Lucius knelt behind Kenneth's desk. He tugged at the bottom drawer. She watched as he pulled on the handle. Curious. Kenneth kept some nude photographs he had taken of her in one of the bottom drawers. She thought he had moved them, in case Beatrice ever went poking around. Perhaps they were still there. Did Lucius know about them? Her eyebrows drew together. Lucius grasp the top edge of the desk for leverage and tugged with all his might, to no avail. He was like a starving animal who smelled food. The telephone rang in the kitchen. He looked up, and she threw herself against the wall outside the doorway. She hurried down the corridor and made her way to the front door, where she slipped on her heels. As far as he knew, she picked up Beatrice and made some stops before they got back to the house. He never looked in the garage, otherwise he would have seen her car. It seemed like his least favorite place. Strange for the son of a mechanic. She waited while the phone rang and eventually stopped. He never came out to answer the phone in the kitchen, nor did she hear his footsteps, so he must still be in the study. She took her heels off once more and crept back to have a look.

She found him still at Kenneth's desk. He rummaged through the center drawer and found a letter opener. With it, he first poked at the lock, perhaps attempting to turn it. When that failed, he worked to pry open the bottom drawer. From where she stood, she was unable to see his efforts, but his body and frustrated expression told her everything she needed to know. His determination, for whatever reason, had made her uneasy. Did he know about the nude photographs of her? Or? Dear God, had he already seen them? She slipped her heels back on. When she stepped into the room, her heels made a sharp tap on the hardwood floor. That got his attention. He sprung up wide-eyed. He gently placed the letter opener on top of the desk with his hand over it. She saw his attempt to hide it. Silly. A coy smile curled inside her.

"What are you up to in here?"

"Uh? Nothing."

He stepped from behind the desk. He had his shirt cuffs rolled like a diligent man at work, and his young pale face was shiny and slick with perspiration. For a brief moment, he reminded her of Kenneth during the winter months, when he had no color, and after a bout of lovemaking, his skin had the same sheen.

"*Nothing?* That's not what it looks like. You seem eager to get inside Kenneth's desk. What do you hope to find there?"

Did he hope to find her, or rather, the nude photographs of her? Her first reaction was horror and embarrassment, but witnessing the teenage boy twist in his own hot soup delighted her. His eyes looked strained. His lips tightened as if he feared secrets might slip out. Her coy inner smile curled even more. He lowered his head, but his gaze remained on her. This delighted her more. A wave of heat traveled up her body and settled into her chest. The texture of her lace brassiere became more apparent as her sensitive nipples tightened.

"I was only snooping. Sorry."

Young man, you'll have to do better than that.

"I know you are well aware that Mr. Crane's desk is off limits. He's been generous to allow you in here in the first place to admire the photographs and to study his art books."

A question struck her. She doubted Kenneth would show Lucius his nude pictures of her. Why the *hell* would he? Kenneth admired the boy as an artist and photographer, but the idea was absurd and obscene. Was that the reason for his obsession with her? Could Kenneth have——?

"I'm sorry. Yes, I'm aware."

"I think you're done in here, wouldn't you agree?"

She crossed her arms.

"Oh, yes. Yes, of course."

She moved into the room, to allow him free travel to the exit, like allowing a timid animal an escape route. He took it with his head lowered.

"Sorry."

He mumbled on his way out of the study.

34

Lucius sat with Mrs. Crane out on the patio. It was early winter, with a few minor flurries, but the ground remained a dull green. The evening temperature was mild, yet they wore their heavier coats. Mrs. Crane sat wrapped in a brown and cream-colored, houndstooth, knee-length coat with fur lining the collar and cuffs. She also brought out a wool throw to cover her legs. He wore his dark gray Navy peacoat. They both looked like two people dressed for a lengthy wait out in the cold.

They had brought out with them a bottle of rosé. Their half-drank glasses sat on the wicker patio table next to the ashtray and her pack of near empty cigarettes. They both stared out into the lifeless backyard.

Beatrice was away at Mount Southington for some skiing with Stephanie Norris and her family. Mr. Crane was again in Hartford for, yet again, another over-night stay. A dull headache came on when Lucius thought of Mr. Crane. It had been almost two months, and he never confronted Mr. Crane about the photographs he found in his study, and Mr. Crane never asked him if he had been snooping. As far as he knew, Mrs. Crane said nothing. It was all a stalemate.

The crisp air stiffened his nose hair. He scanned the bare trees like he did with everything, in search for the right composition. With the squirrels tucked away, the world outside was like one of his photographs, fixed and frozen in time.

The delicate inhalation and soft pucker of moist lips woke him. Mrs. Crane sat comfortably in her padded wicker chair, her arm cocked on the armrest after she took a drag on her cigarette. He wanted to say something, anything, instead he filled both wine glasses and took his from the table. Her gaze remained some place outside or beyond, but there was a slight bend in her lips. Was she smiling? Her eyes told him no. He drank. The wine warmed his chest. His gaze returned to the outside. He wanted to know where her gaze was, so maybe he could join her in that place far away.

"Kenneth needs to balance his priorities. Work and ambition are one thing, but he has a family. He has me."

Was she talking to him, or thinking out loud? It was unimaginable for him to call Mr. Crane, Kenneth. It surprised him that she used his Christian name, unless it was the wine. He imagined when he was older and more on an equal footing, he could address the man by his first name. How was he supposed to answer her? Mr. Crane had to speak for himself. Mrs. Crane should pose her questions to him. He inhaled slow and deep.

"I—I'm happy I'm here with you. I'm sorry to say this, and hope you won't hate me for it, but he doesn't deserve you."

He swallowed at his own declaration. She raised an eyebrow, then snorted, and picked up her glass of wine from the table.

"He was far from deserving of me when we first married. So—you enjoy sitting with me? This old woman—sour with her life, and with her absentee husband."

Her gaze met his. It was one of the few times she spoke playfully and sarcastically.

"Yes."

It was all he could say, but it was true. A cool sweat made his shirt under his coat cling to his back. Her eyebrows rose, then fell, and a slight hum passed her lips.

"If you don't think Kenneth deserves me, an opinion I suppose we both now share, then who does?"

She sounded as though she needed validation that she was desirable. He was unsure if he was still breathing. It was a question she would have never asked, at least not to him, or entertained without the help of the wine. When she gazed at him with her pale sky-blue eyes and waited for his answer, his chest tensed as he struggled to speak.

"Me."

His own voice startled him. A whisper, but a firm declaration just the same.

"I deserve—I mean—I adore you."

The words that followed passed his lips came out like spurts of water from a jug. She chuckled. This time, her dismissiveness seemed strangely encouraging and made him feel closer to her. Her laughter ended with a roll of her eyes and she turned her gaze outward to the unknown, perhaps where she had peered before. She took a drag on her cigarette. He watched her with interest. The angle of her arm as she brought the cigarette to her lips, the way her body eased into the chair's cushions, especially with the more wine she drank, and how she crossed her legs, all captured him.

"You should date Beatrice's friend Stephanie. I know she has an interest in you. She has for some time. The Norrises are decent people, too. Though June can be a bit dull."

She puffed on her cigarette, then cocked her head and blew the smoke upward. He peered out into the yard. He had given up, for the moment, his search for the destination of her gaze, and Stephanie's kiss slipped into his mind. No.

"She's just a girl."

His voice was flat, but his declaration was resounding. Her suggestion filled him with disbelief. What could Stephanie possibly offer him? He wanted to laugh at the absurdity of it, but instead, he wrinkled his lips. From the corner of his eye, he watched her lift her glass and drink. His gaze never left the backyard, but he could still see her. After she lowered her glass, she lifted her chin.

"She *is* a young woman, and you *are* a young man."

"What can she possibly offer me?"

She snorted.

"She can offer you what most men prize—her age."

"She lacks elegance, maturity, sophistication."

"That will come with time."

He glanced at her. Her eyebrow rose, which suggested she doubted Stephanie's capability. Maturity, yes—elegance and sophistication, no. He looked out into the backyard.

"Maybe. I want *what is*, and not *what could be*."

When he glanced back at her, she was staring at him.

"Is that so?"

"Yes."

"I think it's time for one of us to leave."

"What—why?"

She bent forward, crushed her cigarette in the ashtray, sat her empty wineglass on the coffee table, and stood. She glared at him as if his presence was no longer welcome. He sat his glass, still half full of rosé, on the table next to hers and stood.

"All right."

He stepped cautiously and stood before her. In her heels she stood an inch taller than him. She put her hands in her coat pockets. It was like her closing the door on him.

"Do you really want me to go?"

Her hardened gaze penetrated his, but it was different than the ones she gave him when she wanted him to leave. He ran his fingers up the seam of her coat. He slipped his hand in the opening between the buttons and touched her breast. His jaw tightened in anticipation of her slap across his face. When no protest came, he became aware of the rise and fall of her chest. Her face softened into the placid mask she usually wore. The tip of his finger found her hardened nipple that poked from underneath her lace bra. Her nostrils flared and her body tensed. She slipped her hand from her pocket and gently removed his wandering hand from inside her coat.

"You should call Stephanie tomorrow and ask her out on a date. She won't say no."

She sat back in her chair, filled her glass with the rosé, and lit a fresh cigarette. Her gaze was once more away from him, somewhere in the beyond. He might as well be a ghost, or invisible. He cleared his throat.

"Goodnight Mrs. Crane."

He glanced back at her once more before going inside the house. As he lie in his bed, his eyes travelled the abstract shadows of the tree limbs cast across the ceiling by the streetlamp. Although the room was cool, his body was on fire.

The texture of the bedsheets and the weight of the comforter increased his arousal. He had touched her body. She must have enjoyed it, if only in that moment. He stroked himself as he thought about her breast and the stiffness of her nipple. One day, he promised himself, he would have her, *Eleanor, Ella.*

35

After Beatrice peed, she examined her naked self in the bathroom mirror. There was lipstick smudged beyond the boundaries of her lips, as well as two transferred lipstick marks, one on her neck and one on her collarbone. It was her lipstick. Her reflection stared back at her with a tentative smile. Her lips parted and her mouth hung open then she released an astonished breath that shook her body. She had finally done it.

There was no sound of approaching footsteps, but there was a creak on the wood floors in the hallway. Lucius appeared in the open doorway. He was in his white boxers, and his pale flesh was only a shade or two darker. She grinned at the sight of his disheveled hair. What she found most comical, though, was her lipstick smeared across his mouth. His eyes widened and his lips parted at the sight of her complete nakedness. She raised her forearm to cover her small breasts and cupped her hand over her crotch in a sudden attempt at modesty. They had taken off their clothes under the covers of his bed, so they saw little of each other's bodies.

"Hey."

His voice was soft and cautious. It reverberated in the tiled bathroom. Her lips curled into a soft smile, which she quickly vanquished.

"Hey yourself."

She took her bathrobe from the hook on the backside of the door, and slipped it on. His eyebrows rose.

"Are you okay?"

She drew together the robe and tied the cloth belt around her waist.

"Yes. Are you?"

"Yes."

His voice was a hollow whisper.

"Come here, you have lipstick on your face."

She wiped the lipstick from his mouth with a damp washcloth. He chuckled when he glimpsed himself in the mirror, then they both laughed. He combed his fingers through his hair. After she washed her face, he took her by the waist and pulled her close to him. They kissed. His kiss was passionate, but he lacked technique. At least his lips were soft. Passion with the need of practice.

They both brushed their teeth at the sink. He rinsed and spat.

"It's crazy that Mrs. Crane, I mean Eleanor, would drive up to Hartford this late, and in this weather."

She wrinkled her lips. Why must he always bring her up?

"She'll be fine."

"What time do you think they'll come home?"

"I don't know, but we should sleep in our separate rooms in case they come home early."

"All right."

While she lie in bed with the comforter and bedsheets pulled up to her chin, she thought about the condom he had. Where did he get it? He said it was his first time too. Was it? All the moments when it was the three of them, she was unable to think of any times when he and Stephanie were alone long enough to do anything. He took her out on three dates, mostly at the insistence of Eleanor, but Stephanie always told her how things went. She said her father thought Lucius was strange, and he wanted his daughter to see someone else. She smirked at Stephanie's remark that her father thought Lucius was strange. He *is* strange. She decided that was one of his redeeming qualities.

As for any romance, Stephanie told her they kissed, and he even touched her breast, but it was outside her blouse. She said he never took it further, and at moments he seemed distant, as though he was thinking of someone else. Me? She snuggled her covers under her chin and smiled. She imagined Lucius never said or did anything out of respect for her father, and maybe even Eleanor.

What now? What would she tell Stephanie, if anything? If she said anything, Stephanie might tell Eleanor out of spite, or worse, her father. Regardless, she won. They were each other's first. She believed him. It seemed right to her. Were they now boyfriend and girlfriend? She doubted her father and Eleanor would approve.

The floor creaked in the hallway outside her closed door. Her lips curled. She went to her door to see if he came to give her a goodnight kiss. She hoped it was more than a simple visit to the bathroom. When she guessed he was outside her door, she opened it quickly to surprise him.

Eleanor stood there in wet stocking feet, hair disheveled, and the bottom of her dress looked heavy and damp.

"There was an accident, and the roads are closed due to the snow and ice. Even God is against me. Your father wouldn't have wanted me to come to Hartford anyway."

Eleanor gave her a conciliatory smile and sighed.

"Good night."

"Sorry, good night."

She watched her walk quietly down the hallway to her bedroom. There was less poise in her gate. She looked defeated. Beatrice wrinkled her lips and raised her eyebrows. The door down the hallway closed, and Eleanor vanished behind it. She glanced over at Lucius's room. She wondered if he was asleep. A smile returned to her face before she closed her bedroom door.

36

Kenneth stood shirtless in his boxers at the bedroom window of his Hartford apartment. The evening approached, yet the streetlights had yet to come on. The snow had picked up. It came down in large, heavy wet flakes and collected on the outside window ledges. Everything below, cars in the lot, the sidewalks, sat blanketed in white. He brought a half-smoked cigarette to his lips and took a long drag.

She wanted more. They all did, except Phoebe. Mila left frustrated less than twenty minutes ago. She threatened to look for another job. She told him there were other families that would be happy to have her clean their homes or be a nanny for their children. He suggested perhaps she do that. Maybe it was getting too much for the girl to be in his home and to clean and prepare dinner for his family and be around his wife. *His Wife*. It was the title she longed for. He felt flattered and frustrated that maybe his suggestions she took as promises. They were only suggestions made in the heat of sex; he told himself.

Phoebe, that girl, was something else entirely. She wanted to fool around with him, yet she made no demands. She seemed to know where she stood, and that was fine with her. He took the last puff on the cigarette as it burned its way down to the filter. Two streams of smoke blew and burned from his nostrils. That girl! Hard to believe she was Lucius's aunt. Darius's sister. Sure, he could buy that.

"*Phoebe*. Hell, she's got me saying her name."

He snorted. He went to crush out his cigarette in the ashtray on the nightstand. The bedsheets lay clumped at the foot of the bed and half on the floor from his romp with Mila. He smiled and raised an eyebrow when he spotted her panties she left under the bed. She was meticulous. She would never forget any of her clothing. Her panties were a message to other women he might invite to his apartment. If Eleanor came up to see him, he was certain it would thrill Mila if Eleanor found them. He picked them up and sat on the edge of the bed. They were taupe-colored with lace borders, much more elegant than what she usually wore. She must have bought them just for him and their time together. He brought them to his nose. The lace border smelled of her perfume. A change in fragrance. His eyebrow rose. For him, he assumed. The crotch was damp and her scent still lingered. It made him hard. He stretched out on the bed with her panties covering his face and tended to his erection.

37

"What is going on in here?"

Mrs. Crane stood in the doorway in her stocking feet, her heels in hand. She must have known or suspected. She was supposed to be out for another hour, enough time for Lucius and Beatrice to have a moment. They covered themselves with the sheet on Beatrice's bed.

"Out!"

Mrs. Crane pointed to the hallway. She glared at Lucius. He slipped from Beatrice's bed, covered himself with his wadded up pile of clothes and hurried out past Mrs. Crane, who then closed Beatrice's door. Mrs. Crane's voice rose, dull from behind the door. He tried to listen, but was stunned. He hurried to his bedroom, closed the door, and jammed his legs into his trousers. The sharp clack of heels on the hallway floors came beyond the closed door. As he buttoned his shirt, the door swung open and Mrs. Crane entered. She closed the door behind her. Her face was flush and some of her curls had come undone. She glared at him for a moment.

"Is this what it has come to—you taking advantage of the situation—of us?"

He stood silent, heat travelled up from his chest and into his face as he buttoned his shirt. He lowered his head, then rubbed the back of his neck.

"You have a lot of nerve. Mr. Crane brought you into our home. We all accepted you. You have taken advantage of our generosity."

"I'm sorry."

It was all he could say. His eyes rose from the floor to meet her gaze.

"Mr. Crane and I will have to discuss this matter. You and Beatrice are to stay in your rooms until it's time for dinner."

His eyes widened, and his eyebrows rose. He swallowed at her icy gaze. There was a hint of sadness in her pale sky-blue eyes, or maybe it was disappointment.

"Can I stay in the darkroom until dinner?"

"No. You've lost that privilege, at least for today. It will be up to Mr. Crane whether he will allow you to use the darkroom again."

His mouth hung open. He was about to protest, but thought better of it. "Okay."

He got his nerve back enough to raise his chin. She huffed, then left his room. After she closed the door, he listened to her heels strike the floor until they faded. He sat on the edge of his bed and ran his fingers through his hair.

"Damn."

He had to have made her feel foolish. All those times she invited him to sit with her out on the patio. She even offered him wine. She never offered him wine when Mr. Crane was home. If he lost access to the darkroom, that would be a disaster. He glanced at the dresser. The Leica sat in front of the mirror. The lens pointed at him. He felt its stare. Would Mr. Crane take back his camera? His lips drew into a tight line. He held the back of his neck with his fingers laced together. Gone. More things he cherished, gone. What would he say to Mr. Crane? What *could* he possibly say to soften the fact that he had been having sex with his daughter in secret? He never even asked Mr. and Mrs. Crane if he could date Beatrice. At least with that, he would know how they felt about him being romantically involved with her. The muscles of his jaw tightened when he thought of tonight's dinner and how tense it would be.

After Ms. Käthe and Ms. Mila departed, everyone sat at the dinner table awaiting Mr. Crane's arrival. Mrs. Crane sat at the end of the table. Her face was placid, with no indication of her mood. Beatrice fidgeted. She avoided looking at him, and for an instant when their eyes met, they both quickly looked away. He focused on the glass of water that sat in front of his plate. They might send Beatrice away for her final year of high school, but he doubted Mr. Crane would do that. Mrs. Crane would be delighted to be rid of her. As for him, he graduated in less than two months. Would they send him away or allow him to stay? He chewed his lip while they all waited. Then Mr. Crane ambled into the dining room.

"Hello everyone. Sorry I'm late. Dinner looks and smells wonderful."

His tie, still knotted, hung loose around his open collar, and he had his sleeves rolled up his forearms. The tension in Lucius's shoulders abated. Mrs. Crane must not have told him. Or was he pretending to be upbeat to keep from exploding? Perhaps they would get through dinner without any drama, and if they managed, it would only be a momentary reprieve.

"Hello Dear. We're happy you made it home for dinner."

Mrs. Crane's tone carried a hint of sarcasm. Both Lucius and Beatrice straightened up in their seats and glanced at one another.

"Hello-Hi."

They spoke in unison. Mr. Crane pulled out his chair and sat. He first took a sip of wine, then he unfolded his cloth napkin in his lap.

"So, Bea, Lucius, how are you two doing?"

"Um? Fine," Beatrice said.

Lucius was relieved to hear Beatrice's voice, but when Mr. Crane looked his way, he had to say something.

"Same here. I'm okay."

The corners of Mr. Crane's mouth turned down and his eyebrows rose. He looked down at his plate. His steak and vegetables seemed to hold more interest to him.

"Good, good, sounds exciting."

He cut into his sirloin while he spoke.

"How was your day, Dear?" Mrs. Crane asked.

As her words travelled the length of the table, Beatrice and Lucius turned their attention to their plates of food. Lucius waited for Mrs. Crane to fill Mr. Crane in on the day's events. She said nothing the entire time, either out of courtesy toward Mr. Crane, or to make both Lucius and Beatrice sweat. It was punishment in one measure or another. When dinner ended, Mr. Crane inquired as to why Lucius and Beatrice hardly touched their meals. Both only mumbled incoherently. Mr. and Mrs. Crane retired to the screened in patio with their wine and cigarettes as usual. Lucius and Beatrice glanced at one another before heading upstairs to their rooms.

Lucius stood before his bedroom door. He glanced back at Beatrice, who stood outside her room.

"What do you think will happen—to us?"

She stared at him with a grim expression. He sighed. They have been having sex in secret over the past two months.

"We—I messed up. I should have asked your father if I could take you out, then at least he would know we were being honest with him."

"I guess so. If we dated, they would have watched us closely to make sure we weren't fooling around."

He raised his eyebrows. The way she said it made it sounded like she cared more about the sex than anything else.

"Do you think he'll kick me out?"

She scratched a fingernail against the moulding of her bedroom door frame.

"I don't know. My father doesn't get angry easily, or often. You have to do a lot to get him going."

"Don't you think we did enough?"

"We sure did."

Her eyebrow rose. The corner of her lips curled into a soft smile.

"I hope he'll let me stay until I graduate."

Whatever subtle illusion of a smile she had vanished.

"Me, too."

38

Spring was a month away. Lucius would graduate in May. Instead of planning for a momentous occasion, Kenneth planned to send him off to New York as soon as possible. He sat out on the screened in patio with Eleanor. A bottle of wine and a pack of cigarettes sat on the wicker coffee table. He puffed on his cigarette, while Eleanor stared out into the backyard, her glass of wine in one hand and a cigarette in the other.

"Are you sure this is the best course of action?"

Her lit cigarette dangled between her fingers.

He took a sharp breath between his teeth before he blew out the smoke he held.

"It's the only course of action. For Beatrice's sake. Besides, I thought you wanted the boy out of the house."

"I find him amusing. Besides, I thought you admired the young man. Who cares if he dates Beatrice?"

"Apparently he doesn't. They skipped that part and went straight to bed. If he asked me now, I would tell him it's too late for that. Why couldn't he date Stephanie Norris?"

"You can't be serious, Kenneth. That girl, polite as she may be, just does not have *it*."

"Have what?"

He huffed out his words.

"*It.* That *je ne sais quoi*. That attracts Lucius. You can tell the way he looks through the lens of his camera if he's seeing it."

"I think he sees it in you."

"Perhaps. Like what you used to see in me?"

"I still do."

"Do you?"

He took a healthy drink of his wine.

"Of course. Don't be silly."

"I've never been accused of being silly."

"Can we talk about the boy? New York will be a dream for him. It was for me. I have a friend there who is a fashion photographer. Otto Schenker, a crazy eccentric German, but one with an exceptional eye. He's agreed to take Lucius under his wing."

"He sounds like a sadist."

Kenneth chuckled, puffed his cigarette and bent forward so he could flick his ashes into the ashtray. He took the moment to fill his wineglass. Eleanor held out her glass, and he filled hers as well.

"As I was saying, this is an exceptional opportunity for Lucius. He's meant to be a photographer. What kind of photographer, who knows? So far he's mainly shot portraits, but I kind of got a feeling he will love the fashion world."

"Have you spoken to him yet? Does he know what's coming?"

"Yes. I think in the back of his mind he always knew this day was coming. Probably the first day he arrived at our house. Now that he's older, he's been challenging me more. Probably his age. I suppose I was that way too."

He peered out into the backyard. From his periphery, he saw Eleanor take a drag on her cigarette. He wanted to gaze at her like he used to, but found it difficult. She peered into the backyard as well. It always seemed easy for her to look past people. He thought it made her appear aloof and snotty. A trait he strangely found attractive in her. After she took a sip, she lowered her glass and rested her arm on the armrest.

"I suppose."

If she never spoke, she could convince him to question his own existence. He sunk back into the chair's cushions and took a drink. The effects of the wine had yet to soften the sharp edges. He took another drink, sighed and put his head back on the chair.

THREE

39

Otto Schenker's head sunk back into the cushions of a maroon colored sofa in his Manhattan studio. He groaned and sucked in air. A golden-haired model knelt between the older man's parted knees. Her head bobbed with Otto's cock in her mouth. He clenched the cushions. The sofa, a prop paid for and unclaimed by a past client, sat against a wall of windows without curtains or blinds.

"Ja—ja—that's my little French girl."

Through the cracked door to the storeroom Lucius watched as he lie on his side in the dark. He apprenticed for a year under the New York photographer. Otto offered him a place to sleep, if one could call it that. It was a twin-sized mattress on the floor in the small storeroom connected to the Manhattan studio. The first month, he missed his bed at the Cranes, but convinced himself, if he were Tom Sawyer, that's how ole Tom would have roughed it. He doubted Tom Sawyer ever saw a middle-aged man getting blown by a golden-haired girl barely twenty years old, on a modern maroon European-styled sofa. Otto Schenker liked people to watch, and Lucius liked to watch. He sometimes even took pictures with Mr. Crane's old Leica. Two hidden film rolls yet to be developed. Otto never invited any of the girls that came to the studio back to his apartment. He liked to fuck them there on the sofa.

"Oh-oh-oh, scheisse."

Otto's body went stiff, then collapsed into the cushions. The French girl, the model, Helene might have been her name, thumbed the drip of his cum from her cheek into her mouth. Otto photographed her earlier in the day for a cosmetic advertisement. Face cream. Girls her age never wore skin cream, never needed it. He took a liking to her. She told him he reminded her of her uncle. Uncle Otto. Lucius chuckled inside. She asked if he could help her career, with all of his connections, but first she would help him release the tension from his body, to draw the stick from his tight German ass as she told him. Lucius covered his mouth to keep from bursting out with laughter, which would have made the girl aware of his presence in the storeroom.

He moved his arm from under his head and lowered his head to the pillow-less mattress. He watched the two through tired eyes. Their conversation turned to muddled noise. Then they moved out of view. He could only see a fraction of the studio from the storeroom.

"Ja-ja-ja, good night."

Otto's impatient voice. It was all Lucius heard before the studio's metal door slammed shut with a heavy clang and the girl, with her dreams of making it big, pushed out into the night. The shuffle of Otto's loafers echoed off the tall white walls. The distant musical sound of running water came from the sink in the bathroom across the studio. Finally Otto departed, with a softer clang of metal when he closed and locked the door, and left Lucius to the hollow cavity of the studio and its stillness. The muted sound of taxi horns rose from the streets below. City life. Opportunities. A future.

Tomorrow was a big day. Otto Schenker usually attended the various fashion shows in the city, especially the big ones in February and September. Although it was June, and to Lucius's astonishment, Otto invited him to accompany him to a smaller, yet exclusive show. Mrs. Crane had phoned to let him know that she and Beatrice would be in the city and they would like to see him.

He missed Beatrice's graduation due to the demands of the studio. Now that they would be in town, he longed to see them. Beatrice would visit Columbia and New York University, two schools she was interested in. Mrs. Crane told Lucius that Mr. Crane wanted Beatrice to attend the University of Hartford, so she would be closer to home. Although she applied and received a scholarship, Mrs. Crane was certain Beatrice would end up in New York. He wondered why she told him all of this. He swallowed, his eyelids heavy. Did she expect him to look out for her? He was having a tough enough time on his own. Schenker paid him a fraction of what a professional assistant would make, sighting that he had it made, a place to stay, in New York City, for free. His only burden was buying his own food, clothing, and film for the Leica. He snorted. He would still be happy to see them.

A soft sigh passed his lips as he drifted into dreamland. A final waking breath and a mumble.

"Mrs. Crane—Eleanor—Ella."

40

Lucius felt Eleanor's gaze. She arrived at Otto Schenker's studio without Beatrice and told him she would explain after he finished working. He had her sit where the only place there was to sit in the studio, on the sofa. Otto's filthy fuck sofa. He draped a backdrop cloth over it and told her that something had spilled on the seat. Otto's filthy spermatozoa. He imagined the old man's sperm wiggling into the weave of the cushion covers to wait for someone to impregnate when they sat down. She sat and watched him as he directed the two models that came earlier to pay Schenker for portfolio shots. Otto shot them with the Hasselblad, then departed before Mrs. Crane arrived. Lucius wanted to introduce her to the photographer, but it would have to be another time. The models agreed to stay longer and let Lucius photograph them. One a blonde and the other a brunette. Both were tall, with long legs and lithe bodies. Both with foreign accents. He promised them free portfolio prints in addition to Schenker's paid prints. Never turn down free shit in New York City. That was one of the first lessons Otto gave him.

"Okay, very nice, turn to your left, hold, good-good."

He mimicked Otto's direction. He glanced to Mrs. Crane, who sat with her knees together, ankles crossed and her hands in her lap. She peered up at the exposed pipes that ran the length of the ceiling. Painted white, they matched the tall white walls. The paint on the pipes was thick with noticeable brush marks, and white dried drips like frozen semen. Her eyes lowered and met his, as if meant to be. He smiled a soft, toothless smile. She offered nothing back but her gaze with those pale sky-blue eyes. She turned her attention to the models, and he went back to work.

The sun moved to a point where the studio went gray. He only got thirty minutes to shoot both models, twenty frames on a thirty-six exposure roll. It was better than nothing. He lowered the Leica, thanked both models, both girls kissed him on the cheek, which raised an eyebrow on Mrs. Crane's face. She watched them leave. They moved like graceful reeds that swayed in the wind. The heavy metal door shut with a dull clunk.

"That was exhilarating. You've got the start of a beautiful harem."

He chuckled.

"A lot of the models in the city are from all over the place. Many from Europe. They usually kiss Otto and not me. I'm just the peon."

"Not today."

He grinned. He imagined she smiled at him on the inside.

"Nope, not today. What'd you think?"

She went to the dressing area where there was a lighted mirror. Her heels clicked on the concrete floor. She fussed with her hair and examined her makeup.

"Do you think I'm as pretty as those girls?"

He sat the Leica on the corner worktable, next to the case Mr. Crane gave him to protect and transport the camera. He gazed at her. Her back was to him. Her emerald green ruffled skirt cut above her knees danced around her thighs and cascaded over her buttocks as she bent to look into the mirror. She was a sight. His eyes descended her legs to the beige heels she wore with the black lacquered bottoms, then back up her nude colored nylons. She turned around when he said nothing. Her pale sky-blue eyes examined his face as if she could extract his thoughts. She touched the pearl buttons that ran down the length of her green matching blouse with long, sheer green sleeves. It had a broad collar and the top four buttons were unbuttoned, which exposed her collar bones.

"Do you like it?"

"Huh?"

"My dress? I got it at Bloomingdales, here in the city."

"Oh, yes. It's beautiful. You look lovely."

The "You look lovely" comment he picked up from Mr. Crane. A comment he adored and cherished enough to only use it when it felt right. It always felt right regarding Mrs. Crane.

"Lucius—about my question. Do you think I'm as pretty as those girls?"

It was an odd question. He never thought of her as *a girl*. How could he make a comparison? She was *all* woman. He leaned back against the edge of the worktable as he took her in. The inside of his mouth became wet.

"I think you know how I feel about you. That's never wavered."

Her chest rose as she took in a deep breath, then released it in slow exhaustion.

"That's not what I'm asking. We're only discussing beauty and nothing more."

"All right."

He would have given her his answer straight away, but he wanted to apply controlled restraint. Something he knew she would respect. She put her hands on her hips, not in a pose, but perhaps to make herself more visible to him. She bent one of her knees so her hips were on an angle. He supposed she got that from one of the fashion magazines she purchased from time to time.

"Yes."

She tilted her head in a gesture of disbelief, and her gaze held suspicion.

"Yes—yes, you're stunning. You're more beautiful than they are—than they could *ever* be."

Her nostrils flared as if to breathe in his fear, if he had any, which he had none.

"That's sweet, thank you Lucius."

He felt like a child who had given her a crayon drawing.

"Show me some of Otto Schenker's work. Kenneth always spoke so highly of him. He even used the word genius."

His eyebrows rose, and he snorted. He thought Otto Schenker was an excellent photographer, but gifted, or a genius—no. Ever since he left the Crane's house, when she spoke of Mr. Crane, she used his Christian name, Kenneth. It felt odd, like knowing a dirty little secret. He was unsure, but wanted to believe that she thought of him as an adult.

"Sure. He has some portfolios of his latest work in the storeroom. I'll bring them out."

He went into the storeroom past his mattress that lie on the floor and pulled two large hardcover portfolios from a row of deep vertical shelves meant to store large sheets of artist's matting materials in an upright position. She stood at the center of the studio. Some light had come back, but not good enough for him to photograph her. He stood outside the storeroom and gazed at her until she turned around.

"Here's some of his latest work. He's going to put some of these in a gallery showing, so we'll have to be careful how we handle the prints."

She nodded. They both went to the worktable, and he opened the first portfolio. He turned the large prints by pinching the corners on one side. The prints were all black and white photographs of models in contemporary clothing, but the poses and energy were edgier than most of Schenker's commercial work. Her eyes widened, but she said nothing.

"Crazy stuff. I wouldn't have thought to pose the model that way. One of the first things he taught me was the photographer has to *create* the shot. Mr. Crane always told me the photographer has to *wait* for the shot. Schenker told me, if I'm going to think like that, I should be a landscape photographer."

Heat rose in his chest and face. He believed in what Mr. Crane taught him, even though Otto shot it down.

"He's right."

"Who?"

"Otto Schenker."

"Really?"

She tilted her head and squinted her eyes.

"Okay. I understand Schenker's 'you have to create the shot,' but I want to photograph people, not landscapes. I want to capture moments—natural moments without my interference."

She was silent for a moment.

"Lucius, you're more of an artist than I imagined. If something inside you is telling you what is right, then follow your instincts. You can still learn from other photographers, but never forget your internal compass."

His eyebrows rose, and he took in a long breath. Her comment gave him hope, hope that she saw him, a maturing man and not a boy, not a teenager. The scent of her perfume invaded his nostrils. He wanted to kiss her at that moment, but he was afraid. She moved closer to him so their hips touched. When he lifted and turned to the next print, his elbow brushed her breast, not just once, but twice. She said nothing. Inside him was like the inside of a burning house. No where to run. After they looked through both portfolios, he excused himself and went to the bathroom, where he splashed water on his face and examined his reflection.

When he returned, she was looking around the studio. She held her handbag in front of her with both hands. When she saw him, she glanced at her wristwatch.

"They said Beatrice would be finished with the tour of the NYU campus at 1:30. I told her I would return, hopefully with you, then you two could get lunch."

"She didn't want you to stick around?"

"She ran into Robbie Glasser, a boy she went to high school with. Regardless, I doubt she would have wanted me around. It was Kenneth's idea to have the two of us visit both NYU and Columbia. He thought it would be a good opportunity for us to spend time together. To bond. It's too late, if you ask me."

"Oh?"

"So, are you free? Beatrice would love to see you."

She sounded more like Beatrice's servant, set to fetch him, than her college campus chaperone. That aside, it was pleasantly odd to hear *her* request *his* time.

"Yeah, sure."

✺

That night, alone in the studio, his gaze traced the shadows on the ceiling. The light that came from the large bank of windows and filtered through the narrow open doorway to the storeroom acted like a closed down aperture. He calculated f/11 or maybe even to f/16. It would require a slow shutter speed to get a decent exposure.

Vertically stored, long paper backdrop rolls towered upward. His eyes always followed them up, like it was the only place for mice to climb. He stretched out on top of the mattress on the floor among Otto Schenker's photography lights, stands, and other equipment broken down to make the best use of the limited space. Lucius imagined Schenker slept on the same mattress when he worked late and before he acquired the sofa that sat out in the studio.

"Heh."

The sound of his own voice surprised him. When he and Mrs. Crane located Beatrice on the NYU campus, she was talking to Robbie Glasser. He was tall and stocky. Lucius imagined Robbie must have played football in high school. Robbie was younger than him, but he had a deep laugh and firm handshake, which made him feel like the boy's junior. Beatrice invited Robbie to join them for lunch, but he already had plans to meet up with other friends. Lucius was thankful, and supposed Mrs. Crane was as well, but if Beatrice wanted to run off and join Robbie and his friends for lunch, he would be alone with Mrs. Crane. Robbie never offered.

The half muted sound of car horns carried up from the streets and filtered through the narrow open studio windows. He smiled when he thought of how buoyant Beatrice was during lunch. She looked good, a step up toward womanhood from the teenager he knew. She talked with such excitement, while Mrs. Crane was almost entirely silent. Perhaps she wanted Beatrice to have her moment. The memory that clung to him was when Mrs. Crane's leg brushed against his during lunch. He was sure he could still feel the energy from her body transferred to his. His breath entered and exited slow and methodical. The head of his cock dragged against his abdomen as it thickened and rose toward his navel. He imagined how it must feel to be inside her. He held on to that thought and to himself until he reached release.

41

A statuesque blonde in a black leather outfit that barely covered her crotch and nipples led a balding, shirtless, silver chest haired man with a body the shape of a barrel out of the living room and up the stairs to one of the Manhattan brownstone playrooms. As they navigated around the people who sat on the couches, including Lucius, the man lead by the blonde bumped his knee when they passed. The man said nothing, his attention completely on being led to the slaughter. They disappear up the stairs. Guests milled in and out of the open doors on the main floor to watch or to take part.

Almost everyone at the afterparty wore scandalous leather outfits, even Otto, but not Lucius, who wore a t-shirt with a leather jacket and pants he borrowed from Otto. Otto gave him a sour look at his unwillingness to dress for the occasion, but that changed after the old photographer was on his third cocktail. He stumbled in front of Lucius, his leather codpiece at his eye level. Otto held his drink in one hand and put his other on his hip. He swayed unsteadily and jerked his body at every word he spoke.

"Boy. Why are you sitting here?"

He turned. His drink sloshed on Lucius's knee.

"Don't you see the wonderful party around you? Look at these beautiful people. They are frolicking and having fun. You are not. What's wrong with you?"

Otto's German accent softened as the alcohol softened him. He gave Schenker a weary smile. Otto always looked comical when he preached.

"I have told no one you had your birthday recently. Big one. Twenty-one. Would that put you more in the moo-ood if I make an announcement?"

He drew out, mood, and sounded like a cow. Lucius sat up but avoided leaning forward as Otto stood uncomfortably close between his knees, his leather codpiece jutting in his face.

"Oh no, that won't be necessary."

He appeared not to have heard him. Instead, he sipped his cocktail and stared off elsewhere. It was a long stare, as if the man's brain had run a calculation by way of carrier pigeon and he was waiting for the damn bird to return.

"Colette!" Otto shouted.

He held his drinking glass up high. His expression, one first of stupid surprise, then his lips contorted into a broad smile. All teeth. Otto looked down at him. He patted Lucius's head.

"Boy. I must go and have some fun. I suggest you do as well."

With that, Otto made his way around the couch and through the throng of leather clad artists, models, and anxious benefactors. Lucius shook his head and snorted. The two girls that sat on the couch next to him started kissing, then one straddled the other and cupped the face of the girl beneath, all while they tried to devour one another. He stood. His act to give them some privacy was ridiculous. Everyone was pairing off or forming little fuck groups of three to five. One of the waitresses in black leather panties and a tuxedo top walked past him caring a tray of dirty glasses.

"Wait, excuse me. I'll take one."

"Oh, honey, you don't want one of these. I can get you a fresh one. What would you like?"

He took a half full martini glass minus the olive with lipstick on the rim from the tray and raised it as if to make a toast. The waitress shook her head and wrinkled her lips, then walked away. He brought the sticky glass to his lips and drank. It was strong, perhaps too strong, but he liked the taste. He surveyed the room and wondered who wore the color he tasted. It was impossible to tell. Several women wore red lipstick, and a couple of men as well. He wondered where Otto wandered off to and assumed he went upstairs with the woman he had called out to. Bored, he decided to have a look around.

The creek of the wooden floors in the hallways of the Manhattan brownstone reminded him of the floors in the Crane's house. He wondered if anyone knew how to navigate them without a sound and was sure Beatrice could. He stifled a bout of laughter before it erupted from him. The thought of Beatrice in this place was comical and unimaginable. What would she think? What would she do? He covered his mouth when a couple glanced at him suspiciously. Perhaps they thought he was high on something. He followed a girl wearing black fishnets and black leather panties that sat high on her hips like a circus trainer. She might as well have had a leash around his neck, the way he followed her like an animal caught in the hypnotic sway of her hips. Her breasts were bare and had a subtle bounce. He recalled some of the runway models at a lingerie show he attended with Otto. Their bodies and breasts moved the same way. This girl had an edge in her eyes that told him she strutted on an entirely different runway. He followed her into one of the dimly lit rooms.

The bedroom air was stale with the tart scent of climax and sweet sweat. He had yet to drink enough to dull his senses or mitigate any logic. An older man with nice hair like Mr. Crane's, but gray, was naked, stretched out on the bed with his hands cuffed to the headboard. His cock was rigid and veiny. Two long-legged brunettes moved about him on their knees like captors in some twisted version of *Gulliver's Travels*. They only wore black leather corsets. Oiled bare breasts and buttocks shimmered in the dim light of the lamps on the nightstands. One girl atop the bed positioned herself over the man, and faced Lucius with spread knees, while another girl aimed the man's cock upward. The girl lowered her herself onto the man's cock until it disappeared into her raven haired bush. When her buttocks reached his hips, she threw back her head and her mouth opened in a gasp, as if the man's cock might exit past her lips.

A married middle-aged couple, Lucius assumed, since they wore wedding bands, had come into the room to watch. The man stood next to Lucius while the woman he was with squatted in front of him and drew down his tight leather shorts. His half aroused cock sprung out and into her receiving mouth.

The girl Lucius followed surfaced from one of the gloomy corners and came over to him. She stood close in front of him. He could smell smoke on her breath. She took from him the martini with the lipstick on the glass and drank what remained, then sat the glass down. She must have sensed his hesitation, for she put her fingers to his lips to hush him. The scent on her fingers smelled of pussy—hers or another girls, was anyone's guess. She offered him a coy smile before she lowered herself into a squat in front of him and took his pants down. With an upward gaze, her playful expression turned to one of impatience. She tugged his conservative boxers down past his knees. He brought his gaze back to the three on the bed. The girl who guided the man's cock into the other girl straddled the man's face. The one girl fucked the man with more vigor. Her moans rose to cries that filled the bedroom and, most likely, echoed out into the hallway. Lucius licked his lips and felt his cock stiffen. His body twitched when he felt the girl's warm, wet mouth encircle him. From the corner of his eye, the man next to him shrugged his shoulders and tucked his chin.

"Oh, ooh. Gaah-dah."

The middle-aged man next to Lucius came. His body shook as if to shake out every last drop. The man's wife stood, her lips, chin, and collar bone glistened wet with the man's semen. They kissed deep for a moment, as if the man tried to take back what he had given her, then they turned their attention to the trio on the bed. The woman with her glossy lips, the man's wife, Lucius assumed, gave him a coy smile and an inviting wink, while the man rocked on his heels with dreamy eyes and paid no attention to him or the girl who knelt in front of Lucius.

The two women atop the man on the bed, his cock in one and his tongue in the other, cried as they both came in near unison. Lucius muffled a groan of resistance. There was a pull and surge from his testicles. Whatever the girl who squatted in front of him was doing was too much to bear. His body went rigid, his buttocks drew tight, and a sudden rush came from down inside and spewed forth up from the pipes and out. She took all that he gave and swallowed him whole. Her mouth remained on him. She worked from tip to base as if he had more to give. His overly stimulated body became electrified, and he spasmed several times like a kite caught between two crosswinds.

When she finished, she yanked up his boxers, stood and walked from the room as simply as if she had dropped something, picked it up, and was on her way. He noticed the couple next to him. The man's gaze was on the trio on the bed, but the woman's eyes were on him. She licked her lips and her eyes travelled down his body. His semi-erect cock poked from the inside of his boxers. A wet semen spot formed at the tip. He smiled at the woman, then pulled up his pants and left the room to find Otto.

He walked down the hallway, half sedated from his release. On the third floor, a sharp snapping sound came from a room down the hallway. It was like a folded leather belt being quickly pulled tight. Two muscular barefoot men in black leather thongs and collars around their necks framed the open doorway. Their pale shoulders, backs, and bare buttocks seemed to glow under the dim hallway lights. They looked like two unseemly dressed Greek statues. Both men glanced briefly at him when he stepped between them to enter the room.

The room was a larger sitting room and not a bedroom. It seemed that every room in the brownstone had an elegant fireplace of one size or another, but this room had a larger one that was positioned at the center of the far wall. A group of the leather clad guests stood crowded in the corner of the room. The crack of leather came again, followed by a muted grunt. He went to the side of the crowd to see what everyone was looking at. Otto was on his knees. His ankles were bound by leather straps with buckles, and his wrists were bound as well. He held onto the seat of a side chair. His head hung between his shoulders as his testicles hung between his legs. A milky white redhead with long curls who wore a black mask over her eyes, pasties over her nipples, black patent leather panties with matching knee-high boots and gloves drew back the riding crop she held and snapped it across Otto's bare red welted buttocks. Otto took it this time without a whimper, but his body trembled when the whip made contact with his flesh. It seemed Otto tried not to make a sound, so Lucius muttered it for him.

"Scheisse!"

The red-haired woman touched the leather end of the riding crop to Otto's testicles and he lurched. She bent low and seized his cock. Since Otto faced away from the onlookers, it was difficult to tell if he enjoyed being whipped. The woman whispered something to Otto. The way her angular jaw muscles moved suggested whatever she imparted to him would determine his level of punishment. He nodded in quick, traumatic jerks as though someone held a gun to his head. Before the woman released his cock, her forearm muscles tensed, and she squeezed and tugged at him. He raised his head for a moment to release a groan.

Lucius clenched his teeth at each strike. The redhead paused and slowly gazed at each person in the crowd as if she were about to select another recipient of her abuse to either join or replace Otto. Her burning gaze met Lucius's. The corner of her red painted lips, the only other color on her besides black, curled upward. In that moment, he wanted to photograph her, to capture her raw intensity. A woman with shoulder-length blonde hair stepped forward from the group of spectators. She looked wholesome, like anyone's neighbor lady, except for the leather bra and panties she wore. She raised her chin slightly as if she were steeling herself.

"Mistress Scarlet. I'm ready. Pick me."

His lips bent into a subtle smile when he heard the name. The red-haired woman, Mistress Scarlet, he presumed, branded him with her gaze before she turned her attention to the woman. No one else in the room appeared to share his glee. Mistress Scarlet seemed annoyed by his lack of grim enthusiasm that the others shared. After she positioned her new volunteer, kneeling on the chair with her ass and pussy in Otto's face, Lucius slipped past the onlookers. Others who came into the room filled his spot when he departed. The crack of Mistress Scarlet's riding crop followed him out into the hallway. The same two half-naked men still stood on both sides of the doorway like guardians. They gave him a brief glance. He wondered if they were with redhead.

He sucked in the warm night air when he exited the brownstone and descended its steps to the sidewalk. Two women who wore long raincoats, probably to cover their near naked bodies, smoked at the bottom of the stairs. They gave him a cursory glance. He glanced up at the windows. Otto brought him here. Part of him felt he should stick around, but the other part got his feet moving. He headed west to 2nd Avenue to see if he could catch a cab downtown and back to the studio.

42

In a space with exposed brick walls the size of a typical suburban living room, Beatrice stood in front of a white seamless paper backdrop and turned. The two stands that held the backdrop had strips of white tape stuck to them labeled with the name Schenker.

"Good, there. Now twist your upper body toward me."

Lucius stood hunched over a medium format camera mounted on a tripod. He wore black leather pants and a white t-shirt. An outfit she would have never imagined him wearing. He looked like the member of some British rock band. His hair was longer than she was used to. It covered the tops of his ears, but, to her relief, had yet to touch his shoulders.

"Relax your shoulders."

She wanted to giggle, but kept her composure. His own studio space, which was Otto's old one, was a quarter the size of Otto's current studio, but it now belonged to Lucius, and that's all that mattered. It was one of the few times she had seen him actually happy since he moved to New York. She glanced around the space. It was simply a brick box with a steel door and three large windows on the wall that faced the street. He had a small worktable with shelves to sit or store his gear, a chair, a stool, and the two stands with the backdrop given to him by Otto. If he needed any professional lighting, he would have to beg Otto to use his studio and equipment. It was interesting to her that Otto Schenker wanted Lucius to continue living at his studio like a pet.

"Eyes either on the camera or off to my left, please."

She wrinkled her lips but followed his direction. The shutter of the medium format camera made a dull pop, like the sound of one stepping on an inflated paper sack. Lucius turned the small winding crank on the side of the camera to advance the film. He kept his head lowered and his eyes on the viewfinder.

"Okay, tilt your head slightly to your right. Good."

Pop. She wore a silver necklace with broad but thin links from his earlier photoshoot for a client. Her blue dress was adequate enough for her to convince him to let her wear the necklace. The dress the model wore earlier hung on the rack. It was two sizes too small for Beatrice. She asked him if the model was pretty and inquired about her hair color, but he only said that she was a professional. It was like sex, hoping to measure up to a prostitute who knew all the tricks to please a man. She snorted. How many other women had he been with? Did she measure up? He took a few more shots of her.

"Very nice. You pose like a pro."

She smiled at him. His expression she knew well. He was simply being polite.

"Thanks."

He carried the camera on the tripod and positioned it close to the wall, where no one would trip over it.

"I think my father and Eleanor maybe heading for a divorce."

Lucius stopped fussing with the camera and tripod. His eyes widened and his lips parted in a grave expression, but there was an odd glimmer of hope in his gaze.

"Oh? Why do you think that?"

"The past few phone calls. He seemed distracted. He would always ask me how I was getting along with Eleanor. One time, I swear I heard a woman's voice in the background. It almost sounded like Ms. Mila. I'm sure that sounds crazy. I thought maybe it was the television. He has one there—doesn't watch it much, but he has one."

"Ms. Mila?"

"Yes. Did you know she no longer works for us? Either that, or Eleanor fired her. That was after I came to New York for school."

"Would they need both Ms. Mila and Ms. Käthe with only your father and Eleanor there?"

He spoke slow and careful.

"Probably not."

She sighed.

"My father is almost never home, at least from what Eleanor has told me. I know she thinks I take glee in his desertion, but it's not true."

He ran his fingers through his hair and squeezed the back of his neck.

"Is he really that busy?"

"I don't think so. With us out of the house, you would think they would enjoy their time alone."

"It must be lonely for Eleanor."

She snorted and stifled a chuckle.

"Maybe you should visit her."

He raised his eyebrows and tilted his head as if he was contemplating the idea. She played with the silver necklace. It hung between her breasts. She wrinkled her lips.

"I was kidding. Aren't you awfully busy working for Schenker?"

"We could both visit. It would get us out of the city for a day or two. I'm sure Otto wouldn't mind, besides he has a trip planned to Europe in a week or two. Don't you want to know what's going on between your father and Eleanor?"

It was just like him to ask her to go to Connecticut with him, when she knew he would rather visit Eleanor alone. Why was he so fascinated by her? It was like a boy fascinated by a lizard.

"Oh no. I'll only go home during the holidays. I love New York too much. Whatever is going on with them, that's their business."

He was quiet. She went to him.

"My friend is having a party tonight. That's another reason I wanted to see you. I'd like you to come."

He sighed, but then his lips curled into a subtle smile.

"All right. Where and when?"

"It's on the upper west side, 83rd Street. I think she said seven o'clock, but we can get there by 7:30 or eight o'clock. The party should be off to a start by then."

He raised his eyebrows. She almost forgot how cute he looked.

43

Kenneth contemplated his appearance in the bedroom mirror at his Hartford apartment. He made delicate passes with a comb to herd in the few stray strands until his hair was perfect. He then slipped his arms into the sleeves of a clean, pressed white shirt and tossed the wire hanger from the dry cleaners onto the bed. A receipt stapled to the hanger's paper backing had "Kenneth Crane" handwritten on it with "Mila" written next to it. He wondered if she told the cleaners that she was his wife. Ever since she left her employment at his house, she moved to Hartford and frequently visited his apartment. He took advantage of her longing for him. He bought her lingerie, which she was excited to wear for him. She did everything he desired. They fucked on the small dining table. He spreading her on the kitchen counter among half-chopped vegetables to taste her pussy. She mounting him on the sofa in the living room. And they rolled around among the sheets in the bedroom. She was a banquet for his appetite.

His wedding band caught the sunlight coming through the window as he buttoned the cuffs of his shirt. He sighed and his reflection returned a scowl. He rubbed his hands together and rotated his wedding band around his finger. For a moment, he considered removing the ring, but he knew its absence would fool no one. All the women who he slept with or flirted with knew he was married, but they came anyway. Lucius's mom, Paulina, was no exception. What did they expect? What did they hope for? Did they think he would simply divorce Eleanor and then they would have him? Mila certainly did. She still does, by her frequent visits to check on him, her trips to the dry cleaners to drop off and pick up his shirts, her insisting on grocery shopping and cleaning his apartment. He huffed at how he encouraged her. Now the weight of her constant presence had become too much.

Eleanor never demanded his loyalty. She expected it, but in contrast she let out his leash far enough for him to have a dalliance here and there, but nothing deep, nothing that involved—feelings. He snorted. It was always unsettling, her uncanny understanding of the male appetite. She knew how much to feed him and let him run in order to keep him in check. He huffed. When his full attention returned to his reflection, he had mis-buttoned his shirt and had to unbutton it and start again.

After he dressed, he went to the small galley kitchen. It was too early, but he felt he could use a drink. He had a full bottle of wine in the refrigerator, along with a few beers. Neither appealed to him. A knock came at the door. He glanced at the clock on the kitchen wall.

"Right on time."

He could always expect Mila to be punctual. She was German, after all. He snorted. Her past visits have been up and down. Up and down in the bed, and up and down in their arguments and debates regarding what she wanted and what he was willing to give her, which amounted to no more than a sporadic, endless affair. She never seemed to catch on to the reality of things. He was unsure if that was a good or bad thing. Regardless, he had two hours before he had to be in court and hoped they could enjoy themselves.

He swung the door open playfully with a grin. His smile faltered. Phoebe Cook stood out in the hallway, dressed dishy as ever, with her handbag hung from one forearm and some broad dark frame sunglasses folded in her hand.

"Hello Kenny."

"Uh?"

"You're looking a little pale. Are you not feeling well?"

She strutted past him before he could invite her in. She walked to the sunny living room and turned around.

"Did you miss me?"

He closed the door and stepped to the edge of the living room, his lips parted, wordless. She smiled and seemed overly satisfied at the effect she had on him.

"I'm pleasantly surprised to see you. What brings you here? It has to be nearly two months."

"I'm sorry for not keeping in touch. I've been so busy."

He huffed and crossed his arms.

"Busy with Judge Carson?"

She went to the sofa and sat down. He glanced at his wristwatch. Mila would arrive at any moment.

"I'm sorry, I have to leave for work."

She made no move to get up. A knock came at the door. His shoulders and back stiffened.

"Expecting someone? I thought you were leaving?"

On his way back past the kitchen, he sighed and cursed himself, then took a deep breath and opened the door.

"Beatrice? Uh, hello. What are you doing here?"

"Nice to see you too."

She slipped past him and into the apartment, as Phoebe had.

"Sure dear, won't you come in?"

He gestured for her to enter, but she was already past the kitchen and heading to the living room. He wrinkled his lips and closed the door. Beatrice stopped when she saw Phoebe.

"Oh—hello?"

She turned back to him.

"Sorry father, I didn't know you had company."

Phoebe stood to greet Beatrice.

"Beatrice? You must be Kenneth's daughter. How nice to meet you."

Beatrice paused before shaking Phoebe's hand.

"And you are?"

"I'm Phoebe Cook. Lucius's aunt."

Beatrice's face softened with a modicum of understanding.

"From Indiana? What brings you to Connecticut?"

"I live here now, in Hartford."

"Oh? Lucius never mentioned anything."

Kenneth stepped into the living room alongside Beatrice.

"Our city made an impression on Ms. Cook, and she saw more opportunities here than in Bradford, Indiana. I assisted her in finding a job and a reasonably priced room for rent."

"How thoughtful, Father."

Phoebe's lips curled into a conciliatory toothless smile. She tilted her head and raised an eyebrow.

"Your father has been most helpful."

Beatrice glanced at him. He stuffed his hands into his pockets and his shoulders slumped.

"Well, I should be on my way. Kenneth, maybe we can have lunch sometime."

"Sure, that would be nice."

She smiled at Beatrice.

"Nice to meet you."

Beatrice's lips bowed into a skeptical smile.

"Yeah, sure. Nice to meet you."

She strutted past him and Beatrice. He smiled when she touched his arm.

"Call me sometime."

"Sure, great to see you."

He walked her out and when he returned Beatrice sat where Phoebe had been. She had her arms crossed. He sighed. He stood at the edge of the living room, ready to walk her out as well.

"I'm sorry Dear, I was getting ready to head to the office. I wish I knew you were coming. Can I give you a lift somewhere?"

"I passed Ms. Mila on the sidewalk."

Her sharp gaze was on him.

"I asked her if she had come to see you, but she said she wasn't aware that you had an apartment in this particular building, only that you had an apartment in Hartford. 'How nice,' she said. 'I'm going to have to pay your father a visit,' she said. I told her I was sure you would be happy to see her. Anyway, she seemed in a hurry, so we didn't talk long."

She tilted her head and wrinkled her lips. Poised from his many days in the courtroom, he put his hands in his pockets and offered her a warm smile.

"That's very nice. I hope she's doing well."

He retrieved his jacket that was folded over the back of one of the dining room chairs. He eyed her.

"Coming? I've got to get going."

"Do you mind if I wait here for you? You'll be home tonight, won't you? It would be nice riding with you back to the house. I really don't want to take a cab."

His eyes looked around the space as if he were searching for something.

"Yeah, yeah sure. That would be great. I don't have much in the refrigerator, but you remember where the cafe is down the street? I have their menu in the drawer if you want them to deliver."

He took out his wallet and laid a twenty-dollar bill on the counter.

"I'll manage. I'll see you in a few hours?"

"Yes."

He stepped out into the hallway, and the door closed behind him. It felt as though a bomb was ticking in his apartment. Hopefully Mila would skip coming by today. Perhaps she would see his car missing from the apartment parking lot. He clenched his keys in his fist, then plunged them into his pants pocket.

44

The train departed Grand Central Station bound for Hartford. Lucius peered out the window. It would disappoint Beatrice that he was a no show for her friend's party. He had no appetite to be in the company of those around his age. When he arrived in Hartford, he took a cab to the Crane's house, to see Eleanor. It was a three-hour train ride, and an hour in the cab. No one was home. The house key hidden under a planter at the back entrance was missing. He thought he might find her sitting in the enclosed back patio, but it was empty. The cushioned wicker patio chairs, which normally sat askew, sat straight as if Ms. Käthe had cleaned and straighten the furniture, but Eleanor never had anyone clean the patio.

It was near four o'clock in the morning when he stumbled back into Otto's studio. He took off his shoes and socks and slept in his clothes. After a few hours, the studio phone rang.

"Fuck sake."

He got to his knees, then to his feet, and stumbled out and across the cavernous room. His bare feet pattered on the floor.

"Hello?"

He tried to shape the word from his dry throat, but he still sounded groggy. His eyebrows drew together. He imagined it was a client calling, but instead, a familiar voice came through the receiver.

"Good morning Lucius."

"Oh? Eleanor. Hello."

"Did I wake you?"

He rubbed his eyes.

"I'm in your neighborhood. Would you like to have breakfast with me?"

"Ah? Yeah, sure. Can you give me a few minutes?"

"Why don't you meet me at the hotel diner down the street?"

"All right."

"Great, see you there. Goodbye Lucius."

She ended the call before he could say, "Goodbye."

He went to the studio bathroom, finger combed his hair back into shape the best he could, and sniffed his armpits before he hurried across the studio to the storeroom where he slipped on a clean t-shirt. His shirt and trousers he wore to visit her in Connecticut hung wrinkled over the back of a folding chair. All he had was his leather pants to wear with the t-shirt. He sighed and wished he had something more conservative to wear. It would have to do. He slipped his bare feet into his oxfords, laced them, grabbed his wallet and keys and rushed out of Otto's studio.

At the entrance to the hotel diner, he spotted her in a booth near the window. She sat erect and poised as if she were in the company of aristocrats. She wore a cream-colored blouse open at the collar with a pearl necklace. He tugged at his t-shirt. The hostess near the cash register gave him a suspicious glance.

"Can I help you?"

"No, I'm good. I'm meeting someone."

The hostess only gave him a nod. When he arrived at the table where Eleanor sat, she looked him up and down. As he attempted to bend to kiss her cheek, she held up her hand to halt him. He tightened his lips, then slid into the booth opposite her.

"If you hadn't answered the phone, I would think you have been living on the streets. You're not, are you?"

He chuckled and brushed his fingers through his hopeless waves of hair.

"No, no, I'm not. Sleeping in Schenker's studio sometimes feels like the street."

She gazed at him, unblinking. The band of sunlight that came in through the window filtered through her pale sky-blue eyes and illuminated the flesh on her cheek and neck. Her light brown curls caught the light and gold strands appeared woven within them.

"Good—I would hope not."

He felt like a butterfly pinned by her gaze. Her gaze was not one of curiosity, but one of cold academic inquiry.

"So, what brings you to New York?"

The waitress brought a cup of coffee for her and took their order. He gazed at her while she spoke to the waitress. After the waitress left and returned with a cup of coffee for him and then departed once more, Eleanor raised her chin as though she were about to address a child in a matter that was above their comprehension.

"You may or may not be aware that Kenneth and I have run into some difficulties."

"Bea, Beatrice said—"

Her eyebrow rose. He took a sip of his coffee.

"Beatrice said that you and Kenneth weren't getting along."

"Let's just say he's getting along better with other women."

She raised her cup to her lips and drank, but her gaze never left his. It was as if she were looking for a crack in his armor to reveal to her that perhaps he knew—something.

"Oh? Do you think he's having an affair?"

She quickly returned his volley.

"Don't you?"

He raised his eyebrows and shifted in his seat. The span between her eyebrows narrowed and the blue of her eyes became cold. Her subtle expression was one he knew well. He knew his delay or refusal to state his opinion agitated her. One corner of her lips tightened.

"Regardless if you have an opinion or not—I do. I can tolerate Kenneth having a brief fling, but when it becomes more than that, to abandon his family, his *wife*, it becomes traitorous."

His eyes widen.

"So you don't think he's simply choosing work over his family?"

"No."

"Oh?"

She raised her cup to drink. Her gaze left him for a moment to glance out the window. His gaze wandered to the notch at the base of her elegant neck. He imagined the black choker she wore in Kenneth's black and white photographs. The choker, the nylon stockings, the garter belt, was all she wore. He swallowed as images of her dark triangular patch of pubic hair from the photographs came into focus in his mind. He straightened when he heard her voice.

"I have resources that have confirmed my suspicion. That little tart, Ms. Mila. I should have gotten rid of her long ago when she caught his eye. That longing, that lust, like a hungry stray dog. Yet, he is not a stray. That makes it worse. It's one thing when you don't see it or know about it, and another when it's right there in front of you."

She let out an exhausted breath.

"That's the reason for my visit, to meet with my lawyers. I stayed overnight in the city to get away from that damn house."

"You should have called me sooner."

"Why?"

"We could have had dinner. I could have kept you company. There's no reason for you to be alone."

One of her eyebrows rose.

"My dear Lucius—don't be fooled—we *are* all alone."

Dear Lucius? Words he wished he could hear under a different circumstance.

"Aren't you being a little cynical?"

His shoulders stiffened at his accusation. Her gaze hardened like ice on a frozen pond.

"I mean—I understand you must be—under stress. Forget what I said."

The clouds parted in her gaze and her pale sky-blue eyes softened, but her lips still held a tight line. He looked at his coffee cup as he rotated it on the table.

"There is the place I would like to take you. It's a club of sorts. One that might interest you."

His gaze rose, ready to meet hers and any inquiries she might have, but he found her attention elsewhere. She peered out the window.

"Eleanor. You need a release."

That got her attention, and a gaze of ice. Her eyelids drew down.

"I'm not to be toyed with, especially under my current circumstances."

He released a slow, heavy breath.

"I don't mean to add to your frustration. On the contrary, I want to help you. Do you trust me?"

His words were calm, as if to coax a wild animal. She sat back in her chair and crossed her arms.

"Lucius, if you're thinking of taking me to some loud disco, I'm not interested."

"This is something totally different—private. Think of it like going to the theater with your own private booth."

Her eyebrow rose. There was a subtle shift in her shoulders, as if the tension had ebbed.

"All right."

Lucius took Eleanor's hand and lead her down a narrow dark gray hallway with several twisting, blind corners. A faint smell of urine and vomit mixed with cleaning chemicals floated in the stale air of the corridor. He feared she would put a halt to his plans at any moment and abandon their evening. They finally arrived at a service elevator. She glared at him the entire ride up to the eleventh floor. He knocked on a steel door. No one answered, but a shadow darkened the security peephole. A second door down the hall buzzed and unlocked. He glanced at her.

"Come."

They entered a small dark room with glossy, piano-black painted walls. A single bare florescent light bulb faced the ceiling and described the room in gloomy shadows. A comfortable cushioned Chippendale camelback sofa with elegant curved legs and ball-and-claw feet faced a wall hidden by heavy burgundy colored curtains.

"Sit."

She glanced at him in the dim light.

"Please."

He sat and put his hand on the back of the sofa to suggest to her it was okay. She sat and held her clutch handbag in her lap and crossed her ankles. She looked as though she was waiting at a bank or a doctor's office. He smiled inside, then stood and went to the curtains.

"There's no need to be alarmed."

Soft shadows cast a veil over her face, but her apprehension electrified the air. He pulled the ropes that drew open the curtains to reveal a massive industrial size window that was almost floor to ceiling in height. The room beyond was better lit and looked like a torture chamber with two areas designed to restrain someone with leather straps in either a standing, sitting, or kneeling position. He expected her to stand and protest, but she remained silent on the sofa, her head turned to the window.

"It's one-way glass. We can see out, but anyone in the other room can only see their reflection. They use this type of glass for windows on skyscrapers, or so I'm told."

"That's all very interesting Lucius, but what *is* this place? What are we about to watch?"

A loud metal thud and a sheering creak came from the room beyond the one-way glass. A metal door opened and in walked a leather clad milky white, red-haired woman with long curls. She wore an all black outfit composed of a corset, gauntlets, panties, and a matching eye mask. After she seemed to pause for effect, she then strutted in her knee-high boots on spiked heels to the center of the room. Her gauntlets and boots had shiny sharp studs, adding to her dangerous appearance.

Mistress Scarlet turned to the one-way glass. Eleanor straightened on the sofa.

"She can't see us."

As he spoke, the leather clad woman went to the heavy wooden chair with buckled restrains and sat. She put her arms on the armrests and crossed her legs like a queen on a throne. Eleanor snorted.

"Are you sure?"

"Yes. She can't see you, but she knows I'm here."

"You know this woman?"

He settled into a shallow trance as he gazed at Mistress Scarlet.

"Lucius?"

He licked his lips and cleared his throat.

"She knows me intimately, but I don't know her."

Eleanor said nothing.

"We're going to perform for you. She's waiting for me."

He went to the door, and Eleanor rose from the sofa. He raised his hand to reassure her.

"Please wait for me here. You're safe."

She stood holding her clutch handbag with both hands in the dimly lit shadowy viewing room when he closed the steel door with her still standing inside. He went down the hall and entered the door to the room where Mistress Scarlet sat. He glanced at the large mirrored pane of glass and imagined Eleanor behind it. After he took off his button-up shirt, trousers, socks and shoes, he folded them neatly, then placed them on the floor near the wall. He withdrew a thin belt from the pocket of his trousers. A child's belt that was rolled tight.

He stood there for a moment in his white tank top undershirt and boxers. Mistress Scarlet's full attention was on the mirror and the anonymous audience behind it.

"Disrobe and kneel at my feet."

Although this was the third time he had a private session with Mistress Scarlet, her voice still made him tense. He said nothing in return and knew not to speak. He pulled his undershirt over his head and glanced at the mirrored pane before he removed his boxers. His cock hung semi-erect as he imagined Eleanor's pale sky-blue eyes on him. He dropped his boxers on top of his folded clothes and stepped silently to where Mistress Scarlet sat, then he knelt before her.

She stood. He glanced at her when she walked over to a wall rack on which various whips hung. She ran her fingers over the array of instruments. With her back to him, she spoke.

"What you brought with you had better be sufficient, or I will find something that is."

She walked back to where he knelt. He held up the child's belt—his belt—that was wrapped around his hand. She took it from him and uncoiled it.

"Interesting."

During his previous sessions with Mistress Scarlet, she used the same style riding crop she whipped Otto Schenker with when he first saw her punish the old German photographer at the private party Otto took him to. He bent forward so that he was on all fours. This is how they started their previous sessions. He eyed her boots as she circled him like someone walking around a new car to examine it. A metal jingle of the belt buckle whispered in his ear. She stepped behind him unseen, but he felt the smooth leather end of the belt as she ran it across his shoulders and down his back. The room was warm and the air thick. The smell of leather, oil, and wood emanated from the two restraining areas. A chill ran down his back and legs to the balls of his feet when she touched the leather tip of the belt to his skin. It was early. Before she took longer to touch him, which intensified his anticipation.

"On your stomach."

He lowered himself to the floor. She ran her gloved hand over his back, then pressed down as if to pin him to the floor. Snap. Snap. The belt made some initial bites into the backs of his thighs and buttocks.

"Oh. Oh."

He grunted when she hit him, then he laughed. He laughed like he did when Mrs. Crane punished him for his photographs. It was part of the act that he requested of Mistress Scarlet and she agreed, to his surprise.

"You think this is funny?"

The weight of her knee pressed into the center of his back. Kah-snap. The leather belt ripped across his buttocks. His pinned erection ached and caused him to lift his hips. The belt whistled through the air, Kah-snap. Mistress Scarlet ended her strike with a closed hand that drove his hips down to crush his erection against the floor. He let out a huffed, shuddered breath. She struck him twice more. Her closed gloved hand that she drove into his buttocks amplified the sting from the belt.

"On your knees."

When he rose on his knees, his cock ached and pointed at a sharp angle. She stepped to his side. He glanced at her spike heeled boots. She faced the wall where the mirror pane was and Eleanor hidden behind it. What was she doing? Was she taunting whoever she thought was behind the glass?

"Who do you belong to?"

"You."

He answered in a hushed tone too low for Eleanor to hear, then he realized his misstep. The belt crackled as it came down swift and the leather end snapped and bit the flesh of his buttock. His body jerked. That was another no-no. It was like premature ejaculation.

"I didn't hear you. Who do you belong to?"

Her voice, solid like a steel girder one could walk out on and peer down.

"You!"

He raised his voice. It filled and echoed off the walls. Kah-snap. The leather bit into the same tender location. He grunted at the sudden pain on his scalp as Mistress Scarlet grasped a wad of his hair and pulled it tight in her fist.

"You answer when you're spoken to."

Her voice rang within his skull. He answered firm and quick.

"Yes, Mistress."

She stood and walked behind him, her heels made a sharp staccato on the stark dust laden floor. He imagined her winding up to strike him. Time hung in the air. The muscles of his thighs flexed when she touched the leather tip of the belt to his testicles, but otherwise he held still. She knelt alongside him, then seized his cock in a painful grasp. She stroked him hard and tugged at him.

"Don't you fucking come. You don't come unless I say you come."

He clenched his teeth.

"Yes—yes Mistress."

Kah-snap. The leather belt stung his buttocks. Kah-snap. The leather struck his backside once more, but lower and curved inside his thigh and hit his testicles, which sent bolts of electricity through his body. The palm of her leather gauntlet burned the thin skin of his cock. The buildup was fast and surrender was near inevitable. Then she stopped, and he released a breath as quietly as he could, like a rabbit hiding from a fox. He tightened his pelvic muscles for fear that his body would betray him, but he held on to his climax. She went and stood in front of him. He peered down at her boots with pointed toes that ended with silver tips. He tried not to think of how she might employ them for fear ideas would slip into the air and whisper undesirable suggestions. Her black leather panties dropped around her ankles and she stepped out of them. She kicked them off to the side, then she sat in the heavy wooden restraining chair with her knees together at his eye level. The child's belt draped down her leg.

"Crawl to me, then sit back on your heels."

She commanded and taunted him. With locked elbows, she lifted herself until she knelt on the seat. She then stood and stepped up onto each of the chair's broad wooden armrests. From the base of the chair, he gazed up at her as she towered over him from her perch. Her sex, a mound of fiery copper hair. She sneered at him and snapped the folded belt together. It echoed in the room. She lowered her hips, but remained balanced on the armrests even in her high-heeled boots. It was a position she appeared comfortable and familiar with. She unfolded the belt, so it trailed down his back.

"Open your mouth and put your head back."

He did. She massaged her sex, parted her fleshy lips.

"Now drink."

She held herself open and a sudden stream hit him in the face and drizzled warm down his neck and back. His body flexed when first hit. Her aim was accurate. His mouth filled with her piss until it ran over his chin and down his body to wet his chest, abdomen, cock, and thighs. His legs flexed with his sudden urge to stand, but the thought of Eleanor's gaze kept him on his knees.

"Drink! Drink!"

He tried not to choke. When she finished, he lowered his head and her warm piss ran from his mouth. Her boots clomped as she jumped to the floor. She then stood spread legged over him, and took a fist full of his hair and yanked his head back. The fiery coppery hair that hid her sex dripped droplets onto his face. She stepped back and dropped the child's belt across his sore red knees, then strutted out of the room. The metal door boomed behind her.

He wiped his face and glanced at the mirror. The florescent light painted the wall and mirror a sickly yellow. He snorted the urine from his nostrils. Heat filled his face. He rose to his feet with the belt and stepped carefully to his clothes like a beachgoer traversing hot sand.

After he dried his face with his boxers and dressed. He entered the adjoining short hallway and found Mistress Scarlet smoking a cigarette. She stared at him from behind her mask and held out her hand.

"What the hell was that? You were supposed to just use the belt."

"No one tells me what to do. You pay for an experience and I give you one. You're lucky I agreed to spank you like your mommy did. I never take orders."

His eyebrows drew together as he stuffed a handful of bills into her hand.

"The golden shower is extra."

"But?"

Her eyes hardened behind her mask.

"You asked for a memorable evening and I gave you one."

He opened his wallet and passed her another twenty. She dropped her cigarette, crushed it beneath her boot, then left without another word. He went out into the main hallway and to the door to the viewing room to collect Eleanor. He hesitated before turning the knob. His muscles tensed as if he were about to face a tiger. When he entered the dimly lit room, she was gone. On the sofa cushion lay some panties. A whisper escaped past his lips.

"Eleanor."

He was a boy again. He swallowed before he picked up the undergarment. They were plain without lace or any extravagant suggestions that their evening would amount to anything sexual. Why did she leave them? He stuffed them into his pocket and ran from the room.

Down the street, Eleanor climbed into the backseat of a cab.

"Eleanor!"

He ran down the street, one side his shirt came untucked from his waist.

"Eleanor!"

The cab sped away. He flagged down the next cab that rounded the corner and instructed the driver to follow the cab that took Eleanor. Both cabs crawled painfully to the front of a hotel on 56th Street. He opened the door before his cab came to a stop.

"Hey mister, you better pay!"

As he waited for the driver to stop the car, the hotel doorman held the door for Eleanor. She marched inside. Lucius thrust a ten-dollar bill at the driver.

"Keep it."

He hurried from the car to the hotel, and pushed through the revolving doors instead of waiting for the doorman, who looked at him suspiciously. Inside, he tucked his shirt. The scent of Mistress Scarlet's urine clung inside his nostrils. Eleanor boarded the elevator, and he hurried across the open lobby to catch her. He bumped in to a man who nearly fell into the woman he was talking to.

"Hey."

The man behind the counter, who was on the phone, set down the receiver. "Sir? Sir?"

The man at the counter called after him. Lucius leapt onto the elevator car before the doors closed and got them shut before any of the hotel staff could reach him. He huffed to catch his breath.

"My God Lucius. What has gotten into you?"

He backed into the rear of the elevator car and glanced at her. His chest and shoulders rose and fell with each heavy breath until he finally swallowed.

"Why did you leave?"

She peered at him for a moment as if conflicted.

"That was an absurd circus performance."

"I—I thought you would enjoy it."

She huffed and glared at him. Her pale sky-blue eyes gleamed in the soft light inside the elevator.

"What could possibly make you think that?"

Heat rose within him and filled his chest and face. He dug into his pants pocket then cornered her in the elevator and held her panties up in his fist.

"What does this mean?"

She glared at him.

"Eleanor?"

The elevator bell chimed, and the doors opened. He hid his hands behind him, expecting to see awaiting passengers, but no one was there. She stepped around him and out into the hallway. He followed.

"Please, Eleanor."

She stopped at a door in the hallway with a room key in her hand and turned to face him.

"Lucius, this was a mistake. I had no idea you were involved in such activities."

He stood there as if she had slapped him in the face. Had he read her wrong? His eyes burned. He handed her the undergarment.

"I don't understand you."

The elevator bell chimed down the hall and the man from behind the lobby reception desk and a stocky bellhop who accompanied him rushed toward them. The bellhop was shorter than Lucius, but he had a grim, determined expression.

"Mrs. Crane, are you all right? Is this man bothering you?"

Lucius stood between Eleanor and the two men. He felt outnumbered since the man knew who she was. The shorter bellhop glared at Lucius, as if he had done something wrong, and he appeared eager to dispatch his duties, albeit temporarily bestowed on him, and throw Lucius out. Eleanor stepped forward.

"I'm terribly sorry for the misunderstanding. I had dropped something and this young man raced to return it."

The tension in the hotel desk clerk's face softened, yet the shorter bellhop still looked suspicious.

"Oh, I see."

The hotel desk clerk glanced at Lucius.

"Thank you for returning Mrs. Crane's things, but we appreciate polite conduct within the hotel. That means no running. You could have left the item at the front desk."

"The item is of some value."

"I see, yet again, if you consulted with the front desk, someone could have phoned Mrs. Crane's room."

Lucius glanced at Eleanor as if he expected her to say something more to end the interrogation. She smiled at both men.

"Again, I'm sorry for the disturbance. I've had a stressful day and wish to retire. Good night to you all."

She slipped inside her room.

"Goodnight Mrs. Crane."

The door closed on his words.

"Okay, young man, let's go."

The urge to bang on her door surged within him, but the strained gazes of the two men told him it would be pointless. He was at least grateful they kept their hands to themselves, but they rode down with him in the elevator and escorted him out the door. He walked up the block without a glance back and followed the flow of the one-way traffic. At the next corner, he would try to catch a cab.

45

Even after a busy work-filled month, Lucius avoided any contact with Eleanor. As much as he wanted to explain the crazy evening they shared, something told him it was best to put some distance from the affair. He became more preoccupied with Beatrice, who visited him at least once a week after she invited him to her friend's party on the upper west side almost two months ago. It surprised him how she took things in stride since he was a no-show. She instead acted like when they were children chasing one another in the backyard, except now she was the only one doing the chasing.

Otto was out of town, and the studio sat quiet, like a tomb. It put Lucius at ease to know that no one would barge in at any moment. Otto would be gone for two more weeks. He offered Lucius unlimited use of the studio to shoot any of his commercial work while he was away.

Lucius ran a bent comb through his hair in the studio bathroom. No matter how much he tried to smooth the waves, he could never get it as perfect as Mr. Crane's. He even used the same hair cream, but his hair needed a cut to first tame it. When he buttoned up his shirt, he left the top button undone. It was one of the few button up shirts he had. He wore it with some conservative dark gray wool trousers. It was the type of outfit he wore through high school. He looked younger, more innocent. Maybe Beatrice would appreciate his conformity, at least for the evening. He expected her at eight o'clock, although he told her they could meet at the restaurant. For some reason, she liked to drop in at the studio before they went out. It was as if she was waiting for something to happen. Sometimes he would take her picture, but it seemed like something else, like some question hung in the air. He snorted at his reflection. When he came out into the open, white-walled studio, he checked his watch. Any minute. Of all the young women he knew, none of them were as punctual as Beatrice. A soft, familiar, intimate knock came at the steel door. He released a long breath as if he had been holding it for the last hour—then the corners of his lips curled upward. She never used the buzzer. Whenever she knocked, it made the studio feel like his home and not some commercial enterprise. He became accustomed to the hammering thud the door lock made. The first week or two living in Otto's studio, he jumped whenever the door was open, especially if he was in bed or at odd hours.

"Hi—"

He gasped. A white fabric panel Schenker had him hang recently defused the light from the halogen ceiling lamp near the doorway. It pushed back the green-gray cast of the dim hallway lights and illuminated Beatrice in a soft glow. She wore a more conservative dress, with a neckline that exposed her collar bones, yet was high enough to keep an air of sophistication. Her chestnut hair, done up in broad, bouncy curls, gave her a look of the times, with a stylistic contrast to her outfit.

"—Bea."

Her lips pulled into a tight smile, and her eyelids narrowed. It was the look she gave him when she would sneak up on him or outsmart him in some fashion when they were children.

"Hello Lucius."

She walked in and paused only briefly to take him in, then touched his arm as she passed. His nostrils flared at the scent of her perfume. She entered with an energy and freshness as though it was her first time visiting Otto Schenker's photography studio. He admired her gait. Something was different, more refined, more mature. She wore sheer mocha colored stockings with seams up the backs of her legs like the kinds Mrs. Crane wore. When he woke from his reverie, he realized his lips were parted. He licked his lips and closed the door. She spun around, as if surprised by the sound of the door. Her skirt twirled and rose to display a fraction above her knees. She held her small clutch handbag with both hands. He grinned.

"You're in a good mood."

"I am. You look real nice. Did you get your hair done?"

"Thank you. I did. You look nice as well."

She looked him up and down.

"No leather pants tonight? Have you moved past your Sid Vicious faze, or are you simply feeling a little nostalgic?"

He chuckled and brushed his hand down the front of his button-down shirt.

"Do you remember this shirt?"

She nodded. The corner of his lips tightened into a cocked smile. She went to the maroon colored sofa near the windows. Otto's fuck sofa. He stepped forward, but she sat before he could say anything. He snorted. It was the idea that bothered him more than anything. Otto had been gone for a week. Any bodily fluids the old man had spilled on the cushions had long since dried. Who knows, maybe Schenker's jizz came out in dry powder form. His shoulders shuddered at the thought. She crossed her legs and sat back on the sofa. The bottom edge of her stocking welt peeked out from under the hem of her skirt. She made no attempt to hide it. She looked at him with an anxious, familiar gaze, like when they were children and someone had given her a wrapped gift.

"Where would you like to go tonight?"

"We can talk about that later. Come sit next to me. I have something to tell you."

"Oh? Ah—okay."

He went over and sat next to her.

"I think it's been nice that we've been seeing more of each other, don't you?"

"Yeah, sure."

He felt the need to run his fingers through his hair, but after all the time he spent combing it, he instead put his arm on the back of the sofa behind her.

"Have you thought much about us?"

"What do you mean?"

She tilted her head. Her curls brushed and tickled the back of his hand.

"We never spoke about when you left Connecticut, and what my father said to you. Did he threaten you?"

"No, not exactly."

"Did he tell you to stay away from me?"

"Sort of."

"Sort of? What did he say—exactly?"

He sat back on the sofa and took in the large open studio space. It seemed like the first time he took the studio space in as a whole. Maybe it was the angle of where he sat on the sofa. It appeared grander and suggested prospects that were before unimaginable.

"I could tell he knew we slept together. He looked stressed and disappointed, but he said he wanted to help me, which I couldn't believe. Then he mentioned an opportunity in New York. I think it was his way of saying, without telling me directly, he wanted me out."

She sighed. She touched his thigh.

"I'm sorry."

He snorted and touched her shoulder, then gestured out into the open studio space.

"Look at this place. Your father did this. He got me an apprenticeship. I live in the most incredible city in the world. I work for Otto Schenker, one of New York's finest fashion photographers. I've got—"

Her finger pressed against his lips to silence him.

"You've got a good life and I'm happy for you, but I'll ask you again. Have you thought about us?"

His gaze left hers and floated out into the open space.

"Lucius?"

When he touched her back, her muscles tensed under her skin. She seemed poised to stand at any moment and walk out. She released an exhausted breath as if she had been holding it for days, months, years. There was a tug inside his chest urging him to speak.

"Yes, I have."

His words came out in a whisper. The muscles in her back eased under his touch. When he turned back to her, there was still anticipation in her gaze, but her face had softened.

"And?"

"And what Bea?"

This time, her breath came out in a rush. She pulled away.

"You're exhausting. We've been seeing each other every week, yet you haven't tried to kiss me. Why? Is there someone else?"

"Bea, I've been working all the time."

"Don't give me that. You photograph all these beautiful women. You can't tell me that none of them ever flirted with you. I suppose you've never taken any of them out on a date, or slept with any of them."

She crossed her arms. His eyebrows drew together.

"No—no, never. What? Do you think I'm like Schenker? He's filthy and cynical. He doesn't believe in love. Do you think he has that much of an influence over me?"

She relaxed and put her hands in her lap. Her face softened and the tension in her gaze abated.

"So you believe in love. Are you in love with someone?"

He met her gaze, then put his hand in hers.

"No, but I want to love and be loved."

Her lips bowed into a subtle, tight smile. Her fingertips skimmed his cheek. He stroked a loose curl away from her eye. Her stare touched his face like warm sunshine as he tucked her loose curl in with the rest of her hair. He took in a breath and was about to speak, but she leaned into him and her lips melted into his. The kiss was familiar, but more refined, mature, and with innocence replaced with focused passion and intention.

A hunger that lie hidden within him woke and crept forth out of the shadows. He wrapped his arm around her waist and pulled her close. Her want became his need. Their kiss held even as she maneuvered to straddle him. He breathed her in, her breath, the scent of her perfume intoxicated him. She wrapped her arms around his shoulders, and he around her waist, both with a longing of long-lost lovers.

He unzipped the back of her dress while she unbuttoned his shirt. They both squirmed free of their clothes and they helped each other undress. As sudden as their kiss came, she was on her back, wearing only her bra, stockings and garter. Her panties lie atop her crumpled dress, which lie next to his pile of clothes. He caressed her knees and gently squeezed her calves to her ankles. Her lips curved in a soft smile while she watched him with a heavy, dreamy gaze. She opened her legs, and he knelt on the sofa between them. He removed his boxers and his cock angled skyward. She smiled at his arousal. They've been here before, at this place, with one another, in this circumstance. The only difference was time.

"I need to get a condom."

There was a glitter in her eyes.

"It's okay. It's us, Lucius. It's us."

She grasped his forearms. There was a hint of a smile on her face. He aimed himself and with a slow move of his thighs and hips he penetrated her. Her lips parted. He moved into her until their bodies became one. Their connection was complete and perfect. He wished he could descend further, to know the depth of her and what secrets lie there. As he moved between her legs, this was the first time he considered this. Tonight, she had shown him she was much more than he thought he knew, or desired.

As she came, she squeezed her thighs against his ribs and hips, then curled her heels into his buttocks to secure him deep inside her. The texture of her nylons against his flesh and within his hands as he grasped her thighs brought on a sudden rush within him. Her inner muscles spasmed and tighten around him. He wanted to come, to expel himself inside her, but he slipped free of certain destiny and spilled forth onto her abdomen and the lace of her garter belt. Thick pearlescent streams matted her soft patch of pubic hair and ran into the crease of her thigh.

He met her dreamy, sated gaze as she lie there. Her chest rose and fell with an exhausted exhalation. She held her arms out to him and when he descended into her embrace, her legs twined around his waist. He tucked his head into the space between her neck and shoulder, closed his eyes, and inhaled the scent of her perfume. His fingertips ran up the flesh of her hip to meet the lace of her stocking welt and on down her thigh. He breathed her in and thought of Eleanor. Her flesh. Her body underneath him.

Beatrice moved her hips in response to his returned erection.

"Oh!"

A simple delighted acknowledgment slipped past her lips. Her hands moved from where she rested them on his back to down his ribs, and finally to his hips. Her fingers slipped and probed between their bodies, to take hold of his cock and join them once more.

"Lucius—fuck me again."

46

Lucius grabbed the strap of the Leica that hung from his shoulder and held the coffee shop door for a slender gray-haired man who exited with a newspaper and a cup of coffee. The man offered no nod or words of gratitude. Lucius shook his head, then slipped inside. After he placed his order, his eyes swept the interior of the small cafe sandwiched between a shoe repair shop and a bridal shop. A woman who sat in the corner by the window caught his gaze. The morning light gave her milky skin a radiant glow, and her long, curly copper hair bobbed in a pair of playful pigtails. Artsy. He pictured her straddling a drawing horse and sketching a nude model at the Art Students League or some such place. Her expression was gentle and youthful.

The young man who wore an apron behind the counter eyed the camera that hung from Lucius's shoulder as he handed him a cup of coffee and a sandwich wrapped in parchment paper. Lucius went over to the girl.

"Hi, do you mind if I sit here?"

He motioned that there were no other vacant seats. The red-haired girl peered at him for a moment, then one eyebrow on her face rose. She slipped her foot off the seat of the vacant chair so he could sit.

"Sure, why not?"

He sat the Leica in his lap, then he sat sideways so that his body faced the other tables and he glanced at the other patrons in the cafe to avoid crowding the girl. As he drank his coffee and ate his egg sandwich, he smiled briefly at her but otherwise averted his gaze. She chuckled, and he rolled his eyes to the corners to glance at her. He eventually turned to face her. He raised his eyebrows and sipped his coffee.

"Something funny?"

"You."

"Me?"

"You."

"What about me?"

He glanced down at his clothes, brushed his hand over his face, and ran his fingers through his hair. Nothing seemed out of place. He held up his hands in a questioning gesture. She tilted her head and smiled. He raised his eyebrows and wrinkled his lips. What kind of game was this girl playing?

"Apparently you know something that I don't?"

She rested her chin on her palm.

"Clearly."

"Care to share?"

"Maybe."

"Great."

He slumped back in his chair after he took the last bite of his sandwich and balled up the wrapper, then spoke with his mouthful.

"Great."

She laughed.

"Let's just say I haven't seen you around, or heard from you in a while."

He glared at her. She cocked an eyebrow and smirked at him.

"Apparently, someone else spanks your bottom better than I do."

She covered her eyes with her hands and opened her fingers so he could see her eyes. He swallowed and his eyes widened.

"Mistress Scarlet?"

She gave him a single slow nod.

"But?"

"But what?"

"You look so sweet. I thought you were some student hanging out, like most of them do at this coffee shop."

"I am."

She chuckled.

"I'm studying psychology at NYU."

She took a sip of her coffee and looked at him with a smug smile. He turned his seat to face her and leaned into the table as if he had to impart a secret.

"Oh God. Please don't tell me your Mistress Scarlet act is some deviant psychological class project?"

Her eyes narrowed to a familiar, hardened glare.

"Act? Mistress Scarlet is *no act*. She *is* very much a part of me."

He had stepped too close to the fire. He put up his hands in a gesture of surrender.

"Okay-okay. Sorry. That's cool that you're going to NYU. I would have never thought of the girl behind the mask as a college student."

Her face softened, and she tilted her head as if she were inspecting him.

"And what do you do? I know you're friends with Otto, one of my regulars."

"He's my boss and mentor. I'm a photographer."

He held up the Leica and then sat it on the table. She gave it a cursory glance. There was a sparkle in her eyes, or maybe it was only the light from the window.

"So, why haven't I seen you around?"

He cleared his throat and shifted in his seat.

"I haven't been up for a session with you—no offense."

"None taken. Because of what happened last time?"

"Yeah, sort of."

She sighed and shifted in her seat.

"You know, of the few times you came to me, I never felt it was me you wanted the experience with. You said you had a guest in the other room watching us. It was her or him you wanted in the room with you. Wasn't it?"

"Yes. She's someone I can't get out of my head, and maybe I don't want to."

The girl sat back in her chair and looked to be contemplating what he said. With the pleasant light coming through the coffee shop's windows, it was difficult to think of her as Mistress Scarlet.

"Do you have a name other than Mistress Scarlet?"

She peered at him for a moment, as if to contemplate the possible gravity of her answer.

"Grace."

He raised an eyebrow. Her eyes narrowed as if she expected him to laugh.

"It's nice to meet you, Grace. I'm Lucius."

She eyed him with a gaze like someone trying to judge if his name, like a particular piece of clothing, fit him properly. She smiled, took a sip of her coffee, all the while she looked at him over the top of her cup. After she lowered her cup, she licked her lips, and her gaze narrowed.

"You're my only former client that knows my real name. You better not spread it around, or I'll have to crush your nuts."

She smirked. His eyes widened, and he chuckled with a crooked smile.

"Got it! What do you mean, former client?"

"I didn't think I would see you again, so let's just leave it at that."

"Really?"

Her gaze looked tired, and she wrinkled the corner of her lips.

"Really—and too bad. You're kinda cute."

He sat back in his chair as if hit by some loss. His gaze wandered out the window and across the street.

"Maybe you can persuade your lady friend to give you the spanking you desire."

He snorted. She had been looking out the window as well, but then their eyes met. The light set her red hair ablaze and her milky white skin glowed. The light was perfect. She was perfect.

"Can I photograph you? The light is perfect."

Her lips tightened, and she glared at him.

"Go ahead."

He removed the cap on the 50mm lens, set the aperture, then the appropriate corresponding speed, brought the camera to his eye, framed and focused, then waited. As he watched her, he imagined her breathing until he felt it as his own. Click. He lowered the camera.

"I got the shot."

"That's it? Do you want to take another?"

He smiled, both inside and out.

"No—I got the shot. Thank you."

She shrugged.

"Goodbye Lucius."

She stood and slung an oversize beaten canvas handbag over her shoulder. Before she exited the coffee shop, she looked back at him. The brightness of her gaze and the curve of her lips; he had seen before in other women. It was an unspoken invitation.

47

After climbing two flights of stairs and a walk down a narrow dimly lit hallway with worn, chipped tiles, Eleanor arrived at what she hoped was Lucius's apartment. She pressed the doorbell button, and it made a sickly distressed clatter.

The door opened and there he stood, a beautiful young man. It always struck her how he grew from the odd boy Kenneth brought home to the man she now saw before her.

"Hi, c'mon in."

Lucius stepped aside and held the door. His hands were wet, and he appeared to be cooking or cleaning. She stepped inside. The main open space had a kitchen area in one corner. A bistro table with two chairs sat under the window closest to the kitchen. She recognized the Leica camera on the table. On the far adjacent walls, two framed black and white photographs hung, and the wide space between them was a single photograph that was taped to the wall. Her eyebrows rose. Through the doorway, she could see the edge of his bed.

"Hm. Small. Somewhat charming, I suppose. At least it's bright in here."

He chuckled.

"You arrived at the right time. Living on one of the lower floors and with the taller surrounding buildings, I only get about an hour of decent sunlight."

She nodded. Her heels echoed on the hardwood floors.

"You could use an area rug."

He smiled.

"It's on my list. I've always admired the one Kenneth had in his study. If I can find something that size, but less expensive, I'd be happy. Can I make you a cup of tea?"

"That would be lovely."

He went to into the kitchen to fill the kettle and put it on the stove.

"Have you invited Beatrice to see your new place?"

"No, not yet."

"Why?"

"I wanted to get your opinion first. Plus, she seemed too eager and excited to see the new place."

"Isn't that more reason to have shown her?"

"I suppose. I thought maybe you could give me some decorating tips."

"I see."

He came out of the kitchen after he turned the burner on under the kettle.

"Let me give you the full tour."

She followed him into the bedroom, where there was a full-size bed with brass head and footboards, and a simple oak nightstand and dresser. On the nightstand was an imitation Tiffany lamp. It made her smile inside. Attached to the bedroom was a small bathroom with a clawfoot bathtub that barely fit inside. The space alongside the tub was barely wide enough to slip past to reach a small pedestal sink with a mirror. On the back of the sink alongside the faucet was a tube of toothpaste, a toothbrush, a disposable razor, and a can of shaving cream. A bachelor's necessities. When she glanced at him, he was rubbing his hands together like an anxious boy.

"That's it."

He smiled and shrugged. She smiled a soft smile. The entire space was small, but what was more off-putting was the many layers of paint on not just the walls but the moldings.

"It's small, but it's all a single man needs."

When she glanced at him, his eyes were traveling her body. He cleared his throat when their eyes met.

"I suppose."

She followed him back to the main room. The framed photographs caught her attention. She went to examine them. Her eyes narrowed when she saw the old photograph he shot of Beatrice in the backyard wearing her prize opal choker. The only thing that made it bearable to see the photograph again was the distance of time. Beatrice was older, more respectful, and more importantly, out of the house and somewhat out of her life.

"So you never destroyed those photographs as I asked?"

Her back was to him, but she could feel him squirming behind her, like a worm. The floors creaked as he shifted his weight.

"No. I couldn't. I'm sorry."

She sighed. She skipped the small color photograph taped to the wall to first look at the other framed photograph. It was of her, at the beach, when she and Kenneth first took him along with them.

"It doesn't matter anymore, I suppose."

She went to the color photograph.

"Who's this?"

She stood in front of the 4x6 color photograph he taped to the wall. It was a portrait of a fair skin girl with red hair. She looked to be sitting at a table in a restaurant or coffee shop. The girl's gaze and features were tense. Her long red hair and pouty mouth looked familiar to Eleanor.

"She's some girl I met around. I was getting coffee, and she was at the cafe. She let me take her picture."

"Oh? She's attractive in a bohemian sort of way, but she also looks troubled."

The teakettle sang. When she turned around, he was already in the kitchen. He turned off the burner and poured the scalding water into two cups.

"Please sit, and I'll bring it over."

She sat at the bistro table under the window. He brought the steaming cups of tea to the table. The tea bag labels flittered at the end of their strings like cheap kites. The steam rose from the cups and carried with it the scent of orange pekoe. He stood there a moment, teacups in hand, as if he were considering her. She raised an eyebrow. He put down the cups with the Leica camera between them.

"Can I photograph you? The light right now is perfect."

She tilted her head.

"Please, Eleanor."

"Very well."

As he picked up the camera and adjusted the dials, she steeped the tea bag in her cup, then set it aside on the saucer. She glanced up to find the camera in front of his face. He turned the ring on the lens to adjust the focus. She picked up her teacup and held it before her lips. Click. A whisper of delicate metal shutter blades came from across the table. He thumbed the crank on the camera to advance the film. She took a sip. Click. He lowered the camera and set it back on the table with a grin. His eyes sparkled. She lowered her cup and gazed at him.

"Is that all?"

"Yes. I got the shot."

She glanced over at the small color photograph of the red-haired girl at the cafe.

"I know you know more than you're letting on. What's her name? The red-haired girl taped to your wall?"

He snorted and seemed hesitant to answer.

"Grace. Her name is Grace."

"Interesting. She doesn't look like a Grace."

He wore an odd smile, and his eyebrows rose. It was an expression she had seen not too long ago, from behind a one-way glass panel. Her spine stiffened. Long red hair, milky white skin. The girl in the photograph matched the young woman, who wore the scantily clad leather outfit. The same young woman who whipped, punished, and urinated on him, in his mouth no less. She ran her fingertips over her collarbones and at the base of her neck. The memory made her uncomfortably warm. She shifted in her chair. Her thighs rubbed together and her nylons made a faint crisp zipping sound. Heat and electricity intensified between her legs. He moved his lips, but there was no sound. She was still in disbelief that she took off her wet panties and left them for him to find. Deep inside her, she smiled. That night she ran for one reason, to see if he would chase her. He continued to move his lips. She blinked. He chuckled.

"Did you hear what I said?"

She blinked again and snorted.

"Sorry. I was lost in thought."

He lowered his cup of tea.

"Good thoughts I hope."

"It was nothing. Please. What were you saying?"

She had been holding her cup in front of her the entire time. The teacup made a soft clatter when she sat it on the saucer. He sipped his tea and peered at her over the top of the cup. He had been watching her almost the entire time since she arrived. She questioned if he could read her mind.

48

Beatrice stepped from the bedroom into the living room of Lucius's apartment. She wore only her panties and the tie Lucius wore last night for their dinner out. The knot was loose around her neck and the tie hung between her breasts. As she passed the bathroom door, steam escaped and kissed her skin. Lucius hummed inside as he showered.

Out in the main room, she peered at the large collage of black and white photographs taped to the wall between two larger framed black and white prints. Last night they met at the restaurant and got to his apartment late. They skipped the dime tour and headed straight for the bedroom. Her eyes moved over the images. Among them was a small 4x6 color print of a girl with long red hair. The girl was pretty, but she looked tense. A stranger? Beatrice examined the two framed photographs. One was of Eleanor at the beach taken when Lucius and she were children, and one of her when she wore Eleanor's expensive opal choker. She cringed when she looked at the photograph of herself as a young girl. The photograph was beautiful, but all she could remember of that day was after, when Eleanor confronted her with the same photograph as evidence that she had taken the necklace. She drew in an audible breath. Eleanor whipped her good that day. She touched her cheek as she remembered.

Against the wall was a black portfolio case. The leather corners and panels were cracked by time and use. She laid out the case on the floor, unzipped it around its three edges, and opened it like an enormous book. She smiled at the first two pictures, which were of her. One at the beach and the other in the backyard. She flipped through the loose old photographs he must have developed recently, as the prints were clean, flat and the photo paper appeared new.

After she flipped through the prints, she found a raised pocket at the back of the portfolio. She held the flap open and smiled when she heard him singing in the shower. She took out the stack of prints and sleeves of negatives. Her eyes went wide and her mouth hung open. She dropped the photographs and negatives on the open portfolio case. The prints landed and fanned out in disarray.

The topmost prints were nude black and white photographs of the woman she met recently at her father's apartment in Hartford. The woman's name was Phoebe—Aunt Phoebe—Lucius's Aunt Phoebe. In the pictures, the woman lie spread out on a bed. The way the angle was, Lucius must have been standing on the mattress. A fire rushed through her veins. Her lips tightened and her eyebrows drew together. She wanted to burn the mess of photographs. She shoved the topmost photographs to find more underneath. A few of the prints slid across the floor. Another picture of Phoebe showed more of the room. The bed, the nightstand, the lamp—it was her father's bedroom—at his apartment in Hartford. All those nights when he was too busy to come home. Her heart sank. She pushed them aside to find pictures of Phoebe passed out on a couch. Beatrice covered her mouth. Why would her father take pictures of this woman passed out with her skirt raised? Her stomach turned. She felt compelled to look at each photograph, but when she got to the bottom, there was another woman in the last photograph. Her breath caught.

Lying on a bedsheet, wearing only a garter belt and stockings with her legs spread, was Eleanor. Her expression in the black and white photograph was intimate, singular, and met for only one person's gaze, yet recorded for anyone who discovered it. Her face was softer, younger, with eyes not yet hardened by time and circumstance. Beatrice found her breath and exhaled. She touched the rough warped edges of the print. All the corners of the paper were soft and rounded by time. Lucius's singing in the shower drew her attention.

She pushed herself up from the floor and hurried to the bedroom. She threw her dress on, stuffed her stockings and bra into her shoulder bag, and grabbed her heels. The shower knobs screeched from the other side of the bathroom door, followed by the metal clattering of the shower curtain rings. As she hurried from the room, she stopped and stood before the mess of photographs on the floor and the open portfolio case. She dug into her shoulder bag and dropped Lucius's mom's diary atop the nude photograph of Eleanor, and then she ran from the apartment.

49

For two weeks, Lucius tried to reach Beatrice by phone. Any messages he left with her friends seemed to disappear down a dark well. She left his mom's diary on top of the nude photograph of Eleanor, and the rest of the photographs from inside the case lay scattered on the floor. He wanted to explain, but all he could do was give her time, and he hoped she would eventually listen to what he had to say.

"I need to see you."

The phone cord stretched over the top of the kitchen counter and down to where he sat on the floor with his back to the wall. A fiery breath huffed through the receiver.

"I'm not available today, or don't you remember?"

"I remember."

A heavy sigh came over the phone.

"The last time I saw you at the coffee shop, I thought we were done."

"It was *you* who said we were done."

The call was silent. His jaw flexed and his eyebrows drew together.

"How'd my picture turn out?"

He glanced across the living room. Between the two framed photographs, one of Beatrice and the other of Eleanor, was a grouping of black and white prints of various sizes taped to the wall. Stuck within the center of the chaotic mess was the 4x6 color photograph of her taken at the coffee shop.

"It's beautiful. The light on your face and hair is perfect."

"Really?"

"Really."

"Hm. Can I see it? Invite me over."

Grace's voice brightened. He chuckled. Her playful request was a far cry from her Mistress Scarlet voice and persona.

"So, does that mean I can see you?"

There was a silent pause again.

"Yes, but not here, and not like before. Maybe we can have coffee at your place. Well?"

He imagined her dressed in her leather outfit, ready to abuse her next client, all the while teasing and talking to him like they were high school kids flirting. He held back the laughter that brewed inside him.

"Okay."

"Okay what?"

He chuckled.

"Grace, would you like to have coffee at my place?"

"I thought you would never ask."

Grace ran her fingertips through the ends of her hair, adjusted the ribbon choker around her neck with a silver heart pendant, picked at her t-shirt, and tugged the sleeves of her jean jacket as she stood before Lucius's apartment door. She waited a moment, then pushed the buzzer. The doorbell made a sick metallic clatter. There were footsteps on the other side of the door, and when it swung open, Lucius stood there with a smile. With her Chuck Taylors on, they were about the same height. He was barefoot with jeans and a raggedy faded orange t-shirt, but his face was smooth and clean shaven. It was impossible for her to hold back her smile.

"Hi, c'mon in."

She walked in, gave the kitchen area a cursory glance, then her gaze went straight to the two walls where the two framed photographs hung at both ends of a large grouping of prints randomly taped to the wall.

"Not bad, about as bright as mine. Did the ad or realtor say sun-drenched?"

He raised an eyebrow but made no comment. She nodded.

"Yeah, same here."

She pointed at the photographs.

"Mind if I have a look?"

"Go ahead. The coffee is ready. How do you take it?"

She took off her jean jacket and tossed it over the back of a chair. Braless, her nipples pointed through her t-shirt. She smirked at him.

"Guess."

"Black?"

"Nope, lots of cream, lots of sugar."

He chuckled. His gaze briefly wandered down her shirt.

"You got it."

When he went to get the coffee, she turned her attention to the photographs. Her gaze went straight to the center and the only color photograph, which was the one he took of her at the coffee shop. She smiled softly, amazed that he only took one picture. He was right. It was perfect. The way the light lit her hair and face made her look angelic. She wrinkled her lips at how tense of an expression she had that day, but that aside she had to admit it was possibly the best picture ever taken of her.

"You're right. The picture turned out great. How come it's so small?"

She raised her voice and glanced over her shoulder. He was in the refrigerator getting the cream.

"Diamonds are small."

She tilted her head and smirked at him.

"That's sweet. *Really*. How come it's so small?"

He was stirring the cream and sugar into her coffee.

"I rarely shoot in color, if you haven't noticed. It's what I had loaded in the camera at the time. Honestly, I was trying to finish the roll. When I looked over the negatives, I asked a friend of mine at the camera store to pull a single print on their instant print machine, one like they use at the drugstores."

She wrinkled her lips and put her hands on her hips.

"Are you saying you took my picture just so you could finish up the roll of film?"

He brought their cups of coffee to where she stood.

"To be honest, yes. I shot mostly street scenes and a few locations in the park, and then there you were."

His eyes were wide and bright. She shook her head and chuckled.

"You're ridiculous."

She took the cup of coffee he held out to her. They stood side by side and looked over the photographs.

"That picture has got me thinking more about shooting in color, but I am more comfortable with black and white."

"Maybe you should experiment more. You can take my picture again."

She held her cup with both hands and sipped her coffee. It was good. He made it just like she liked it, not too sweet and not too much cream, so the flavor of the coffee came through. The two larger framed black and white photographs equally caught her attention. Both were like question marks at the beginning and ending of a sentence—a Spanish sentence.

"Who's the woman at the beach? Is the other picture of her as a girl? The choker she's wearing looks expensive."

She touched the ribbon and heart choker around her neck. He pointed with his cup.

"That one is a picture of Ms. Eleanor Crane. Her and her husband, Kenneth, took me in after my parents died in a car crash. Mr. Crane, Kenneth, was the one who taught me about photography, and gave me one of his cameras."

He pointed to the bistro table where a silver bodied camera sat.

"Sorry to hear about your parents."

"It's okay."

"I thought dear Otto taught you everything about photography. Is Kenneth a fashion photographer as well?"

"No, a lawyer."

She burst into laughter.

"You're joking?"

He chuckled.

"No, he's a lawyer and a damn good one, but if he chose to be a photographer, he would be great. He has a good eye and sensibility."

"Sounds like you."

"Does it?"

He moved closer so that their arms touched. She stepped forward for a closer examination of the larger black and white framed photograph of Eleanor at the beach.

"She's pretty, but there is something in those eyes."

"Oh? What do you see?"

"You see it too, don't you?"

"I do. What is it *you* see?"

"A kind of danger. Like looking at a sunbathing crocodile lying there. It doesn't move, but if you get too close, it will snap you, and you're done."

He laughed.

"Is that really what you see?"

She tilted her head and further contemplated the picture.

"Yes, or something like that."

"That's funny coming from you."

She had given him the look she intended, for his smile dissolved.

"What do you see?"

He turned and gazed at the picture. His chin rose as though he had contemplated the picture many times before and had become a sort of scholar.

"Mrs. Crane—Eleanor—is an elegant woman who prides herself on being fashionable and well put together. She can be demanding, but no more so than the demands she puts on herself. She has great taste and style. She is—"

Grace raised an eyebrow, and he must have noticed her disbelief in his admiration for Mrs. Crane.

"Are you in love with her?"

"What?"

"You are."

"No. I love her like—"

"Like what? And don't say 'mother' because we both know that's not true."

He raised his eyebrows and was silent for a moment. His lips wrinkled as if he misplaced his train of thought.

"She's special to me. Let's just leave it at that."

"Uh, huh?"

She smirked to let him know she had finished torturing him, and he gave her an awkward smile. She went over to the other framed portrait.

"Who's this?"

"That's Beatrice Crane. She's Eleanor's step-daughter. We were kids when I shot that. I was eleven."

"You were really only eleven."

"Yes."

"That necklace. It looks expensive. Did her daddy get it for her?"

"Oh, no, it was Mrs. Crane's. Beatrice wasn't supposed to have it. We got in trouble over the whole thing. Mrs. Crane found my pictures, and we both got spanked."

"She hit you?"

"She hit the both of us. Beatrice was mad at me. Mad at the photographs I shot of her."

Grace looked closer at the photograph. Her lips were tight, but bowed into a smile. He moved in alongside her as if to see what she was looking at.

"Lucius, you're an amazing photographer. Your pictures are incredible. They're loaded with emotion."

He leaned toward her with heavy eyelids and puckered lips. She put up her hand to stop him and sloshed some of her coffee onto the floor.

"Whoa."

He went to the kitchen and got some paper towels.

"Sorry about that."

His eyebrows rose and drew together.

"No, I'm sorry. I thought…"

She faced him and held her cup with both hands.

"It's okay. I guess you might have had that impression, since I insisted you invite me to your place. Look—I don't want a boyfriend, let's make that clear."

"Uh? Oh? Sure, I understand."

He stood up with the wet coffee stained paper towel in his hand, and lowered his chin. She touched his cheek. It was a gentle touch.

"We can still have fun, as long as you don't get attached. Got it?"

"You make it sound like I'm some kind of barnacle."

She chuckled, and he joined her.

"Oh, you would be surprised. I've had my share of barnacles. So you understand?"

"Yes."

He looked at her, but his gaze seemed somewhere beyond. She chuckled and shook her head. He wrinkled his lips into a crumpled smile.

"You're too cute for your own good."

His eyebrows rose, and in the dimly lit apartment, the sun broke through the gloom on his face and crept across his lips to expose a soft smile. She put her coffee cup in his open hand so he stood there, hands full, with the paper towel in the other. She put her hand on his cheek and moved close to him until the compressed space between them became electrified. Two bodies in magnetic proximity. She licked her lips and gazed into his eyes. His breath was soft on her face. She could see in his eyes that he wanted more than what she would give, but who knew, maybe this would be enough. She squeezed at his crotch and he lurched in surprise and spilled more of her coffee.

"Whoa."

He patted his jeans where some of the coffee landed. They both laughed, and she helped him clean up the mess. After they put their half-drank cups in the sink, she took his hand and tugged him to the bedroom, to get the other thing she had come for. There would be time later to ask him for the photograph he took of her.

50

Beatrice sat in the kitchen of her upper west-side apartment, barefoot, with one heel up on the chair's seat. She held the phone to her ear while she picked at her toes and rubbed her foot. She knew something was coming, but was unsure who would call her first. To her surprise, it was Eleanor. Her throat was dry as she listened.

"Have you spoken to your father?"

"No."

"I'm sorry to say our marriage has ended. Kenneth and I have agreed to a divorce. I will keep the house, and he has made his Hartford apartment his full-time residence. You should know that any of your belongings at the house are safe, and there is no rush to move anything."

"Oh God, Eleanor. I'm sorry things turned out the way they did. I love my father, but you deserve better."

She was astonished at her sympathy for the woman. The same woman who often made her feel unwelcome, and the same woman who she prayed misfortune would come to, and it did.

"That's kind of you to say."

She shifted on the kitchen chair and knit her fingers between her toes on the foot she had propped up on the seat.

"I know it's no surprise to you I don't do well with children, but now that you're a young woman, a smart and beautiful young woman I might add, it would be nice if we could be friends and have some sort of relationship. That is, if you would like to."

She wanted to tell Eleanor that it would be best if they never saw one another again, but other words came out.

"Sure, that would be nice."

"Good. That warms my heart."

Her words surprised Beatrice. She never knew Eleanor possessed a heart.

"Have you heard from Lucius?"

"No, not for a while. Well, I almost saw him."

Beatrice said nothing about storming out the last time she saw him, the last time they made love, and when she found the nude photographs of his Aunt Phoebe and the one nude photograph of Eleanor. For a second she considered asking Eleanor about the nude photograph, but knowing her father's appetite for such things, she let it drop.

"Almost? Did you see him or not?"

"I was going to drop by, but I saw this redhead coming out of his apartment. She was tall, as tall as him. I turned away from her in the hallway and stood facing one of the other apartment doors. She passed behind me without a word or a glance. I don't think she was one of his models. She was attractive, but hard looking in the face. I couldn't imagine Lucius wanting to photograph her. Who is she? Do you know? Sorry, why would you? I didn't think he liked redheads."

Beatrice was sure the red-haired girl was the same one in the small photograph Lucius had taped to his apartment wall, but she wanted to know if Eleanor knew anything about it. There was silence at the other end until a faint bird chirp came over the receiver. She imagined Eleanor in her wicker chair out on the patio with the phone.

"I'm sorry. I don't know who she is."

Her words sounded more contemplative than merely curious or disinterested, and the time it took her to answer made it seem more so. She knew something. Beatrice was sure of it.

"I figured as much. Well, thank you for calling. I must head out soon. I've got some things to take care of."

"Beatrice, I'm pleased we had a friendly conversation. I have a couple of trips to make to New York to finalize things for your father's and my divorce. Maybe we can get together for lunch."

"That would be nice."

The two women said their goodbyes. Beatrice got up and hung up the receiver on the wall-mounted phone. She gazed out the kitchen window that looked out onto the courtyard of the apartment complex. An old woman sat alone on a bench. She again imagined Eleanor sitting alone out in the screened patio of their old Connecticut home.

51

Eleanor glanced back down the narrow dim lit hallway where she followed Lucius months ago. She had first knocked on the steel door where Lucius had knocked to gain access to the viewing room where she had watched him. Not knowing who or what she might face, she wore high-waisted knit pants and a long sleeve shirt. She wished she had worn sneakers or boat shoes instead of her heels. She peered at the glass peephole, then knocked again. A shadow passed over the small glass aperture. The door opened and its dry hinges screeched and echoed in the hallway.

The same redheaded young woman with milky white skin who she watched from the viewing room stood in the doorway in her black leather outfit that barely covered her nipples and crotch. She also wore knee-high tall boots, leather gloves, and a leather mask that covered half her face and had large diamond cutouts around her eyes. The florescent light cast a yellowish tint on the walls. A second industrial steel door stood closed on the opposite wall. The leather clad woman stood there with one hand on her hip and the other on the door. Her lips curled into a mocking smile.

"Avon calling?"

Eleanor pushed her way into the room.

"Mistress Scarlet, or should I call you Grace?"

Her eyes narrowed from behind her leather mask.

"So you're Mrs. Robinson? Or perhaps Mommie Dearest. I thought I recognized you."

"I beg your pardon?"

"From behind the glass. So you're the one who has Lucius tied around her little finger."

"You don't know what you're talking about."

"Don't I? I bet he would have loved it if you were the one to beat him instead of me."

An uneasy smile formed inside her.

"Don't be absurd."

Grace put her hands on her hips.

"You know what? I can see it in your eyes. You and I are not that different."

Grace looked her up and down.

"Sure, you may be some rich bitch, but that doesn't change the fact that you like to punish people. Maybe it's a prerequisite, and I'm the getting-by college student anomaly."

Eleanor huffed and shook her head.

"Think what you may, but I'm here to tell you to stay away from Lucius. I don't want him to throw away his life with the likes of you."

Grace stood tense with her fists balled. Eleanor hoped the girl would make a move. She was far from being a brawler, but it would give her a reason to smack this girl and set her straight. Behind her leather mask, Grace's green-eyed gaze grew fiery and her jaw and lips tightened.

"I know he's obsessed with you, but I'm the one fucking him and giving him what he needs."

She glared at Grace. Grace smirked.

"He's a skilled lover. I bet you didn't know that."

"Stay away from Lucius. Do you hear me?"

"Why should you care? Or is it you don't want me to steal your boy-toy? You know, toys are meant to be played with."

Grace tilted her head and sneered. Heat rose within Eleanor.

"Lucius doesn't need you. I'm not leaving here until you tell me you will never see him again."

Grace huffed, and her gaze was sharp and dangerous.

"No one tells me what to do. Why don't you crawl back to the Hamptons or whatever couture rock you crawled out from under? I've got a client waiting."

She marched to the inner steel door and yanked it open. Its hinges screeched, and she disappeared inside. Eleanor's chest tightened, and she huffed, then caught the door before it closed and she followed Grace in. Restrained to the bulky wooden chair was a naked, balding man with silvery-hair and rounded belly. The man in the chair gazed forward as he waited for his session with Mistress Scarlet to begin. Eleanor grabbed Grace's arm and spun her around so the two women were in each other's faces.

"You may have ignored other people, but you will not ignore me. You will do as I say."

Grace slapped Eleanor with a gloved hand, upsetting her hair and caused some of her curls to come unpinned. Heat rose in her cheek where Grace hit her. She gave it back to her, slapping Grace across her mouth. Grace touched her lips, then snarled at Eleanor before she grabbed her wrists and pulled her to the ground. Eleanor landed unceremoniously on her rump. Grace tried to straddle her, but she pushed her away and got back on her feet.

She took off her heels and tossed them aside. The man strapped to the chair made several darting glances at the two women, always returning his gaze forward with a look of uncertainty. Grace swung at her, but Eleanor captured her wrist and kicked her in the midriff, which sent Grace landing on top of the restrained man. Grace held her stomach and slumped to the floor between the man's legs. Blood dripped from the man's nostrils and sprayed as he cried out.

"What's going on? I only booked a session with Mistress Scarlet."

"Don't you mean Sweet Grace here?"

"Huh? Who's Sweet Grace?"

Eleanor shook her head and grabbed a handful of Grace's hair and dragged her to the rack of assorted whips. Grace screamed and clawed at her wrist and arm, but Eleanor held on. The younger woman finally tripped her, and both women were wrestling on the floor. Grace got to her feet first. She reached for a bullwhip, but Eleanor yanked back on Grace's hair, keeping her out of reach. Grace grabbed hold of a riding crop. She whipped it back, and it snapped loud when it contacted Eleanor's legs. Eleanor was grateful that she wore the pair of high-waisted knit pants she purchased at Bergdorf

Goodman the last time she visited New York. The leather end of the riding crop still stung her legs.

"Would someone please tell me what's going on?"

The man groaned and muttered behind them. Eleanor got a hold of Grace's wrist. She slapped the younger woman several times in the face while Grace clawed at her and got a hold of her hair and pulled until Eleanor cried out. Eleanor tore at Grace's mask and finally ripped it from her face.

"Oh, you cunt!"

It was all Grace could say before Eleanor got the riding crop from her and turned it on her. She lashed the young woman. Red welts appeared on the girl's arms, shoulder and then cheek, until she cowered on the floor against the wall. Grace cried uncontrollably.

"Okay, okay, okay-okay, please."

Her words trailed off into muddled sobs. Eleanor tossed the riding crop. It flipped and hit the other wooden restraining area and landed somewhere in the shadows of the room. She flipped her hair back that hung in her face.

"It would be a shame if I have to come back, wouldn't it?"

Grace held up her shaking hand.

"I won't talk to Lucius again. He's all yours, you crazy bitch."

Eleanor found her heels, slipped them on, and marched from the room. She slammed the metal doors with their screechy hinges behind her.

52

The hands of Otto Schenker's Omega wristwatch approached nine o'clock. Lucius worked his jacket cuff over the borrowed watch and smiled at one of the female servers, who carried a tray of champagne flutes. Denise Eccles, owner and gallery manager of Eccles Fine Art on 47th Street, leaned into him and touched his forearm.

"We sold another one!"

Her eyes were wide and bright, and her thin lip smile painted a deep red. She strolled away to work the room. Denise was like a bee that knew where the nectar was. She wore all black of various textures: black heels, black opaque stockings, a black skirt and a black shawl over a silky black blouse. She could preside over his funeral. He glanced at the white walls where his oversized prints of Beatrice hung in their thin black frames with white linen mats. He captured those moments at his studio and in his apartment. Her smile was radiant and carried bucketsful of joy. Her eyes saw him, knew and understood him, and wanted him. All of her energy came through the photographs with raw sincerity. The nudes he shot of her were more playful than seductive, perhaps because he shot them the morning after a blissful night of sex. Like the others, her energy came through honest and vulnerable.

"I can't believe she let you photograph her nude, let alone put her on display."

Lucius turned around to find Eleanor fixed before one of the large nudes. Her expression was placid, and her pale sky-blue gaze was dull and overcast. He glanced at the large photograph of Beatrice behind her. Even in black and white, the morning sun that lit Beatrice's face warmed her soft smile and bright eyes. She wore his dress shirt unbuttoned; her left breast and nipple exposed, and her hair tossed in a delightful mess of curls.

"Bea knows the stakes when she models for me."

Eleanor raised an eyebrow, and the corner of her lips tightened.

"I haven't seen her. Does she know about your opening?"

He brushed back the bottom of his jacket and slipped his hands into his pants pockets. It was difficult for him to look at her.

"Not exactly."

She snorted.

"Lucius? She's the main subject of your show."

"I know. She has seen some of the enlarged prints."

"That's not good enough. They could be for your private collection for all she knows."

"Eleanor, the truth is—I wanted *you* to see my work. I wanted *you* to judge it."

"That's flattering, Lucius, but you might not like my opinion."

"Tell me."

She glanced around the room.

"I wasn't aware you were so taken by Beatrice."

He cleared his throat and lowered his chin as if he was preparing to impart some secret, then leaned slightly toward her.

"I wish they were photographs of you."

"You can't be serious. Besides, it seems you found your muse in Beatrice."

"No, don't say that."

"Lucius, I think it's time for me to go."

He peered at the gallery's hardwood floor as if some answer lie there, perhaps wedged in the grooves or seams. She headed for the entrance.

"Wait!"

She stepped out the door as he hurried to catch her, but Denise stopped him. She was all smiles.

"We sold another print."

He grabbed her arms and kissed her cheek.

"That's wonderful, Denise, but I have to run."

"What? Why?"

"I'm sorry. I'll call you tomorrow."

He hurried from the gallery. A cab pulled to the curb where Eleanor stood. He skipped some steps and nearly fell.

"Eleanor! Wait!"

She slipped into the back of the cab when he grabbed the door handle and swung the door open. His body heaved as he struggled to catch his breath.

"Wait, just wait. Please, Eleanor."

She silently glared at him, but made no objection when he got in the backseat next to her. As his breath slowed to a reasonable rate and blood seemed to return to his head, he thought he was crazy, crazy for chasing her. He swallowed gulps of air.

"I'm sorry Eleanor. I'm sorry I said that, but—"

But it was a lie. He was far from being sorry.

"Miss?"

The taxi driver eyed them from the rearview mirror of the cab.

"It's fine, drive please."

"Where are we going?"

"I'm going to my hotel room. It's been a long day and a most unusual evening. Where shall I tell the driver to drop you?"

He glanced in the direction the taxi was traveling.

"Which hotel?"

"The Hilton."

Her voice was flat. He relaxed back into the seat.

"That's fine. You can drop me there."

She narrowed her gaze at him. He combed his fingers through his hair and prayed that she would allow him to ride with her to the hotel.

"All right."

She turned to gaze out the window. He brushed his fingers through his hair once more and rubbed his palms over his pant legs. She remained silent, so he took the opportunity to think. When the taxi stopped at the entrance to the hotel, he got out to hold the door open for her and to hand the driver the fair.

She took long strides to the hotel entrance with her dress flowing behind her. He hurried to catch up.

"Eleanor, wait."

She stopped before the door and turned on him.

"Go home Lucius."

He grabbed her elbow. The doorman gave him a look and he let go of her.

"We need to talk."

"Oh? Do we?"

She smiled at the doorman, who stepped in front of him. Lucius shook his head and walked away. While the doorman held the door for people exiting, Lucius ducked into one of the unmanned doors. He straightened and buttoned his jacket before he strode across the lobby to follow her to the elevators.

He stepped into the elevator car as the doors were closing, and they shuttered and opened back up. In the car stood a couple and their three kids. They smiled at him for reaching the elevator in time. He moved to the back corner opposite of where she stood. She crossed her arms and glared at him. The yellow light above gave her skin a greenish cast. He brushed his hair back with his fingers and leaned back against the wall. The couple and their kids made hushed chitchat. They looked like they were from out of town, Midwest maybe.

When the car stopped and doors opened, she touched the man's arm.

"Excuse me, please."

The man glanced over his shoulder at her.

"Certainly."

He shuffled, and his family moved closer to Lucius to let her out, which pinned Lucius in the corner.

"Sorry, excuse me too. I'm getting out as well."

The doors nearly closed on his arm before he got out. He smiled at the family before he followed Eleanor down the hallway. When she got in her room, she held the door for him. Her gaze had softened, perhaps conceding to his *need to talk*.

"Thank you."

She closed the door and walked past him to turn on the lamps on the writing desk and nightstand. She then put down her handbag and slipped off her heels before pouring herself a drink from the room's minibar. Without a glance his way, she took off her necklace, earrings, bracelet, and then rings and deposited them on the small writing desk. They clattered like coins. He unbuttoned his jacket and sat on the bed. The room had nice furnishings and smelled of vanilla. She stepped in her stocking feet to the window and pulled the long wooden rods to close the curtains. The rods dangled and clattered soft and hollow like wooden wind chimes. She unbuttoned the top two buttons of her blouse and went to the writing desk to retrieve her drink. She leaned her butt against the edge of the desk, crossed her arm to support the one in which she held the glass tumbler, and drank. Her pale sky-blue eyes fell on him. She drew in a long, impatient breath.

"Lucius, I am deathly tired. Please tell me what this is all about, so I can retire. I have an early morning drive home."

He peered down at his hands in his lap.

"All the times you visited New York. The evenings out we shared. I know you feel something for me. Those moments at home out on the patio, with Kenneth at work, and you inviting me to a glass of wine."

She snorted, shook her head, and took a drink.

"I'm not a boy anymore. I'm a man."

"Kenneth is a man."

She huffed and peered off into the room at nothing in particular.

"At least he *was* a man. Now he's just a damn fool."

"I won't argue with that. He has no idea what he's given up."

She snorted and glanced hard at him. Her gaze was like fiery ice. She finished her drink and went to the minibar to pour herself another. Even in her stocking feet, she moved gracefully. Without her heels, made her seem more approachable. His cock stiffened. His palms pressed into the mattress, and he shifted in his seat on the bed and crossed his legs. He returned his hands to his lap to cover the rise in his trousers.

"Kenneth seems to know what he wants. Maybe he's right. Perhaps I'm no longer the woman he fell in love with. Perhaps I'm nothing."

She sat on the edge of the bed next to the nightstand with her drink in hand. She took a healthy swallow before she sat the tumbler down. He raised an eyebrow. She seemed on a quest to dull her nerves.

"You're not nothing. You're everything. You're incredible. When you enter the room—"

She stifled a chuckle and glanced at him with a raised eyebrow.

"That's sweet Lucius, but whatever crush you have for me is merely that. You're a young man who can have lots of girls, and you should. Now, if you would kindly go, I would like to get ready for bed."

"I'm sorry Eleanor. I'm not leaving."

She snorted and shook her head. Some of her curls came loose and fell alongside her face. She turned and glared at him for a moment.

"I'm going to get ready for bed, and you're leaving before I turn out the lights."

She stood, unzipped and stepped out of her skirt, and unbuttoned her blouse, then tossed both on the back of the accent chair, and sat back down in her bra, slip, and stockings. He still sat on the bed. She wrinkled her lips and pulled her stockings down from under her slip, then worked each one down her legs. He licked his lips and when he looked up, her gaze was on him. She must have watched him as he watched her. After she rolled up her loose stockings, he closed the space between them. Their bodies touched, and he put his hand on her thigh.

"Don't deny me Eleanor. I've waited all my life for you."

He spoke in a heated whisper with his face close to hers. In her gaze, he found no answers, yet she made no objections. He pressed his lips to hers, tender at first, then he kissed her rough and deep with a hunger, and when he moved his lips from hers to kiss her neck, she gasped. Her body stiffened when he moved his hand up between her thighs to take hold of her sex. Her panties were wet. He fumbled his fingers at her panties and attempted to slip his fingers under the lace to touch her where he most desired. She grasped his wrist and tore his hand away, then shoved his shoulder. He caught himself before he fell back on the bed.

"Enough! Enough of this madness."

She slapped him across the face. She rose to her feet and stood over him. "Get out!"

He stood slowly and backed away from her. Her gaze was electric. He feared lightning could leap from her eyes and strike him dead. He ran his fingers over his lips, ducked his head, and walked from her room. Out in the hallway, as he made his way to the elevators, he had difficulty swallowing and gravity increased to match his desire to run. Time seemed to stretch during the elevator ride down and the walk through the lobby. Outside, the blaring sound of car horns woke him until he gasped and sucked in mouthfuls of air. He walked in long strides with no idea of where he was going. Finally, he ran.

53

Kenneth came into the living room with two open bottles of beer. He handed one to Lucius, who sat on the sofa, then he sat in the easy chair. It was the first time Lucius visited him at the Hartford apartment. Lucius took a sip from the bottle of beer and glanced around the space.

"This is different than what I imagined—smaller."

Kenneth chuckled.

"Yeah? Originally, I intended to have a simple small space for occasional over-night stays, so I could be close to the office and the courthouse."

Lucius raised his eyebrows and wrinkled his lips before taking another sip of beer.

"I was sorry to hear about your divorce. Is this—now—your permanent home?"

Kenneth shifted in his seat and took a drink.

"I'm afraid so, at least for now."

Lucius knit his fingers together as he clenched the bottle with both hands. He stared at it as if he was inspecting the label.

"Something on your mind?"

"I learned that my Aunt Phoebe is living here, here in Hartford. Are you and her together? I remember at the airport long ago, when I took pictures of you two together. There was something I saw then."

Kenneth braced his elbow on the armrest of the easy chair. He was cornered, and he knew it. There was nowhere to run, nowhere to hide, no stories he could make up.

"I'm sorry, I didn't tell you that your Aunt Phoebe moved to Hartford. I left it up to her discretion."

Lucius looked up at him without a word. Kenneth cleared his throat.

"Yes, we ended up seeing each other. She soon got bored with me and sought other lawyers to fool around with, and that not being enough, she moved on to some judges. If their wives find out, it will be some mess. Your Aunt Phoebe sure knows how to leave a wake behind her."

Lucius huffed. His gaze returned to the bottle in his grasp.

"For what it's worth, I regret taking things as far as I did with her. After I helped her move to Hartford, that should have been the end of it. I'm sorry things played out as they did."

Lucius's shoulders softened, and Kenneth could see the tension leave the young man's face. He looked as though he traded a mask of anger and frustration for one of doubt and worry.

"Something else?"

"I got my mom's diary back. There were pages torn from it."

Kenneth released a long, heavy breath.

"She mentioned an affair with a man, a tall, handsome professional man, perhaps—a lawyer."

Kenneth sat his beer on the coffee table, stood and went to the kitchen. From inside a drawer, under a manual for his countertop blender, were twelve torn pages. He slipped them free from under the manual, and gazed at the words for a moment, not reading the pages, but to take in the woman's handwriting who wrote them. He returned to the living room and placed the pages on the coffee table in front of Lucius.

"I know you want to know if I am *that* man. The answer is, yes."

Lucius put down his bottle of beer and stared at the pages with a look of someone who regretted his own curiosity. He expected Lucius to be angry, instead he looked confused.

"There's more in those pages. Something I never knew. The timing when your mother was pregnant with you. Well—I often wondered, but she told me a different story than what she wrote in those pages. What's written in those pages confirmed my initial belief."

Lucius met his gaze.

"Lucius, you're my son."

Lucius's eyebrows knit together, and his lips parted. He flexed his hand into a fist.

"What? No—no."

Kenneth went over to him and put his hand on his shoulder.

"It's true. I understand if you want to hit me."

Lucius held the sides of his face and stared at Kenneth with glassy eyes, then stood and stepped away.

"No, this can't be true."

Kenneth rose.

"We could do a paternity test to be sure, but your mother's words are good enough for me. I wish she would have told me."

Lucius glanced around as if he searched for the meaning of it all hidden somewhere in the room.

"Lucius, it's going to be okay."

"No, it's not. Everything is upside down. I can't be Beatrice's brother. I just can't."

He looked as though he could double over at any moment.

"Why not? You couldn't ask for a better sister."

He gave Kenneth a look of astonishment. A sense of uncertainty slipped in to cast a cloud over Kenneth's belief. He almost wanted to reread the torn out pages from Paulina's diary. Lucius dug his fingers through his hair.

"Mr. Crane—"

It had been months since Lucius called him, "Mr. Crane." Kenneth's back stiffened and he drew in a slow breath.

"I wanted to see you not only to ask about my Aunt Phoebe, but something more important. Now—I—I can't."

"You can tell me anything, Lucius. I've laid all my cards on the table."

Lucius worked his lips as if he had a mouth full of sand. He then let out a sigh.

"I came to see you—to ask for Bea's hand in marriage, and to get your blessing. Can you believe it? To get *your* blessing to marry *my* sister!"

Kenneth shook his head. He stared at Lucius as if he were some impossible math problem he desperately needed to solve. Lucius took a step as if he were getting ready to bolt out the door, but Kenneth stopped him.

"Sit down."

Both men gazed at one another with strained eyes. Lucius backed toward the sofa and sat down when the backs of his legs made contact with the seat. Kenneth sighed then smiled.

"That's wonderful news."

"Huh? Are you crazy? Sure, no one knows I'm your son, but I can't marry my sister. That would be madness. Oh, dear God."

"Calm down Lucius. Beatrice is not my daughter."

"What?"

Kenneth's lips drew into a thin line, and his eyebrows knit together. He never wanted to say those words, but he knew it was true. His late wife, Theresa (Tess), slept around, and he knew it was true. There was no possibility that Beatrice could be his daughter. The pain was too great, so he closed his eyes, buried the truth deep inside himself, and loved Beatrice with all of his being. Lucius looked at him with wide eyes and an open mouth.

"It's true. I've often put my work above my family. My late wife, Tess, before I married Eleanor, had an ongoing affair. It was some time before I got my head out of my ass and knew about it. It's something—to smile and enjoy the time with your family, all the while not knowing the betrayal. I let it go on for some time and wondered if her lover would put her in a position where she would eventually divorce me. That never happened. So she had her windswept romance with this man, and I eventually welcomed the advances from other women to drown in a sea of debauchery."

Lucius looked as though some of the tension had drained out of him, but there was something still there.

"But I'm older than Beatrice, so you were with my mom before your wife's affair."

Kenneth gazed out into the open living room and sighed.

"That's true. I had a couple of affairs while I was married to Tess. All brief, until I met your mother, Paulina. I suppose that's why I wasn't angry at

Tess, and allowed her to have her fling. I know I wasn't giving her the joy she needed and deserved. Sure, we had good times, but not enough of them."

Lucius shifted on the sofa so that he sat on the edge of the seat.

"Mr. Crane—"

"Lucius, you have my blessing to marry Beatrice, but on one condition."

"Uh? What's that? But—"

"There is no sense causing any more hurt than what we already shared. Would you want to hurt Beatrice by telling her I'm not really her father? Regarding you being my son, well, after you two marry—son or son-in-law, what does it matter?"

Lucius's eyebrows raised, and he wrinkled his lips.

"There is one more thing I need to tell you."

Kenneth crossed his arms.

"Okay?"

Lucius rubbed his hands together.

"Bea is pregnant."

His face was tight and his eyes strained. Kenneth gazed at him for a moment. His jaw knotted.

"Is that the reason you two are getting married?"

"Oh, no-no. We've been dating for some time. It feels right. We get along so well."

Kenneth snorted. His lips curled into a subtle smile, then he released a long sigh.

"That's good to hear. I'm happy for you both. Congratulations, I should say."

He held out his hand. Lucius stood and the two men shook until Kenneth pulled him into his arms and gave Lucius a big hug.

"I'm sorry I can't change the past, but we can all work hard for a beautiful future—son."

"I would like that. It feels good for you to call me 'Son,' but it may take some time for me to call you 'Dad.'"

"That's all right."

Kenneth squeezed his shoulder. They both picked up their bottles of beer from the coffee table and toasted.

"So, when will you pop the question?"

"When I get back to New York this evening. We have dinner plans."

"What about a ring? You *do* have one, don't you?"

"I have a jeweler holding one for me. I'll pick it up as soon as I get back."

"Thank you for respecting my opinion regarding Beatrice. You're an honorable man, Lucius. Never lose that quality. When you get back to New York, let me know how things go, will you?"

Lucius smiled.

"I will."

54

The following day after his visit with Kenneth in Hartford, Lucius drove from New York City back out to Connecticut. He walked across the field of wet cemetery grass from the street where he parked his car, to his parents' graves. The soft ground seemed to pull at him. He smiled when he saw the trail that he rode his bike on as a teenager, when he visited their graves. Those visits were few, but held lengthy conversations. He filled in their responses to his questions with memories of what they might have said about this or that. When he departed, there was a sense of reassurance, of parental advice given, albeit his own.

Leaves and twigs covered the headstone, and grains of sand had seeped into the stone-carved letters. Lucius brushed away the debris the best he could, then his gaze traced each letter—Darius Riley Cook.

"Dad? Wow, that sounds strange. Did you know or have some suspicion that I wasn't your son? It's hard to believe you and Kenneth had the same fucked up situation. Both of you with wives who bore children from other men. Kenneth put work over family, and you, you were just a controlling asshole. You pushed mom into another man's arms, or should I say, into Kenneth's arms. Still, Darius, I suppose now I should call you Darius. You deserve some sympathy. I'm sorry you died in that car crash without the chance to change things. Whether you would have, no one will ever know."

He closed his eyes and pinched the bridge of his nose as if he felt a headache coming on.

"Mom. Did you intend for your secret to come out? You must have realized that someone could and *would* find your diary someday and read what you wrote. Were you hoping it would be me? I can't imagine you would want Darius to find out."

His eyes blurred, and a tear crested his bottom eyelid and started down his cheek. He brushed the tear away when it tickled the edge of his lips. A brief laugh blurted out of him. He glanced at both of their carved names as though they now stood alive before him.

"Not to worry. These are tears of joy. I wanted to let you both know that I'm engaged."

He eyed the headstone. His eyes followed the veins in the marble.

"Yes, that's right. I proposed last night over dinner, and she said, 'yes.' Oh, thank you. I'm pleased that you're both happy and wish the best for the both of us. You promise you'll be at the wedding? Really? That's wonderful."

Tears wet his cheeks, and he laughed.

55

Lucius drove the old black Mercedes that used to belong to Mr. Crane. He turned into the Crane's driveway. From behind the wheel, he took in the house from its foundation to the tops of its skyward reaching chimneys. The beautiful rows of flowers that lined the house in previous years were sparse, and their blossoms were less vibrant. Perhaps the early evening shadows dulled the colors, but there was still the question of the lack of attentiveness to the gardening.

He eased the Mercedes up to the garage, put it in park, and keyed off the engine. After the engine fell silent, he released a heavy breath, one he felt he held for the entire drive from New York. This would be the first time he would see Eleanor since she came to his gallery opening in Manhattan. That was a night he wished he could forget. He was at least relieved that she agreed to see him, even inviting him to dinner. They needed to talk.

Ms. Käthe would be in the midst of preparing dinner. After Lucius exited the Mercedes, he thought he could smell her cooking from out in the driveway. It was only a memory, but a good one. When he rang the doorbell, it was Eleanor who answered and not Ms. Käthe. Eleanor dressed impeccably, as always, wore a satin black evening dress with sleeves that went to her elbows and a flowing pleated skirt that ended halfway up her calves. Wrapped around her pale exposed neck was her black-beaded opal choker that Beatrice first wore all those years ago in the backyard when they were children. His eyes widened.

"Hello Lucius."

Her striking, pale sky-blue eyes were bright and her lips bowed into a smile. He struggled to remember any other time that she made him feel so welcome and wanted.

"Hello Eleanor. Good to see you. You look radiant."

Her smile tightened.

"Please come in."

He offered her a polite smile and kissed her cheek. They stood in the entranceway. He glanced into the adjacent sitting room. The house was different.

"Dinner is almost ready. Shall we?"

"Of course."

He followed her. He was always following her, even when he knew the way. It was nice, though. The sway of her hips, the rise and fall of the flowing hem of her dress, the full contours of the backs of her calves made plump by the height of her heels, and the poise of her shoulders. He could watch her for an eternity. The scent of her perfume trailed behind her and made him dizzy with desire.

"Here we are."

She gestured at the two place settings at the opposite ends of the table. One was where she usually sat, and the other was where Mr. Crane, Kenneth, used to sit. She had already decided that he would sit in her former husband's chair.

It was striking to see that there were no other place settings but the two. When he and Beatrice were children, Eleanor had Ms. Käthe and Ms. Mila set the entire table for eight even though there were only the four of them, providing Mr. Crane made it home for dinner.

He pulled out her chair and seated her.

"Thank you, Dear."

Her voice was sweet and low. He smiled inside, then he sat in Kenneth's old seat. Before he could speak, there was the clomping of heels on the kitchen tiles and Ms. Käthe appeared, holding a large serving plate of roasted chicken and vegetables. Her eyes brightened briefly when she saw him.

"Good evening, Lucius, or should I say, Mr. Cook? Pleasant to see you."

"Hello Ms. Käthe. Please, Lucius is perfectly fine. Good to see you."

Ms. Käthe held the platter while Eleanor and Lucius filled their plates. Then she disappeared back into the kitchen.

"May I do the honors?"

"Please."

He rose with his empty wineglass and went to her and poured them both a glass of wine, then returned to his seat. No rings adorned her fingers, only a single bracelet slid about her arm. It was an odd state of affairs, since their last encounter in New York at his gallery opening and his aggressive Hail Marry attempt to woo her into having sex with him. It still gnawed at him, but after Kenneth's blessing and Beatrice's response to his proposal, he was content to settle with a friendship of sorts, and that seemed to be what she wanted all along. Maybe, at best, a close companionship, but one with a mutual understanding that there would be a wall between them, or at least a fence tall enough to disallow any physical intimacy.

She raised her glass of wine to make a surprising toast.

"To getting reacquainted."

He raised an eyebrow, then his chin, and finally his glass to meet hers. They went on to discuss his life in New York, then on to how she was managing in such an enormous house. Ms. Käthe came up often in the conversation. In that she has been a loyal servant and now a quasi-companion. She made it sound as though Ms. Käthe has taken on Kenneth's role in handling all the tasks around the house that required a masculine sensibility, or rather ones that perhaps she considered beneath her. It made him chuckle, but he did so in a manner as not to appear mocking. After they finished dinner, Eleanor leaned slightly to her side in a subtle, playful way. Her fingertips caressed her collarbones below her black-beaded opal choker. He stared at her and blinked softly. She was stunning, and there was no denying it.

"Would you like to join me for a glass of wine out on the patio? That is, if you don't have to rush off."

"I'm in no hurry. That would be lovely."

He kept his tone level and polite, and followed her out to the patio. He carried the bottle of wine and their glasses, and she her pack of cigarettes.

When they passed through the kitchen, it was clean and tidy and Ms. Käthe was nowhere to be found. She must have crept out silently.

In the screened patio, they sat in the cushioned wicker chairs. He sat in the chair that Kenneth usually occupied, but Kenneth seldom sat in for some time, leading up to his and Eleanor's divorce. It seemed obvious to Lucius, but Beatrice dismissed his concern, for it was common for her father to be absent for spans of time due to the demands of his job and the location of his office.

Lucius sat on the edge of his seat, opened the bottle, and filled their wineglasses, while Eleanor lit a cigarette. They both sat back in the cushions of the patio wicker chairs and quietly contemplated the evening. He took two sips of wine to fortify himself and waited. She blew a stream of smoke toward the ceiling. She then slid the hem of her dress up to massage her calf. The bottom edge of her stocking welt appeared. He swallowed and gazed at her profile, then cleared his throat.

"There's something I want to tell you."

She stared off into the backyard. The evening shadows crept in. Her lack of response, albeit typical, still left him cold. The space between his eyebrows narrowed. He took another sip of wine.

"I have asked Beatrice to marry me."

It puzzled him as to why he withheld Beatrice's answer, or to state simply that they *were* to marry.

She raised an eyebrow. The curve of her lips flattened. She took a long drag on her cigarette and again blew a stream of smoke toward the ceiling. This time with force.

"Why?"

"I love her and she loves me."

She snorted and huffed.

"I saw Kenneth in Hartford, and he has given me his blessing."

"I see. Do you think his word means anything?"

The air hung still and lifeless within the screened patio.

"Has Beatrice given you an answer?"

"Yes."

The word came out dry and reedy passed his lips. She said nothing. She raised the wineglass to her lips and paused as if to take in the fragrance before she drank.

"It won't work out, just as things did not work out between Kenneth and me. She can't give you what you need, just as I wasn't or willing to give Kenneth what he wanted or needed."

His jaw tightened and his eyes burned.

"How do you know what I need? Why can't you be happy for us?"

She took a long drag on her cigarette. The smoke escaped her lips, this time delicate, like the smoke from a little country house on some desolate wintry hillside.

"Eleanor, I'm not sure what to say."

He sat his wineglass on the wicker coffee table next to the bottle.

"I don't know what you want from me. I've given—"

Her gaze met his and silenced him. It was not her icy blue gaze, but one of a pale blue sky, one of promise. He sighed.

"It's getting late. Thank you for a wonderful dinner. It was good to see you."

He rose, and she grasped his arm.

"Not yet. Not like this. Please."

He never heard her ask for anything in such a sweet, pleading tone. She gently pushed out her cigarette into the ashtray, sat her wineglass next to his, and stood so they were eye to eye. She touched his arm.

"Won't you at let me show you some changes I've made to the house? You might also like to visit your old bedroom. It is as you left it."

A gentle smile formed on her lips. The tension ebbed from his shoulders.

"All right."

He followed her through the house. Enchanted by her movements and when she turned to glance at him, he felt a tug in his chest. If she ran, would he chase after her? It was unfair to Beatrice, the spell Eleanor had over him.

She had redecorated the family room and sitting room. She turned Kenneth's study into a library filled with new books and new furniture. Any photographs with Kenneth in them were missing from the walls and replaced with paintings. When they reached the top of the stairs, she turned to him.

"Did Kenneth tell you I moved all of his photography things into storage for him to deal with? It's an empty room now, no windows, like a prison cell."

He was uncertain how to respond.

"Oh?"

"Next summer I have grand plans for the outdoor landscaping. Currently, I have little desire, as you can imagine, due to the collapse of my marriage, to tend to the flowers and bushes. Ms. Käthe has done her best with her lack of gardening skills."

He snorted. He wants to laugh at his mental picture of Ms. Käthe in garden gloves holding garden sheers.

"Indeed."

They arrived at his old bedroom, but neither of them entered. He poked his head inside, then smiled at her.

"Like you said, just as I left it."

"I left Beatrice's room untouched as well. They remind me of photographs, with memories frozen in time."

"Memories, yes."

The hallway table outside the master bedroom, where she kept a vase of white gardenias, was no longer there. She grasped the door handle to the master bedroom, and eased the door open, then stepped into the murk of shadows and turned on the lights. Evening had set in and the outdoor streetlights had come on. The room was exquisite. She had decorated the walls with suede wallpaper that had a lotus print. All the furniture was new and arranged in a different layout. There were Bronze Tiffany floor lamps with colorful shades, an elegantly carved dark wood canopy bed, a mirrored sitting area for her to brush her hair and do her makeup, and a tall full-length mirror with a carved wood frame rested against one wall. She stepped into the room and stood near the corner of the bed. She held one of the tall bedposts. There was an avidity in her pale sky-blue eyes, like that of an anticipating bride. He glanced around and raised his eyebrows.

"It's beautiful."

"Thank you. I intend to do more to the other rooms downstairs, but I first needed to do something special in here."

He nodded. There were no signs of Kenneth anywhere in the room.

"I had the bathroom made over as well. Have a look."

He felt self-conscious, merely standing inside the room beyond the doorway. His knees felt weak. He had only been in the master bedroom a few times when he lived at the house, and now that she had made it over, it felt like the first time. The interior was uniquely hers and she emanated from its core. She remained at the corner of the bed while he went to inspect the adjoining bathroom. She had replaced the tiled-in tub with a clawfoot one. The shower, vanity, and mirror were also new, along with the tiles. He breathed in the perfume scented bathroom. Images of her soaking in the elegant clawfoot bathtub played on the walls of his mind. Her beautiful legs surfacing from the creamy bubbles of her bath. He closed his eyes and inhaled deep to hold on to and savor the image, just as he tried to hold on to the image of his missed attempt to first photograph her.

He remembered what Kenneth had said.

"Sorry Lucius. I guess she's the one that got away."

When Mr. Crane asked Eleanor if she would pose for Lucius, her reply was, "We'll see."

There was hope there, but Lucius knew now how misguided that hope was.

"Beautiful. It's beautiful. The bathroom is beautiful."

When he came out of the bathroom, Eleanor stood by the bedpost, but she had slipped out of her dress and heels. A deep purple sheer bra revealed the pink of her areolae surrounding her nipples, and her sheer panties did nothing to hide the dark triangular patch of hair between her thighs. A matching purple garter belt held up her light gray stockings. His breath froze and a single unspoken word shot through his mind—beautiful.

"What do you think?"

Her lips curled into a coy smile at his inability to speak.

"Come here."

His legs were wooden and his feet moved as if weighted with lead. He swallowed. His mouth was dry. Her black dress lie carefully placed across an accent chair near the window like an unspoken promise. He stood speechless.

"Isn't this how you always wanted me?"

Her perfume eased his thoughts and captivated him. A moment he never wanted to end. He struggled to keep eye contact. Her pale sky-blue eyes penetrated him. He wanted to look at all of her, from head to toe, to consume her visible naked flesh and relish in his desires to explore her hidden topography. A warmth crept up into his chest and face when his gaze descended her body.

"Yes."

She took his hand and placed it on her breast. She drew in a sharp breath when his fingertips touched her stiff nipple under the sheer fabric of her bra. He pinched at the stiff protrusion, which caused her chin to raise. She sucked in a breath and remained still as his fingers probed under the lace. His heart raced as her nipple bowed under and sprang between his fingers. His fingertips traced her abdomen, then he drew his hand away.

Sharp fragments of her rejection in New York soured his thoughts. Shame for how he aggressively touched her made him shrink inside. He peered into her eyes, those pale sky-blue eyes which were darkened by the shadows of the dimly lit room, to find a calm sea of emotion. Her face gave no clues, not even the subtle ones he learned to read. He touched her shoulder, traced her collarbone, then down her sternum to touch her breast. She made no attempt to stop him, nor did she pull away. Her lips once again parted and her breath carried the scent of wine.

She touched his forearm as if to reassure him. She then reached behind her and unclasped her bra. The straps fell down her arms to her elbows. She slipped free of her bra and dropped it to her side. He took off his jacket and dropped it on the floor. With his eyes, he measured the weight of her perfectly shaped breasts. She stepped closer and put her arms around his shoulders. Her breath sent shimmers of electricity across his cheeks and lips, and when she kissed him, her lips were soft as he had imagined. He put his hands on her hips and she moved her body into him and their kiss deepened. The heat of her breasts came through the fabric of his shirt. She raised her chin to expose her neck so that he could kiss her there, then she ran her fingers through his hair. As he kissed her neck and shoulder, he took in the scent of her perfume. His eyelids opened slowly, weighted with lust, and his gaze fell on the full-length mirror that stood against the wall. An image of him peered back with a near naked Eleanor in his embrace. It was like looking into an alternate world, a fantasy world, one he had dreamed about for a lifetime. He held her hips and gently pushed her away.

First, he saw her smudged lipstick, then her piercing, pale sky-blue gaze. Her eyebrows drew in slightly and her lips parted as she drew in a slow breath.

"What is it?"

He ran his fingers through his hair and drew away his gaze from the mirror. As he hoped reality would play itself out, he gulped in a mouthful of air.

"I can't do this."

His mind struggled to comprehend his own words.

"I—I can't do this."

She touched his face, but he grabbed her wrist.

"But this is what you always wanted."

"No, not like this. Besides, it's too late. I'm sorry Eleanor."

He picked up his jacket from the floor.

"Lucius."

Her voice was firm, and her pale sky-blue gaze froze to ice.

"You're being ridiculous. You're ruining an enchanting evening we could have together."

He shook his head. He dug inside his jacket and slipped from the inside pocket the old black and white nude photograph Kenneth took of her before they got married. There was a crease down the center and the corners were curled.

"I've carried this with me for so long. I don't need it anymore. This belongs to you or to Kenneth, not to me. I know you'll never belong to me. I've lusted after you, and I've loved you, but it was a mistake coming here."

He held out the warped photograph. She only stared at him as if he were a child attempting to show or explain something without the facility to do so. He sucked in a breath and put the photograph on top of the bedspread.

"I'm sorry Eleanor."

He rushed from the room and down the hallway. His oxfords clunked on the wooden floors.

"Lucius?"

She rushed after him in her stocking feet. As he approached the bottom of the stairs, she appeared at the top landing.

"Lucius! Don't go. Don't marry Beatrice. You're making a mistake."

She hurried down the stairs, bare-breasted in only her garter belt, panties, and stockings. It was a tragedy to see such a woman brought to a point of desperation. He rushed to the door before she reached the bottom of the staircase. He tugged at the doorknob until he got outside and took long strides to the old Mercedes. When he got to the driver's side door, she stood in the doorway with her hands covering her breasts. The light in the vestibule cast her face in shadow. She stood there, silent. Maybe she expected him to stop being petulant and return to her.

He got in the car before he could allow his yearning for her to cloud his judgement. She stood there motionless, framed in the doorway, as he drove off. He imagined her hand raised to call him back, but he was unsure, and told himself it was only a dream.

56

Beatrice remembered two things on her wedding day. All the cheering and clapping, and being joyfully tugged by Lucius down the main aisle of St. Paul's, then out the double doors, and into the bright sunlight. The only thing brighter was their smiles. Down the stairs they ran past the cheers through a blizzard of rice to the awaiting Rolls-Royce her father arranged for, to give his little girl the most romantic wedding he could. The closeness her father and Lucius had gotten in the previous months overjoyed her. Her father treated Lucius like his own son, which warmed her heart and put her at ease about marrying the boy who came to live with her family. Her face hurt from all the smiling, but Lucius was right there, sharing in the joyful pain. She slipped into the back seat first, and he helped her gather the trailing portion of her dress before he slipped in next to her. She grabbed his face, and they kissed to the cheers of the guests gathered around on the sidewalk.

The driver of the Rolls-Royce took a moment before departing, so photographers could take pictures of the couple in the car. They waved with fixed smiles at the two wedding photographers. Otto had gotten his shots inside the church, and of the couple exiting. He gave them a wave before going to his car to race ahead to the reception hall.

As the Rolls-Royce rolled forward, Beatrice went to kiss Lucius, but her lips landed on his cheek. His gaze was out the window across the car-lined street. She touched his cheek and chuckled.

"Everything okay? You look as though you've seen a ghost."

He snorted.

"Oh, no, I'm good. I just thought I saw Eleanor. I guess I was mistaken."
He kissed her.

"Do you really think she would have attended the wedding?"

"No—not at all."

"Do you think she'll be at the reception?"

"I don't think so."

"Does that bother you?"

"No Bea. This is the happiest day of my life."

They kissed as the Rolls-Royce picked up speed. The church, the guest, the ceremony, and even Eleanor, if she was there on the sidewalk, vanished.

57

Lucius entered the viewing room at the Wynn Funeral Home with Kenneth. More people were present than he imagined would attend Eleanor's funeral. Most of them he had never seen before. Kenneth made the rounds to thank those who attended. Old friends and acquaintances of the Cranes, he assumed. Funny how people visit you when you're dead, but make little effort when you're alive. Maybe deep down inside they despised her, and their attendance was more for show, or worse, to take glee in her death. He snorted and his lips tightened at the corners until his gaze met Ms. Käthe's. She smiled when their eyes met. At first, he nearly passed over her. He had never seen her in any other outfit than what she wore at the Crane's house to cook and clean. He went over to her.

"Hello Lucius."

Her thick German accent had a warm tone. Ms. Käthe held his shoulders and gave him a brief hug.

"Hello Ms. Käthe. Nice to see you."

"Nice to see you too, my boy."

Her makeup hid some of the redness around her eyes.

"I'm sorry about what happened. I mean, in the manner in which you found her."

Ms. Käthe sighed. Her stocky chest rose and fell.

"She took pills. Very sad."

His breath seized.

"But why?"

"I'm not sure. Loneliness, I guess."

Ms. Käthe patted his forearm. A woman came over and interrupted them. She wanted to speak to Ms. Käthe.

"Goodbye, dear Lucius. Take good care of yourself."

It was the kindest thing she ever said to him.

"Thank you. Goodbye Ms. Käthe."

Everyone else in the room was engaged in quiet conversation. He glanced at the various bouquets of flowers and plants, then strolled over to inspect them. It gave him time. A moment he needed before he could gaze upon her lifeless body. He straightened his posture. She hated when he slouched.

St. Paul's Evangelical Lutheran Church had sent a peace lily. Kenneth's firm had sent an arrangement with yellow blossoms, and at the end of the row he found the arrangement of white gardenias he had a local florist deliver. He went to inspect them. They sat on a glass side table near two easy chairs. The white petals, with their scent of creamy coconut and spice, haunted him with vivid memories that stirred inside him. They teleported him back to the time when he was eleven and glanced through the narrow open doorway to the Crane's master bedroom. There and then, he spied on Mr. and Mrs. Crane in bed. Her eyes, those pale sky-blue eyes, gazed toward him as he stood in the shadows behind the bedroom door. He never asked if she saw him, but in that moment, he felt connected to her.

A hand fell on his shoulder, and Kenneth appeared at his side.

"Take all the time you need. I said my goodbyes. I'll be out in the entrance hall."

Lucius nodded. It was odd seeing Kenneth, Mr. Crane, without his wedding band. It still struck him that Kenneth threw away something amazing. Kenneth gave him a comforting smile, then left him alone by the vase of white gardenias. He took in the scent of the flowers one last time. The petals kissed his nose. He then went over to where Eleanor's body lie. The casket was a rich mahogany with elegantly carved corners and polished brass handles that ran down the sides. It was befitting of the woman's body it contained.

He put his hand out as if to run his fingers along the deep polished wood, but only touched the casket when he stood before the open end. He was thankful, and not, that Eleanor chose to be buried and not cremated. A cremation would have allowed him to remember her as he last saw her, and not like this. The foundation they applied was too dark, and her eyeshadow a shade more flamboyant than she would have ever worn. At least they put her in one of her favorite dresses, most likely with the guidance of Ms. Käthe, or Kenneth, if he got involved. He liked to think Kenneth at least did that for her.

He wished he could gaze into her eyes one last time. Those pale sky-blue eyes. His vision blurred, and when he blinked, a tear landed on the back of his hand. He removed the coiled child's belt from his jacket pocket. The dry flaked paint was like scales on the leather.

"Did you ever love me?"

The same answer came as when she was alive—silence. He sighed, then tucked the belt inside the casket under her arm. He was about to touch her hands positioned over her heart, but caught himself. The fewer memories of her in this cold, lifeless state, the better. He wiped away his tears.

After he walked away, the desire to turn and look at her once more was great, but he kept going until he was out in the lobby where Kenneth came over to him.

"Are you okay?"

"Yes. I'm ready to go."

"Will you be back for her service?"

"No. I don't think so."

Kenneth gazed at him a moment, as if to give him time to change his mind.

"All right. Take care of yourself—"

He could see in Kenneth's eyes that the man wanted to call him son, but held his tongue. Maybe he considered this was not the appropriate time.

"Thanks. See you soon?"

Kenneth's eyes brightened.

"See you soon."

Outside, Lucius released a sharp breath, took several steps, then stopped. The sun broke through the clouds and had pushed away the early morning gloom to reveal a sky of soft pale blue—a familiar blue. He sighed and his lips curled into a subtle smile.

"Goodbye."

His oxfords made soft scuffs as he continued on the stone path. In the adjacent parking lot, Ms. Mila stood smoking a cigarette next to Kenneth's car. When they made eye contact, he offered her a gentle wave, and she waved back. He strolled to a smaller lot where a large, black, classic Mercedes sedan sat parked. It was a similar sedan, like the one Mr. Crane owned when Lucius was a boy. As he approached the car, the silhouette of a woman's head and shoulders became visible through the back window. He stepped alongside the car and got behind the wheel.

When he settled in the driver's seat, he touched Beatrice's cheek, and she gave him a warm, tight-lipped smile. Eleanor's black opal choker was around her neck. Now, as a woman, it fit her perfectly. She kissed his hand.

"Everything okay?"

He gave her a warm smile.

"Everything is better than okay."

He started the car's engine. When he gripped the steering wheel, his white-gold wedding band gleamed in the afternoon sunlight. After he put the car into drive, he reached over and rested his hand on Beatrice's rounded belly. Her eyes brightened and her smile broadened. She put her hand over his, then they drove off.

About the Author

James Walter Lee is an award-winning American author. He is the founder and editor of two publishing imprints, Zennea Press and 2nd Sight Press. He holds a Master's in Fine Arts from The New York Academy of Art and a Bachelor's in Fine Arts from the College for Creative Studies. James is also an avid photographer and lives in Pennsylvania. For more about James Walter Lee, please visit jameswalterlee.com.

www.ingramcontent.com/pod-product-compliance
Lightning Source LLC
Chambersburg PA
CBHW030615250626
47154CB00013B/1977